Club Deception

CLUB DECEPTION

SARAH SKILTON

GRAND CENTRAL
PUBLISHING

New York Boston

Copyright © 2017 by Sarah Skilton
Cover illustration by Sylvan Steenbrink. Cover design by Elizabeth Turner. Cover copyright © 2017 by Hachette Book Group, Inc.

Grand Central Publishing
Hachette Book Group
1290 Avenue of the Americas, New York, NY 10104
grandcentralpublishing.com
twitter.com/grandcentralpub

First Trade Paperback Edition: July 2017

Grand Central Publishing is a division of Hachette Book Group, Inc. The Grand Central Publishing name and logo is a trademark of Hachette Book Group, Inc.

The publisher is not responsible for websites (or their content) that are not owned by the publisher.

The Hachette Speakers Bureau provides a wide range of authors for speaking events. To find out more, go to www.hachettespeakersbureau.com or call (866) 376-6591.

Library of Congress Cataloging-in-Publication Data
Names: Skilton, Sarah, author.
Title: Club deception / Sarah Skilton.
Description: First trade paperback edition. | New York : Grand Central Publishing, 2017.
Identifiers: LCCN 2017008123| ISBN 9781455597017 (softcover) | ISBN 9781478915973 (audio download) | ISBN 9781455597000 (ebook)
Subjects: LCSH: Secret societies—Fiction. | Magicians—Fiction. | BISAC: FICTION / Contemporary Women.
Classification: LCC PS3619.K5565 C58 2017 | DDC 813/.6—dc23
LC record available at https://lccn.loc.gov/2017008123

ISBNs: 978-1-4555-9701-7 (trade paperback), 978-1-4555-9700-0 (ebook), 978-1-4789-1597-3 (audiobook, downloadable)

Printed in the United States of America

LSC-C

10 9 8 7 6 5 4 3 2 1

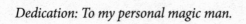

Dedication: To my personal magic man.

The art of the magician is not found in the simple deception, but in what surrounds it, the construction of a reality which supports the illusion.

—Jim Steinmeyer, *Art & Artifice*

THE MAGICIAN'S WIFE sat in Interview Room A with her legs crossed at the thigh and ankle. Though the room was equipped with a video recorder and two-way mirror, the soft lighting and broad, cushioned furniture provided a more comfortable atmosphere than did the harsh fluorescents, low ceilings, and plastic chairs used in the official interrogation room down the hall. Merely a person of interest, the magician's wife had not been charged with a crime. Yet.

The detective guessed she was in her forties. Her thick, honey-blond hair skimmed the top of her collarbone, and she was disheveled in an uncalculated, attractive way that suggested some kind of postcoital slackening. Her makeup was smeared, too, just a little—a thumb had recently pressed against her lower lip, perhaps; a hand had tangled in her hair.

She wore a faded Liz Phair EXILE IN GUYVILLE T-shirt and dark jean shorts with white stitching on the pockets. On her feet she wore severe-looking, open-toed black stilettos with leather straps that crisscrossed up her calves and made every inch of her bare legs—she looked at least five foot nine—even more elongated.

The combination of '90s casual meets kinky footwear made her look like she was half in one world and half in another. He knew the detectives they'd passed in the hall were already working on a nickname for her and he wanted to be ready. *Real Housewife of Silver Lake? No. Dominatrix Day Off.*

The arresting officer told the detective she'd chosen the shoes specifically. She'd been given the option of wearing something more practical but she'd declined, which was odd since she'd had no idea how long she'd be at RHD, the Robbery/Homicide Division of the LAPD, which investigated crimes of a high profile or particularly unusual nature. This one fell into both categories.

"You're taking the news pretty well." The detective flipped his chair around and straddled it so he could lean toward the magician's wife without coming across as threatening. The back of the chair served as a good barrier, and a place to rest his elbows.

She frowned. "I'm not rending my garments, so I must not be upset?"

"I was just remarking upon your relative composure."

"No, you're saying I'm not believable as a widow. How would you like me to act?"

"I'm not saying you should act one way or another."

"I could hold a press conference. That's what Houdini's wife did. Bess. Would that make you feel better?" The magician's wife was babbling now, swivel-eyed, lost in her own world. "She used her husband's death to drum up publicity for a séance, starring him, of course. Said he'd come back in exactly one year to haunt her. To be fair, it's probably what Houdini would have wanted."

He felt a sting of pity for her. "Mrs. Fredericksson…"

"Claire."

"Claire, I think you're in shock. It's understandable. Can I get you anything? Coffee, water, cigarette? Of course, we'd have to go outside for that." He rattled them off by rote, but her eyes lit up at the mention of the last item.

Just as quickly, she glanced away. "No, better not."

"No cigarette? You sure?"

She ran a tired hand through her messy blond hair. "Let's just get this over with."

"How long were you married to Jonathan?"

"Twenty-two—no, twenty-three years."

"How long was he a magician?"

"As long as I've known him."

"Did he ever tell you how he did his tricks?" It was probably irrelevant, but his curiosity overruled his common sense.

Claire obviously wished he'd resisted. She picked at the frayed hem of her jean shorts and made him wait for a long beat before answering. "Once I know how a trick is done I lose all interest in it. That's a quote from someone. I don't remember who."

"So you weren't his assistant?"

"God, no. Have you *seen* what magicians do to women?"

He raised his hands apologetically. "I meant no disrespect."

"They're called torture illusions. Originated in the twenties, a perfect response to women's suffrage. What a relief it must have been to see those uppity females getting stabbed, sawed in half, hypnotized, *vivisected*—"

"Mrs. Fredericksson," he interrupted. "I'm not here for a history lesson. I'm here to figure out who poisoned your husband."

She swallowed, had the good sense to look abashed. "I didn't kill him and I don't know who did."

"Women are far more likely to use poison than men are. And you just told me magicians hate women, so let's elaborate on that."

She shook her head imperiously. "No, that's not what I said. They don't hate women. Quite the contrary. But there are people who hate *magicians*. That's the question you should be asking. That's how you find the person who did this."

"Okay, who hates magicians?"

"Other magicians, of course." She paused. "Every magician has another magician he hates. Doesn't matter if you're a hobbyist or a top performer, a stage illusionist or a close-up expert. Somewhere, for whatever reason, another magician hates you."

He regarded her carefully. "You've given this speech before."

"I try to warn the new wives. Most of them have no idea what they're getting into."

"What are they getting into?"

She dismissed him with a wave. "Oh, I don't know. Disillusionment. Misdirection. Now you see him, now you don't."

"I thought that was every marriage."

"A lot of magicians—the good ones, anyway—lead a double life. It can be disconcerting to discover. On the other hand…he might make us float. He might make us fly." She sounded far away, and her pale-green eyes shimmered like gemstones. He was certain a tear would slip down her cheek but she kept it at bay, perhaps through sheer willpower.

"Is that why you married Jonathan?" he asked.

"No." She looked straight at him. "I wanted to disappear. And that was the only way I knew how."

SIX WEEKS EARLIER

Jessica

THERE WAS A girl in a fish tank in the lobby of the Standard hotel.

It was not an illusion; it was downtown Los Angeles, Jessica's new home.

The large, waterless aquarium sat behind the concierge desk. The girl inside looked about twenty-two, not much younger than Jessica, and she was sexy in an understated way. Warm pink lighting washed over her, making her white tank top and formfitting shorts look pink, too. She didn't dance or pose or strip or anything. As far as Jessica could tell, the girl just went about her life: texting, reading, uploading pictures to Instagram, and napping on her side, knees curled up to her chest.

Sweet gig. Wonder how she got it?

"Single or double?" asked the clerk. He looked fresh off the set of a teeth-whitening ad, and his gaze slid up and down the exposed V of skin where Jessica's burgundy wraparound crossed her slim frame.

She winked, and proceeded to break his heart. "Honeymoon suite."

Cal's place was a disaster, so for the next week she and Cal would be living in a hotel, just like when they first met.

His loft apartment on Sunset and Vine was bright and

open, all floor-to-ceiling windows, sleek granite countertops, and wood paneling on the floor and cabinets, but the furniture was dusty and sun-faded: par for the course when you've been traveling the world for three years straight.

Unopened boxes of custom-made playing cards were stacked in precarious towers throughout the living room. Large posters of Cardini (THE SUAVE DECEIVER), Thurston (THE WONDER SHOW OF THE UNIVERSE), Blackstone (THE WORLD'S MASTER MAGICIAN), and Alexander (THE MAN WHO KNOWS) sat against the wall in chipped, gilded frames (*"The man who knows" what?* Jessica thought).

An antique armoire crouched in the corner, battle-ready and prepared to die to keep its owner's secrets.

On the floor:

Swords, box cutters, trunks, saws, heaps of magic books.

Rope.

A straitjacket.

On the dining room table:

Bicycle playing cards, with red and blue backs, pristine in their plastic wrappers. Pens that opened on both sides. Creased dollar bills.

"Bit of a shambles, isn't it? My bachelor pad," Cal had said as he ran a hand through his dark hair, mussing it up into points. "Or is the proper term *man cave?*"

"It's a *magician* cave." Jessica laughed, clasping his hand in hers. "Normal bachelors don't live like this."

He pretended to be shocked. "Are you saying I'm not normal?"

"Thank God," she answered.

A promotional poster for MASKELYNE & COOKE'S MYSTERIES AT THE EGYPTIAN HALL IN LONDON caught her eye. "Did you get to see them?"

"Before my time, sadly. As you can see, I have a lot of picture hanging to do. *These two*"—he pointed to Blackstone and Thurston—"have to be kept apart. They despise each other." Indeed, the two magicians positioned on opposite sides of the room seemed to glower at one another. Both posters featured impish red devils whispering instructions in their respective magician's ear, as though adding fuel to the fire of their animosity.

Jessica grinned. "I'll try to remember that."

"Let's go someplace lush while I have the place sorted," Cal suggested. His subtle, velvety British accent curled around Jessica's ears and lulled her into a hypnotic state, and he'd slipped his credit card inside the back pocket of her skintight Levi's before she could blink.

"But—we just got here. I'm tired from the flight," she protested.

"All the more reason to rest comfortably. Call for room service, hit the spa." He kissed her forehead. "Book a suite at The Standard downtown. It'll cost a bomb but the view's brilliant."

She thought their current view was pretty brilliant. "What about you?"

"I'll come by after I dig through some boxes."

She pulled his face down toward hers for a proper kiss, only to be interrupted by the chirp of his cell phone.

His producers needed him in Santa Barbara to shoot B-roll for his TV pilot, which was why, an hour later, Jessica found herself checking in to The Standard by herself.

The room was classy and modern but sterile. The furniture cut the space into segments, all hard lines and muted colors, separate and formal; it reminded her of the furniture on *Mad Men*. She sat by the window, sipping a Perrier and watching the sun go down. On Flower Street below, the sign for The Standard hung upside down. Maybe only people who could afford rooms got to see it properly?

She didn't blame Cal for racing off. His upcoming TV special was a huge step for his career, and the reason he'd returned to Los Angeles after such a long absence.

On top of the hotel dresser, next to the TV, her phone vibrated.

Just seeing Cal's name on the screen lit a flame inside her like a matchstick striking a box.

She tapped ANSWER. "Hey, babe, when will you be here?"

"Not for a while, I'm afraid." She could picture his handsome face lined with regret, his tie loosened after a long evening of performing. "Traffic's a nightmare."

"Shit, really?"

"Really. Why don't you get dolled up and pop round the club? The WAGs are dying to meet you."

"Who?"

"Right, sorry, wives and girlfriends."

"I'd rather wait and go with you," she said.

"You'll go the club, have a lovely time, and return to the hotel. You'll wait up for me, and…"

She smirked. "And what?"

"And when I get home, I'll do the rope trick." His voice was a caress. "You remember the rope trick, don't you, pet?"

Her heart began to race. "Yes," she whispered. Sometimes it seemed to be the only word she could form around him.

"It's settled, then."

Now he sounded a little *too* cocky, which shook her out of her reverie. "You know," she said with a laugh, "one day that's not going to work."

"Until that day…charge a taxi to the room and have the driver wait till you're inside the club, the area's a bit dodgy."

"Okay."

"Make a good impression on the ladies, and you'll have a set of friends for life."

She released a breath she didn't realize she'd been holding. "Now you're making me nervous."

"Just be your adorable, charming self, and ask to speak with Claire."

"What does she look like? And how do you know she'll be there?"

"She's a Hitchcock blonde, my age, and she's *always* there."

Purchased in the late 1980s by the Brotherhood of Arcana, Club Deception was a hidden, members-only club built out of a converted speakeasy in downtown Los Angeles for use strictly by magicians and their guests. It contained a small apartment for monthlong residencies; a lecture hall where visiting magicians were expected to teach classes; a library culled from the works of John Mulholland (including copies of every issue he edited of *The Sphinx* until "retiring" to join the CIA); a small museum of magic patents and curiosities; a luxurious, private screening room with red velvet armchairs, chaise lounges, and a champagne fountain; and a midsize performance stage that only opened its doors to outsiders twice a year, for the Close-Up Magic Competition in the spring and the Stage Show Magic Competition in the fall.

Membership dues were ten thousand dollars a year and admittance required sponsorship from an existing member, as well as successful completion of a grueling audition. The dress code was strict: jackets and ties for gents, evening gowns for ladies. Those who arrived in anything else would be sent home.

As a first-time visitor, the only thing Jessica knew about Club Deception was that she couldn't find it. The air was strangely cool—after ninety-nine-degree weather all day, she'd expected the evening to continue in that vein, as it did in the Midwest. But the instant the sun went down, all warmth left with it. The lone streetlamp nearby was cracked, and her taxi had departed despite the tip she'd given the driver to stick around.

The address Cal had texted her didn't seem to correspond to anything. She wandered alone and lost until she realized the entrance didn't face the street but the alley, with the numbers written sideways, one per brick, going up the side of the building.

Needless to say, the name of the club wasn't on a sign above the door. At least he'd warned her about the sliding door with the peephole in it, upon which she knocked.

The slot opened and the face of a young woman appeared. Or rather, a rectangular screen *projecting* the face of a young woman appeared. The face's owner presumably sat at a desk elsewhere in the mysterious building. The woman wore heaps of mascara seemingly designed to balance out the sparseness of her arched, plucked eyebrows.

"Hiya." Jessica beamed, pleased at having solved the puzzle. "How's it going?"

"Password?" the receptionist asked in a bored tone.

"Huh?" She leaned closer to the small circular speaker under the screen.

"The password, what is it?"

"I didn't know there was one."

"Then you must be in the wrong place."

"What? No." Jessica stood a little taller in her peach chiffon dress and matching heels, and announced in a proud voice, "I'm with Calum Clarke."

"Then he would've told you the password."

"But…"

"I'm going to have to ask you to leave." The receptionist gave her a disdainful look. "And next time? Wear a bra."

Shocked, Jessica stumbled backward into someone and felt three fingers press into her shoulder, right at the tendon, to hold her in place.

"The password is *ephemera*," said a flat, definitive, female voice. "I know because I chose it."

The receptionist's expression changed from haughty to horrified. On-screen, she pressed a buzzer that unlocked the heavy door.

The fingers on Jessica's shoulders squeezed gently and released. "Off you go."

Jessica stepped inside the dark lobby, followed by her savior: a tall, leggy blonde (*But is she a Hitchcock blonde? What does that even mean?*) whose tousled hair, pale-pink lipstick, aquamarine eyeliner, and intense green eyes suggested undersea tumult. She wore a black leather dress with blink-and-you-miss-them slashes of material cut out across the tops of her full breasts. Her black heels appeared to contain the missing straps. Leather cords, visible through a thigh-high slit in the gown, wrapped tightly up her calves and secured the precariously high heels in place. She reminded Jessica of a fawn in the woods learning to walk on thin, wobbly legs—but there was nothing doe-like about her eyes. This was a deer who shot back.

The lobby contained nothing but a polished chandelier, an unused pool table, a coat check, and a desk for the receptionist. Midnight-blue wallpaper with a vintage gold-leaf design gave the place a turn-of-the-century parlor look. At the clutter-free, antique secretary desk with foldout table, the receptionist had dissolved into a stuttering mess. She nearly fell off her small mahogany armchair in her haste to approach them.

"I'm so sorry, Mrs. Fredericksson. I didn't know she was with you."

"Well, now you do." Her voice was soft and slightly hoarse, as though she'd come from a smoke-filled blues lounge.

"It's okay," Jessica said quickly. "Are you Claire?" she asked, hoping to redirect the blonde's attention.

"What? Yes." But Claire wouldn't be deterred from berating the receptionist. "If I hear you speak to a guest that way again, you better start polishing your résumé."

"It's really okay—" Jessica said.

"This is Cal's *wife*," Claire snapped.

The receptionist looked shocked. "I…" she stuttered, "I…had no idea he got remarried."

Claire's blond eyebrows shot up. "Why would you have?"

"Will she…is she…what rooms does she have access to?"

"Any room she wants."

Claire half pushed, half guided Jessica to the left, where a thin elevator door opened for her. Noticing Jessica's perplexed expression, she said, "Be glad it's not a trapdoor and a stepladder anymore. Welcome to Manderley."

"Um, okay…" Jessica gingerly walked inside the elevator and turned around. "Will we both fit?"

But Claire had vanished, leaving only a faint scent of lavender and lime in her wake.

The elevator doors closed, and Club Deception swallowed Jessica whole.

***

Upon arriving downstairs at the dimly lit bar, Jessica's attention flew to the enormous gilt-framed lithographs of Carter the Great, Chung Ling Soo, Harry Houdini, Alexander Herrmann, and Dante (who, as in Cal's posters of Thurston and Blackstone at home, was surrounded by vibrant red demons). They glowed like stained-glass windows, hauntingly beautiful, suspended by near-invisible wires that hung from the ceiling. At first glance they appeared to float.

Until she'd met Cal, Jessica had never traveled beyond the Midwest, but she'd seen photos of European cathedrals, and it was these houses of worship that came to mind while standing in Club Deception. The sense of history...the reverential admiration...the hush in the air...

Club Deception was the Vatican of magic clubs.

The elevator doors began to close. She stepped out of their way and gazed up. And up. The ceiling had to be thirty feet tall.

Each private table and set of chairs was nestled in its own recessed alcove along the wall, reachable only by thin staircases of freestanding rectangles that lit up upon contact. When not in use, they, too, appeared invisible. She imagined them flickering to life in a pattern of movement, like the sidewalk panels in the music video for "Billie Jean."

At the top, Jessica could just make out a separate balcony overlooking the room. But there didn't seem to be any way to access it.

To her left, a door opened and three magicians emerged. She craned her neck to look past them into the room. It looked like a hall of mirrors from floor to ceiling. The door shut behind them, its dark coloring merging with the wall. Without a telltale doorknob, she'd be hard-pressed to find it again.

She felt like a visitor inside someone else's hallucinatory dream.

A drink would help. She approached the L-shaped bar, whose smooth, see-through surface revealed vintage magic coins from around the world embedded within, trapped like glossy relics. The cocktail menu, printed on the back of an enlarged Ace of Spades card, listed modern drink specials as well as a few classics (Gin Rickeys, Sidecars, Dirty Martinis, Gimlets, and absinthe). Below the list was a recipe for "the magic trick of the week." This week's was Twisting the Aces by Dai Vernon. Members were encouraged to discuss it and practice it together. (Cal referred to this as "sessioning.")

Men of all ages in suits and ties sat together, hunched over their tables, nursing drinks and manipulating decks of cards. She stood transfixed and delighted in the center of the room.

A pale, Ichabod Crane–looking fellow in a loose suit approached her. He was thin, but not in a charismatic way like Cal. This guy was cadaverous, sunken, and the bags under his eyes reminded her of bruises. She guessed he was about fifty. "Care to see a little sleight of hand?"

"Sure," Jessica replied, and followed him to a low, circular ceramic table between two blood-red velvet love seats framed in wood trim.

Ichabod pulled out a deck of cards. His movements were elegant but his hands trembled as he cut and fanned the cards. Jessica selected one, memorized it, and returned it to the deck. A flourish of movement, a dramatic pause, and he produced it again.

She clapped and smiled, impressed. At the same time, however, she was keenly aware a trick was happening. With Cal, you didn't realize a trick had happened until halfway through the next day, and even then you second-guessed yourself.

During the magician's demonstration, a bartender sauntered over with a tray of Martinis. Then, turning his back to Ichabod, the bartender dropped a napkin into Jessica's lap, a message written on it in aquamarine eyeliner: "Say 'You flashed.'"

"You flashed," Jessica read aloud without thinking.

Ichabod set his drink down on the ceramic table with a clatter. "What?"

"You…flashed?" she repeated, equally confused, then showed him the napkin. "I don't even know what that means."

He whirled around, scanning the bar. "Oh, I get it," he said angrily. "Ha-ha, very funny."

Jessica followed his gaze. There was Claire, sitting by herself on the farthest bar stool. Her endless legs crossed at both the knee and ankle so she could swivel in her chair without, well, flashing anyone.

Jessica turned her attention back to the magician. He sipped from his drink, looking sulky.

"To *flash* means to accidentally reveal the technique behind a trick," he groused.

"You didn't, though," she assured him. "Honest. You were good."

"Oh, who needs this?" He tucked his cards away in his suit pocket, then rolled up his dark-green velvet close-up mat and placed it inside his briefcase. "Go laugh in your corner. She's waiting for you."

Flustered, Jessica stood up and cut across the room toward Claire. "Where did you go? Why didn't you walk in with me?"

She thought of the inaccessible balcony. Had Claire entered the bar from up there, and if so, how?

"I wanted to watch you experience the club for the first time. It's rare for me to get to see that."

All the fight left her, replaced by self-consciousness. "Oh. Did I pass the test?"

A warm smile spread across Claire's lips. "With flying colors. You were appropriately awed."

The vintage poster above Claire featured a dishy redhead brandishing a sword. Unlike the grandiose proclamations of Thurston and Blackstone, her advertisement read simply, ADELAIDE HERRMANN AND COMPANY.

"A woman," Jessica remarked with surprise. "Who's she?"

"Ah, yes. The patron saint of magician wives. She started out assisting her husband, Alexander, during the vaudeville era. We also have a poster of Ionia the Enchantress in the women's bathroom." She seemed proud of this fact. "It took six months for the board to approve it, but it was worth every fight."

"What kind of magic did Ionia do?"

"Grand illusions, pantomime. Her first husband was in the circus but she wised up and hitched herself to an Austrian royal later on."

"Outside, you said you chose the password?"

Claire nodded. "My husband is president of the club, and he farms out that particular chore to me." Claire explained how the password, altered daily, worked. Members received a Snapchat message that disappeared after it was viewed.

It had apparently slipped Cal's mind to tell her about it, and Jessica felt a flicker of irritation as she remembered standing in the alley feeling foolish. This in turn reminded her she was still irritated with Claire. She glanced over at the Ichabod Crane fellow. "Wasn't it kind of mean to show that guy up?"

"Of course not," said Claire. "You can't be expected to spend your time humoring amateurs. Not when you're married to Cal."

"How could you tell he was an amateur?"

"His execution was sloppy, his hands shook like we were in the middle of an earthquake, and he had no charm. If I had to guess, I'd say he's a lawyer or an accountant in real life, and he gets off on the idea of playing magician two nights a week. He pays extra dues for the privilege of coming here on a probationary basis until he passes the skills test, which I'm guessing he'll never be able to do."

"Ouch."

Claire drained the clear liquid of her drink, until only a thin slice of lime remained at the bottom. She motioned to the bartender. "Another gin for me, and she'll have a Bellini."

"I will?" asked Jessica.

"You want your insides to match your outsides, don't you?"

"Fuck me," Jessica said happily. "How'd you know? Are you a mentalist or something?"

Claire cringed at Jessica's choice of words and looked at her like a Realtor assessing a property. "*No*, I leave that to the professionals. But I do have a functioning nose. Let's see. Peach dress, peach nails, peach body wash, peach conditioner," she rattled off. "At least you're consistent."

Now it was Jessica's turn to cringe. She looped a strand of brunette hair tightly around her finger, self-conscious again. "Did I put on too much? Is it bad?"

"Not at all," Claire said. "You're newly wed. You want to be perfect for Cal tonight, no matter how late he gets home, don't you? Prepped and ready for him in all your peaches 'n' cream, peachy-creamy glory."

The bartender gaped at them, his mouth open. Eventually, he found his voice. "Did I hear you married Cal?" he asked.

Jessica beamed. "That's right." She dangled her left hand out for him so he could admire the band tattooed on her ring finger.

He gave a quick nod. "Nice."

The bartender's eyes darted to Claire's. She returned his gaze, her expression unreadable.

"I'm surprised he came back," he said carefully.

"What do you mean?" Jessica asked.

"Oh, just—nothing. Anyway." The bartender slapped his thin cotton towel against the side of the bar. "Congratulations. Um, a Bellini, right?"

"With an ounce of Aperol if you've got it," Jessica said. "Thanks."

Once he was out of earshot, she leaned in toward Claire.

"What was he talking about, 'surprised he came back'?"

"When he skipped town," Claire said, "no one expected to see him again. Not after what happened with Brandy."

Jessica swallowed. "Oh." She knew very little about Cal's first wife, who had passed away.

An awkward silence fell between them.

"Aperol," Claire remarked, once they'd been served. "I wouldn't have thought to add that."

"IBA contemporary classic."

"Where'd you bartend?"

"The Gold Coast Hotel? In Chicago?"

"Are you asking me or telling me?"

"Both. I'm telling you, while asking if you've heard of it. I'm being polite."

"Oh, you're being polite. I thought you were being insecure."

Jessica lowered her head. "Maybe a little. It's kind of intimidating, being here."

Claire's expression softened. "Hmm. I can help you with that." She clinked her glass to Jessica's. Their bare arms brushed against each other's.

Before the first drop of alcohol hit her tongue, she felt intoxicated—by Los Angeles, by the club, by Claire. Were all the women in LA this beautiful? She wanted Claire to like her—and she had no idea how to make that happen.

"First lesson." Claire set her drink on the bar. "Every magician has another magician he hates. Doesn't matter if you're a hobbyist or a top performer, a stage illusionist or a close-up expert. Somewhere, for whatever reason, another magician hates you." She paused. "*Your* job is to back up your husband on any move he makes against this magician."

"Was...did Brandy do that kind of thing? For him?"

Claire ignored the question. "Your job is *also* to remind him he's talented and worthy of respect, because the outside world won't always provide that reassurance. With Cal, it shouldn't be a problem. He was made for TV."

Saddened by the earlier part of Claire's lesson, Jessica asked, "The magicians all hate each other?"

"Not exactly, but there have always been rivalries. I mean, look at the posters: the Greatest this, the Greatest that, the World's Best. It makes for good business, but it's also a pain. For us, I mean."

"How do you know who wins?" Jessica asked.

"No one wins."

"Or, like, what if they're equally good?"

"Then you just have to wait for the other one to die. That's how Kellar beat Herrmann." Claire nodded to the poster of Adelaide, Herrmann's wife. "Did wonders for *her* career, at least."

"How do you mean?"

"She took over the act."

"But if Herrmann wasn't around to know that Kellar beat him, how can that count?"

Claire regarded her, all warmth gone. "It counts." She cleared her throat. "Second lesson: Invest in a strapless bra."

Jessica crossed her arms over her chest, mortified. She'd figured the receptionist was just being spiteful. Apparently not.

"I don't mind if you go without; you're perky enough to pull it off. The other WAGs might, though. Especially on dress-swap day."

Blushing, Jessica knocked back the rest of her drink and wiped her mouth with the back of her hand. "How many are there?"

"How many who?"

"Wives and girlfriends."

"Oh, *WAGs* doesn't stand for 'wives and girlfriends.' It stands for '*widows* and girlfriends.' Wives don't exist to these guys. Once you tie the knot, and the chase is over, you're dead to them."

The room felt chilly all of a sudden. "Wait, what? But you just said…and what about *your* husband?"

"What about him?"

"Where is he?"

"I have no idea."

Jessica was dumbfounded. "He's not here?"

Once again, Claire ignored the question. Instead, she expertly turned the spotlight around: "Let me guess: Cal's working tonight."

"How'd you know?"

"They're always working tonight." She stood up and tossed a ten-dollar tip on the bar. "Want to have a look around?"

Jessica nodded, unable to concentrate on anything beyond the word *widow*.

We barely touched down in California and he left me on my own, my first night in a new city.

Their five weeks of bliss, first in Chicago, and then on their honeymoon, were over. They were on his turf now.

A shiver ran through her.

What if I uprooted my entire life for a man who no longer sees me?

Claire

JONATHAN WOULD EXPECT a recap of the other magicians' comings and goings tonight; Claire was his spy in the House of Houdini, but considering he was currently making the master bed creak and groan, she didn't feel particularly inclined to analyze which of his competitors for Stage Magician of the Year were worthy of discussion.

A dainty, red-soled set of heels, no larger than size fives, sat in the foyer of their secluded Silver Lake home, flanking Jonathan's custom-made leather shoes. His laces draped over his companion's Louboutins like tentacles, reaching toward the bedroom door and the noises within.

Claire kicked off her own heels—size nine and a half—and lay on the Chesterfield in the living room. She pressed a cool, wet cloth to her forehead.

She considered calling Eden at Rice University. It was late in Texas, though, and would serve only to prove Claire had been drinking. She had to learn to settle for their weekly phone call, and be grateful that (a) she *got* a weekly phone call, and (b) she and Eden hadn't erred on the other side of lunacy and become one of those mother-daughter BFF texting duos who attended Botox parties together. Her daughter's independence made her proud. The kids who couldn't sign up for classes or decipher a bus schedule without Mommy's guidance, and the parents who enabled them, made Claire want to shoot herself.

She missed Eden—sometimes to the point of breathlessness—but texting seemed exhausting. She was fine communicating the old-fashioned way.

As if sensing her need for connection, her phone lit up.

It was Cal.

She took a deep breath and held it a second before answering.

"She's gorgeous, isn't she? Just completely darling," Cal gushed before she even said hello.

Claire lay back and placed the washcloth over her eyes. She felt a headache coming on. "Where are you?"

"Driving back from Santa Barbara. Got the Bluetooth on, don't fret."

"I wasn't. But I'm touched you thought I would."

"What'd you think of Jessie?"

"Who?" Claire asked. "Oh, you mean Legally Brunette?"

"Play nice," he admonished. "I'm counting on you to make her feel at home."

"You know me. I'm a one-woman pie-baking neighborhood Welcome Wagon."

"Can you at least include her in things, as a favor to me, if nothing else?"

"I didn't realize I owed you any favors."

He sighed. "She's alone here, she could use a girlfriend."

Claire didn't respond right away, pondering the best way to make an effective gagging noise over the phone.

"Are you there?" he asked.

"*Girl* is definitely the right word. She still has some baby fat in those cute widdle cheeks."

"Hey, now…"

"A *cocktail waitress*? Really, Cal?"

"Tending bar was just her day job—night job, whatever. But she's also a small-business owner. Self-taught."

"A real autodidact, I'm sure. 'Massages 'N' More,' winky-face?"

"No! She runs a scrapbooking service, and she's fantastic at it."

"A professional scrapbooker from the Midwest." Claire guf-fawed, sitting up and sending her washcloth to the wood floor. "It's *perfect*."

"It's quite clever, actually. Rich toffs who can't or don't have the time to compile their family histories pay her to do it for them. She interviews family members, edits their photos to-gether with music, that sort of thing."

"And to think I was living my life, unaware of the booming market for scrapbooking videographers. This changes every-thing."

"In Chicago she had loads of clients. They'll love her even more out here."

"Look, to be honest, I can't get a good handle on her, which makes me think other people won't, either."

"What are you on about?" He sounded genuinely per-plexed. (*Whipped into obliviousness*, Claire concluded.)

From the master bedroom came a loud noise, followed by the after-chase of shrieks and laughter. Maybe Jonathan had fallen off the bed.

If you injure your hands, I'll kill you, she thought.

"Claire?" Cal pressed.

"Right. I can't decide if she's wholesome or trashy. She's like a *Twin Peaks* waitress who turns tricks on the side."

"Didn't they all turn tricks on the side?"

"No, you're thinking of the perfume counter. I mean, surely you've noticed? She cusses like a Mamet character but looks like a JCPenney catalog model. Who's secretly dating a biker gang." Claire chuckled at her own joke.

"The whole lot of them, is she, not just one?" he asked drily.

"Exactly."

"Are you quite done?"

"Please, I have a million of 'em." She cleared her throat. "She's like a debauched Dairy Queen samples girl who's about to—"

"Enough," he snapped.

"Wait, that's the one that offended you? I didn't even finish! Was it the Dairy Queen remark? Hit a little close to home?"

He sighed. "Yes, she grew up in Wisconsin. With their... cheeses and whatnot."

"Curds," Claire said, unable to contain her laughter. "*Cheese curds.*"

"Someone born and bred in Modesto doesn't get to throw stones."

"...Good point."

"Your jibes are technically accurate. Yes, she's both adorable and mischievous. Embrace the contradiction. And yes, before you ask, she's got some ink. On her back."

"Eden and her friends call those tramp stamps."

"Eden will change her mind one day, if she hasn't already."

"I don't think so."

"Besides, I have a tattoo now," he revealed. "On my ring finger. We got them instead of wedding bands."

"That's right, I saw hers tonight. I must have blocked it out."

"This way I'll never lose it since I won't have to take it off during shows."

"What about the TV special?"

"They'll cover it with makeup."

Jonathan and his gal pal were making the headboard bang against the wall now, but it wasn't particularly rhythmic, which meant his partner likely wasn't getting much out of it. Some men never grasped the importance of tempo; her husband joined their ranks when he'd had too much to drink.

"I'm going to go." She suddenly felt very tired.

"Be happy for me," Cal begged.

"I made a Mrs. Danvers joke and she didn't *get* it—"

"I'd have thought you'd be chuffed. Any excuse to feel smug—"

"Nothing I've said tonight is half as vicious as whatever Brandy's thinking."

"Brandy's not thinking anything because Brandy is dead," he said angrily. "Sod it. I fell in love with someone kind and sweet this time around. Is that so horrible?"

Claire held the phone away from her face for a moment and closed her eyes.

"No, of course not. But…it won't be easy for me."

He was quiet now. "I know."

They didn't speak for a moment.

"Do you really hate her?" Cal asked, sounding melancholy and far away.

There was a time Claire would've said whatever he needed to hear to make him stop sulking, but that time was long since passed.

"She's half your age."

"She isn't! And let's face it, sometimes younger can be…preferable."

"'Younger can be preferable'? Do you *hear* yourself?"

"I just mean less cynical, less jaded."

She snorted. "For now. And what happened to 'she's so kind, she's so sweet'? Was that just code for 'nubile'?"

"Give me a little credit here."

"I just…I never thought I'd see you turn into Jonathan."

"Why haven't you told him to bugger off yet? Eden's in college—"

"She just got there—"

"—point is, she's out of the house and you don't have to

pretend for her anymore. Wasn't that the plan?" Cal said. "I thought by the time I got back, you'd have…" He trailed off, and Claire glanced toward the bedroom, which was now strangely silent.

"She's a freshman. It's barely been a month. I can't pull the rug out from under her the second she leaves home. And Magician of the Year is his to lose this time, I can feel it."

"Why is it so important to you that he win?" Cal asked.

She chose her words carefully. "It just *is*. And if I'm going to end things I want to end them on my own terms."

"But—"

"You support me, and I'll support you, okay?"

"Right. I'm off."

"Are we saying good night angry, or are we good?" she asked. Old habits died hard, and she disliked ending the call on bad terms, especially when he'd only just returned.

"We're fucking marvelous," he grated out.

"Just answer me one thing. What do you *talk* about? Can she keep up?"

"She keeps up fine. And she keeps *me* up twenty-four seven—"

"Oh, ewww." Claire threw her phone onto the couch, silencing him.

She wanted to be glad for Cal, but his happiness only highlighted her lack of it.

They used to be unhappy together.

She turned on the TV in the hope of drowning out the renewed noises emanating from the bedroom.

She flipped to a late-night talk show. The guest was an up-and-coming, fresh-faced card sharp, Patrick Blake; Claire had recorded the segment last week but hadn't gotten around to watching until tonight. Patrick was twenty-nine now, but when Claire had known him he'd been twenty-six.

As president of Club Deception, Claire's husband ran a semester-long internship for young magicians. In reality it was a free-labor program, consisting of rides to and from the airport, dry-cleaning pickup, and walking the dog. In exchange for "school credit" or some other bullshit, he chewed up the young men and spat them out; they had nothing he needed or wanted (unlike his female assistants) so he forced them into indentured servitude. Sometimes he'd even host a party and let them work as servers, allowing his protégés to eavesdrop on a Who's Who of Magic. He'd occasionally drop crumbs of advice, or demonstrate some classic tricks, but never patiently enough for anyone to learn from or duplicate them. The poor saps signed nondisclosure agreements on the first day of work, allowing the program to continue in perpetuity, since no one could warn the next victim.

Patrick Blake had lasted nine weeks, and made no secret of the fact that he was attracted to Claire. He planted little chocolate hearts around the house for her to find and she felt silly and flattered whenever she brought one to her mouth as he watched. Ultimately, she suspected his flirtations were vengeance-based. He'd wanted to be able to say, *I banged the asshole's wife*. He wouldn't have been sticking it to her; he'd have been sticking it to Jonathan. Claire was simply the delivery system.

Still, his presence helped curb her loneliness. Claire and Patrick shared a vice Jonathan disapproved of, smoking, and had spent stolen moments on the porch, wordlessly trying to outdo each other's Zippo lighter tricks. Flintwheel. Snap Flick. And her favorite, the Hot Hand: flipping the lid open, slamming the opened Zippo wheel into her palm at a forty-five-degree angle, bumping it with her free hand to light it, then flipping it around and snuffing it out with a satisfying clap. Patrick's specialty was the Trip Roll, in which he held the lighter upside down, flicked it open, rolled it along one of his fingers so it spun into the correct hand position, and lit it.

In the end, she'd hesitated to return his advances, so Patrick had skipped town, toured the college circuit for a while, and apparently made a name for himself in the art of cardistry. Cardists focused strictly on cards. Fans, extravagant cuts and shuffles, all were exceptionally executed maneuvers meant to display technique, hard work, and skill. The concept wasn't new, only the name (and the attitude). Cardists were the first to tell you they weren't magicians. As Patrick explained to the confused talk-show host on TV, "Magic's for old men."

He was trying to be controversial—forge an identity as the young upstart declaring war on the establishment. But Claire knew if his downloadable tutorials didn't wind up paying the bills he'd return to traditional magic in a heartbeat.

To the tune of "Kiss Off" by the Violent Femmes, Patrick demonstrated some of his moves, separating the deck into ten sections in a delicate, patterned combination with his fingers. The cards seemed to hover in the air before seamlessly sliding back together. The audience gasped and roared with approval. "This is a skill you have to *practice*, pure and simple," he said once the applause died down. "Don't get me wrong, a lot of magicians have skill, but just as many of them rely on props. Hocus-pocus in a box, you know? If you spend enough money, you, too, can become a 'monarch of magic.'" He used sarcastic air quotes and Claire smiled at his nerve. It was a direct dig at her husband, who had given himself that title in all his promo posters. (Jonathan had stolen it from Servais Le Roy, the Monarch of Mystery.)

She felt proud of Patrick, and sorry for herself that she'd never curled one finger around the belt loop of his jeans and pulled him into the walk-in pantry during one of Jonny's whiskey-'n'-poker nights at the house.

As a good-bye present, he'd left her his grandfather's post-war Zippo metallique, which had a hand-painted Scotty dog on it. It was far too expensive to carry around but she kept it in her bedside drawer, to remind her she had options Jonathan knew nothing about.

The moment the cacophony of "*Yes! Yes!*" crescendoed and died, Claire stalked down the hall toward the master bed-room. On the way, she passed a litany of framed awards, trophies, and medals hanging on the wall, depicting Jonny's stellar and varied career. The rest of their house was decorated in a low-key, midcentury style. This wall of fame served as the only indicator that a magician dwelled within.

Claire yanked the bedroom door open and walked in.

"Oh, shit." A young woman frantically pulled the silk sheets up to her armpits.

"Is this the new box jumper?" Claire asked, walking toward the bed. "She sounded limber enough."

"Oh, she got the job, just not as my assistant," hissed Jonathan. He remained sprawled atop the sheets in all his glory.

"What's a 'box jumper'?" the young woman asked.

"Never mind, dear." Claire tugged the sheet loose from under her husband's calves and threw it over his naked hips to cover him up.

Then she sat atop the bed, pinning the sheets in place and effectively trapping the lovers. "How drunk are you?" Claire asked.

"We took a limo," Jonathan replied.

"So we'll need to pick up your car tomorrow. Fan-tas-tic." Claire hit the syllables like a rubber band snapping, and the young woman flinched as though she'd been hit.

Claire turned her gaze on the girl. "Let me guess, he told you I was a lesbian, and that sometimes for kicks, I bring a woman home for both of us, so it's okay for him to do the same. We're Sartre and Simone de Beauvoir! Am I close?"

The young woman glanced nervously between them. "Um, no, he just said you were out of town."

"Oh. That's a new one."

Jonathan shrugged. "It's quicker."

"Anyway, a threesome at Oxford in the early nineties does not a lesbian make, no matter what he thinks," Claire said.

"Did you catch that?" Jonathan thundered. "She went to *Oxford*. She studied *literature*. It's all very impressive."

"Okay…?" The young woman's eyes darted back and forth nervously.

"Did you come in here to show off?" Jonathan asked his wife. "You forgot your diploma."

"It's in my other dress."

"You don't think you're Simone de Beauvoir," Jonathan said, jabbing a fingertip against Claire's collarbone. "You think you're Véra Nabokov. See? I can play this game, too."

"I can't be Véra Nabokov because that would require you to be a genius."

"Touché."

"What's happening?" the girl blurted out. "Should I leave?"

"Do you have a name?" Claire asked.

"Becca." Becca paddled her feet against the sheets, trying to loosen them, but Claire's thighs held them in place.

"Hi, Becca. Where did you meet my husband?"

"At a party. He's a really good magician," Becca said meekly.

Claire stared back. "He is, isn't he?"

Despite having fled Modesto at eighteen (and immediately expunging the word *hella* from her vocabulary), she retained a hint of the flat, affectless Northern California accent she'd grown up around. Sounding detached came in handy at times; it helped her save face in certain situations, and she was grateful for it.

"I should probably go." Becca made another attempt at escape.

Claire ignored her. "You need to be up at five thirty, Jonny, remember?" She leaned across her husband's body to set the alarm. He was reasonably fit, if slightly doughy, and that, combined with the smattering of blond hair on his chest and legs, made him look like a pampered Nordic prince. When they'd first met, he reminded her of Stellan Skarsgård in *The Unbearable Lightness of Being.*

"Maybe I should go," Becca said.

They stared at her impassively. No one moved.

"*Can* I go?" she pleaded.

"You already have," Claire said. "As far as I'm concerned."

"I didn't think you'd be here," Jonathan slurred. "I thought you'd be out with Cal, celebrating his return."

"Is that what this is about? A preemptive lay in case Cal pushed me up against a wall somewhere? You're insane."

"Why'd he have to come back?" Jonathan looked on the verge of tears suddenly. "Everything was better when he was gone."

She hadn't been exaggerating when she told Jessica every magician had another one he hated. Jonathan was obsessed with Cal, and the possibility of beating him out. At anything. (At everything.) At first, Claire assumed it was leftover jealousy from Cal and Claire's decades-long friendship, but it also had to do with the respect afforded to close-up magicians. As Patrick had crudely pointed out on his television spot, close-up guys were known for pure hand skill, whereas stage magicians were carried by using large, self-working props.

Cal, of course, rarely gave Jonathan much thought, which rankled Jonathan most of all.

Cal's absence the past three years had only heightened his mythology in the minds of those he'd left behind. Now the prodigal son had returned, with a new wife in tow. (Claire kept that fact to herself. If Jonathan feared Cal was planning to whisk Claire away now that he'd returned to Los Angeles, so much the better. He deserved to worry.)

Claire shifted on the bed so her back was toward Becca. "Unzip me."

"What the hell?" Becca muttered. "I thought you said you *weren't* a lesbian." Nevertheless, she complied, determining it was easier not to argue.

Claire tossed her dress to floor, where it pooled into a misshapen black hole, sucking in all remaining light from the rest of the room. In nothing but a slip, she got under the covers, trapping Becca in the middle of the bed between her and Jonathan.

"What are you doing, my dear?" asked Jonathan sleepily.

"I'm not sleeping in Eden's room and I'll be damned if I take the guest room in my own house."

"Okay, I'm outie," declared Becca, jerking free from the sheets in a burst of panic and leaping out of the bed. She made a mad dash for the bathroom, naked ass wiggling.

"There are fresh towels in the left-hand drawer," Claire called after her.

Jonathan barked out a drunken laugh and flopped onto his stomach, apparently down for the count. He'd wake up tomorrow as he always did with a pillow crease on his face, looking like a moron.

Claire moved him onto his back, then followed suit and stared up at the ceiling.

Her husband was objectively good-looking, she knew; or at

least, he'd looked good to her once. But twenty years of watching him piss on their marriage vows had altered his face in her mind to Dorian Gray levels of grotesquery.

Jonathan was erudite, charming, passionate, and smart.

Claire was smarter.

Jonathan was a very good magician.

Claire was better.

If not for one twist of fate, her incapacitating stage fright, the countless trophies Jonathan had accumulated in their time together might have been engraved with her name, not his.

He was her proxy onstage; she needed him to give life to her routines, or they would wither and die, never to find an audience. It was her ideas that catapulted him to board president and two-time runner-up for Stage Magician of the Year; her patter he memorized; her stage direction he followed, however grudgingly.

If he finally succeeded in grabbing the brass ring next month, it would be as though Claire had finally won. Before she divorced the son of a bitch, she needed to prove it, to herself if to no one else. She needed to know she was the best.

Jessica

WHEN JESSICA WAS six, growing up in Waukesha, Wisconsin, her mother told her that her dad, a mysterious figure whom Jessica had never met, was a magician who traveled the world with exotic animals, a team of beautiful assistants, and a water tank, from which he had to escape every night or die trying.

Her mother spoke in a loud, animated voice, and to Jessica's young ears, her intoxicated enthusiasm was indistinguishable from passion and therefore rang with truth.

Likewise, it never occurred to her to ask why, if he was the star of his own show, he never sent them any money. Or why risking death by drowning every night was preferable to being part of a family, or even sitting down with them for dinner once a month. His name was William Deverell (the Great) and he'd proved strangely ungoogleable.

In elementary school, to her mother's irritation, Jessica recorded every magic TV special she could find. She also borrowed DVDs from the library in nearby Cutler Park, scouring them for mentions or glimpses, anything that could be connected to a Deverell. While Mom slept off a bender or worked long hours at the Kroger (then the Cracker Barrel, then Sam's Club, then Sunset Laundry, and ultimately as a late-night cleaning lady at an insurance agency, where she could be alone and sip from a flask while she vacuumed and dusted), Jessica researched her dad and, in the process of pursuing him, learned the skills she needed to become entirely self-sufficient.

He must not have been famous enough to make it on TV, she concluded at age thirteen. *Which means he has to be tracked down in person.* But globe-trotting magicians and their entourages didn't perform in Waukesha, Wisconsin, on the regular. So she took the train to Chicago and walked right into Magic, Inc., one of the oldest magic stores in North America. The older woman behind the register was sympathetic to Jessica's plight but unable to recall meeting any magicians of that name.

To soften the blow, she gave Jessica a free ticket to a stage show at the Arie Crown Theater. The headliner was known as the Monarch of Magic. His tricks may not necessarily have been new, but they gave Jessica an extraordinary rush. Seeing magic *live* was to question the solidness of the world around you. (TV didn't compare because a part of you always suspected trick camera angles or false editing at play.) The shared experience with an enraptured audience, surrounded by pulsing music, lights, and smoke and mirrors, was addictive!

By fifteen, armed with only a learner's permit, Jessica risked juvie each weekend by dragging her friends on road trips to Milwaukee, Chicago, and Indianapolis, to carnivals where magicians performed alongside jugglers, sword swallowers, clowns, and burlesque dancers. She and her friends wasted none of their time or money on the Tilt-A-Whirl, Thunder Bolt, or potato sack slides. They were on a mission. And then one night, after a year of searching the Midwest on increasingly distant road trips, she realized she wasn't doing it to find her dad, not anymore.

She loved magicians. They made people happy, wanted

nothing more than to bring joy and astonishment to others. They lived for her delight; gave her a feeling she never got at home, of being wanted.

For her eighteenth birthday, her friends took her to a two-hour magic show in Madison, with warm-up acts, an MC, and a headliner, and arranged for her to assist during the first card trick. Afterward, Jessica got a larger-than-life-size image of a Queen of Hearts playing card tattooed on her back. She wanted the memory of that night—her friends' love and support, her own light-headed joy—engraved on her skin.

Home at three a.m., Jessica was startled to discover her mother waiting up for her.

To the consternation of the backyard chickens, which she'd enclosed with her inside the mosquito-screened front porch, Jessica's mother paced angrily from side to side. Clutching a bottle of Green Mark vodka, she hurled her questions:

"You're looking for him, aren't you? Do you think I don't know what you've been doing all these years? Do you think I'm stupid?"

The chickens squawked and fluttered.

"Of course not," Jessica replied carefully. Her fresh tattoo leaked beneath its bandage. She was desperate to put a cold compress and some Aquaphor on it as the tattoo artist instructed, but if her mother sensed her distraction, things would get ugly, fast.

"You haven't been spending your weekends at Priya's," her mother hissed, her finger stabbing the air.

"If you knew, why didn't you stop me? Why did you let me go?"

"One less thing on *my* plate. But you're wasting your time, looking for him."

It turned out Jessica's father wasn't a magician.

If William Deverell the Great knew any magic tricks,

Jessica's mother assured Jessica, he'd twisted them for his own gain.

He was a con man. A thief.

She didn't even know his real name.

When she'd met him in San Francisco, he'd gone by the name William Deverell. However, he used different names for different "careers," among them a limousine driver, a bouncer, a purveyor of antiquities, and a document forger. The name Deverell was fake, which meant Jessica's name was fake, too. She was the only branch in the Deverell family tree.

She was eighteen now so maybe it was time, so her mother said, that Jessica stopped being a goddamn idiot expecting him to show up with a goddamn top hat, goddamn cane, and goddamn bunny rabbit.

Despite the shock of it all and the crude way it was delivered, Jessica wouldn't have traded her years of searching for this cold truth, because the story of a magician father had sustained her for most of her life, kept her dreaming and hoping and burning for something better when she'd most needed to.

Ultimately, it would lead her to California.

* * *

After one semester at University of Illinois Urbana-Champaign, she dropped out, armed herself with a fake ID (like father, like daughter), and made a life for herself in Chicago, bartending at the stylish Gold Coast Hotel overlooking Lake Michigan.

For five years she took online courses. She dated bland, square-jawed fraternity brothers from Northwestern and Concordia who seemed to think drinks at The Ogden to watch a Blackhawks game was a good date night. They were future bankers, future stockbrokers, and future venture capitalists, and she couldn't imagine herself staying with any of them once they truly *became* those things. The Art Institute boys weren't much better. Their fragile adoration made her feel trapped, and she kept their conversations to surface-level banalities. If they knew her family history, they'd only end up putting her on a tragedy-pedestal. One of them referred to her as his muse, so she gently broke things off. Let him feast on *that* for a year.

So when Calum Clarke arrived at the hotel, it was as though she'd conjured him out of her collective disappointment in men; men who thought her Queen of Hearts tattoo was kind of trashy; men who grabbed her ass in front of their buddies; men who had no clue about what she wanted or needed, only what they could extract from her.

Not only was Calum the best-looking man she'd ever seen—dark-haired and dashing—but he was a magician, *and* he was British. Just like *The Prestige*. He was pure fantasy, this lanky yet masculine illusionist with the James Bond accent—but she wasn't allowed to go near him! Her manager made it clear the first night of Calum's weeklong engagement that servers and bartenders were not to bother him. The magician had been hired and flown in at great expense by the hotel, for VIP guests *only*.

All Jessica could do was stand behind the bar, night after night, in dizzying envy while the rich crowd lined up outside (cocktails in hand, excitement swirling), entered the theater, and emerged forty-five minutes later, invigorated, glowing, forever changed.

Every show, every night, was torture.

Somehow she made it to Friday evening.

After clocking in, reapplying her lipstick, adjusting her skirt, and memorizing the night's drink specials, she scanned the dining area and felt a familiar, painful knot of lust tightening in her stomach. There he was, devastatingly gorgeous in his tuxedo, his soft-looking, wavy dark hair aching to be touched; his perfectly smooth face, sculpted cheekbones, and cleft chin begging to be kissed and caressed. He may have been too skinny for some girls' taste, but he pushed all her buttons.

As usual, he ate dinner by himself, at a table by the window. He rolled a poker chip smoothly along his knuckles, then swept it back up and around his hand to start over again. His movements were effortless and sensual, in a smooth rhythm. She unconsciously swayed on her feet to match the tempo. Over and around. Over and around.

And Jessica's manager was nowhere in sight.

He'd be gone after tomorrow night, so what did she have to lose?

She waited until the server dropped off his check, and then she strode over, bare legs shivering in the air-conditioned room, trying the fake-it-till-you-make-it mode of confidence.

"Hi! Sorry to bother you, but do you have a few minutes for a drink? On the house."

Cal sprang to his feet and pulled out a chair for her like a butler in an old film. "I don't drink, but I'd fancy some company."

Her eyes nearly rolled back in a haze of pleasure. His accent was delicious.

She saw now that what she'd thought was a poker chip was a sobriety chip. She could've kicked herself, but his smile looked genuine, and his cautious brown eyes revealed a hint of humility that put her at ease.

There's no way you could've known about the sobriety thing. Forget about it and just be yourself.

Up close he seemed closer to late thirties than early but she didn't give a damn. Chivalry was chivalry, and he had it for days. There were a few wrinkles around his eyes, but that made him seem illustrious instead of insipid like her college-aged boyfriends. He smelled faintly of fresh cedar, which reminded her, pleasantly, of Cook County Forest Preserve after a rainstorm. She'd have given up a week's pay to see him in a tight T-shirt and jeans, drenched.

His lips were a dream, full and soft looking.

Trying to keep her breathing steady, she sat and clasped her hands under her chin. "I'm Jessica, by the way."

"Pleasure to meet you, Jessica. I'm Calum."

"I know."

(He was sitting under a poster advertising his performance.)

He glanced at the poster and shook his head with embarrassment. "Right."

"So, I came over here because I wanted to apologize."

"Whatever for?"

"I've been dying to see your show, but…" She lowered her voice, glanced around for eavesdroppers. "My manager said it wouldn't look right to the guests."

"I see."

"I've been catching bits and pieces all week, though, and after each show I jotted down some of the things people have been saying as they left." She reached into her apron pocket and pulled out a fistful of napkins. "I thought maybe you'd like to read them? Everyone especially seemed to love the Bottle Cap trick."

His bottom lip dropped in surprise.

She stared at his mouth, picturing his lips gliding up and

down her neck. When she handed over the napkins, he reached toward her at the same time, and their fingers grazed, sending a jolt of longing through her.

"Aren't you a doll," Cal said in a quiet, sincere voice. "I'm going to hold on to these so next time I botch a show I can re-read them."

She was *positive* he had never botched a show.

"I'm sorry you missed it, too," he continued. "But I'm, frankly, a tad relieved."

"Why's that?"

"I don't see how it could possibly live up to expectations."

Gorgeous *and* modest. Her desire for his hands on her was so pure and unflinching she could almost, *almost* feel it happening.

"I'm willing to take that risk," she said. Her smile faded. "Maybe next time, huh?"

"Tell you what. If *you're* willing to take that risk, *I'm* willing to as well. What about a staff-only show at the end of the night? Invite anyone you like. If you're free, that is."

She had never been more available.

True to his word, Calum stayed put onstage following the final curtain that Friday night. He didn't return his velvet close-up pad, his Linking Rings routine, or any other prop to his steel-framed briefcase.

The bar manager protested, of course—"We have a band on the weekends, they need to set up"—but Cal convinced him to allow a fifteen-minute version of his show for the hotel staff. The cameraman who'd been shooting footage all week (rumor had it Cal was putting together a TV show to air in the fall) continued filming, albeit with a cocktail in his hand. He was officially off the clock, but a few more spontaneous reaction shots from "regular people" would be valuable as cutaways.

"Would you mind terribly helping me?" Cal asked Jessica, who sat in the front row with another bartender and two waiters.

She had a half-empty beer in hand and he told her to bring it up with her. She knew what that meant: the famous Bottle Cap trick, at last.

"The cap, too, if you please."

To her co-workers' enjoyment, Jessica threw her head back and swigged the last drops. Cal took the glass bottle and bottle cap from her and showed them to the audience, then asked Jessica to confirm their ordinariness. They'd come from her own hands, from her own bar. They couldn't have been more normal.

Calum held the bottle in his left hand, and with his right, he tapped the bottle cap once, twice, against the bottom of the bottle. It made a clicking sound each time.

On the third tap, silence.

He held the bottle up: the cap was inside.

And it was never coming out.

Jessica shrieked, her eyes shiny with delight. He handed her the bottle so she could study it.

She shook it up and down—*rattle, rattle, rattle*, went the cap—and passed it around to her pals.

Contrary to his professed fear, the trick didn't disappoint. Not even close.

For his next illusion, he asked Jessica to pick a card and sign her name on it with his Sharpie. She selected the Two of Hearts. Calum placed the card in the middle of the deck, snapped his fingers, and asked Jessica to turn over the top card. There it was, having risen through the ranks: the Two of Hearts.

He lost the card six more times; in the front, the back, and the middle of the deck, only for it to rise to the top over and over.

During a moment of heart-stopping tension, Jessica turned the top card over a seventh time and discovered that the front of the card was blank. The staff collectively leaned forward in their seats. The next card was blank, too. And the next. Cal spread the deck out on his close-up pad for all to see: a full set of red backs and white fronts, all blank. The signed card and its original siblings were gone.

He waited a beat, then pointed to the ceiling.

Everyone looked up.

"No. Motherfucking. Way," Jessica squealed.

"Yes. Bloody. Way," he said back.

Her signed card was stuck to the side of a tall pillar above them.

The audience responded with cheers and yells.

Jessica glanced down and saw that the original deck was now spread out where the blank one used to be.

"This, too," she called out, motioning to her friends. "Look back here again."

A fresh wave of applause broke and washed over them as everyone realized Cal had set them up for a second surprise.

It could've gone on all night; everyone wanted it to, but the bar manager made a fuss and Cal politely gathered his items together.

Jessica's heart stampeded in her chest as she realized it was now or never.

"Want to get out of here?" she asked.

He smiled back.

They walked along Lakeshore Drive, Jessica still buzzing off his performance. She'd never seen magic so close up before. She thought of his fingers, long, firm, and dexterous...

"Are you at university?" he asked.

It took her a moment to realize he'd asked her a question. "Nah. I figured if there was anything I was passionate about I could teach it to myself, you know?"

He nodded. "Cheers to that. I felt the same way when I was your age."

She swallowed, disappointed. Was pointing out their age difference his way of telling her he wasn't interested?

"I've been mixing drinks for my mom since I was fourteen, but it's really just to support my other job," she said, and told him about her scrapbooking business. It was more than she normally revealed, but Cal was different. She wanted him to know she was more than a waitress. "I started it because I like seeing how other families live." She paused. "Normal families."

"No such thing."

"Mine may have been a bit further from the norm. When I turned eighteen, my mom said, 'All right, it's up to you now, kid.' Got this the same week. I've always loved magic," she added shyly.

She lifted up the back of her shirt to show him her tattoo.

He traced the outline of the playing card with his fingertip. She arched toward his touch, couldn't prevent a happy sigh from escaping her lips.

He rubbed the image of the queen with his thumb, in smooth, tiny circle-eights.

She inhaled with pleasure. *He's actually touching me.* The skin-to-skin contact made the muggy, oppressive July heat feel decadent. The thin sheen of sweat on her back only added to the charged moment.

"I think we come from the same tribe," he remarked, never ceasing the steady stroke of his thumb against her skin.

"Alcoholic mother?"

"Father."

"Was yours around, at least?" she asked.

"He wasn't exactly the sort of bloke you wanted around."

"Is that why you don't drink?"

His thumb abruptly stopped moving.

Oh, God! Why did I ask that? "Sorry, sorry! Too personal?"

"It's probably one of the reasons, yeah."

She didn't push further, but the mood was broken. She pulled her shirt back down.

They sat on a bench facing Lake Michigan. The skyline to the left was dazzling at night. Jessica's favorite was the Smurfit-Stone Building, lit up like a diamond.

To her surprise, Cal returned to the subject of fathers. "He wasn't around unless you count Saturday Shockers. A phrase coined by my mum, by the way, not me."

"Ooh, what were Saturday Shockers?"

"Saturday Shockers were the one day a month my dad would spend time with us. The first shock was, 'Would he show up?' More often than not, the answer was no. The second shock was, 'Will he be pissed?' (Yes.) The third shock was, 'Where will he take us?' My sister and me. Usually it would be, 'Hey, I've an idea, let's go down the pub!' Because we weren't going to get in the way of his footie-and-drinking schedule, I can tell you that."

"Footie?"

"Soccer. Other times it would be, 'Off to the cinema, then.'"

She shrugged. "Movies are fun."

"Not *Alien*. When I was *five*."

She giggled, horrified. "No. With the—?" She mimed "alien bursting out of stomach."

His eyes crinkled with delight at her reaction. "Nightmares for months. Another time it was a funeral. *We went to a funeral.* For someone we didn't know."

She bit back a shriek. "Nooo."

"Yeah. Lovely outing, not at all upsetting. He was pleased about the free food. Considered it one of his best shockers."

They laughed together and Jessica felt a warmth swim through her veins. In the short time they'd known each other, he'd made her laugh more than her last three boyfriends combined. She could listen to him talk for hours, and she ached for more stories, wanted to learn everything she could about him.

"Were you always a magician?" she asked.

"Always," he said. "First thing I did in the delivery room was ask the nurse to pick a card. And I cut my own umbilical cord with my fingers." He made a scissoring motion and Jessica grabbed his hand to make him stop.

"Come on," she said.

"I was a layabout, really. Left school at sixteen after my O-levels and crewed on ships, mucking about for five years. Cooking, cleaning, trimming the sails. Saw the Mediterranean, the Caribbean, a bit of Norway."

"Wow," Jessica said quietly. "I haven't been anywhere."

Cal began fiddling with a red silk cloth. Where it had come from, Jessica couldn't guess. His movements were fluid, unhurried. Staring out at the water, never glancing down, he pushed the thin, long red silk into his fist until it vanished, and opened his hand, revealing it to be empty.

"Again," Jessica whispered.

He looked down, apparently surprised to see he'd been practicing a trick.

"Sorry, just a habit."

"Again," she repeated, daring to place her hand on his knee.

The silk was in his breast pocket now, bright and vibrant.

"I need to get some rest." He sighed.

Her shoulders drooped. It was late and he was right, but…it felt like a dismissal.

Until he pressed the scrap of silk into her hand, and covered her small fingers with his large, warm ones. "You keep it."

"What should I do with it?"

His gaze was dark. "I can think of a few things," he said.

At work the next afternoon, she opened her purse and saw that her driver's license was missing from her wallet.

In its place was a hotel room key.

At eleven twenty-eight, exactly ten minutes after his final show, Jessica slid her key card into his door slot and held her breath. She wore a miniskirt and a cropped biker jacket. His red scrap of silk served as a halter top.

He appeared in seconds, his tie off, barefoot, dress shirt rumpled, holding her driver's license like a white flag between his first and second fingers.

"Here, you can have it, you don't have to come in, that was awful of me, really, I never should have presumed…" But in the same breath he gasped, "You're the best thing I've seen in years, Jessie."

He looked down, embarrassed, and she put her finger against his lips.

Hearing him call her Jessie in that worshipful voice had cemented her decision. "I didn't come here for my driver's license."

He looked up and allowed their eyes to meet. "Oh," he said.

He pushed the door shut behind her. The click of the lock echoed in the silent room.

He canceled the rest of his tour.

She never made it back to work.

Seeing him now, framed by the light of their bedroom door-way at the Standard hotel, brought back a hundred happy memories. With the hotel setting such a distinct reminder of their beginning, all her fears about Claire's widows and girl-friends dissolved into the ether. They were together, which meant they were home. Any city, anywhere.

There was Cal, unbuttoning his shirt and placing his slacks on a hanger in the closet. There was Cal, rummaging through his metallic briefcase. There was Cal, retrieving the object he'd promised her eight hours before: soft as silk, strong as cable.

"Hey, baby," she called softly.

Moonlight cascaded over his face as he wrapped the rope around his fists and pulled taut, making a line so tight it vi-brated. "You'll have to keep quiet, though. We can't get kicked out of The Standard."

Kaimi

AT CAPACITY, THE Dorset Theatre in Hollywood held
fifty-five people. Today fifty-four of them were men—
specifically, magicians—who'd paid a whopping $365 each to attend Landon the Libertine's sold-out seminar, "Luck Be a Lady."

The fifty-fifth audience member (and sole woman) was
Kaimi Lee, a freelance art appraiser and broker who'd been invited as Landon's guest. Landon needed Kaimi to auction off a
peculiar item his late father had left him.

He'd contacted her the week before through her now-defunct email account at the University of Hawaii at Manoa
and suggested they grab a bite after his seminar. He promised
to make it worth her while, and she was holding him to it.

A glance at the info sheets and tear-away phone numbers
tacked up to the lobby's bulletin board told Kaimi today was a
special occasion for the small, unassuming Dorset. Most afternoons it seemed to serve as a rental space for improv classes or
a background for showcases wherein struggling actors bludgeoned their friends, family, and the occasional agent with
monologues from *Fame* and *Angels in America*. The theater
was a bit shoddy, with peeling light-green paint on the walls,
and a collection of vases filled with fake flowers resting on
every available surface. The squat, 1970s-era building sat on
Santa Monica Boulevard across from the army/navy surplus

store. Five more uninspiring theaters flanked it, collectively known as Theatre Row.

Ahead of her in line were hipsters with lopsided bangs, USC frat boys in polo shirts and khakis, and semi-nerdy, earnest men in their thirties who clutched binders with printouts inside. More than a few fiddled with decks of cards. The vibe reminded Kaimi of the comic-book stores she used to go to with her junior high boyfriend; in both places she'd felt like she was on the periphery of a society she'd never understand and never be allowed to join because the only membership requirement was a penis.

"Luck Be a Lady" must be the name of an elaborate card trick they want to learn, she thought. *Better be a helluva trick to justify charging $365.* Maybe the ticket price included a DVD or instruction pamphlet. The only magic Kaimi had seen was the Kona Kozy Comedy & Magic Show at the Voodoo Room on the Big Island, so she had little idea what to expect.

She eavesdropped on an argument taking place behind her in line, between two nasal-voiced young magicians.

"Red Hot Mama is not a closer. It's an opener, dude. That's why it's also known as Chicago *Opener*. A good closer should be your strongest piece."

"But it still has to fit within the rest of the show."

"No, it has to be better. It has to stand out."

"Within a *theme*. Or else it's random as shit and rapes the whole thing."

Violent, sexist hyperbole: It's what's for dinner! She couldn't resist interrupting. "He's totes right, dude. No one likes random-as-shit closers that rape everything!"

Before they could respond, the doors opened and Kaimi got swept along with the crowd. There were no assigned seats, so she chose one by the aisle in the back to facilitate a fast escape if necessary.

The curtain rose right on time, which she appreciated.

Raucous applause greeted Landon the Libertine, an extremely handsome black man in his late twenties with tight, twisted curls and neatly trimmed facial hair. He exuded the friendly yet brusque confidence of an inspirational speaker trying to convince regular Joes that they, too, could make a fortune flipping houses.

Clad in tight jeans and high-top Margiela leather kicks, Landon traversed the small stage with charisma and self-possession that would put a faith healer to shame.

Kaimi was instantly suspicious.

He was too slick for his own good.

Intermittent music (Kanye West's "Stronger"; Drake's "All Me"; Rihanna's "What's My Name"; and of course a remixed cover of Sinatra's "Luck Be a Lady") amped the crowd up further and segued into the seventy-five-minute presentation.

"Hey guys, thanks for coming out today. Great crowd, great crowd. To kick things off, I'ma quote Jim Steinmeyer, who said, 'There was no magic ever created without establishing a trust with an audience—without seducing them first.' Okay, but what does that mean, right? Establish trust, and *then* seduce? Well, it means your magic game has got to be *on*. Assuming your magic's on point, though, and you put the time and effort into my techniques, you will see an increase in the number of dates this year over last year, and next year over this year."

Record scratch. Wait, what? More dates than last year? What is this?

Kaimi looked around at the other audience members, who paid rapt attention to Landon. They'd even ceased shuffling their cards.

"A dollar a day," Landon shouted. "That's less than a Starbucks! Surely you care more about increasing your dating velocity than a jolt of caffeine, am I right?"

My new client is a goddamn pickup artist.

Hence the $365 ticket price: For a mere dollar a day in fees (paid in one lump sum, of course), Landon was guaranteeing his audience more dates this year than they'd had last year. She wasn't at a magic class. "Luck Be a Lady" was a seminar on how to seduce women via magic tricks.

"Let's be real, 'more dates than last year' is not a fixed sum. It'll be different for everyone sitting here today. It'll be different for you than it will be for your neighbor over there. Yeah, look around. The guy with the chinstrap, he looks like a douche to you, but maybe that works for him, you don't know. On the other hand, if he had zero dates last year, he'll get at least *a* date this year. I'm not a miracle worker."

(Laughter.)

She wanted to run screaming into the street. But he was a client, her only client, and beggars couldn't be choosers. Still, that didn't mean she had to like it, or listen to it. Unfortunately, all of that charisma was impossible to block out. She wished she'd brought headphones.

"If you walk out the door right now and, starting today, September first, until September first of next year, you haven't increased your Rolodex, your little black book, your Facebook honeys, or whatever system you use to keep track of girlfriends, I will personally—personally!—refund your money. You've got to give it the full year, though, no welching on that, because only by applying my techniques and perfecting them will you see results. And if your magic's shit, well, I can't help you with that."

(More laughter.)

Make it stop, Kaimi thought, grinding her teeth and digging her fingernails into her palms.

At that point, Landon's seminar unabashedly morphed into an infomercial for his newsletter.

"And if you subscribe to the newsletter—sign up today at my website—you'll get *additional information*, top-secret *bonus information* that I don't have time for today, in your in-box, once a week. Today's seminar is about the basics. Think of it as an appetizer to get you started. The newsletter material is the main course, the dessert, and the after-dinner drinks. The newsletter is so good, so *very* good, I can't talk about it here, because come on, y'all are magicians—don't tell me one of y'all didn't bring in a camera phone or mini recording device or spy pen or something. The newsletter contains valuable stuff, I can't risk giving this information out at the seminar, it's too detailed, it's too *good* to hand out for three hundred sixty-five dollars. But people who've attended this seminar *will* get a discount on the newsletter, so be sure to go to my website after you leave tonight and get all the details on *that*."

The cadence of his words fell into a hypnotic rhythm. Kaimi closed her eyes and started to nod off. Twenty minutes later, she tuned back in—without wanting to—because the call-and-response going on was too enthusiastic to be ignored.

"Who's our target?" Landon demanded, his voice breaking.

"Half plus seven," the audience yelled back.

"Half plus seven. You know why?"

"Because she's not too young, and she's not too old."

"That's right! You've been paying attention! Half your age, plus seven. If you're forty, you should be aiming for twenty-seven-year-olds. If you're thirty, you should be aiming for twenty-five-year-olds, you get me? If you're twelve, you best believe you want a thirteen-year-old. She could teach you somethin'."

(Laughter.)

"No twelve-year-olds are here, are they? Shoot, they gonna shut me down if I'm giving love advice to twelve-year-olds.

"So. Half plus seven, that's your goal. If you're fifty, you want a thirty-two-year-old, right? That's George Clooney's rule, did you know that? That's not even my rule! But if you want to be like George Clooney, this is your way in. I'm telling you.

"Next we talked about using magic as a conversation starter, you know, bridge that gap, have a reason to chat her up. More important, to chat her *friends* up. You've *got* to flirt with the underdog. Flirt with the friend. Flirt with the enemy. Do not flirt with the target. Make *her* come to *you*.

"Never, ever, *ever* choose the prettiest girl to help you with a trick. Know why? Active disinterest creates a jealousy plotline. If you ignore the prettiest girl and make her stay down in the seats, she'll spend the whole set hot and *bothered* wondering, *Why didn't he pick me? Doesn't he think I'm pretty? What did I do wrong?*

"You're making the other girl, the homely girl, laugh, she's having a great time, you're being funny and charming with her, and meanwhile the woman you're actually into is Kermit the *Frog* with envy, thinking, *That should be* me *up there.*

"She's into *you* now, playa. She's insecure and ripe for the picking!"

Gross. Kaimi stood up and got the hell out of there.

She could still hear Landon spewing nonsense as she exited the lobby.

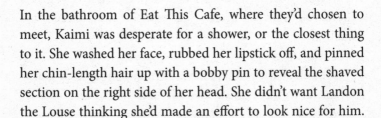

In the bathroom of Eat This Cafe, where they'd chosen to meet, Kaimi was desperate for a shower, or the closest thing to it. She washed her face, rubbed her lipstick off, and pinned her chin-length hair up with a bobby pin to reveal the shaved section on the right side of her head. She didn't want Landon the Louse thinking she'd made an effort to look nice for him.

With upscale clients she was happy to play the part, wear nice makeup, and cover the punk side of her hairdo, but for this guy? Forget it. Pinning her hair up also revealed the fact that she had a quadruple helix piercing in her ear. No need to protect Landon's eyes from *that*, either.

The head shave and piercings were new. Visible, daily reminders that she'd never again be, or even *resemble*, the demure, naive, and outright stupid girl she'd been in grad school.

Landon arrived ten minutes late. She saw him first and watched him searching for her. His worried eyes darted around the restaurant, and he seemed smaller, more life-size, now that he wasn't onstage. He also looked tired. Expending so much confidence and energy over a long, uninterrupted stretch of time must have taken a toll.

With a deep breath and a quick reminder to herself (*You need this job, you need this job*), she strode over to greet him.

"You're here," she said flatly.

He held out his hand. "Hi, Kammy, thanks for your patience," he said warmly.

She corrected his pronunciation. "Kai-may. Like 'My Way' from your favorite singer. It's a Hawaiian name."

"But you're Korean, right?"

"Korean *American*, third generation. We aren't super traditional. I lived in LA till I was twelve, but my parents always wanted to move to Hawaii, so my name was their way of making sure it happened, I guess." She hadn't meant to say all that. The less he knew about her, the better.

"Cool, cool. Hey listen, I'm sorry it took me so long to get out of there."

"I understand. You were probably being swarmed with 'honeys,'" she said sarcastically.

"What? Uh, no, just some guys wanting to talk about forced spreads—"

"Jesus!"

"It's a card term," he interjected quickly, and showed her the deck in his hand as if to prove it. His hands were so large that the deck fit in his palm without her noticing it. "Anyway, sorry again to keep you waiting."

She was thrown by his apology, and therefore irritated by it; he wasn't allowed to behave the way he had onstage and then switch to someone decent in private.

Why is he being nice? What's his angle? With her makeup removed and shaved head on display, she'd purposefully "uglified" herself (in the tame, predictable view of men like Landon, at least) so there was no reason for him to be gentle with her.

Still, she had to admit that if Landon's pickup techniques worked—and that was a big "if"—it wasn't because of some secret, or his ability to do magic tricks. It was because of the way he looked. Up close, he was startlingly attractive; his perfectly symmetrical face, clear brown skin, and charming smile were distracting, and unfair. *Who among his prey would stand a chance?*

She motioned to the hostess that they were ready for a table.

When they reached it, Landon pulled Kaimi's chair out for her.

But it felt like a slimy, premeditated gesture instead of a considerate one.

She made a point of grabbing the chair herself.

"What'd you think of the show?" he asked once their drinks had been ordered. Iced tea for her, water with lemon for him.

"'Half plus seven'?" she said. "Really? You're incapable of enjoying the company of someone born the same decade as you? It would just be too disgusting to spend time with a girl who might actually share the same cultural references and touchstones?"

He lowered his voice. "Hey, c'mon, between you and me, I don't believe the half-plus-seven thing."

"You were selling it pretty hard."

"Because that's what I do. Sell it. It's just a persona, for the job. If I legitimize what they think they want, they'll subscribe to my newsletter, which is where I make my real money."

She rolled her eyes. "Yeah, I sort of figured that out the seventeenth time you mentioned the newsletter. But if you legitimize what you think they want, you make life even harder for women than it already is." *Asshole.*

He took a long sip of his water. His voice was likely shot from the show. "But it's not real. It's my day job. I'm sort of like a con artist, if you want to look at it that way."

"Don't you mean pickup artist?"

"No, it's not like that, really. I can explain it to you, if you want—"

She brushed him off with a flick of her hand. "No, forget it, I don't care. Let's talk about why we're here. You need help selling some artwork?"

"Not artwork like a painting, but…It's a rare and unique magical item."

She took a deep breath. "Okay…" Her specialty was the Old Masters, but beggars couldn't be choosers. "Let's see it."

He retrieved an acid-free manila envelope from his briefcase (at least he wasn't clueless about storage) but hesitated to hand it over.

She rolled her eyes. "If we're going to work together you'll have to trust me with the merchandise."

He reluctantly slid the manila envelope across the table to her. She undid the clasp and reached inside with her thumb and forefinger, expecting to pull out an eight-by-ten photo of some kind of historical artifact. Instead the item itself was inside, held together in a plastic, see-through dust cover: a sheaf of five wrinkled papers, covered with small, ink-splattered writing, diagrams, and margin notes. Oddly, the set was torn diagonally in half.

She frowned. "Where's the rest of it?"

"There is no rest of it. This is all I've got."

She squinted at the pages in the poor lighting of the café. "I'll need a QDE to verify this, but I want to say 1905?"

He nodded. "Close. It's 1902."

"And these wormholes look real. Congrats, you're the proud owner of some old paper." She knew she shouldn't antagonize a potential source of income, but the meeting felt hopeless. It's not like she could look this up on Artnet for estimates or comps. And unless the potential QDE or graphologist she hired could verify, she had nothing.

He bristled. "Trust me, these are worth a lot."

"What is it, then?"

He leaned in, expecting her to follow suit. But she remained fixed, straight-backed in her chair on the opposite side of the table.

"Never-before-published, unedited, handwritten pages by S. W. Erdnase." He stared at her and raised his eyebrows, waiting for a reaction.

"Am I supposed to know who that is?"

Landon plucked a green book from his briefcase and plopped it down in front of her.

She read the title aloud. "*The Expert at the Card Table.* Who's S. W. Erdnase?"

"Good question. No one knows."

"What do you mean, 'no one knows'?"

"The book's a classic. You can find it on the shelves of every magician and card cheat in the world, but no one knows who Erdnase was. Some people think his real name was E. S. Andrews—you know, S. W. Erdnase spelled backward—and others believe it combines the names of two people who were too scared to reveal their identities and lose social standing back in the day, since the book was written for card cheats."

"Okay. Well, there's always hope in the art world that a master's lost work will resurface, but does anyone reference these elsewhere? Are people looking for them?"

"No, but wouldn't that make it even more valuable? New Erdnase material that's never been circulated or even hinted at…any magician would lose his *mind* to get his hands on it."

"Do you have other samples of his handwriting? How do you know it's authentic?"

"That's where you come in."

She leaned back and folded her arms. "I'll have to hire a graphologist and QDE—qualified document examiner—and that'll cost extra."

She was sort of hoping he'd call the whole thing off, but it didn't seem to faze him.

"Do whatever you need to."

"You said in your email that your father bequeathed them to you?"

"That's right."

"They didn't belong to him, though, did they?" It was a stab in the dark, but his reaction told her she was right.

"Well…" He smiled. "That's sort of the tricky part."

"Uh-huh. Why are they torn? Was there some kind of struggle?"

"Look, I don't know how he acquired them. But *I* didn't steal them, okay? They simply came into my possession, and now I want to unload them. For the right price."

"Is it a shakedown?" she demanded. "You sell the first half, then raise the price for the second half?"

"No, I'm telling you, there is no second half. If there was, he'd have left it to me. But I can't exactly sell them to a historical society. They're going to want to know the origin and chain of sale and all that."

"Yeah, how dare they?" she asked sarcastically.

"Is this going to be a problem for you? Because I figured with your arrest, you'd be cool with it—"

She stood up, furious. "How do you know about that?"

Landon laughed, which made it ten times worse. "Relax, Kaimi."

On second thought, *that's* what made it ten times worse.

"Wow." She fanned herself with her napkin and made an exaggerated swooning motion. "Nothing turns me on more than being told to relax by a *guy* I *just met*."

"Okay, okay, I apologize."

"It's not a problem for me *ethically*," she explained. "But it *does* limit the number of people we can sell to."

"All it means is that when you ask around, you tread carefully."

"Meaning…what? Is there some kind of magician black market? Because you'd be better at that than I am. Why do you even need me?"

"Because you're a woman."

She pulled at the skin next to her eyebrows. "I'm scared to ask why that's relevant."

"I can't approach any of these guys directly. It's too risky. I need a go-between, I need you to get to them through their wives."

"How do I do *that*?"

"Club Deception has a monthly brunch for the wives and girlfriends of magician members. I'll get you the password and you can buddy up to them, feel the place out. You'll have to pose as my girlfriend."

Oh, the joy my life is, she thought. "Can I take a sample page with me?"

He snatched the envelope from her and placed it back inside his briefcase. "The pages stay with me," he said seriously. "They don't leave my sight until they're sold."

"At least send me a jpeg in case I need to prove their existence."

He nodded. "Okay. A *quarter* of a page. I don't want any digital copies floating around or no one will be motivated to buy."

I can do this, she realized. *Pose as his girlfriend, befriend some of the so-called magician wives, and laugh all the way to the bank.*

Because if she found a willing buyer, and the papers were worth as much as Landon seemed to think they were, Kaimi didn't need Landon at all.

She would steal the papers from him and sell them herself.

Plus, it would be *pure pleasure* to rip him off.

"Smile," Kaimi said, and leapt into frame to take a selfie with Landon.

Reflexively, he grinned for her camera phone. *Click.*

"What was that for?" he asked.

"Maintaining the illusion."

She pocketed her phone, got up from the table, and left him to pay the check.

Felix

FROM THE OUTSIDE, Merlin's Wonderporium on Ventura Boulevard appeared to be a year-round Halloween store. The costumes in the window were top-notch, designed to lure in tourists seeking *Guardians of the Galaxy* masks or *Avengers* shields, but the bait and switch only lasted a few feet. Once you moved beyond the dress-up area, Merlin's Wonderporium became another store entirely, mired in the past.

Dusty straitjackets, handcuffs, and vintage coins filled the padlocked display cases in the center of the room. Old issues of *Mahatma*, *Sphinx*, *Genii*, and *Linking Ring*, encased in plastic, pressed against one another in three-foot-long collectors' boxes, color-coded by month and year, all the way back to 1953.

The employees, all men, were skilled at sleight of hand and happy to show off any products for sale.

Felix Vicario, however, had recently been forbidden from demonstrating tricks. He sat behind the cash register, mournfully surfing porn on the owner's slow-ass 2010 desktop computer. Normally he spent his downtime perfecting his overhand shuffles or coin rolls, but any of those movements might draw an audience, which was currently numero uno on the Forbidden List.

He wasn't allowed to showcase products to customers (even the "Hyuks" items—whoopee cushions and yo-yos—were off-limits). Without that ability, his only shot at earning commission was to match prospective customers with the right book for their skill level and interest. While Felix was stuck behind the counter ringing up orders, his asshole colleague, "Free Range" Spencer, got the advantage of moving about the floor and picking people off as they walked in.

Sometimes Felix killed time on Tragic Magic, a Tumblr account dedicated to the most humiliating/hilarious clips of magician failures throughout the world.

But mostly he looked at porn.

The incident that got him banned from demonstrating tricks had occurred a week earlier.

His nemesis was a product called Foiled (retailing for $57.95) in which a magician wears a piece of foil covering his face, but, because of his psychic powers, proceeds to do anything he could do *without* a piece of foil covering his eyes, such as walk around a magic store. True, Felix hadn't finished watching the instructional video or bothered to take Foiled for a test drive, but he was certain he'd guessed the method and he really wanted to impress the Georgetown girl and her parents visiting from DC.

He must've missed a step, because the trick blew up in his face.

With the foil wrapped tightly over his eyes, nose, and mouth, he tripped and fell headfirst into what should've been the counter. Unfortunately, it wasn't, and while attempting to regain his balance, he pawed the father's groin; the father yelled and pushed Felix backward, directly into the footstool he'd used earlier to remove a cape from the wall. The footstool banged his Achilles tendon and re-routed him into a stand-alone Hyuks display of gross-out toys, the containers of which toppled over onto the floor and split open. That, in turn, sent him crashing into the very counter that should've broken his fall in the first place. He knocked himself unconscious and landed with a thud facedown on the thin red carpet, surrounded by fake vomit and poop, which was how the paramedics found him after Georgetown Girl called 911.

Besides playing the security camera footage for the other employees to laugh at, Felix's boss, Roy, was deducting the cost of the damaged merchandise from Felix's paychecks. It would be another week or two until his debt was clear, which was the only reason he still had a job.

From the moment he returned from the ER, concussed and bruised, the pranks and mockery hadn't stopped.

Earlier today, Free Range Spencer had left out a Zorro mask on the counter, claiming Roy had offered to raise Felix's pay by a dollar per hour if he wore it on the job.

Racists, he thought. He was born and raised thirty miles north in Castaic, and had only been to Mexico twice. But *dinero* was *dinero*, and the quicker he replaced the Hyuks items, the cracked countertop, and the ruined Foiled, the quicker he'd have cash on hand to shore up his own collection of illusions.

Besides, what was the big deal? He'd seen dudes dressed as the Statue of Liberty during tax season, spinning signs up and down Ventura. At least a Zorro mask was manly, and at least he was inside, where it was air-conditioned.

Three hours later, Roy arrived for an inventory check.

"What on God's green earth possessed you to put on that mask?" he hollered. "Have you been ringing up customers that way?"

"Spence said you…aw, man, fuck you guys." Felix tore off the mask (retailing for $34.57, now added to his debt) and threw it at Spencer, who was practically crying with laughter. Spencer picked up a magic wand and made a slashing Z-mark in the air.

"You're having crap luck with masks," Spencer taunted. "First Foiled, now this. Have you considered another line of work?"

"You know, I was reading somewhere there's a shortage of clowns," Roy added. "Supply and demand's in your favor."

Felix and Spencer simultaneously gasped.

The c-word was the worst insult one could sling in their line of work. A tense silence filled the shop.

Then Spencer doubled down. "Try this on for size." He chucked a handful of multiplying sponge balls (unnervingly similar to clown noses) at Felix, who batted them away.

A year ago, when he played catcher for the 66ers, he'd had respect, a sports agent, and a shot at the majors. Now he used his muscular arms to fend off *sponge balls*.

"Laugh it up," he growled, "but just answer me this: Which one of us gets mad pussy, and which one of us has to take a class to learn how? Huh?"

"Landon's system *works*," Spencer gritted out.

Felix dug a hand into his pocket and retrieved the old school phone numbers he'd gotten that week, tossing the scraps of paper like confetti. "Runyon Canyon. All fit, all fine."

"Get out of here before I fire you," Roy said mildly, though he took a moment to pick up one of the numbers and slide it in his wallet.

"Can't be late for your internship," Spencer scoffed.

Three times a week, Felix interned with Jonathan Fredericksson, Club Deception's president. He was surprised that one of the biggest names in magic had hired him sight unseen after a brief phone interview, but he wasn't going to look a gift horse in the butt or whatever.

His roommates thought he was insane for taking a non-paying position, but what they didn't understand was that it got him a free, all-access pass to the club, whose annual fees were unreal. Of course, Jonathan hadn't taken him yet, and he hadn't provided any one-on-one lessons, either (both advertised as a "trade-off" for his work), but maybe Felix had to prove himself worthy first.

His main tasks so far had been to walk Doctor Faustus, Jonathan's pug mix, and get him groomed once a week. And the same Doctor Faustus was currently tied to a parking meter outside Merlin's Wonderporium with intestinal distress. So all Felix had to show for his internship thus far was a pocketful of phone numbers from the cute girls who walked their dogs at Runyon Canyon, and an unreimbursed vet's bill for $209.

His first real assignment was to ghostwrite Jonathan's "Letter from the President" for the Club Deception online newsletter, using the theme of autumn renewal to inform members about an upcoming magic swap. Jonathan had assured him eight hundred words would suffice and that it shouldn't take more than half an hour of his time, but it had already taken three days to write the first sentence. So far all Felix had was, "One man's trash is another man's treasure," but wasn't that copyrighted? And the word *trash* didn't set the right tone, he was pretty sure. The letter was due this afternoon.

With a sigh, he gathered his deck of cards and Doctor Faustus's Beggin' Strips, and headed out the door.

The drive to the top of Edgecliffe went way too quickly. He could normally count on a forty-minute delay any time of day, any day of the week, except when he actually wanted one.

The swift commute seemed to have worked in his favor,

however. Jonathan's black SUV wasn't parked in the driveway yet. Maybe if he was quick, Felix could get away with
securing the dog in the backyard with a water dish, and
leaving a note—proof he'd shown up as promised, but without any of the fallout from neglecting to write the column.
Right?

He knocked.

Nothing.

He waited ten seconds and rang the doorbell.

The house was small but somehow intimidating, with its
corner glass windows, solar panels, and thermal roof. Not
that Jonathan was particularly eco-friendly, driving around
in his ugly-ass gas guzzler, so this must have been his wife's
influence. The dense, packed trees surrounding the property
provided shade and privacy, making the house seem secluded.
Felix wouldn't mind lying down and taking a nap right on the
grass.

"Yo, Mr. Fredericksson, you there?" he shouted. It was
pointless, but he wanted to cover all his bases.

Nothing.

He knocked a second and third time, loudly.

The door suddenly swung open to reveal the irritated face
of Mrs. Fredericksson. She held a glass of red wine in her
hand.

"What's next, a flare gun?" she asked in a slightly hoarse
voice.

Felix had seen her in passing a few times, usually on her
way out, dressed to the nines. But now she stood in front of
him, barefoot, in jean shorts and an old SMASHING PUMPKINS
T-shirt. It was a tomboy outfit, but there was nothing boyish
about her; you could tell she had a great figure. Her breasts
pushed against the confines of the T-shirt's fabric, stretching and reshaping the band's heart-shaped logo. Her blond

hair fell in thick, loose curls. She looked like a 1950s calendar pinup about to hop on the hood of a car.

He took off his sunglasses and tried to joke his way out of his discomfort. "Thought I'd break a window next."

She stared back: no smile.

"Uh…sorry for the racket. I guess he's not here? I'll come back another time."

She looked behind him and motioned with her wineglass, causing the wine to slosh against the sides. "Where's the dog?"

"Oh, right." He fought the urge to smack his forehead. "He's in the car."

Her eyebrows shot up. "The car? In this heat?"

He quickly retrieved Doctor Faustus and led him to the door.

Mrs. Fredericksson gave the dog a perfunctory pat on the head as he walked inside. "You don't leave him in the car a lot, do you?"

"No, *never.*"

"Well, not 'never.'"

"I swear, just this once while I knocked."

"And yelled. And rang the doorbell. And pounded on the door."

She was treating him like a gardener, which would have irritated him more if he weren't also terrified of her. "Ma'am? Are you going to tell your husband?"

She chuckled. "No, I'm not going to tattle on you. And please call me Claire."

The sun descended behind a tree, and in the fuzzy light of the porch lamp she looked even softer, classier, prettier. She took a long sip of her wine, lingering, and leaned against the frame of the door. He didn't know what to do.

Until the next words fell from her shiny, red-stained lips. "You may as well come in." Claire held the door for him and he looked down at her bare feet as he crossed the threshold. Even barefoot, she was tall; Felix was six foot one but he didn't tower over her the way he did most women.

"Something to drink?" she asked.

He closed the front door and followed her down the hall like a puppy. "I'm not much of a wine drinker…"

She looked back. "We also have milk. No cookies, though, unless you bake them yourself, which you're welcome to do."

He wasn't sure if she was teasing him. His whole day—his whole week, his whole *year*, it felt like—had been one big mockery fest, though, and why should Mr. Fredericksson's wife be any different?

They reached the kitchen. She opened the refrigerator door and gave him an expectant look.

"Oh, uh, beer's fine."

"'Beer me, bro,'" she translated in a dumb-jock voice.

He was insulted. "Hey, I'm no frat dude."

"But you played baseball, right? I think Jonathan said—"

"Yeah."

She turned and tossed him a bottle of Corona Light over the opposite shoulder, trusting him to catch it, which he did, more at ease now that she'd displayed a sense of playfulness. Maybe not everyone had it out for him today after all.

"Opener's in the drawer." She motioned to a pullout section of the island near his hip, but he placed the edge of the bottle top against the counter, smacked it firmly, and opened the beer that way.

She raised her glass in a toast. "Felix, right? Felix the baseball player."

"I was a catcher till I wrecked my knees. My teammates called me El Gato." The nickname was a cruel joke now. "The Cat's" luck had run out, nine lives gone, and he no longer landed on his feet. After months of physical therapy and no results, he'd been forced to start over.

"I've never met an athlete-turned-magician before. Real estate and used cars not doing it for you?"

"Something like that." Actually, to Felix it made perfect sense. He couldn't imagine holding a nine-to-five job, despite growing up in a household where those were prized. Dad an acupuncturist, Mom a paralegal, even his show-off *hermanita* had her class elections, volunteer work, and after-school jobs.

What Color Is Your Parachute? had asked "What do you most love to do?" and since baseball was out, the first image that had popped into his mind was the fifth-grade talent show at Castaic Elementary, where he'd won first place with Hippity-Hop Rabbits, a store-bought routine consisting of two wooden rabbits that magically changed places and colors. The award had led to his first kiss, and birthday party gigs for classmates. A job at Merlin's Wonderporium and an internship with Mr. Fredericksson, and here he was. Boom.

He wasn't about to lay all that on Claire, though. Felix set down his beer and reached inside his front pocket for the crumpled sheet of paper containing his pathetic attempt at Jonathan's "Letter from the President."

He opened it and slid it across the island to her.

Claire squinted at it, confused. "He asked you to write this for him? Lazy bastard."

He wasn't sure if he was supposed to agree with her.

She scanned the page and tapped her fingers on the table, reminding him of a teacher. "This is really bad."

"I know! That's why I haven't finished it. What should I do?"

She finished the last of her wine and placed her glass in the sink. "How about this: You do my chores and I'll do yours."

"Uh, what are your chores?"

She went into another room, and when she returned, she was carrying an overflowing basket of laundry.

Holy shit, if you thought walking the dog was humiliating…

"Separate the darks from the lights, and then separate the reds and blacks."

He gaped at her.

"They're clean," she added. "I assume you know how to fold?"

"Uh, I can't."

"What do you mean, you 'can't'?"

"I'm color-blind."

It was her turn to gape. "A color-blind magician. Where did he *find* you?"

"It's not like I can't tell the difference between hearts, clovers, spades, and diamonds. The shapes are different."

"Did you just say 'clovers'? Are you…" She cleared her throat. "Are you aware there might be another name for them besides clovers?"

"Of course," he said solemnly. "Puppy-dog paws."

Her eyes widened.

"What?" he asked.

"God help us. They're *clubs*."

He grinned. "Gotcha."

She rewarded him with a throaty laugh. "And the color-blind thing—that was a joke, too, right?"

"Just with greens. Like, right now…" He leaned in slightly. "I'm not sure if your eyes are blue or green."

"I guess you'll have to keep wondering."

"It would help if Mr. F gave me something worthwhile to work on, or at least got me into Club Deception like he promised."

She leaned against the kitchen island. "I can get you into the club."

"Right now?"

"No, not right now. Sort the clothes, whatever you can do, and order something for dinner." She smacked her hand against the fridge on her way out, so he'd notice the take-out menus held there with magnets.

He wasn't sure where she'd gone or when she was coming back. He folded all the clothes and called Jonathan's favorite pho place for delivery.

When Claire returned, she carried a deck of cards and a small contraption, both of which she dumped on the table with a clatter.

"Your column's written," she said. "Show me the tricks you're having trouble with."

"What makes you think I'm having trouble?"

"Jonathan has trouble with things all the time, and you're no Jonathan. So…"

He sat beside her. *Can't argue there.* "I can't decide if I should use Brainwave or Invisible Deck for my prediction trick."

"I prefer Brainwave," she offered. "Visually, it's more interesting."

"But then you can't have dual reality with the volunteer onstage."

"Why would you want to? That's like running when you're not being chased."

He nodded. "And then there's Secrest Count."

"One deck or two?"

"And Twisting the Aces," he admitted. "And my Zarrow Shuffle…"

"Okay, one thing at a time." And she picked up the cards.

He'd heard that magicians' wives weren't the same as laypeople, but Mrs. Fredericksson took it to a whole new level. She was the first female knuckle buster he'd ever met.

For the next half hour they went over Twisting the Aces, in which the magician holds all four Aces in his hand, facedown, then turns them 180 degrees clockwise to reveal that one of them has magically turned faceup. The construction required proficiency in at least three types of lifts and turnovers.

Next she picked up the device she'd brought in, a palm-size square with four finger levers.

"'Musician's Friend,'" Felix read aloud, giving her a side-long glance. "Look, they spelled *magician* wrong."

"Cute," she said, and he mentally scolded himself. *Don't be cute with her. Only be actually funny.*

"It's to strengthen your fingers, build speed and dexterity. Most people don't think about those things, but it'll help. Here." She placed her hand over his, lacing their fingers together and curling his hand around the levers.

He swallowed. "Good to know."

The way her fingers slid through his made him think of legs intertwining, hips slamming against each other, fingers laced together and pinned against sheets.

She molded his hand into different positions and pressed on his fingers as she taught him how to best use the grip. "You can squeeze it with your whole hand, like this; you can work on individual fingers, like this; you can build up calluses, like this; or you can work on the muscles of your hand and fore-arm, like this."

He almost joked about other ways of building up hand and forearm muscles but stopped himself just in time; it wouldn't have impressed her. It wouldn't have even warranted a "cute."

When she let go of his hand, he was surprised by the strips of tension already shooting through the tendons of his wrist.

"Take it home. Use it when you're watching TV, on the treadmill, whenever you've got a free moment. You'll see re-sults pretty quickly."

"Won't he get mad?"

"He won't even notice."

"I'm beginning to think I should've interned with *you*," he remarked. "And, uh, that reminds me…I have a bill from the vet." He reached in his other pocket for it. She didn't take it from him, and he felt foolish holding it in the air.

"I'll let him know to bill my card next time, he's a friend of mine." She finally took the receipt from his outstretched hand and wrote him a check for the amount. "But you know, Felix, you shouldn't let Jonathan jerk you around. Life's too short."

They stared at each other for a moment.

She got up abruptly, opened the cupboard, and pulled out some dinner plates.

He moved to her, bridging the distance between them, and reached for the dishes. "Let me do that."

They were so close, he could smell her perfume: a light floral scent with just a trace of lime.

She allowed him two plates but held the third to her chest. "It just occurred to me…I'm so used to setting the table for three…" She was still, seeming pensive and a little dazed.

They looked at each other again, an unmistakable current pulling them together. He reached out to trace the outline of her lips with his thumb.

Before he could make contact, the sound of the garage door opening stopped him.

She turned away and put the third plate back in the cupboard.

With a deep breath, he stepped back and set the two plates on the table at opposite ends, miles apart from each other. "I better go. Thanks for your help, Mrs. F."

She nodded, still looking at the cupboard. She didn't ask him to call her Claire that time, or even open her mouth to say good-bye.

Claire

WHEN CLAIRE WAS pregnant with Eden, she and Jonathan lived *la vie bohème* in a two-room shack on Washington Boulevard near the beach. They couldn't afford air-conditioning, but keeping the windows open provided a cross breeze from the Pacific. It also provided constant noise from tourists, beach bums, hot dog vendors, skate rats, doomsday prophets, patrol officers, and, of course, the criminals they sought.

The days were long.

Jonathan was a fixture along the Venice boardwalk, busking from sunup to sundown. Part fakir, part improv artist, he tailored his fifteen-minute shows to whatever was popular with the crowd. *Eat glass? I can do that! Walk on hot coals? Why, that's my specialty! Balloon animals for the kiddos? You're in luck!* It was grueling, sometimes demeaning work, but he put every ounce of energy he possessed into it, and audiences loved him.

While her husband scraped and bowed, Claire searched used-book stores and video vaults for classic magic tricks Jonathan could learn, update, and personalize.

She wrote new scripts by hand in a yellow legal pad and altered the patter to fit Jonathan's style. She sewed hidden pockets into his clothes and tore out items from the *Daily*

Breeze so his jokes could reference current events. Unused sections of the newspaper were set aside for use in a torn-and-restored newspaper effect.

When Jonathan returned home at night, he and Claire sprawled on their foldout couch bed and separated the ones, fives, tens, and twenties from his hat and placed them inside envelopes marked FOOD, RENT, and BUSINESS EXPENSES. One month's business expense was an ironing board so Jonathan could press his shirts and look formal at a moment's notice, should a high-end gig surface. It doubled as their dinner table.

Some nights they stole away to a secluded spot on the beach and made love under the stars. Their undignified living conditions didn't bother them; they considered it a paper-thin facade, temporary and flimsy as a theater set, a stopgap between her parents' house in Modesto and their upcoming North American magic tour.

Jonathan's favorite magician was Doug Henning, whose elaborate, traveling stage show—with a full menagerie, two tractor-trailers, and fifteen sets—he'd seen as a child. Jonathan wanted to follow in his hero's footsteps, and he wanted his family with him.

Claire adored the idea, and adored her husband for suggesting it. The entire world would be their daughter's classroom and play yard. What better gift could two parents bestow?

The Plan, once Eden was old enough to walk and talk, was to live on the road: a traveling utopia of three.

The Plan was for Eden and Claire to perform in Jonathan's show.

The Plan fell apart in six weeks.

During Jonathan's lengthy solo tours, Claire accepted her husband's dalliances, what Daisy and Tom Buchanan called sprees, so long as they didn't follow him home. After all, it was her fault she wasn't beside him.

He called home twice a week and FedExed Claire a video of every show. As she'd done in the past, she critiqued his act and helped him strengthen it. She also researched his competition, both to avoid replication and to improve upon others' work. Her notes and suggestions evolved into the backbone of Jonathan: Monarch of Magic, Coming to a City Near You.

She campaigned for his Club Deception presidency, and wrote his platform and election statements, molding and remolding his stances as she went along. She threw cocktail parties and hosted brunches for the WAGs. As king and queen of the club, with near-constant bookings in Beverly Hills, Vegas, Chicago, Miami, and New York, plus a beautiful, secluded house in Silver Lake, Jonathan and Claire had achieved what her father had long ago deemed impossible: a thriving, well-respected career in magic.

The only thing Jonathan didn't have was a TV pilot with a series option, the way Cal did, and nothing could convince him he hadn't been robbed.

"So Cal's back, huh?" Jonathan asked. "For good?"

They lay in bed together on Sunday morning, the *Los Angeles Times* stacked between them like the Berlin Wall, eating from a breakfast tray Jonathan had compiled: strawberries, slivers of cantaloupe, and rosemary/olive bread from La Brea Bakery.

Claire peeked over the top of the newspaper that divided them. "Looks like it." She still hadn't mentioned Cal's new wife.

It was entertaining to watch Jonathan writhe with paranoia. He deserved it after shoving his one-night stand—Becca the brain trust—in her face the other night. She knew she'd be divorcing him soon, but *he* didn't know that, so the fact that he didn't try harder to be even minimally considerate was grating.

She returned to her crossword puzzle.

He used his butter knife to push down the newspaper sheet and peer over it.

"You know he stole my TV show."

She snorted. "No one *stole* anything from you."

"Explain to me how someone can be away from the spotlight for three years and get a *TV deal*, when I've been here the whole time, taking meetings and pitching ideas and playing all those damn tennis games with network executives."

"Maybe they didn't like your topspin."

"Thanks, that's very helpful."

It was obvious he wasn't going to leave her in peace to finish her crossword, so she tossed the sheet to the floor. "He set up the deal before he took off, and he was willing to let camera crews follow him around for *years*."

"You're defending him again."

"I'm not defending him, I'm explaining to you how it happened."

"I tell you I'm upset about something, and your first response is to side with him."

"Like I said, he gave them access to everything."

"I would've given them access."

"Well, they didn't ask you, did they? And anyway, I wouldn't have let you, not with Eden still in the house."

"So you're saying the reason I don't have a TV series is because of you, then."

"Oh, for chrissake…his Coins Across is flawless," she snapped. "Yours isn't."

"Aha. The truth comes out."

Sometimes Claire thought her husband would rather fight than have sex. His eyes shone with glee if he succeeded in getting her to raise her voice, because if *ice-cold wifey* lost her composure, he automatically won the argument. That was the main reason she hadn't swooped in on him and Becca like a shrieking Valkyrie the other night. She *refused* to rant and rave in his presence.

"And his Bottle Cap routine kills, anytime, anywhere," Claire added calmly. "They were looking for off-the-cuff magic in urban settings that plays well on TV and in sports bars. Not stage shows."

He responded in an obnoxious falsetto, meant to be her. "'The close-up magicians are so dreamy. They don't rely on smoke and mirrors or big props. Why can't you be like *them*, Jonny?'"

She ignored him and wrenched open her bedside drawer. Inside was a printed piece of paper, which she slapped onto Jonathan's stomach. "Here's your column, by the way. I know you think words should simply fall out of the sky for you to use, but you should be more careful whom you trust."

"I asked Felix to do it because I thought you were too busy working on the new routine. It wasn't meant as a slight, my dear."

"You may not have asked me, but you got it from me anyway. If people knew how much I helped you…"

"*Assisted* me…"

"You'd be kicked out of the competition. Or forced to give me top billing."

Two types of awards were handed out at the annual Magician of the Year competition: Best Reproduction of a Classic, and Best Original.

In a rare acknowledgment that magicians stole each other's

acts all the time (going so far as to poach each other's prop masters, architects, engineers, and assistants), a category for outright thievery existed. It was called Best Reproduction of a Classic.

The prize money for Best Reproduction of a Classic—fifty thousand dollars—came in the form of a grant from the Brotherhood of Arcana's Historical Society, whose motto was "Keeping the Past Alive."

The Original category, on the other hand, encouraged innovation and risk taking. The prize money was double, one hundred thousand dollars, and came with a lifetime membership to Club Deception. Presentation was considered to be the most important component in an original act. It had to provide such a startling experience that no one could guess the illusion's ancestry, if indeed it had one.

Jonathan regarded Claire as he bit off a piece of strawberry and chewed it. He took his time, as if nothing in the world could compel him to eat at a normal pace. Finally, he spoke. "Yes, yes, you've been the woman behind the curtain this whole time, fixing my shows, spying on the competition, securing me awards—but never *the* award. Isn't that right? If you're so integral to the operation, how come I always fall short?"

Jonny had competed five times in the past ten years and never won.

Cal had won twice—the only close-up magician to do so since the contest's inception. Of course, the money was exhausted before he'd received it. He and Brandy hadn't so much spent money as set it on fire.

"You've come in second, though," Claire reminded Jonathan. "And that was all me."

"When I'm onstage, Claire? I'm up there *alone*."

"And when you're offstage, you're *never* alone, are you?"

He crossed his arms. "Is this about Becky?"

"Becca."

"See, I care so little for her I don't even remember her name. Look, her uncle is a talent manager, she can *help* us."

"Oh, that makes everything okay, then."

"You were never bothered before, so what's the problem?"

"I was bothered by Indiana, I'll tell you that," she retorted, on the verge of losing control.

"That was years ago!"

Maybe for you. She took a few deep breaths. Jonathan had an uncanny ability to brush aside truly rotten business while fixating on the tiniest of slights. When she was calm again, she said in a steady tone, "You need to focus. That's the problem."

"I *am* focused. I don't like Schrödinger's Cat. Find me something else."

Claire closed her eyes and counted slowly to five. It wasn't a matter of finding something—to win Best Original Magic Act, the routine had to be created whole cloth. And she'd already spent months on Schrödinger's Cat.

"You haven't even read the whole proposal."

"Cats are too unpredictable."

"I'm telling you, this is how you win."

He paused, appearing to consider the truth of her words. "Sometimes I think you want me to win more than I do."

She stiffened. "Fine, do a Classic instead. I'm done."

"Okay, okay," he said quickly. "I'll give it some more thought. I promise."

She allowed herself to relax slightly. In her fantasy, updated hourly, the judges would present him with the grand prize check, and when he turned to embrace her, thank her, she would smile and present him with divorce papers.

Jonathan set their breakfast tray on the floor, placing the empty orange juice glasses beside it. Then he sat against the headboard and pulled her toward him so he could reach her shoulders and give her a massage. She shifted to grant him better access, winding up between his knees as he pressed his thumbs into the knot of muscles along her back and neck.

"I never would have brought her home if I'd known you would be here," he murmured in her ear.

"This is a strange apology."

"Why *were* you home so early?"

"It wasn't that early. After midnight."

"Yes, but you're usually there till two."

"I got bored." She sighed.

"Really?"

"There's no competition right now. Best Original is yours to lose. *If* you do my routine."

"What about the stupid Hipster?" he asked. "Any closer to figuring out who he is?"

The so-called Hipster Magician had blanketed the web with short, sardonic video explanations of magic tricks. There was no instructional element involved; they were simply mean-spirited spoilers.

Fear of exposure didn't usually bother professionals, but his web presence—two million hits in the past six months—was impossible to brush aside. The guy was slick, polished, and aware. *An insider.* Maybe even a club member. Wearing a deliberately ironic/cheap eye mask, skinny jeans, and bright leather sneakers, he named the magicians he was exposing, six so far, showed clips from their live shows, and then destroyed them piece by piece, trick by trick. Everyone who made a living from magic wanted him shut down, permanently.

"No," said Claire, "but I'll bring it up at brunch today, see if anyone knows anything."

Sitting behind her, his legs framing hers, Jonathan continued the shoulder massage for a too-brief moment before reaching under her nightgown and cupping her breasts in his hands. Would it have killed him to give her an actual massage first? Not the bare minimum to qualify for the term, and then straight to her tits?

Nevertheless, when he began rubbing his thumbs in a circular motion, she shifted her hips backward so she was flush against his lap. He was half hard already.

An idea forming, she turned to face him and straddle his lap.

Surprised, he leaned forward to taste her lips, but she dodged him. He raised an eyebrow. "No kissing these days?"

She made her eyes go wide. "You mean you haven't filled your quota?"

"Ouch."

She held on to the bed frame behind him and settled into position. Jonathan let out a soft moan.

Claire enjoyed it, too, but for different reasons.

He doesn't know it, but this is the last time.

Make it count, Claire.

Jonathan inevitably rolled them over so he was on top. He made love the same way he performed: utterly confident and strong, oblivious to the fact that he was up there because of her. And in bed, oblivious to the fact that whatever pleasure she generated for herself had little to do with him.

Occasionally she thought about a younger version of Jonathan while the present-day version pounded away at her. Jonathan from the old days was a turn-on, before his smile seemed nothing but smug to her, before his gaze was nothing but patronizing.

She arched upward and kissed him with all the ardor and affection she'd once felt, conjuring it in her heart and making him feel the emotions spill from her with every movement of her lips and tongue, tasting him and dragging him toward his orgasm like a current of waves.

When she was certain he'd been swept up in an irreversible undertow, she wrenched her mouth free and whispered into his ear, "Oh, Cal…Cal!"

Jonathan's eyes widened. He stopped moving, tried to back out of her embrace, but she clamped her legs tighter around his hips. His expression of hurt and frustration nearly made her laugh.

He glared at her. "Never do that again."

Don't worry, I won't.

She smiled and pushed at his chest with her fingertips. "Off you go. I have to get ready. Brunch in an hour."

Knowing she'd spoiled his orgasm was even better than having one of her own.

Jessica

AT THE SAME moment her husband's name was being invoked in another woman's bed, Jessica woke to the feel of Cal's lips on her belly. The air-conditioning was turned up high, so his kisses provided a warm balm.

"Mmm, hi." She smiled and stretched languidly.

"Hi, yourself. Did I wake you?"

"I don't mind."

Cal kissed his way up her body to her neck, then across her cheekbone and over to her lips. He tasted like fresh coffee with a hint of toothpaste. He always got up early to work in the guest room/rehearsal space, but returned to bed before she woke up so they could start the day properly.

Though they were visible in the morning light, she didn't worry about the little scars dotting her arms and legs. She'd had them since childhood, although she'd have preferred to forget where they came from. He never mentioned them or asked about them, which made her love him even more. It was almost as though, in his gaze, they ceased to exist. Their marriage had healed her in infinite ways.

His loft—*their* loft—had been transformed, cleared out, and organized, just as he'd promised. The Cardini poster remained on the wall, which held a new coat of paint, but he'd made plenty of room for Jessica to add her own artwork and embellishments, and he'd altered the kitchen nook into an office for her. It was partitioned off by a Japanese-style room divider that could be taken down at night or when entertaining guests. So far, though, they hadn't had a single visitor, which Jessica found curious.

Also peculiar was the lack of evidence of his previous marriage. Not that she wanted it shoved down her throat, but shouldn't there be *something* from that time period remaining in his life? Was it so strange to want to at least see a photo of the woman? It wasn't like they'd divorced or something; she'd died.

"You should go to the brunch today. Claire really wants you to come."

She squinted at him. "Did she say that?"

He gave a half nod that did little to reassure her.

She couldn't pretend his absence at the club her first night in LA didn't bother her. "Don't pat me on the butt and send me off like you did last week. Come with me. Introduce me to people."

He smiled against her neck. "I'm not invited to the *ladies' brunch*."

"You know what I mean. Or, I know. We could have a dinner party, you could invite all your friends, and—"

"That's not a good idea." He was abrupt. "I don't—parties are difficult for me."

Her tone softened. "Because of alcohol? It doesn't have to be dinner. It could be really casual. A lunch thing, just pop and sandwiches."

"It's not that. My friends—well, they don't really understand how much I've changed since I lived here before. I think it might be—awkward."

"Why would it be awkward?"

He didn't acknowledge her question. It reminded her, disquietingly, of Claire. It seemed they both simply ignored her when they didn't like what she had to say. "When I'm done filming and editing the show, we'll paint the town red, okay? Just you and me."

"But that's not what I'm saying."

"I'm proud you're my wife. Never doubt that. I just want to keep you to myself a little while longer."

She sighed. They'd clearly have to revisit the topic later. "Okay."

"And you'll go to brunch today?"

"I don't know what to wear. None of my dresses work with bras. They'll call me the bra-less wonder."

He stroked her hair. "Can *I* call you the bra-less wonder?"

She smiled and let her misgivings roll away. "You can call me anything you want."

"I think you should go bra-less, *and* I think you should ice your nipples right before you walk in."

She threw her head back and laughed. He punctuated his comment by leaning down and giving each pink bud a lip-smacking kiss.

"I just don't get what the problem is. They're not very big," Jessica said shyly, covering her breasts with her arm.

"They're perfect, and you're beautiful." He studied her eyes for a moment. "I bet people have told you that so often you don't even hear it. It's just white noise."

People *had* told her that her whole life, but never in a gentle way, more in a honking-from-a-car-and-leering kind of way.

And anyway, she'd never heard it from someone who mattered. Not her mother. Not her nonexistent father.

"I hear it when it's you," she said quietly.

When Jessica arrived at Club Deception, the valets refused payment or even a tip, and parked Cal's Beemer at the reserved spot nearest the entrance. Word must have gotten around about her identity—she was being treated like royalty.

It was strange seeing the club in daylight, all its dusty flaws laid bare. Claire in daylight, however, was as intimidating as ever. She leaned against the brick wall, smoking a Marlboro Light.

She wore stilettos, a pressed black pencil skirt, and a white scoop-neck blouse with chiffon cap sleeves. Her hair loose, tousled, and sun-streaked, she looked like a surfer chick goddess in designer clothes. Jessica felt self-conscious about her own French braid, which felt childish in comparison, practically like pigtails.

Before Jessica could greet her, Claire pushed off the wall and gestured with her cigarette. "For brunch, we use the Gold Room. There's a separate door around back." She gave Jessica a chance to catch up (an improvement, at least, over last time) and led her around the side of the building toward a door marked EMERGENCY EXIT.

"Good," said Jessica. "The girl at the front desk hates me."

"She's pointless, don't worry about her."

Jessica choked back a startled laugh. "I think I'm going to bring her cupcakes, show her there's no hard feelings."

"Don't be ridiculous. I'll just have her fired and you can start fresh."

Jessica halted in her tracks. "What? No! That's horrible!"

Claire smiled. "I prefer 'efficient.'" She leaned a hand on Jessica's shoulder so she could balance on one foot. Then she stubbed out her cigarette against the sole of her high-heeled shoe. "No ashtrays, can you believe it?"

The movement was so at odds with Claire's previous decorum, Jessica was rendered speechless.

Claire flicked the dead cigarette away and deftly entered a security code into the panel at the door. Inside, Jessica heard a friendly, raucous mixture of voices down the hall. She realized how eager she was to meet the other magicians' wives and girlfriends. Cal was right: She'd been in the city for nearly ten days; it was time to make friends, beyond whatever Claire was.

She strode forward to join the party, but Claire encircled her wrist and held her back. "Just so you're aware, the parking spot you're in is usually mine, but I took a cab today."

"Oh, okay." Standing close to the other woman in the darkened hall, Jessica inhaled a faint whiff of citrus, with something darker underneath.

As the child of an alcoholic, she immediately recognized the smell of liquored-up breakfast tea. As a former bartender, she knew the liquor was Cointreau. The knowledge brought with it a familiar fear, and the accompanying urge to prevent Claire from embarrassing herself. The tricky part would be protecting Claire while not letting on that she was doing so. Alkies couldn't stand being babysat. It was a risk she had to take, though.

Besides doing right by Cal's friend, Jessica wanted Claire to like her; teach her how to project the same fearless, sexy poise that Claire possessed, at least under normal circumstances; show her how to be the ultimate WAG. But first, she had to determine whether Claire was a happy drunk or a mean one.

Claire tottered into the Gold Room, which lived up to its name. The ceiling, floor, and walls were etched with thin, intricate, swirling, golden mandalas. Looking at them gave Jessica the sensation of falling. Upon each dining table sat a gold vase containing a single gold rose—made of silk—surrounded by gold-etched plates, gold-edged cutlery, gold champagne glasses.

Claire's entrance provoked shouts and cheers. Her comrades encircled her. Cast adrift to find a table, Jessica chose the one closest to the stage. In her haste, she didn't realize the average age at the table was somewhere between seventy and death.

"She's been putting it off for years, and I just can't see a way out of it anymore. Not if we're going to sell the house," one of the older ladies said to her companions. A black cane rested against her chair.

"Who's putting what off?" asked Jessica, sitting down.

The women turned to regard her.

"What's your name, dear?"

"Jessica. Pleased to meet you," she said in a rush.

"Jessica...?"

"Sorry. Clarke. I'm still getting used to it." She blushed.

The table fell silent.

"As in Calum Clarke?" Jessica clarified. "He's—"

"Oh, we know who Calum Clarke is, dear," said the woman with the black cane. "We've probably known him since before you were born."

"Well, I don't know about *that*," she said quietly, regretting her choice of table.

"I'm Cynthia," the woman continued, lowering her bifocals to peer at Jessica. "How long have you been Mrs. Clarke?"

"Since August."

Another silence. Someone coughed and another woman dabbed at her mouth with a napkin.

"What's the matter?" Jessica blurted out. She was getting pretty sick of people's reactions to her, not to mention the fact that Cal wasn't there to back her up. The receptionist had been shocked to hear Cal had remarried. The bartender had been surprised he'd come back to California. And now the establishment WAGs were acting salty.

"Perhaps second time's the charm," Cynthia said drily. "At any rate, it's nice to have a new face joining us today." She raised her champagne glass and tilted it toward Jessica. "Welcome."

There was a pause before the other ladies followed suit.

Then they returned to their previous conversation.

"If she would just let us go through the boxes, we could pare down the photos into something manageable."

"When we put *my* mother-in-law in a home, they wouldn't let her bring more than five picture frames."

"She has plenty of framed photos on the wall, that's not the problem. It's the shoe boxes from the sixties and seventies that are driving me up the wall."

Jessica ventured into the fray again. "Your mother's got too many loose photographs?" she asked Cynthia.

"That's right," Cynthia replied. "And she refuses to toss any of them."

"I could digitize them for her," said Jessica. "That way you can still keep them but they won't take up any space. I used to run a business cataloging old photos back in Chicago. And I'll do it for free if you promise to refer me to your friends."

Cynthia's eyes lit up. "Do you know how to use Photoshop? Can you brighten some of the images, or zoom in closer on the faces?"

"Absolutely." All her clients requested that the past be airbrushed.

For the next ten minutes, Jessica chatted with Cynthia about the scrapbooking packages she offered and handed out new business cards to everyone at the table.

"Good morning," Claire said quietly from the podium. A screech of feedback from the mike startled her, and secured the room's attention. Claire gingerly tested the mike, tapping her finger on the mouthpiece.

"Hi. Uh, hi, everyone." She cleared her throat and took a sip from her drink, which was amber-colored and garnished with a bright-orange spiral, peeled from a carrot. Jessica wondered what it was. But mostly she wanted to know why Claire looked so out of place at the podium. Minutes ago she'd ruthlessly cut Jessica down about a parking space, but now she struggled to deliver a simple greeting. She currently read from a stack of notecards, rarely looking up to address her audience.

"When it pours, it...I mean, when it rains it pours," Claire said. "It's been, uh, six months since, um, anyone new has come to brunch, I think, right? But today we have *two* young ladies joining our ranks."

Jessica's ears perked up. *Hooray, I'm not the only newbie.*

"So give them your heartfelt sympathy, I mean, a heartfelt welcome." There were some chuckles and Claire looked somewhat relieved. "Here with us today for the first time is, and please stand up so we can see you...Kaimi Lee. Did I say that correctly? Yes? Oh, good. Kaimi Lee."

A striking Korean American woman wearing a bubble-hem black dress with a bright floral pattern stood and gave a mock salute, her expression wry. Jessica was delighted to see that Kaimi looked about her age. Finally, someone to chill with who could relate to the changes in Jessica's life since meeting Cal.

"Kaimi is...can this be, uh, true? You've recently started dating *Landon Gage*."

Kaimi shrugged as if to say, *You're as surprised as I am.*

"You can have him," someone shouted.

"Boo," someone else added, though Jessica wasn't sure if they were booing the woman who'd just spoken, or the fact that Kaimi was dating Landon. Did Cal know him?

"None of that," Claire said firmly, and for a split second she seemed like her formidable self again. It didn't last long. Right now, she could not have been less suited to commanding the attention of a room. "Whatever you think of his…self-help seminars, let's show some respect for the, uh, woman who finally tamed him. Big applause, I mean, big *round* of applause, for, uh, Kaimi 'the lion tamer' Lee."

"Do you need a drink, Kaimi?" someone else shouted, and this time the room erupted in laughter.

Kaimi was a good sport. "How about ten?" she asked, which immediately won over the crowd and restored the good nature of the room.

"Next up," said Claire, "is Jessica Clarke, who happens to be Cal's…um, that is, *Calum* Clarke's wife."

"Say it ain't so," came a wail from a faraway table. There were at least eight tables, seating ten women per table. Laughter filled the air again, broken by overlapping catcalls.

"Where is she?"

"Who's the lucky bitch?" hooted a woman wearing a vintage girdle and corset. "Show yourself."

Jessica stood up and gave a little wave. She sought out Kaimi in the crowd, hoping to make eye contact, but the other newbie was buried in her iPhone.

"Look at her. She's precious."

Claire wagged her finger. "Curb it. You're going to scare her off. Especially you, Table Six."

The occupants of Table Six cheered at being singled out.

Claire cut them off. "There will be plenty of time to, uh, harass her later. Next order of business: The so-called Hipster Magician is becoming a real, um, problem."

Groans from the crowd.

"I know. But he's got three million views as of this morning. Obviously, this—this affects all our livelihoods. Our *husbands'* livelihoods," she quickly corrected. "You may not have been affected yet, but, you kn—know, your husband could be next."

"If you see something, say something," Kaimi piped up sarcastically. "Like terrorism."

Jessica bit her lip. She didn't think it was the right comment to make in a room full of magician lovers.

Claire shot Kaimi a sharp glance. "Keep your eyes and ears open. If you see or hear anything, no matter how insig—" She stumbled on the word, and Jessica's back stiffened. "—insignificant it might seem, or anyone who might know him, my door's always open. Drop by my table today, email, call...No one's throwing blame around. Anonymous help is, um, always grateful. I mean, we're always, the board of directors, is grateful for it, and we can act on it without casting blame or getting anyone in trouble.

"Okay. Next item." She rolled her eyes, crumpled up her final notecard, and dropped it on the floor. "The ventriloquists' wives still want in. And to the surprise of no one, the nays have it, for the, uh, forty-seventh time in a row."

"Why do we have to vote on this every month?" groused a woman in the second row. She wore a hat with vibrant bird feathers on it.

"It's not that bad of an idea. It would bring in additional membership dues," another woman pointed out.

"See that chocolate fountain over there? The one we hardly use because we don't remember it exists? That means we don't need additional funds," said Claire rapidly. "Especially if we all turn in our dues on time. With that, I'm going to open the floor."

Claire looked desperate to be done. But before she could exit the stage, a voice demanded, "Tell us what you're drinking!" Table Six, naturally.

"Carrot juice and rum, a new one from the boys upstairs. It's called the Rabbit."

"Like the sex toy," squealed another Table Sixer.

Claire didn't bother to respond. The mike gave a final screech of feedback when she attempted to rid herself of it. Claire's hand shook, making it difficult to return it to its holder. Jessica smoothly walked over, took Claire's drink from her, and slid the mike into the base.

"Can I try a sip?" she asked, to make her actions appear self-serving instead of sympathetic.

"Grab your own glass," Claire said haltingly. "Grab a *gallon*."

"That's okay, I just want a taste." She'd decided to stay sober this morning so she could be on her toes around Claire.

"Any particular reason you sat with the old hens?" Claire murmured.

"Yes. Lead generation."

Claire's wispy blond eyebrows shot up. "How about that. You *are* a businesswoman."

Jessica basked in the approval. She didn't care if the affection came from booze; she knew from years of witnessing her mother's mood swings that sometimes that was the only way to get affection at all.

And here her ex-boyfriends all thought she had *daddy* issues.

"Let me tell you who's who," Claire offered.

"Table Six looked fun."

"Oh, Lord. Okay. May as well get it over with. Just. Come here a second."

Jessica's heart pounded double-time as Claire steered her to a secluded section of the floor. She loved being privy to secrets.

"You know they're swingers, right?" Claire asked quietly.

"They're *what*?"

"I'm pretty sure you heard me."

"Like, real swingers? I thought that was something people did in the seventies and then never mentioned again."

"Uh, no, it's alive and well. Cal didn't tell you?"

"No, he didn't say anything."

He'd been so insistent that she attend today. It seemed odd that he'd leave it out.

"Hmm. Be careful what you say; they construe anything remotely friendly as an invitation. Just be firm if you're not into it."

"Come with me," Jessica begged.

"Oh, no. I'm going to freshen my drink. I'll give you five minutes before I rescue you."

Jessica panicked. "I don't have a watch."

But Claire was gone, and ten other WAGs had taken her place. Specifically, the ten WAGs from Table Six. There was no escape.

The ladies circled Jessica like hyenas. The corseted one was their leader. She leaned in and kissed Jessica on both cheeks. Jessica froze, not knowing which way to turn her head, and fearing a collision of nose and lips.

"Hi, sweetie. I'm Brianna. We're a loud group but a fun one."

"What do you think about a spa day later this month?" cooed a woman in a red leather dress. "I'm Helen but you can call me Hel."

"On Wheels," cackled another lady, who wore a peculiar combination of plaid tights and ruffled skirt. "I'm Elizabeth."

"How did you and Cal meet?" Brianna asked.

"At one of his shows," Jessica said. It was easier than giving a full explanation.

"He *married* a wand fucker? Good for him."

For some reason this struck the group as hilarious. Jessica looked among them, uncertain whether she was being teased or honored.

"And what do you do?" Elizabeth prompted.

Something told Jessica to keep her business cards tucked away. The less contact info they had for her, the better. "I just moved here, so I'm still settling in, finding my footing."

"Must be fun to play house," Hel remarked.

"Yeah, that worked out nicely for you, didn't it?" Elizabeth added with a hint of bitterness.

"What do you mean?" Jessica asked.

"Soon you won't have to do *anything*. For the rest of your life. Not with Cal's TV show coming together."

"It isn't a sure thing, he's just shooting the pilot," Jessica said. "And I plan to contribute. I like working, being creative," she continued, but no one was listening to her.

Elizabeth placed a conspiratorial arm around her shoulder. Unlike with Claire, whose proximity she instinctually welcomed, Jessica felt trapped by the gesture. "You know," the lady said, "we're the real source of power here at the club. The shadow government. We have to support each other. Any way we can."

"Give it a rest." Another woman clutched Jessica's arm, and Jessica fought an overpowering instinct to jerk free; *talk about space invaders*. "Her husband's running for board treasurer and she wants your vote."

"I don't think I can vote on that stuff," Jessica said, prying loose one arm from her neck and one from her arm.

"But we can all use our influence with our husbands to encourage them to vote a certain way."

"Some of them never even open the ballots; they're too busy to check the mail. So we vote as their proxy."

"Is that legal?" Jessica asked.

"Listen to her. This is a clubhouse for boys who play with cards, sweetheart, it's not the Federal Reserve. Anyway, vote Christiansen next January for treasurer. And if you ever need anything from me, don't hesitate to ask…"

Brianna, the leader, interrupted her. "Okay, I'm just going to ask. Everyone's thinking it."

"Bree, don't—"

"Is it true Cal gave up sex for *three years* as penance?"

Penance? Penance for what? Before she could ask, Brianna bombarded her with further questions.

"Do you know if he wanked?"

The others tried to shush her.

"Seriously, did he wank at least?"

"Oh, my God, Brianna…"

"*What*, isn't that what British people call it? Anyway, I don't believe it. Three years without pussy? No way. Not our Cal."

Jessica frowned. *Our Cal?*

Lost in memories, they closed Jessica out of the circle. It was as if she weren't there.

"Can you imagine Cal unleashed after all that time?"

"He was probably bursting."

"No offense to Brandy, of course, may she rest in peace—"

"She certainly didn't rest while she was alive."

"No rest for the wicked!"

Elizabeth pivoted toward Jessica, including her in the conversation again. Her eyes gleamed. "What was it like? The first time you and Cal…?"

Snorts and gasps exploded from the others. "Don't ask her that!"

"Did you pass out?"

"Was it like getting your ovaries punched?"

Gross! Jessica was so stunned she couldn't respond. They were acting like Cal was some kind of demented sex beast. Worse, they were acting like they knew it firsthand.

Mercifully, Claire showed up and put a stop to the interrogation. "All right, quit hogging her, she needs to make the rounds."

"Jesus," muttered Jessica, when they were out of earshot. "Those chicks were fucking nuts."

"You stole their favorite toy, what do you expect?"

"Their favorite *toy*?"

"Anyway…"

Claire pointed out cliques of other women at each of the tables. Jessica was certain she must've met several nice, normal people, but they were eclipsed by the strangeness of her encounter with the swingers.

"Our Cal"? What the frigging hell? "Gave up sex as penance"?

Was that the reason he'd told her to come today? So he could ease her into the concept of, of…*swinging* by shuttling her off to the brunch and letting other people do his dirty work for him?

My friends don't really understand how much I've changed since I lived here before. I think it might be—awkward, he'd said.

O-M-G. Had he and Brandy thrown *sex parties*? (*"No rest for the wicked!"*) Did his friends think he was still into that? (*Was* he still into that? And did he expect her to be a part of it?)

Claire droned on and on. "The women at *this* table are married to the daredevils: endurance artists, bullet catchers, blah blah blah. Over there are the Cruise Ship Wives. It's more like a support group with them. Their husbands and boyfriends are gone half the time. They're raking in the dough, but…"

"Mo' money, mo' problems?" Jessica asked.

Claire seemed pained by the question. "Sure, why not," she answered at last. "I'm going to the ladies' room."

Jessica was relieved to see Kaimi approach. At last, someone normal, who'd been thrown to the sharks as well.

"Hi," she bubbled, "I am so glad you're here. I can't even tell you."

"What? Oh, yeah. Yeah, me too," Kaimi said. "It's nice to meet someone who's new to this whole thing. So, what kind of magic does your husband do?"

"Mostly close-up, a bit of stand-up," Jessica said.

Kaimi's eyes widened. "Oh, very cool. Mostly cards, or coins?"

"A bit of both. How about yours?"

"Landon? Oh, he's…he does magic, yes, but he's mainly, a…motivational speaker," Kaimi said slowly. "That's how we met." Her teeth seemed clenched.

"Are you okay?" Jessica asked.

"Here he is!" Kaimi chirped, and thrust her iPhone in Jessica's face. On the screen was a photo of Kaimi with a seriously hot black guy. Kaimi smiled so hard in the photo it hurt Jessica's cheeks to look at the image.

"You guys seem really happy," she offered.

"We sure are," Kaimi almost shouted. In a calmer voice, she added, "We should plan a get-together, just the two of us, so we can really sit down and chat."

"I'd love that. Does tomorrow work?" Jessica knew she sounded desperate, but didn't care.

"Sure, sounds good." They traded phones and swapped numbers.

After another hour of mingling, the crowds dispersed and Claire stood at the fire exit, shaking hands and saying good-bye to everyone as they passed. "Don't forget to pick up a pamphlet on alcoholism. More magicians die of it than anything else. Well, that and poverty. Know the signs; educate yourselves."

Jessica found the PSA slightly contradictory to the general tone of the meeting, and apparently she wasn't the only one.

The woman with the bird-feather hat murmured to a friend, "She's one to talk."

"That's so nasty," giggled the other lady.

The woman with the bird-feather hat leaned closer to Jessica, fairly dripping with schadenfreude. "She has to be absolutely blotto or she can't speak in front of a crowd. That's why Brandy always used to do the talking for her. One-on-one she's okay but more than a few people and—pfft. *And* it's why she never drives herself to brunches."

"Looks like we're the only ones left. Top up?" asked Claire, holding out a pitcher of gin and lemonade.

"I'm good, thanks."

"You survived your first brunch. How do you feel?"

"'Survived' sounds about right."

Claire seemed astonished. "That bad?"

"Just...a lot to take in."

"You may come to find more value in it the longer you're married," Claire said.

"Oh, yeah?" Jessica asked wearily.

"Well, let's face it, nothing you could possibly do or say will ever be as interesting as the fact that your husband's a magician. Who would want to talk about anything else once that's out of the bag? It's easy to lose your identity. People here understand how that feels."

"But the only thing anyone wanted to talk about *was* Cal," Jessica groaned. *And everyone he's slept with.*

"Next time we'll make sure you mingle with other people, not just Table Six."

Jessica wasn't sure she could think about a next time just yet. But at least she had some job leads, and she'd met Kaimi. She had a lunch date with her to look forward to.

Claire was full-on loopy by that point, so Jessica was about to offer her a ride home when Claire asked, "Want to see the best part? Maybe this will convince you."

"Sure."

Claire practically skipped past the bar toward a large golden door labeled WARDROBE. She swung the doors open, revealing an enormous walk-in closet filled with beautiful gowns, as well as shelves filled with hats, gloves, shoes, and handbags. Although most of the items befit black-tie gatherings and cocktail parties, there was a selection of cute, casual day dresses, plaid scarves, thin leather belts, chunky necklaces, drop-leaf earrings, miniskirts, and kitten-heeled shoes that looked perfect for lounging.

Jessica danced over and clasped her hands in delight. "This. Is. Awesome."

"I know." Claire giggled. At last they felt like equals, drooling over fashion.

"The rules are simple. Leave a dress, take a dress," said Claire.

This she could get behind. "Like the penny dish at 7-Eleven!"

"…Right. This is our lending library."

Claire's phone buzzed and her face lit up when she saw who was calling. "Sorry, it's my daughter, away at school." She answered and said, "Hey, baby." To Jessica she whispered, "Go nuts. Try on anything you like."

Jessica couldn't resist running her hands along the dresses and fabrics, which seemed to come from several different eras and explained the variety of colorful outfits she'd seen earlier. Silky, floor-length gowns, velvet and lace, beaded fringe, rayon, cotton, fleece and fur... The genuinely vintage pieces—hairpin sets, beaded headbands, elbow-length satin gloves, a lone, pearl-buttoned cardigan—looked brittle yet delicate (*What if I wreck them?*), so for the time being she limited herself to modern materials.

Then she saw it: a Bill Blass ready-to-wear coral-red halter-neck dress with a center split. It was loose and flowing, and would nicely showcase her bare shoulders. It didn't need a bra, and would look perfect with a pair of gold, peep-toe slingbacks and matching gold bracelet.

Jessica slid the dress on, tied a knot at the neck, and admired herself in the mirror. *Presto-Chango.* Best of all, it reminded her of the red scrap of silk of she'd worn the first time she and Cal made love back in Chicago.

"What are you doing?" Claire demanded.

Jessica whirled around, startled. "You said I could try on any dress I wanted."

"Take it off. Just take it off." Claire's fingers reached out and attacked, pulling on the knot at Jessica's neck, tugging the fabric loose. "That's not for you. You don't wear that. Ever."

Jessica backed away, almost tripping over the open boxes of shoes behind her. "What's wrong with you? Why are you being totally sus?"

"'Totally sus'?" Claire roared. "Are you speaking a language from earth?"

It reminded her of Cal repeating her words as though they were nonsense words, as though Jessica were incomprehensible; from a less intelligent generation.

"*Totally sus* means suspicious," she said, not backing down. "Shady. Not cool. Your *daughter* would know what I meant."

Claire was stone-faced. "Take the dress off. Now."

"Why should I?"

"Because it was Brandy's. She *started* this group with me,

and I'll be damned if I'm going to let you parade around the club wearing it."

The ex-wife again! "Why didn't you just say so?"

Claire was silent for a long time, staring into space. Jessica wasn't sure if she'd even heard her. Then, to Jessica's shock, she slid down the wall onto the floor and put her face in her hands and cried. Her entire body shook.

It turned out Claire was not a mean drunk or a happy drunk; she was a lonely one. Why else would Jessica be the last one here with her instead of women she'd known much longer? Despite the fact that Claire had manufactured a sorority in which to belong, none of the other wives could take the place of its co-creator. Least of all Jessica.

She stood rooted to the spot, unsure of what to do. The best course seemed to stand completely still. Any word or movement risked unleashing another tirade from hell.

Finally Claire raised her head. Her face was wet and her eyes dripped. No longer a goddess of any kind, just perfectly, imperfectly human. "Please take it off." She sniffed. "I'm asking you, okay? I'm imploring you."

When she'd changed back into her original outfit, Jessica sat next to Claire on the floor.

Claire had spent the time alone composing herself. Her mascara was smeared, but other than that her face was bone-dry, pale as sand.

"Are you okay?" Jessica said.

Claire's green eyes were red-rimmed but clear, and her voice was calm and detached. "My best friend's husband married a foulmouthed, tatted-up trophy wife. How am I supposed to feel?"

"Maybe he's *my* trophy," Jessica snapped. "Ever think of that? Maybe my life thus far fucking sucked and he's the prize I get for leaving it behind! I'm sorry about your friend, but he's *my* husband now, not your friend's, or any of those swinger chicks', so get over it."

Claire got up and slowly walked inside the bathroom.

Jessica closed her eyes and waited for the sound of retching to stop.

Then she followed Claire into the bathroom, placed several paper towels under the faucet, squeezed them out, and pressed them gently to Claire's forehead.

Felix

MONDAY AFTER WORK, traffic was worse than usual, and usual was already a *dolor en el culo*, pain in the ass.

His cell phone rang but he let it go to voicemail. One of his exes looking to hook up. He didn't have time for any foolishness if he wanted to get his magic career launched.

Desperate to escape the 101, Felix exited at Cahuenga and took a circuitous route toward Edgecliffe Drive. He considered stopping by the Frederickssons'—maybe the hot-as-hell missus was home again and could help him with his dollar-bill trick—but when he saw Jonathan's SUV in the driveway, he passed right by and continued home to Glendale. *It's prob'ly not a good sign when you avoid knocking on your mentor's door because your mentor is there.*

He'd used Claire's finger-strengthening device all last week at the shop. His tendons ached but he could already see improvement in his card passes and coin work. He was even considering adding pool balls to his collection of props; those were heavy and dangerous but so cool when used right.

He wanted to let her know he appreciated the help, give her an update on his progress, and ask for more advice. Who knew what other tips she'd throw his way, if he could arrange to see her again? He liked replaying their time together in his head, especially the way she'd tossed him the bottle of beer behind her back, trusting him to catch it. She was sort of a bombshell, and sort of terrifying, but there was something more to her that defied characterization, something sad underneath her toughness. It was a sorrow he wanted to lighten.

He couldn't decide if he'd rather kiss Claire or make her laugh. Her incredulity-turned-laughter when he'd punked her into thinking he didn't know the correct word for clubs had lifted him to the ceiling. Getting another laugh out of her would require effort, and he liked planning how he would do it.

He'd never wondered about those things before. Never asked himself what a girl might want from him, instead of what he could *get*. Never weighed the goal of sex against a higher, longer-term objective. (*It's still a good goal*, he reassured himself. *But Claire is so much more interesting than that.*)

She made every one of his exes seem duller than dirt.

As usual, his housemates had a few people over around nine o'clock. A few people turned into ten, then twenty, then thirty, and by two a.m. it was a bangin' house party. The five-bedroom, twenty-four-hundred-square-foot house on Hillside had no neighbors, so the Pussy Palace ("Party Palace" if girls were around) was free and clear to rock the night away, every night of the week, which it happily did. The spare bedroom held two fridges filled with beer, and its wall was covered in lipstick kisses from anyone who wanted to leave one.

Felix locked himself in his room and put on his noise-canceling headphones, but it was impossible to get any practice done. The first few months he'd lived there, he'd joined the carousing; it had felt like a continuation of his baseball days, a necessary transition into "civilian life," but now it made him helpless and angry.

Despite his unusual profession, Felix had the closest thing

to a corporate job of anyone living there. Cousin Paco had inherited his dad's successful turboscape company (mulch re-fills and soil erosion) but paid a manager to run it while he designed graffiti-based T-shirts on the side. Chicks dug the free merch he had lying around. Aspiring actor Jamie, a good-looking white boy from Riverside whom Felix had roomed with at Cal State, spent all day calling the Central Casting hot-line and all night partying. Scooter was a DJ who traveled back and forth among San Diego, LA, SF, and Vegas for club gigs. He partied for a *living*.

In comparison, Felix was a suit, and suits needed sleep to function. He appreciated the rent-free living arrangement, but he also felt handcuffed by it. If he didn't move out, he'd never enjoy the peace and quiet necessary to become a "worker," the term for a magician who made a full-time living. But his hourly wage at Merlin's Wonderporium would never pay enough cash to leave.

The vicious cycle continued.

The next morning, Tuesday, was his day off. Felix slept in late, pulled on some boxers, grabbed his cell phone, and ventured downstairs. A couple of guests from the night before were sprawled outside on deck chairs by the pool, or passed out on the living room carpet. The sound of laughter rose up from the kitchen. When he walked through the swinging double doors and he saw why, his stomach dropped.

His housemates had gone through his mail, and plastered the kitchen walls with pages from *Clowning 4 Cash* magazine. Tuning out their cackles, he walked past them to the fridge for his eggs, but they were all gone—well, eleven out of twelve were. He slammed the fridge door shut.

"What the hell, *cabrones*," he groaned, "I bought those *yesterday*."

Cousin Paco pointed an accusatory finger at Felix. "*Payaso*," he hissed. Clown!

"Dude, *why do you have this*?" Scooter said, chucking the magazine at Paco.

"'The hottest source of information for today's clowning professional,'" Paco quoted from the cover.

"I hope it's the *only* source of information for today's clowning professional," added Jamie.

They tossed around what remained of the issue like a game of hot potato. ("Get it away!" / "Burn it!" / "I don't want it touching me!")

"Does this mean you're giving up on magic?" Jamie asked. "Because this is the creepiest thing I've ever seen, man. For real. But, you know, do what you gotta do…"

As a fellow performer, Jamie understood the bizarre ups and downs that came with creative work. Jamie's own career had stalled three years back after he was cast as a customer who orders the riblets platter in an Applebee's commercial. But even Jamie didn't want to align himself with a clown.

Paco wrapped an arm around Felix's shoulder. "I want to cry, *primo*. You were my hero when you played ball. Then you get into magic, fine, whatever, sort of weird, but I hook you up with this sweet pad, never knowing I'm living with a *payaso*! Does *Tía* know about this?"

"You got one of those flowers that when you lean in to smell it, it shoots water at you?" asked Scooter. "I want to see it."

"Dude, Pennywise haunts my soul," Paco said, and everyone paused to agree.

Felix went around pulling the articles off the counters and wall.

"Ugggh, I'm not a clown." He crumpled the pages and lowered his voice to a harsh whisper. "And that's no joke, man, you can't go around calling me that or throwing that word around. The c-word's not good for business."

Jamie laughed. "The c-word ain't what you think it is, bro."

"It's for my insurance, assholes. I had to join the AAC, American Association of Clowns, so I could get an insurance plan."

"Whoever heard of clown insurance?" Jamie howled.

"Does it protect you from death by clown?" Scooter asked.

"Look, there's no union for magicians, we don't have a choice but to join up with the clowns. You gotta have insurance if you want to play at like Hotel Bel-Air and those places. If something goes wrong with a fire trick or someone gets hurt, you need protection."

"Since when are you doing magic at Hotel Bel-Air?"

"It could happen! And they won't hire you if you don't have it."

"Yeah, but that still doesn't explain this shit." Paco tore out a particularly upsetting page from the magazine (an opinion piece with the clown's profile picture in the upper corner), threw it to the ground, and stomped on it.

"The subscription comes automatic when you join," Felix explained.

"I don't want this in my place, *primo*," said Paco. "You got to, like, *intercept* this shit from the mailbox and get rid of it before it comes through the door."

I have to get out of here, he realized. *It's not just the parties; everyone's up in my business all the time.* Plus whenever he brought groceries home, his housemates gobbled them all up and never paid him back. *Paco's right: I'm never going to get gigs at Hotel Bel-Air or even freaking Motel 6 if I stay here a minute longer.*

Absurdly, he thought of the apartment at Club Deception,

used by visiting lecturers. What a dream it would be to live there, surrounded by magic day and night.

Felix's cell phone rang.

Scooter was closest and snatched it up. "Is it one of your overflow honeys? Let me talk to her."

"No," said Felix, reaching over. "C'mon."

Scooter held the phone out of reach and hit ANSWER and then SPEAKER so everyone could hear. "Yo."

"Um, hello," came a female voice. "To whom am I speaking?"

"They call me Scooter 'cause I move *fast*."

Pause. "Aren't scooters typically used by kindergartners?" the woman asked.

Paco fell into hysterics. "You got pwned, bro!"

Felix motioned angrily to Scooter: *Give it.* He recognized the voice on the phone, and so did his dick.

"Not the way *I* ride 'em—" Scooter managed to get out before being interrupted.

"Okay, Scooter, is Felix available? You can tell him it's Mrs. Fredericksson calling. Unless of course he can already hear me."

"Hi, Mrs. F." Felix snatched the phone from Scooter and tapped the speaker function off.

"Ahh, that's better. Do you remember me?" she said. "We met the other day?"

"Yeah, of course. Sorry about my roommate."

"No problem. I had a roommate like that once."

"How are you? What can I do for you?"

She got right to the point. "Do you own a suit?"

"Of course, a bunch of 'em." *Why do I keep saying "of course"?*

"A nice one? Fits you well?"

"Definitely."

"Want to see the club tonight?"

"*Yes.*" He might not be able to move out yet, but he could escape for the night.

"Meet me at five and I'll walk you in."

"Seriously? Thank you."

"It's a good suit, right? Because if not, I can bring you one," she said.

"No, it's good, it's good. I'll see you soon. Thanks again."

He turned off his phone and victoriously spiked it on the carpet. "Yes. Yes! See, douchebags? I'm going to Club Mother-fucking Deception tonight. For free. The internship was all worth it. This is where it starts, *vatos.*"

"Can you stop at Whole Foods on the way back?" asked his cousin. "Rocky loves their coconut marshmallows." Rocky was the wild raccoon that sometimes crawled through the broken living room window at night. They hadn't seen him in a while and were worried something had happened. "Maybe we can lure him back if you put some of that coco-marsh out by the screen."

"I don't think I'll have time for that," said Felix. "Yo, anyone got a suit I could borrow?"

Felix arrived at four forty-five, and the valet guys were still setting up. Claire didn't show until ten minutes after, but she was worth the wait in a high-slit, sleeveless black dress that looked painted on. He savored watching her walk toward him in spiked heels. Strangely, she had a men's tie draped over her arm, and she didn't bother greeting Felix before popping his collar and undoing the knot in the tie he wore: a skinny seersucker in a bright check pattern.

"You look nice." She removed the offending item, looped it around her own neck for safekeeping, and replaced it with a muted pink-and-gray-striped Armani. Her hands lingered briefly, smoothing the silk material down his chest. She stepped back and admired her handiwork. "Now you look nicer."

She lifted the skinny tie off her neck and tossed it in the trash bin by the entrance.

Startled, he laughed. "That's my roommate's."

"Scooter won't miss it. I did you both a favor."

"It's Jamie's, actually—"

"Whoever's it is, it's not right for you. Don't you want to make a good impression your first time here?" she asked.

He bowed. "Yes, ma'am."

She squinted at him. "You are over twenty-one, right?"

"Twenty-seven."

"Good. Tonight the bar serves nothing but whiskey. Hope you're into that."

"No milk?"

"Excuse me?"

He looked away. *Real smooth, Felix.* His callback to their first meeting meant nothing to her. *She hasn't spent the last week reliving it the way you have,* he reprimanded himself. "Sorry, nothing."

After Claire gave the password at the door, Felix followed her inside. It was still light out, but the club plunged him into darkness, as though he'd left the real world behind for a fantasy. He inhaled the cool air and smiled. *Finally!*

Claire spread out her arms. "Well, here we are. Tuesdays are a bit slow until the lecture at six."

Via a full-length mirror on the wall, they watched themselves advance toward the elevator. She smiled at their images as they passed. They looked good together, like a real couple. Her legs were smooth and endless, and he was happy to note that even though she wore killer heels, he was still taller.

Perhaps it was their elegant attire, the low lighting, or the atmosphere of enchantment, but he felt as though anything was possible tonight. He touched her bare back with his fingertips as the elevator doors closed.

"Your tab follows you from room to room, but I'd keep it to two drinks for the night so you don't get sloppy," Claire said.

The doors opened and they stepped out into the main room. Felix's eyes widened as he took in the spectacle of hanging lithographs, a seemingly freestanding staircase, and alcoves embedded in the walls.

"M. C. Escher must've designed this place," he muttered.

A thin man stood by himself in a darkened corner, glaring daggers at Claire. Felix frowned. "What's his problem?"

Claire cocked her head. "Who?"

"That *flaco* creeper at two o'clock."

She subtly shifted her gaze. "Oh. Him. I exposed one of his tricks the other night." She chuckled. "He'll get over it." She gave Felix's new tie a final straightening and patted him on the chest. "Have fun."

"Aren't you coming with me?"

She seemed surprised. "Do you want me to?"

He didn't need to look around to know she was the only woman he wanted to spend time with tonight.

"Where's Jonathan?" he asked.

"Backstage, I imagine. He's introducing the lecture if you want to say hello. You have about ten minutes before it starts."

"Okay, cool. Walk me there?"

She hesitated. "All right. How's your Zarrow coming along?"

She remembered! "Still pretty rough."

"Try angling them a bit more. If the top card buckles, you're doing it wrong."

"Show me?"

Again she looked surprised. "If you like."

They found a quiet table under a portrait of The Mysterious Dante. (Real name: Harry August Jansen.)

"Cards?" she asked.

He handed her his deck and she went over the move with him a few times. His back was to the wall, and her back was to anyone who might see them. *Why is she shy about her card handling? She has no reason to be.*

"What's on your mind?" Claire asked.

He placed his hands on the table, leaned forward. "I want to intern with you instead."

She coughed. "Oh, no…"

"Just hear me out. Please? I've been doing his errands for weeks now, and getting his sh—his *clothes* dry-cleaned, and he hasn't taught me *one* thing about—and *you're* the one who got me in tonight, and—"

She was already shaking her head. "Not going to happen."

"Why not?"

"Because I can't do anything for you. He's the magician."

"But…"

"My advice? Get out before he turns you mean."

"Is that what he's done to you?" Felix asked quietly. "Turned you mean?"

She stared at him and then stood up from the table. "I think it's time we went our separate ways." She pointed to a hallway on the left-hand side. "Third door on the right, just past the theater doors. It'll be marked PERFORMERS ONLY. He's in there if you want to quit. Or grovel. Your choice."

Flustered and uncertain, Felix left their table and followed her instructions. He pushed the door open with his arm.

In the corner of the greenroom, Jonathan sat on a sagging couch, some *chola* in his lap, kissing his neck. Felix's heart pounded fiercely against his chest, and blood roared in his ears.

Claire is right outside. Claire with the perfect Zarrow Shuffle and painted-on dress, and instead of walking her through the club and treating her like the prize she is, Jonathan's hiding out here, humiliating *her.*

He burst back through the door, fists clenched, and nearly ran into Claire.

"I thought I'd better come with," she said. "Explain how you got in the club, in case he was angry—"

"Don't go in there." He pleaded with his eyes.

"Why, what's wrong?" Claire asked.

"Because…I…"

"Is he with a girl?" she asked.

His shoulders drooped. "How'd you know?"

"Did anyone else see?"

"Just me."

"That's good, at least." She sighed.

He couldn't stop moving, pacing, flexing his fingers. "Can I punch him? I really want to punch him."

She looked alarmed. "No. Leave it alone."

"But—"

"Don't do anything; he's about to go on."

"I could wait outside and jump him when he leaves tonight—"

She tugged on his hand, led him away from the door. "Not smart. He's litigious. He once sued another magician for copying one of his jokes. And it wasn't even one of his jokes."

"No one deserves that kind of disrespect," he whispered heatedly. "Especially you."

"I appreciate the concern, but it's not your fight."

Adrenaline and anger surging through him, Felix swayed from side to side like a boxer warming up. "Why aren't you mad? Why don't you want to do something about it?"

She frowned. "Who said I don't want to do something about it?"

Just then Jonathan's deep, overly enunciated voice could be heard over the intercom like a late-night radio host: "Good evening, my fellow mages. If you'll move to theater two, our Tuesday-night business lecture is about to begin. Tonight's topic is strolling magic etiquette, with special guest Brent Wilson all the way from Louisville."

The theater doors opened and a group of people made their way through the hall. Claire flattened her back against the wall to let them pass. Felix instinctually moved in front of her, to protect her. Magicians pushed past them, pinning them together. She spread her legs just wide enough for Felix to press one of his thighs between them. Their movements hidden from view, she rocked almost imperceptibly against him.

He didn't dare breathe.

"Have you been doing your finger exercises?" she said into his ear.

He couldn't speak, resorted to nodding.

"Prove it," she said, and guided his hand under her dress and up her thigh.

He rolled through three stop signs on the way to her house, but still she beat him there. When he arrived she stood on the porch, fumbling with the house key.

As he approached her, she dropped the keys and Felix took her face in his hands so he could kiss her at last.

She hadn't been drinking but she tasted like champagne, like success, heightened and saturated. She was the parts of Los Angeles he only saw on postcards even though he lived there. The parts that felt dream-like and glamorous instead of day-to-day.

He didn't know how to impress her. His career in baseball

meant nothing to her, and he couldn't astound her as a magician; even if she weren't married to Jonathan, she was surrounded by dozens of other award-winning professionals, and she knew more about the art than he would learn in a decade.

That left him with sex. He would find out what she liked and master it. He wanted to fuck the sadness out of her, at least for a little while, and then maybe she'd agree to see him again, and then maybe she'd agree to mentor him...

"Lights off," Claire said once they entered the house.

"No." He switched the dimmer back up. "I want to look at you."

"My house, my rules."

Darkness fell on them again. He lifted her up and set her smoothly down on the couch. The leather squeaked a little as they settled in. Claire's fumbling at the door had evolved into certainty; she removed his tie with nimble hands, and this time it stayed off.

He shed his suit jacket and undid the buttons on his stiff cotton dress shirt.

"I'm older than you..." she began.

He kissed her neck, her throat, her jaw. "I don't care."

"I've only been with two other men. Does that bother you?"

He kissed her deeply and threaded his fingers through her impossibly soft golden hair. He wondered how those tresses would feel brushing against his chest, his abs, lower, lower... but not tonight. Tonight was all about her. "They were lucky," he assured her, "and so am I."

"It feels like more than that because I have a, um, rich inner life."

"Okay...?"

The confusion must have shown on his face, because she felt the need to translate, bluntly: "I think about other people when I screw my husband."

She lay back on the couch, her hair splayed above her on the cushions like she was underwater. Her legs remained trapped together by the tight material of her dress. She looked like a beautiful, otherworldly mermaid.

He remembered the breathy gasp she'd made in the darkened hallway of the club when he penetrated her with his finger. The way her tongue darted out to wet her lips. Every nerve ending in his body urged him to finish what he'd started, but instead he sat back on his knees and removed the thin buckles of her high-heeled shoes. Repositioned himself and pulled her feet into his lap.

He pressed both his thumbs into the smooth arch of her right foot. Her left foot wrapped around the bulge in his pants. Even her feet were sexy. He'd never understood that particular fetish until now. But any part of her body he was allowed to touch tonight, he was going to touch.

"And he gives foot massages." She sighed with appreciation.

He leaned over to kiss her, and she arched up to meet him.

"I *know* you can find a better use for that tongue," she said after a few minutes of back-and-forth.

He dove lower. She yanked her dress up her thighs as high as it could go. He slid off her lacy thong and positioned his face in the perfect spot to write *c-l-a-r-e* with his tongue.

Her throaty laughter interrupted his thoughts.

"What? What's the matter?"

"You spelled my name wrong."

"I did?"

"Stick to the alphabet. You know the alphabet, right?" The twinkle in her eyes told him not to be offended. Plus he was intoxicated by the taste and feel of her skin.

"Yes, I know the alphabet." But when he started again, he didn't write the letter A. Instead, he used his tongue to spell *M-r-s-F-r-e-d-e-r-i-c-k-s—*

"Oh, God, don't stop," she pleaded. "Right there. Don't stop. Two *s*'s. Two...*s*'s..."

Claire's body tensed, and she scraped her nails down his strong, tattooed back.

Just as his tongue rounded the curve on the final *s*—

The door opened, and light flooded the room.

"What the hell is this?" boomed a voice. Jonathan stood in the doorway, livid.

"Dammit, Jonathan, I was so close," Claire wailed, pounding her fists on Felix's back. "What are you doing here?"

She fell against the cushions and tugged her dress back down her thighs. Felix hid his erection with a pillow.

"I introduced the lecture and came home. To find *his* car in *our* driveway and his *face* in your—"

"You don't have a leg to stand on," Claire said dangerously.

Jonathan traversed the room surprisingly fast and stabbed the air in front of Felix's face with his finger. "You're fired."

"Oh, for crying out loud," snapped Claire, sitting up and tucking her feet underneath her. "Fired from what? Walking Doctor Faustus? Picking up your Vitaminwater? Big loss."

"Get out." Jonathan gripped Felix by the arm and attempted to jerk him to his feet.

Felix broke Jonathan's hold and shoved the other man away. Jonathan stumbled backward, knocking into the armchair opposite the couch. He glared at the thwarted lovers, apparently coming to terms with the fact that Felix wouldn't simply be tossed out.

"You made your point," he said to Claire. "So I'm supposed to what, call ahead? And then what? Play the happy cuckold? Watch you from the closet?"

"I don't care what you do. The house is fair game now, according to you and Becca."

Becca must be the chica at the club, Felix thought.

"Don't you realize that if I thought for even a *second* you were still interested in me, I would stop? I always would have."

Claire made a sound between a snort and a guffaw.

Jonathan looked at Felix for corroboration. "Have you ever, in all the weeks you've been coming here, seen her show an ounce of affection for me?"

"Oh, because you're a paragon of warmth and devotion," Claire retorted.

Felix sank down into the couch. They were putting each other on trial, and for some insane reason he was forced to be the judge.

Jonathan's eyes were tiny pinpricks of rage, though his voice remained calm. "You know what your problem is, Claire?"

She brushed at something invisible on the armrest of the couch. "I'm sure you'll tell me."

"It's not the women. It's not how many weeks of the year I spend traveling—earning money for *all of us*, by the way. You think you married the wrong person. You think if you'd just married Cal everything would be *perfect*."

Felix's jaw dropped. "Calum Clarke? You know him? That is *so cool*."

"Not now," she hissed.

"But that's the guy, right? With the TV show? Everyone at the store is obsessed with him."

"Get out of my house," Jonathan barked.

"Now you've done it." Claire smirked. "That's worse than him catching us, bringing up Cal's TV show."

"I'm not leaving until I know Mrs. Fredericksson is safe," Felix announced. He stood up and the pillow on his lap fell to the wooden floor. Thankfully, his boner had subsided by then.

"Oh, she's safe from me," said Jonathan. "I wouldn't touch her to smack her."

Felix saw red. "She taught me more in one afternoon than

you have all month. And you treat her like dirt! What's your problem, man?"

Jonathan was silent for a moment, his impassive expression rivaling Claire's. Felix wondered if they had contests over who could look less upset.

"Let me ask you a question about *Mrs. Fredericksson*," said Jonathan. "If she's so good at magic, why doesn't she perform, huh?"

"Stop it," said Claire.

"No really, ask yourself, if she's so talented and smart, why isn't *she* a magician? She has the skills and the knowledge. She's easy on the eyes. So what happened? Why isn't she the one up there, if she's so great?"

"There aren't that many women in magic," Felix said carefully.

"Do you really think that would stop her?"

He shook his head.

"I'll tell you why she's not up there. Claire is useless onstage. Did you know, once upon a time, she was going to be my partner? Oh, yes. That was the idea, wasn't it, honey? Are you familiar with Vice Versa, Felix?"

He was. It was a transpo illusion in which a man and his female assistant swapped places. But this felt like a trick, so he didn't respond. It was unsettling how much Jonathan was talking to him right now, after weeks of near-silent interaction.

"Well, we created an hour-long show surrounding her version. The high point was when I suspend my lovely wife in midair before making her vanish and reappear in a box hanging over the stage. We rehearsed for months. The show was exemplary. We booked a twenty-city tour. All the venues were scheduled, advances paid, tickets sold. Sold *out*, in some cases."

Claire jumped in. "He's angry because I refused to be a

stage mom. But our baby was not a trained seal put on earth to make us money."

Jonathan's voice got louder. "On the very first night, she freezes. Right in the middle of the show. Couldn't do a single illusion in front of an audience. Even with a *mask* on. What's to be scared of?"

Felix winced. There was of course a parallel phenomenon in baseball, a problem no one talked about it, because if you acknowledged its existence in any way, it might happen to you. A year removed from his time on the baseball field, and he still felt superstitious thinking the words: *the yips*.

The worst part about the yips, and maybe also about stage fright, was that there was no cure. He wanted to tell her this, so she'd know he understood and didn't judge her for it, but Claire spoke up before he could.

"It wasn't right for Eden," Claire yelled. "She needed to be in a stable environment, needed playdates and preschool. Life on the road is no place for a three-year-old."

"She loved it. She didn't know any different. You just like to be the martyr who saved our baby girl from her awful father when all along it was *you* who couldn't handle it." Jonathan turned conspiratorially to Felix, as though they were pals now, sharing a beer together. "I should've known long before that it would never work. I mean, look at her, she's enormous."

Felix couldn't believe what he was hearing. "She's beautiful."

"Shit, clearly she's attractive, that's not what I mean. What I mean is *she's enormous*. She's almost six feet tall."

"Five ten," Claire corrected irritably. "But please, keep talking about me as though I'm not in the room."

"That's extra-large in magic. Five foot three *or less*. That's the only height you can use. What was I thinking? She can't be sawed in half. She certainly can't fit inside any of the equipment, she's too *big*."

"You could've made it work, if you built your own props," said Felix. "If you wanted it to work, it could have."

"Thank you," said Claire.

"Would you please get the hell out of here?" Jonathan roared at Felix.

Felix stayed where he was and looked at Claire for guidance.

"It's okay," she told him.

"Are you sure?" He touched her arm.

"Yes. Thank you for asking."

Outside, Felix moved his car half a block down, then returned to the front porch to stand by the door and listen. He wanted to make sure Jonathan didn't start whaling on Claire. Their voices were low, but he could make out every word:

"I'm packing a bag," Jonathan said. "You'll hear from my attorney first thing tomorrow."

"*You're* divorcing *me*?" Claire cried. "Ohhhh, no, you don't, that is *not* how this is going to play out…"

They shouted at each other for a while, and Felix moved behind a tree just in time to see Jonathan, with a suitcase in one arm and Doctor Faustus in the other, stomp over to his TrailBlazer and peel out of the driveway. Uncertain what to do, but eager to leave now that Claire wasn't in danger, he got into his car and drove down Edgecliffe Drive into downtown and past Club Deception. The place, the people, the dream, all seemed less mysterious now, yet more out of reach to him than ever before.

How had he fallen so far, so fast? Internship, gone; affair that had barely started, over; career in magic, kaput. Jonathan would probably get him banned from the club and he was sure he'd be fired from Merlin's Wonderporium any day now, and then what would he do? Beg Paco for a job at Turbocare, shoveling mulch for the rest of his life?

I could've at least spelled her name right. Now she thinks I'm stupid.

At home, depressed and horny, he drank several shots of tequila and passed out atop his messy sheets, still in Jamie's suit.

But when the phone rang a few hours later, waking him from fitful sleep, it was *her*.

Heart pounding, tongue a thick sour mass inside his mouth, he tapped ANSWER. "Are you okay? Did he hurt you?"

"No, no, we're fine... What's wrong with your voice?"

"It's three in the morning."

"Oh. Right. Listen. I've been thinking, how would you like to be Magician of the Year?"

Jessica

THE MORNING AFTER her first WAG brunch, Jessica woke up alone on the couch. Cal had gotten home so late the night before, she'd fallen asleep in front of the TV waiting for him. He'd placed a blanket over her but as usual they were ships passing in the night. She'd tossed and turned, cognizant enough to realize she wasn't in the bedroom, but too tired and heavy-limbed to get up and walk across the hall. Now he'd be out all day on postproduction for his TV special, just like yesterday, and the day before that, so of course they hadn't had the chance to talk about Claire's meltdown, the odd response she'd received from the older WAGs at her table, or the salivating sex fiends of Table Six.

Claire's explanation ran on repeat in her head, spinning faster and faster.

You stole their favorite toy.

It was time to face facts: She'd married a man she didn't know because the unknown was better than the things she *did* know. About her family, her life, herself.

Jessica stretched and looked at the clock above the TV: ten forty-five. As much as she wanted to, she couldn't spend the day in bed stewing, catching up on sleep, and waiting for Cal's return. She was supposed to meet Kaimi for lunch in Los Feliz. After that, she had an appointment with Cynthia's mother,

Evelyn, at a nursing home in mid-Wilshire, to discuss organizing and digitizing Evelyn's photos.

First up, coffee. As part of his commitment to sobriety—and because he never did anything halfway, case in point: his rapid-fire marriage to Jessica—Cal only drank decaf. Jessica kept a small box of Starbucks VIAs in the cupboard for her own caffeine needs. The finished concoction reminded her of the Nescafé her mom used to buy in bulk from Kroger; it had the same plastic smell and frothy pond scum surface at the top of the mug, but it got the job done.

She filled a mug with water to heat in the microwave, then opened the cupboard for the packet of instant when *wham*—dozens of beer bottle caps hailed down on her like stinging wasps. Jessica screamed and covered her face. The bottle caps fell and scattered, creating a field of sharp edges on the kitchen floor.

Why the fuck does he have all these?

Oh, right. The Bottle Cap trick. She crawled around cleaning the caps up, and decided to buy a real cup of coffee on her way to lunch.

After scrubbing her face and brushing her teeth, she fumbled for her contact lens case only to see a *severed thumb* in the corner of the bathroom floor.

"Oh my God, oh my God…" Jessica hopped up and down, hyperventilating, then pushed at the horrible thing with her toe, squealed, and crouched down for a closer look—it wasn't a severed thumb, just a fake plastic thumb, cut off at the first knuckle. She chucked it in the trash with no regrets.

Outside Cal's loft, a FedEx courier stood in the hall.

"Can I help you?" she asked.

"Are you Jessica?"

She nodded.

He held out an electronic signature reader, which she signed.

The battered, partially ripped brown box, held together with frayed duct tape, was postmarked Waukesha, Wisconsin. *A wedding gift?* she thought idly. *Right on time, Mom. And such pretty packaging. You shouldn't have. Really.*

"Looks like your mail arrived, too." He nodded to a stack of envelopes by the door.

"Thanks."

Jessica gathered the stack in her arms and slammed the door behind her, praying she would survive the morning before the house exploded or a bunch of doves fell from the ceiling.

The magazine on top was facedown, so she turned it over, then promptly screamed for the third time that day. On the cover was a clown, wearing full makeup and clown regalia, holding a tiny umbrella. *Clowning 4 Cash* magazine.

She chucked the mail to the floor and took off so quickly she forgot all about the package from Waukesha, Wisconsin.

Inexplicably, there was bumper-to-bumper traffic on the Harbor Freeway. Rush hour should've been over. *Why isn't anyone at work? What do people do all day in Los Angeles?*

"Hotel California" played on the radio. She switched to another station. "Alone" by Heart finished, and "Hotel California" started up. She switched to a third station just in time for the guitar solo from "Hotel California."

To pass the time, she surveyed her new city. None of the houses on either side of the freeway matched. Stucco seemed to be the dominant theme, but within the black wrought-iron fences and rose gardens she saw Spanish, Mediterranean, French, and Tudor-style architecture side by side, or integrated in one property, proving that in LA any set piece from the outside world could be plunked down between any other set pieces.

At the Mickey D's drive-through on Fountain Avenue, she

splurged on hash browns to go with her coffee, and pulled up to the pay window with a pounding headache. *Relief comes soon*, she promised herself, grateful that despite her horrible morning she was still on track to meet Kaimi on time.

She dug through her purse, realized her credit card was still on her desk at the loft, cursed, and searched the car for cash.

Nothing in the cup holder or sunglasses holder above the rearview mirror.

She unbuckled her seat belt and twisted her body to dip down to the backseat, where she was rewarded with the discovery of a five-dollar bill.

She handed it through the window to the clerk.

He unfolded it and gave her a suspicious look. "What is this?"

"A five. It was only two-something, right?"

"This isn't five bucks. This is…I don't know what this is. Hey, Larry," he yelled to a co-worker. "Come look at this."

Larry, whose name tag identified him as the shift manager, walked over. "What's going on?"

"Check this out. Do you think it's counterfeit?"

"No, it's weirder."

The guy behind Jessica honked and shouted at them to hurry up as Jessica finally noticed what had perplexed the clerk so much. The bill she'd given him was divided into fourths, containing the print work of a five, a one, a ten, *and* a twenty, all on the same sheet.

"Wait, don't, that's mine." She snatched it back from a perplexed Larry and shoved it in the back pocket of her cutoff jeans. In the armrest, a coin slot beckoned her, so she frantically raided it for quarters.

When she leaned her arm out the window to pay again, one of the coins split open, revealing a second coin inside.

"Goddammit," she muttered.

The number of legitimate coins in her possession added up to a buck twelve, enough for coffee and nothing else.

When Jessica pulled into the restaurant parking lot, her stomach grumbled and she hoped the menu had something more substantial than salads or smoothies, both of which seemed to be the dominant meal choice for women in LA. She'd kill for a Chicago-style hot dog and a vanilla shake to dip her fries in, especially since she'd been denied her hash browns that morning.

Kaimi seemed to have a similar mind-set; her choice for lunch was a place called Home on Riverside Drive, which boasted honey-breaded chicken with Belgian waffles on its all-day breakfast menu. This boded well for their potential friendship.

"Thank you for having a normal appetite," Jessica said when she reached their table. Kaimi sat outside on the expansive, shaded patio, wearing a loose, bat-sleeved sweater, red-framed glasses, and ripped skinny jeans. She raised her Mimosa in greeting.

Jessica ordered the same and got carded. *Can this day get any more mortifying?*

"Really?" Thankfully her license was in her purse. "I'm almost twenty-seven."

"Deverell?" Kaimi asked, reading from the card. "You didn't take Cal's name?"

"Fast as I could. I'm waiting on my new license."

Once Jessica's age had been verified, they settled in for a good old-fashioned chat. Even before the OJ and champagne bubbled up to her head, she felt relaxed around Kaimi; no need to guard her words or behavior the way she did around Claire.

"Oh, my God, can I vent to you about my morning?" she asked.

"Go for it," said Kaimi.

"Every magic trick Cal owns fucking attacked me today."

Kaimi stifled a laugh. "What?"

"His props are, like, scattered around the house, lying in wait for me like a bunch of fucking spiders. And it wasn't just in the house! It was in the car, too. Fake coins everywhere, fake dollar bills! Which reminds me—this is so embarrassing—I don't have any money on me because I raced out of there so fast I forgot my credit card. I'll owe you big-time. I'm so sorry."

"Don't worry about it. You can just pay for the next lunch."

The implication that they might make this a regular thing made her feel better, less unhinged.

"Thanks. I mean, what if Cal had needed those trick coins today? I could've lost them. They were in a regular coin slot, not even in a box marked SNEAKY COINS."

She knew she was fixating on small things, stupid things, instead of the real issue, the fact that she'd married a stranger. A good-looking stranger, sure; a kind stranger, too—so far, at least—but a stranger nonetheless.

"Do you ever feel as though you barely know Landon? Or like…he's hiding things from you, and you're just…alone?" she asked hopefully. Maybe this feeling wasn't singular to her. Maybe it was suffered by every woman who became involved with a magician.

Kaimi cleared her throat. "Landon's kind of an open book, for better or worse. But I know what you mean. I had a boyfriend like that in grad school. I could never tell what he was thinking, or what he was going to do next. It was hell."

"It sucks. What brought you out to California?" Jessica asked.

"I'm a native, actually."

"Oh, cool! I wasn't sure they existed."

"I know. Everyone seems to come from someplace else. But I've spent the last fifteen years in Hawaii."

"Lucky duck. I'm from Wisconsin. This is my first time on the West Coast, but it's in my blood. My parents met in California. They didn't stay together, but I've always wanted to come here."

The waiter returned to take their orders. Kaimi asked for a crispy onion burger and Jessica ordered the chicken/waffle combo.

When he left, Kaimi leaned forward, her eyes glittering with curiosity. "So, what'd you think of the other wives and girlfriends?"

"Some were nice, and some were completely bonkers," Jessica said, relieved to have someone to compare notes with.

"Did you meet the Chest Hair Woman?"

"*What?* No." She lowered her voice. "Is she like…a sideshow freak? Am I even allowed to use that word?"

"Oh, no, sorry, *she* doesn't have chest hair. But her husband does a trick in his set where he has someone pick a card and return it to the deck, right? But instead of *finding* the card, he rips open his shirt and the card symbol is *shaved into his chest*, a diamond and a three. And guess who has to shave it for him every month?"

"Oh, my God, awesome. I missed all the best people. Meanwhile I was stuck in *suckville* with the creepy swingers."

"Swingers? Really?"

"I think my husband…used to…swing. A while back." She closed her eyes briefly. *I can't believe I said that out loud.*

Kaimi's expression didn't change, and no judgment passed across her face. "Who am I kidding? Landon did, too, probably. I mean, he's *noticeably* been around the block."

"I was going to ask you more about him. I guess he's got

a reputation or something? But if you're dating him, he must have at least some redeeming qualities," she said sincerely.

Kaimi rolled her eyes. "I have a theory about that, too."

"Tell me."

"Take a look at this." Kaimi pulled up Landon's Facebook profile on her smartphone and showed it to Jessica.

"Only sixty-three friends?"

"I know. I figured he'd have ten thousand. But look at his childhood photos."

Jessica scrolled through the album of vintage images and chuckled. Landon was a plump kid wearing glasses and purple suspenders. "Nerd alert."

"Right? And I think that's common. With magicians. Maybe they started doing magic to break the ice, have a little game, and when it suddenly worked, when they started getting dates, they went a little overboard. They've been starved for girls for years so now they overcompensate, because who wouldn't?"

Jessica considered this. "Yeah, maybe." She scrolled to a more recent photo. "Plus, hello. Criminally hot now."

Their food arrived and they dug in.

Between mouthfuls, Kaimi told Jessica about a rare set of card-manipulation papers she represented, written by a long-dead card cheat named S. W. Erdnase. They weren't cheap but Kaimi figured she may as well ask: Would Cal be interested in buying them?

"I have no idea. I'll be happy to ask after his premiere, though. Right now he's completely absorbed," Jessica explained. "And we wouldn't have the money till after anyway."

"Okay, but just so you're aware, I'm talking to other people, too, so if someone else wants them, they could get snatched up before then."

"I'll definitely ask him." *Assuming we ever see each other during daylight hours.*

"Could you let me know at the next WAG brunch?"

Jessica's fingers twisted her paper napkin into tense shapes. "I'm not sure I'm ready to go back yet."

"Please don't leave me alone with the crazy wives," Kaimi begged.

"I'll do my best."

"If you can't make it, just call me on my office line."

She handed Jessica her business card. It read:

KAIMI LEE

RESTORER OF ANTIQUE ARTIFACTS

FINDER OF LOST THINGS

On the drive to the nursing home for her next appointment, "Hotel California" came on and Jessica didn't bother to change the station. Why fight it?

Once again she looked intently out the window. For a place often blamed for the country's moral decline, Los Angeles was pretty religious. On a single block there was a Mormon temple, a Zen Buddhist pagoda, and a Korean United Methodist Church. There was also a towering cathedral at the top of Highland Avenue just before the lanes merged into the 101 freeway, and a glowing white cross hovered mysteriously in the mountains above the Hollywood Bowl.

Cynthia's mother lived at the Sunshine Estates between mid-Wilshire and K-town. Built in 1924, the Estates still looked grand from far away, but the crown molding was crumbling and the marquee sign on the roof had long since burned out.

The streets surrounding the nursing home were named for East Coast states and schools (Vermont, New Hampshire, Harvard), but the industrial buildings, video stores, cash advances, doctors' offices, and nightclubs all had signs in Korean script, occasionally interrupted by Que Ricos!, the short, squat, orange-lidded Mexican taco stands. Little Armenia was just up the road. It was like a cheaper, dirtier Epcot village.

She parked at Johnie's Coffee Shop, an old-fashioned diner with a blue-and-white-striped awning. It looked incredibly appealing until she saw it was dark inside. Not a single person was there. A large sign in the window read, AVAILABLE FOR FILMING, with a phone number underneath. It was a fake; a shell rented out for movies and TV shows. There was something sad and lonely about it. She wondered if it had ever been real.

Feeling tired and out of sorts, she walked around the corner to her destination. The sidewalk was wide and eggshell white, with baby jacaranda trees stamped in black square boxes every twenty feet or so. Lavender blossoms had fallen to the street, where they got smeared like waxed paper under the wheels of cars.

"I'm here to see Evelyn White," she told the fifty-something receptionist in the lobby. "Could you tell me where her room is?"

The receptionist checked Jessica's name off a list and walked her to the elevator. "Second floor, first door on the right."

In the elevator was a bulletin board with the days' activities (Social Hour, Bridge, Naptime, Movie) and menus (Today's breakfast: orange juice and Malt-O Meal).

In the hallway of the second floor, the lingering smell of disinfectant and stale Cheerios pushed Jessica to discomfort. *I don't belong here.* She'd never known her grandparents, had never gone to their houses on summer breaks or been spoiled by them at birthdays or Christmases. From her scrapbooking jobs she'd learned just enough to know what she'd been missing out on. But she pushed her forlorn thoughts away before knocking on Evelyn's door, plastering a smile on her face.

To her relief, Cynthia answered.

"My mother's just in the bathroom, but please come in and sit down."

For the next several minutes they went over Cynthia's hopes for her mother's photos. Cynthia rifled through a large box absentmindedly. Jessica looked at the clock on the wall. Both women ignored the sounds emanating from the bathroom. Evelyn's bedside table contained at least six bottles of prescription drugs.

"Oh, look," said Cynthia. "This'll interest you."

She held out an old photo for Jessica to look at. It had been taken outside Club Deception (there was no photography allowed inside the building). There were ten people in the picture, and Jessica's eyes immediately focused on a young Cal, his hair thicker, his teeth a little more crooked (did he have them fixed after he moved to the States?), and she smiled despite herself. *My handsome husband.* Within the group, Claire stood between a man who was probably her husband and a brunette woman with a pixie haircut.

It was Brandy. It had to be.

Everyone else was from Cynthia's generation. Claire, Claire's husband, Cal, and Cal's wife were the new class. Claire was pregnant, and Jessica remembered from the WAG brunch that Claire's daughter was in college, which meant the photo was at least eighteen years old.

Brandy was stunning—disaffected, and cool, all sharp, high cheekbones and dark, mischievous eyes. She seemed to be staring right at Jessica and laughing. Everything about her was luxurious, like an elegant Swiss chocolate.

Jessica felt about as exotic as a handful of Skittles.

Why was Brandy's arm around Claire instead of Cal?

Evelyn emerged from the bathroom at last, clad in a nightgown. Her hair was neatly combed but she seemed either sleepy or highly medicated; her gait was unsteady and her hands trembled. Cynthia was no spring chicken herself; with the aid of her black cane, she guided Evelyn by the elbow to her bed.

"This is the woman I was telling you about, Mother. Her name's Jessica, and she's come to help with the photos. She's part of the club, she married Calum Clarke."

Evelyn's still features sprang to life and her face snapped toward Jessica. Her voice was anxious and very loud.

"Calum Clarke? The one who killed his wife?"

Kaimi

THE NEXT BUYER Kaimi was scheduled to speak with
that day had wanted to meet at Yoga Booty Ballet class, but
Kaimi had declined, citing her lunch date with Jessica. So at
one o'clock they met at the juice bar inside a health club off
Fountain Avenue.

The young woman who'd DM'd her on Facebook on behalf
of her magician lover wore teeny-tiny shorts and a red racer-
back tank top that read SQUAT DAMN in white cursive. She
held out a perfectly manicured hand.

"I'm Becca. You're Kimmie?"

"Kaimi. Thanks for meeting me."

Becca's hairline was sweaty and her roots were visible under the headband she wore high on her forehead. She held out
a chocolate bar that was half eaten. It said 4.20 on the wrapper. "Pot choc?"

"No thanks, I'm good."

"It's medical. Man, they didn't have *anything* like Yoga
Booty back in Joliet. My muscles are *so* 'oww,' right now and I
have to go to work after this so I need a little help, you know?"

"Where do you work?" Kaimi asked, genuinely curious.

"At Lil Folks preschool in Santa Monica. I wish I worked
at the Brentwood one, though—their parents are *way* more
tapped in to the business."

Kaimi tried her best not to react. Luckily, Becca required no encouragement to continue.

"My boyfriend wants me to quit and work for him, but doing a magic show isn't really *acting*, you know? My uncle, he manages my career, said to forget it. Right now my hours are good. I can work out and go on auditions in the morning."

"And get stoned before looking after our nation's greatest resource," said Kaimi cheerfully.

Becca wasn't so high that she couldn't sense sarcasm. "It's not like they *know*. Anyway, I told him I'd help out with this because his wife is a mega-beeyotch and he doesn't trust her." She puffed up proudly. "He needs me to handle it for him. He's trusting me with *everything*. So give me the deets on the drawings or whatever."

Reluctantly, Kaimi laid out the information in the simplest possible terms.

That night, she and Landon met for drinks at the Polo Lounge so she could update him on her progress. She'd spent two hours primping and making herself look both stereotypically Hawaiian (*hello, absurd peony in my hair*) and submissive. She wore a demure, loose-fitting floral dress with simple white flats, and one tiny pearl earring in each ear. She basically looked like a Honolulu airport greeter, minus the leis. She needed Landon to let down his guard around her.

She'd been doing additional research on the papers as well as the man, the myth, the legend, and discovered that Erdnase's identity was the most notorious mystery in magic. More than a century after the book first appeared, there was still nobody who could claim to know its origins. Karl Johnson, author of the 2005 book *The Magician and the Cardsharp*, asserted, "It was as if Erdnase had made some devilish bargain to erase his identity in order to guarantee the immortality of his work." Unpublished, handwritten, heretofore unknown pages by Erdnase were *priceless*. Her QDE had confirmed the papers' age, and that would have to suffice; buyer beware and all that. Granted, she didn't understand the magic terminology they contained, but the point was they truly seemed to have come from the greatest card master the world had ever known. There could be techniques in it nobody else could replicate; information that would offer unparalleled advantages to a card cheat, or career-defining, life-changing status to a magician.

She pulled up to the iconic, Pepto-Bismol–pink Beverly Hills Hotel in her rental Kia, and her heart fluttered in her chest. *This isn't a date*, she berated herself. *Your body thinks it is because of all the prep time, and because you've been pretending for days now that you're seeing each other.* They'd simultaneously selected "In a relationship" for their Facebook statuses (complete with the psychotic-looking smiley photo she'd snapped on her phone) in case anyone from the club tried to friend her. She'd pointedly ignored the comments his FB update elicited. All sixty-three of his friends had an opinion.

Landon had reserved a corner table for their tête-à-tête. He looked fit and debonair in a dark-gray vest and slacks, no tie. He had more facial hair than when she'd seen him last: a bit of stubble with a neatly trimmed mustache.

She briskly walked over. "I'll tell you who I've spoken to so far and you can let me know which ones sound the most promising."

He stifled a laugh. "What's with the flower?"

"What's with the chinstrap?" she retorted.

He looked offended. "It's not a chinstrap, it's a little scruff."

He stroked the short, neatly trimmed 'stache portion with his fingers. "Deliberate scruff, nicely maintained."

"The purpose of scruff is that it's not deliberate, it's haphazard."

And then she was laughing all of a sudden. She couldn't help it. Their hostile greeting had devolved into an argument about *facial hair*.

"Most ladies like a little scruff," he said.

She counted herself among them, and it was imperative he *never* find that out. The guy was magically delicious. Problem was, he knew it.

"Do I seem like most ladies?"

"Not at all."

She sat down at the table, smoothing her shapeless dress down her thighs. She hated engaging in small talk but if it helped loosen him up, she'd suffer through it.

"Can we start over?" she asked. "Hi, how's it going?"

"That's better. Fine, how are you?"

"Phenomenal. So, Claire Fredericksson," she said. "She was running the wives' brunch, so that's the first person I approached."

"Ahh, Claire. The vagician," Landon said fondly.

"The *what*?"

"Female magician." He put his hands up defensively. "Not my word."

"So don't use it!"

"She's also the wife of the board president."

"Jonathan Fredericksson," Kaimi cut in.

"Right. Apparently Claire writes all his material. It's the best-kept secret in magic."

"I thought Erdnase was the best-kept secret in magic."

"Okay, Claire is the *second*-best-kept secret in magic."

"How come you know about it?"

"My buddy Patrick Blake, he used to intern for Jonathan. Hated him so much he quit stage work altogether. He's a close-up guy now, only works with cards."

She pursed her lips. "My, my."

"Yeah, they're kind of the snobs of magic. Anyway, he said Claire's the real deal."

"Well, she didn't think her husband would want the papers. Told me to ask Calum Clarke instead. But then get this…" Kaimi leaned in and lowered her voice. "Jonathan's *mistress* found me and said he *was* interested, and to only go through *her* with the info."

Landon's jaw dropped. "Whoa."

"I know. I also reached out to a collector in London, and I had lunch with Cal's wife, Jessica, already."

Landon nodded, pleased. "Good thinking. Jonathan hates him. Make sure you let it slip that Cal wants them. He'll set fire to himself rather than let Cal win."

"Will do."

"What'd you think of the new wife?"

"Total sweetheart. Way too sweet to be swimming with sharks."

He grinned. "I knew those WAG brunches were trouble."

She smiled back before she could stop herself. "Yeah, a whole room of women with opinions. That must terrify you."

She wondered if suggesting they meet for drinks instead of dinner was part of his manipulation technique. Drinks were casual, dinner was serious. Did he want her to think he had a "real" date planned later that evening?

Who cares! She forced herself to concentrate. "Jessica couldn't commit him to anything, but she'll get back to me, and if the show takes off they'll have the cash on hand."

"Anyone else?"

"I have three more people on my list, and as soon I as know more, you will, too."

"Cool. Now I have a question for you. What's with you looking all girlie tonight? Why'd you cover up your hair?"

"That's two questions."

"The shaved thing you had going on was cool. It suits you."

"Any other critiques you'd like to share?" she asked crisply.

"I'm not critiquing, I'm just saying I liked how you were last time. You know, with your funky style and all the earrings."

"I should change the way I look because you like me *better* that way?"

"No, would you stop putting words in my mouth? I'm saying you should be yourself, that's all."

Landon's glass of sangria arrived. Kaimi threw caution to the wind and ordered a Ramos Gin Fizz.

Landon didn't touch his drink.

"Go ahead," she said.

"I'll wait for yours to arrive," he replied.

"Suit yourself. Why are there so few women in magic?" she asked. "Why is it so rare that you have to make up a *gross term* for it?"

"You may as well ask why there aren't any dudes who are cat ladies," he said.

"What do you mean?"

"You're acting like it's a real shame, like women are missing out. But women don't *want* to be magicians, so they don't become them. It's that simple."

"Why don't women want to be magicians?"

"Magicians are dorky. They're nerds. They spend all their time alone, practicing their routines."

She heard Jessica's voice in her head: *Nerd alert!* "Not true. Some of them are sexy and mysterious."

He gave her a sly glance. "Anyone in particular you're thinking of?"

"Ha. So women shouldn't aspire to the same level of nerdiness as men? They have to be responsible, humorless 'adults'? They can't be artists?"

He laughed. "You're relentless. I never said any of that."

"If magicians are so dorky and nerdy—your words—is that why you target them for your seminar? Because you think that without you they won't get any lovin'?"

"Are you saying they don't deserve love? That's pretty harsh."

"They deserve love as much as anyone"—*which isn't much*, she thought—"but why do they have to trick women to get it? Why can't they be themselves? You just accused me of not being real, but isn't that what you're advising to all of them?"

"I never said, *Don't be real*. It all boils down to, *Don't choose the prettiest girl to assist you onstage. Go against your instincts, and give someone else a shot*."

"But only so the prettiest girl will be jealous!"

"That's what courtship *is*, Kaimi. Wanting someone for yourself, wanting them not to be interested in other people. That's what spurs action. Jealousy is as old as love."

"I think the real reason there are no female magicians is because men don't like being fooled by other men. But they *hate* being fooled by a woman."

She assumed he would brush off her idea without considering it, but to her surprise, he nodded. "Men are kind of assholes."

Kaimi's Ramos Gin Fizz arrived and Landon took Kaimi's menu away from her and handed it to the waitress.

"Want to get some food?" he asked.

"I am a bit hungry," she acknowledged.

"What do you like? Meat, veggies?"

Kaimi sighed. "Don't do that thing where you order for me."

"But you said you've never been here, and I know what's good."

"But you don't know what I like."

"That's why I asked, so I can tailor it to you. Why do you have to make it a thing?"

"Fine, just order. But if I don't like it, I'm throwing it in your face."

"Wow, okay." He laughed, and she snorted, picturing him smeared with food.

"I mean it."

There was something exasperatingly mesmerizing about Landon. He was beautiful but also outspoken. He made no apologies for his beliefs, yet when presented with a conflicting point of view, he was willing to listen or even concede, which was rare.

He addressed their waitress. "She'll have the short rib banh mi, and I'll have the filet mignon."

"Reverse it and we're good to go," Kaimi interrupted.

The waitress glanced between them for a second, then left them to their bickering.

"I'm old-fashioned, so what?" Landon asked. "I think it's nice for the guy to order. And open doors, pull out chairs, that sort of thing."

She shook her head. "You're such a liar. What happened to, 'You got her now, playa!'?" she quoted from his lecture.

"Come on, do I sound anything like that when I'm being real? Here, with you?"

"Are you? Being real? How am I supposed to tell?"

"Because I code-switch with the best of them."

She examined him carefully. "What do you mean?"

"White father, black mother. I've been straddling two worlds my whole life. Didn't you notice I talk differently at my seminar than I do in regular conversation?"

"Yeah, but I figured that was part of your so-called persona."

"*That's* a con job, *this* is my personal life. I can talk 'white' and 'black,' 'gangsta' and 'corporate,' depending on the situation. Magic helped a lot, too. The kids at school, they all assumed I was black, until parent/teacher night or whatever when Dad would come by. Here's this white guy in a polo shirt, calling himself my old man, and it threw their world out of alignment. Thought I was fronting. Thought I was a liar, too, just like you do. 'What *are* you?' they'd say. And I'd say, 'I'm magic.' And I'd show 'em a card trick. It defused the situation, distracted them, made me okay again. I didn't have to answer that shit. Because I had magic."

Kaimi's throat constricted. She pictured him as a kid, which she could do because of his Facebook photos. He'd been round and soft, all glasses and high socks, begging to be picked on. *What are you?* She pictured the other kids' contemptuous, taunting faces. Such a horrible question. *What are you?* He'd been brave, is what he'd been. Brave, and clever.

He took a long sip of his sangria.

"Why are you telling me this?" she asked.

"Because I want you to like me," he said. "I like you. Or at least, I liked the girl I met last week. With the piercings and the badass shaved head. Who are you trying to be right now?"

She frowned. "You don't know anything about me."

"So tell me some things. You got any siblings?"

"A sister. She's older by fifteen years."

"I always wanted a sibling," he said wistfully. "Always."

"My parents had me when they were on the wrong side of forty, and they could never control me. And Grace, my sister, was always on their side, so it felt like I had three parents instead of two."

"You said the other day your family's not very traditional?"

"Well, I'm not bilingual or anything but we honor *some* traditions. I mean, we had a *dol*—a big first birthday party—but they canceled my coming-of-age day when I was a teenager. Ha. 'Not mature enough yet,' they said. I was a bit of a wild child."

"How were you wild? Like, sneaking out at night?"

"I used to shoplift." She frowned. She hadn't meant to let that slip. "Just a bad patch in junior high. I never got caught, except by Grace, who made me confess."

"Why'd you shoplift?"

"The point is, my parents signed me up for art classes after school and in the summer, to keep me out of trouble. I was an expensive mistake. I feel bad now for what I put them through."

"That's how you got interested in art?"

"Yeah, except I was terrible at it. Those who can't, appraise."

Maybe it was the frothy cocktail, or the fact that he'd told her so much about his life, but she decided to open up a little more. *None of it matters. I won't be seeing him again after tonight.* "I haven't spoken to Grace in a while. A lot of family drama going on right now."

"You'll work it out," he said.

"How do you know?" She couldn't pretend it didn't feel good to hear those words, though.

He smiled, just a little. "'Cause you're a hustler. Like me."

She bristled. "I am not a hustler."

"Of course you are." He stood up. "Excuse me a sec, I have to visit the men's room. Don't eat all my food when it arrives."

"*You're* the hustler," she called to his retreating back.

She was dazed by their conversation, by her desire to stay in her seat and wait for him to return so they could continue talking. *Get up*, she ordered herself. *Get up, get up, before you run out of time.*

His suit jacket was slung over the back of his chair, the wallet in plain view in the pocket. She quickly opened it, found his valet ticket, and darted for the front of the hotel. They brought around his Prius (*a Prius!*) and handed her the keys. She told the valet she'd forgotten her purse, ducked back inside the hotel, and took photos of his house key with her phone. She'd be creating a copy of it based on the images. They needed to be to scale, so she used her own valet ticket as context for the sizing. Giddy and light-headed—the gin helped in that regard—she returned to the valet stand. She played stupid, returned his keys to the valets, and said she'd be staying longer. Back to her table she ran, and slipped Landon's wallet back inside his coat pocket.

Landon returned a moment later and seemed happy to see her.

She theatrically pulled the peony from her hair and placed it on the table as a centerpiece. "Better?" she asked.

"Much better," he said.

They ate half of their respective meals, then swapped plates. Both were delicious, which was annoying; he'd chosen well. Seeing her finish every morsel of the filet mignon, he grinned and all but said, *I told you so.*

Landon paid the check, which she didn't protest; it was a business expense, and if he got to feel like a big old-fashioned manly man in the process, then fine.

Without access to the University of Hawaii's 3-D printer, Kaimi would have to use a do-it-yourself method to copy his key.

She set up shop at the kitchen table of the one-bedroom apartment she was renting by the week. Furnished, corporate, and utilitarian, the Oakwoods sat on a gated, sprawling compound between Universal City and Burbank. According to the rental manager, during pilot season (January to April) they housed actors from New York, Texas, and the Midwest who'd come to town to maximize their chances of landing a role for the following season's TV shows. Luckily, in the fall the buildings were much less crowded. Except for the occasional child star with eerily perfect posture, teeth, and clothing, Kaimi rarely ran into neighbors. She liked the quiet, and having access to the pool and hot tub at night.

At her makeshift worktable, she regarded her supplies and got to work. Using a metal soda can, paper, scissors, glue, Blu Tack, her laptop computer, a standard printer, and a hard-backed ruler, she constructed a facsimile of Landon's key. The trick was to go slow, cut only large and vague shapes at first, then slowly add the precise grooves. It was like arts and crafts at a summer camp for spies.

An hour later, lying in bed, she was pleased with her efforts. One thing bothered her: Landon had proven to be a charming dinner companion, astonishingly easy to talk to.

She almost had a change of heart about robbing him.

Almost.

Claire

DID I REALLY send my husband of twenty years packing so I could transform his young, dumb, full-of-cum apprentice into Stage Magician of the Year?

Claire stood in the shower and turned the knob as close to freezing as she could stand. She needed a jolt to the heart, needed to blast through the surreal fog of her situation. Cold water smacked her in the face like shards of glass raining down, but she forced herself to stay put as a full-body shudder rolled through her.

Felix had no formal training and even less experience. She couldn't have picked a more difficult challenge for herself if she'd tried. Did empty-nest syndrome come with a side effect of insanity? She felt like one of those idiots who rarely left the couch but signed up to hike the Grand Canyon. At least the idiots would be rescued by helicopter (albeit ordered to pay a steep fine). She had no such backup plan.

The events of the night before made her reasons for staying with Jonathan all those years null and void—a pointless prison sentence where she'd played both prisoner and jailer.

No, that wasn't quite true; she would never have divorced him with a child in the house. One way or another she'd have muddled through until Eden left for college. No sense pretending otherwise.

Annnnnd the curtain rises on opening night of Pygmalion in Hell, *starring Claire Fredericksson. In a surprise twist, an understudy will play the role of Claire for each and every performance because Claire is incapable of getting onstage.*

That was the real problem, the true problem, the only problem. What a different life she could have led if not for that. *Participating* in magic instead of observing it. Even Jonathan's philandering could've been prevented had their joint magic show gone forward, she was certain. Eden would've seen the world. Claire and Jonathan could've built a magic empire together, publicly.

It wasn't as though she hadn't tried to fix herself. She'd made attempts throughout her entire adult life. Visualization and breathing exercises briefly got her hopes up, only to crush them again. Beta-blockers made her faint. Xanax made her strangely hyper, with an added bonus of hand tremors. Alcohol was an obvious destroyer of skill and subtlety, both required to succeed in magic. (Though of course that didn't stop some magicians from performing while tipsy; she just wasn't one of them.)

No, there was no cure for what ailed her. She had needed Jonathan. Now she needed Felix. In fact, it was imperative that he win because the prize money might be her only source of income for the rest of the year. Whatever settlement came from their divorce would take months to sort out.

Maybe young, dumb, and full of cum isn't so bad. It has its uses.

For one thing, she could control him. She knew how to shake him up. (You had to give Jonathan credit for consistency; when Felix stepped backstage to the greenroom, Claire was fairly certain he'd find Jonathan in a compromising position. The way he'd reacted told her everything she needed to know about their burgeoning partnership.)

He'll do exactly what I ask for the routine because he doesn't have the knowledge or ability to suggest alternatives, and because he wants me to be happy.

It didn't hurt that he was easy on the eyes, as Jonathan would say; or that in the brief time they'd spent on the couch, he'd nearly sent her over the edge. (However inept his spelling, he was eager but unhurried; he was going to *take his time*, which was admirable, but dammit, why couldn't he have finished?)

She didn't know how much of her attraction to him had to do with Felix and how much had to do with her missed opportunity with Patrick Blake. Either reason was irrelevant now; she couldn't screw around with a student. They had to pour all their energy and resources into making him an expert on the Schrödinger's Cat routine.

Besides, revenge sex was fleeting. Besting Jonathan for Magician of the Year was eternal.

The stream from the shower remained ice-cold, causing her skin to tingle, but this time she shuddered with delight. Jonny's self-aggrandizing walkout last night was better than serving him with divorce papers, she decided. *Let him believe he got the last word. In a month's time I'll be the one laughing.*

She scrubbed her arms, legs, and feet into raw smoothness with her mesh loofah, trying to wipe away through sheer, punishing insistence the image of Felix's bottom lip, which was so full and supple you could bounce a quarter off it. If only they'd had five more seconds…

The phone rang in the bedroom, and she turned off the water to hear the caller ID announce it was Eden.

Claire frantically toweled off and pulled on a robe, then picked up the phone on the seventh ring, out of breath.

"Hey, baby, everything okay?" She tried to hide the panic

in her voice, her mind already conjuring up disasters she couldn't protect her beloved daughter from.

"Yeah, why?"

Her pulse slowly returned to normal. "You usually call on Sundays. I thought something had happened."

"No, I'm fine. What, I can't call just 'cuz?" she teased.

"Of course you can. How'd your civ test go?"

Eden was majoring in civil engineering and minoring in theater. Unencumbered by her mother's affliction, she enjoyed the spotlight and would have preferred her degree in reverse, but Jonathan and Claire had made it a requirement of her tuition checks that theater take a backseat to something more practical.

"Okay. I got a B-minus on the civ test, but an A on my partner scene. Which, I think, tells you all you need to know about that," she said cheekily.

"Yeah yeah yeah, don't you know we have copies of all your tests forwarded to us?"

"Mom! You do not."

She got a kick out of scandalizing Eden. "Sure we do. It's a new perk for parents. We also GPS'd your phone and set up a camera over your bed. Don't look for it, you'll never find it."

Eden laughed. "Stop."

"Tell me about the boy."

"Well, okay. There's not much to tell. We went to Pasha with a group and split the meze platter. His roommate's cute, too, though. Ugh. I don't know."

"Date them both."

"Ladies and gentlemen, my mother. Who has been telling me to play the field since I was nine."

"Keeps 'em on their toes. If they know there's competition, they'll rise to the occasion of treating you better than the other guy. And you shouldn't be looking to settle down anytime soon anyway."

"I know, I know. So the reason I'm calling is I was thinking about Aunt Brandy. Remember when I was eight and she took me to the Halloween parade in West Hollywood with Uncle Cal and we stayed out till four in the morning?"

"I almost called the cops."

"It was the best!"

"It wasn't 'the best'; you spent the next two days ill from all the candy they let you have, and you had nightmares about the costumes for a week."

"Really?"

"Really." Eden had woken at six a.m. in her own throw-up, her face and hair crusted with it, frightened and confused; Jonathan was still asleep from a flurry of shows the previous night, Halloween being to magicians what Christmas Eve was to Santa Claus, and Claire had spent the day tending to their daughter, feeding her sips of water, holding a cold washcloth to her forehead, and promising her it would end soon. All Eden could remember was the fun that preceded the nightmare, of course. Wasn't that parenthood in a nutshell? (Wasn't that life with Brandy in a nutshell?)

"It was three years ago, wasn't it? When her heart stopped?"

"That's right." Claire swallowed around the painful lump in her throat. As euphemisms went, it wasn't bad, and it also had the distinction of being true. Brandy's heart *had* stopped. Just not from a genetic defect, as they'd led Eden to believe.

What was it Brandy used to say whenever she lit a cigarette and someone told her, "Smoking will kill you"?

"Living will kill you. Piece by piece. If you're lucky, it'll start with your heart. The rest's easier after that."

In a way, she got her wish.

Eden's voice pulled her back from the abyss. "I'll light a candle for her tonight at chapel."

"Thanks, baby."

"Is Dad there?

"No, he's in Atlantic City." Another euphemism. This one meant, "Living elsewhere until you come home and we break the news to you in person." The last decision they'd made as a couple was to keep Eden in the dark about their breakup until they could all be in the same room. He wouldn't renege on that deal. When it came to their daughter, they didn't waver. After all, they'd kept that nasty business in Indiana hidden from her for over a decade.

"You guys working twenty-four seven on Magician of the Year?" she asked with affection and familiarity.

Claire swallowed again. "Something like that."

"Then I should probably let you go." ("I should probably let you go," was Eden's new way of hanging up, and it made Claire feel impossibly un-chic.)

"Just remember, 'Beer before liquor, never been sicker. Liquor before beer, you're in the clear.'"

She could almost see Eden roll her eyes on the other end. Eden never drank, as far as Claire knew. She was a serious girl, bright and hardworking, introverted except when called upon to become someone else in a play. Claire missed her so sharply she had to continually and deliberately misinterpret her absence. If she recognized Eden's departure for Rice University as the beginning of more and longer departures, instead of a temporary educational necessity, she probably wouldn't get out of bed.

"Love you, Mom. Say hi to Dad."

"Love you, too."

Click.

Claire stood in her robe, the phone heavy in her hand. Should she give in and make the call? The past two years they'd acknowledged their mutual loss on this day, but it might be overstepping now that Wifey: The Sequel was around. She might even pick up Cal's phone and chirp, *Clarke residence, Jessica speaking.*

Cal replaced Brandy, scrubbing her from his life. It still infuriated her that Cal had burned all his photos of Brandy. He claimed to have copies of videos they'd made, but that may have been a lie to placate her. She had several bound albums from over the years, but almost nothing digital, nothing that would last. Sometimes she couldn't remember how Brandy's hair had looked in the last year of her life. What color had she dyed it by then? How short had it been?

The doorbell rang.

She expected Doctor Faustus to bark and run over, and then remembered that Jonathan had abducted him last night.

Aware that she wore no makeup, no bra, and no underwear, she tightened the knot keeping her robe closed and looked through the peephole.

There was Felix, as though he'd materialized to fulfill her longings in the shower. He wore a backward baseball cap, jeans, Converse without socks, and a blue-sleeved baseball tee. If not for the manly stubble on his face and the fact that she could see his pecs through this shirt, he'd have looked like a paperboy stopping by to collect his wages.

When she opened the door, he took off his baseball cap and held it to his chest in a facsimile of antiquated manners. "Hi."

She ushered him inside and shut the door. "Did anyone see you?"

"No, why?"

"Are you sure?"

"What's the problem?"

"No one can know I'm helping you. Do you understand? What about your roommates, do they know where you are right now?"

"No. Well, Jamie does. He won't care. And I might've mentioned it to Paco."

"Which one's Paco?"

"My cousin. He owns the Party Palace, uh, the house."

"Well, let's not leave out Scooter. Let me guess, he dropped you off, so now *he* knows what we're doing, too."

"Relax, okay? I drove myself and I parked a block away."

"Oh," she conceded. "Good thinking." *At least he knows enough to do that.*

"Jonathan's not here, is he?" Felix said, peering behind her.

"No, and he's not coming back."

His gaze swept over her body and he grinned wolfishly. "Nice robe."

She pulled tighter on her belt, which served only to draw Felix's attention closer; the thin silk stretched across her curves made it obvious she wore nothing underneath.

"Don't cover up on my account," he said, and let his top teeth graze across his delectable bottom lip.

She stared, mesmerized. "Why don't you sit down, and I'll get changed?" she said, not moving.

He took advantage of her hesitancy to place his hand above her on the wall, reminding them both he was taller than she was, but still giving her room to maneuver away if she wanted to.

"Wait, I need to ask you something: And it's not that I'm not psyched, but…why are you doing this for me? Magician of the Year is a huge deal."

"Nature abhors a vacuum," she replied.

"…Right."

"Do you know what that means, Felix?"

"Yeah, isn't it like global warming?"

She blinked. *Don't torture yourself, just move ahead with the proposal.*

"I assume by your presence that you're in?" she asked.

"Definitely. I just need to know how it's going to work."

"Simple. I hand you a gift-wrapped, brand-new, ten-minute act. I'll coach you through every second of it. But you have to commit; lessons every day, no exceptions. The contest is in less than a month, and the grand prize is one hundred thousand dollars."

He whistled.

"I think we should split it seventy–thirty," she finished.

"Sixty–forty. I'm doing all the hard work."

"*I'm* doing all the hard work. In fact, I've already done it. In or out?"

He considered this. "Sixty-five–thirty-five."

"Deal."

"Seal it with a kiss?" he suggested.

"Sure." Their mouths brushed against each other. His lips were warm and pliable.

She came back for more.

His stubble burned her, and she wanted to burn everywhere.

He tugged on the silk ties of her robe, and it fell open with no resistance.

Cold air hit her naked breasts, causing her nipples to tighten. Felix lowered his face to lavish them with attention. He tugged on one of them with his lips, sucking on it like candy, like he was trying to pull it from her body. She cried out when his stubble abraded her; it felt even better than she'd imagined. Her pleasure was short-lived, though. *This is a mistake. If we do this, he'll expect it every time and we'll never get anything done.*

"We need to focus," she managed to get out.

He smiled around her other nipple. "I am focused."

"On the routine."

He sighed and stood back while she quickly retied her robe.

Brandy screamed at her from the great beyond: *If you don't bone him to death, right now, I'll freeze you out in the afterlife. I will not invite you to a single party.*

Cal and Jonathan seemed to think younger was better. Maybe it was time to find out if they were right.

Felix looked right at her. They could probably see his sincerity from space. "I meant what I said last night. I think you're beautiful, and I want to show you."

Forget the paperboy. Now he looked like an Abercrombie & Fitch model who'd sneaked off set to smoke a blunt; his gaze was heavy-lidded and full of promise.

None of that mattered, though. The competition had to take priority.

"Stage name," she blurted out.

"What?"

"You need a stage name."

He stepped back, confused, and she retightened her robe as a reflex. "Felix doesn't cut it. I mean really, what sounds better, Harry Jansen or Dante?"

"Where did this come from?"

"You're right, we'll worry about that later. I'm going to change." She dashed into the master bedroom and locked the door behind her. When she emerged, wearing decidedly unsexy old sweatpants and an oversize T-shirt, he was waiting for her on the couch, looking hopeful.

"Up," she said. "To the kitchen." The couch held too many tempting memories of the night before.

She fixed them both coffees, grabbed a deck of cards, and sat opposite Felix at the table. In the skylight of the kitchen his eyes were clearly bloodshot.

"First off, no drinking until the contest's over," she said.

"Seriously?"

"Seriously. You can't be hungover when I'm trying to teach

you things. Okay. So. The judges for the contest are older than God with twice the memories," Claire said. She absentmindedly riffled the cards.

"Should I be writing this down?" He sounded nervous.

"Just listen for now."

"They're tough to please, is what you're saying?"

"Yes, sort of how doctors make the worst patients. When magicians go to magic shows, they don't go to be astonished or mystified. They know when they're being misdirected. They know when the patter's been lifted word-for-word from last month's issue of *Genii*. They know women always pick the Queen of Hearts. They know when a card's been marked, palmed, crimped, reversed, or sleeved. They know when the deck's been switched, false-cut, false-shuffled, or Svengali'd. They know how the balls multiply and the rings link. They know how the knives, razors, and bullets penetrate; how the swords are swallowed and the glass eaten.

"When magicians go to magic shows they just hope the sap onstage doesn't embarrass their profession. At their worst, they go to magic shows to find fault and burn the other magician. Did he flash? Did he fumble? Did he miss his cue, wreck the punch line?

"At their best, magicians go to magic shows because in their heart of hearts, they still want. And what they want is to see something *new*.

"They remember what it was like when they were kids, watching magic shows on Saturday morning, transfixed by every Cut-and-Restored Rope, Metamorphosis and Impossible Escape, Vanished Lady, Quick Change, Miser's Dream, Coins Across, and Egg Bag. So. Understand? That's what we're going to give them."

"Something new?" Felix guessed. He looked pleased with himself.

"*No*. We're going to make them *believe* it's something new. We're going to take them back to those Saturday mornings before they knew everything. *We're going to give them back their childhoods.* That's how you win. That's the only way to win."

He looked at the floor. "That's kind of a lot to ask."

"Let me worry about that. Do you want to hear about Schrödinger's Cat?"

His brow furrowed. "Schroeder? From *Charlie Brown*?"

Dear God. "Schrödinger's Cat. It's a famous thought experiment." *Though apparently not famous enough.* "It's the name of your act." *My act.* "It's a paradox in quantum mechanics theory in which a cat is discovered to be simultaneously dead and alive while covered up inside a box. His condition is predicated on whether some other event in a different time and place does or does not occur. That connection is called entanglement."

"Um. What?" said Felix. He looked ill.

"It's okay. I'll show you. Here." She got up from the table and described the show to him. She paced and gestured, her face flushed with excitement at the telling of it, of sharing it with someone besides Jonathan. It was her pride and joy. Her finest contribution to the art of magic. She watched his reactions carefully as she explained the opening, the intermediate illusions, the rising action, and of course the twist ending.

When she finished, he didn't speak.

"What do you think?" she asked, bouncing on the balls of her feet. A standing ovation wouldn't have been out of order.

He did stand, but it was to flee. Head ducked, he nearly toppled his chair in the effort to leave. "I'm out of here. Sorry."

"What? *Why?*"

"What you're asking…is impossible. I want to do it, I *thought* I could do it, but we don't have enough time, there's no *way* I can learn that before the contest."

She followed him to the door. "Are you allergic to cats? We can work around that…"

"I can't even impress the customers at the magic shop, okay? This is nuts."

"Okay, okay, it's okay. Let's talk this through," she said calmly, though she felt anything but. She couldn't let him derail her plans. She *wouldn't*. "Forget the magic shop for a moment. In fact, you shouldn't even be working there. You don't have time for that. Call them tomorrow and give your notice, effective immediately."

His panic grew. "I can't! I need money for groceries and I've been trying to save up first and last month's rent so I can move out of my cousin's place."

"Not a problem. I'll loan you whatever you need." Before he could protest, she added, "You're not a kept man, I'll take it out of your share of the prize money."

"What if we don't win?"

"It's an investment I'm willing to make, and you never need to pay it back. But that's moot, because we're going to win. *You're* going to win, and I'll be with you every step of the way."

"How can you be so sure?"

"After you quit the shop tomorrow, come over and we'll go over the routine again, in detail, however long it takes, and make a list of the techniques you need to learn. You'll see that with enough practice and hard work, you *can* do this. I know you can."

"I think you picked the wrong guy, Mrs. Fredericksson."

She wanted to slap him. He was being a coward and he was going to screw everything up. When he opened the door to leave, she dug her fingernails into the side of her arm so that she wouldn't do it to him.

"But this is what you wanted," she cried. "You said you wanted to intern with me, and now you can."

"Not like this. Not with all this pressure."

"At least think about it. Take the rest of the day to think about it. Catch up on your sleep and I'll call you this evening, all right? Felix? Felix!"

"Yeah, whatever. Bye, Mrs. F."

She forced herself to wait until nightfall before picking up the phone. Every word out of her mouth would be a gamble. She needed to choose them with great care. The prospects of money, fame, or collegial respect hadn't been enough to persuade him. That left her with one other option.

When he answered, she didn't bother telling him who it was.

"What are you thinking?" she asked.

He sighed. "I'm thinking about all those people in the audience, the judges, the other *magicians*, burning me with their eyes…"

She regretted painting such a brutal picture of the audience and their lust for catastrophe. She'd be sure to downplay it in the future.

Oh, God. What if her stage fright somehow…manifested in him? What if it was contagious? She felt queasy imagining rows and rows of spectators' eyes; the force of their gazes a living thing, making her joints lock up and her mouth fill with cotton.

She fought to redirect him before he could sense in her the same fears he was experiencing.

"When you played baseball, you faced much tougher crowds, much bigger crowds. This'll be nothing. And it's only ten minutes."

He didn't respond.

Hail Mary time. "Do you know how much fun you can have in ten minutes?" She elongated the words, like honey dripping off a spoon. "We had a lot fun on the couch with *our* ten minutes."

"Yeah, we did," he admitted.

"Do you know what I've been thinking about all day?"

"No, what's that?"

"How wet I got when you untied my robe." She held the phone away from her mouth and bit her lip, certain she'd gone too far, that he'd see through her blatant ploy. But his reaction told her it was quite the opposite.

His breath quickened. "Keep going."

"Why, do you like the sound of my voice when I'm touching myself?"

"Fuck yeah," he whispered. "I like the sound of your voice *all* the time."

"Are you by yourself?"

"Yeah, everyone's at a movie."

"Mmm, lucky me."

He laughed, but quickly got serious. "What are you wearing?"

"A silk chemise. It's the same material as my robe this morning, but it's gold, and it has a much, *much* shorter skirt." In reality she wore a frayed camisole and plaid pajama bottoms, but what he didn't know wouldn't hurt him.

He sighed with longing. "I bet you look hot."

"I wish you were here to take it off me, pull the straps down my shoulders."

"Oh, God," he moaned. "I wish I was, too."

Were, she mentally corrected. *You wish you were. It's not the past tense.* "What are *you* wearing?" she purred.

"Uh, just my jeans."

"No shirt? I like picturing that."

"I like picturing you, too."

"Why don't you undo the top button of your jeans and get more comfortable."

"Okay." His breathing was ragged.

She lay on her back and looked up at the ceiling. She was uniquely well suited for phone sex—it being a style of performance that didn't involve strangers looking at her. All she needed were her wits, her imagination, and—why not?—her hand. It didn't technically violate her no-sex-with-the-student rule. They weren't even in the same part of the city.

"For your first lesson we're going to see how well you take direction."

Jessica

CYNTHIA HAD APOLOGIZED profusely for her mother's outburst, of course. They ducked into the hallway, where Jessica paced back and forth, clenching and unclenching her hands. Cynthia's face was red, and she spoke in rapid, hushed tones.

"I'm so sorry. She has dementia and she's not herself. No one really thinks he had anything to do with Brandy's death, it was just a rumor going around at the time, it was on the news I think, and she picked up on it. We never know what she's going to retain, and...I'm sorry. I understand if you don't want to stay but I hope you'll consider coming back another time. We could really use your help. But it's up to you, naturally, and...again, I'm so sorry. What a horrible thing to have happened."

Jessica promised to think about it, and immediately took her leave. All she wanted to do was go home, pull the covers up over her head, and sleep for three days. Maybe by the time she woke up Cal would be finished with his motherfucking (bloody) TV show and they could finally see each other for more than twenty minutes. He could tell her about his first wife and reassure her that nothing sinister had caused her death.

On the drive back she argued with herself.

"No one really thinks he did it," huh? Why the frosty reception at the WAG brunch, then? Why was everyone I met surprised he'd come back to LA—the scene of the crime—with a new wife in tow? A naive, foolish young wife who worships him…oh, God, I'm the stereotype of a trusting, gullible victim and he's going to kill me next!

Shut the fuck up. He didn't murder anyone. Evelyn's on a lot of meds, her memory's shot, and she doesn't know what she's talking about. It's not true. There's no way it could ever be true.

Yes, he's been busy. Yes, he's been ignoring you since you arrived in California, but that's because he has a once-in-a-lifetime opportunity with this show and he doesn't want to screw it up. He's doing it for both of you. And when you do see him, he's your dream guy—funny, and loving, and generous. He's given you a great home, a car, a place to do your work, all his support, and the best sex of your life.

Everything he has, he's shared with you.

Except information.

How many times had he cut off her questions before they got started? How many times had he given her the runaround?

Mind racing, she pulled into the parking garage of Cal's building. The other car (Brandy's car? It was disturbing how much she didn't know) wasn't there yet. *Good.* Her breathing sped up and she moved quickly, out of the car, into the elevator, and up to his loft. She could google all of it, right now, before he came home. He'd never have to know she'd researched him, and when the time was right they could talk about it, all of it, but in the meantime she'd have peace of mind. Everyone googled each other, it was just life in the Internet age.

Upon entering the apartment, she tripped over the scattered pieces of mail she'd left by the door earlier that morning.

She dropped to her knees and picked up the envelopes and magazines, plus the battered-looking box her mother had sent from Wisconsin. She carried the pile over to her workstation and stacked it beneath her desk, out of the way.

Then she returned to the front door and locked it. That way she'd hear him knock first (he'd left his keys behind) and she could shut off the computer before he saw what she was up to.

Feeling a bit dizzy, she sat down and began to type.

Calum Clarke wife death

Calum Clarke wife murder

Calum Clarke Brandy death

She couldn't believe she was typing the words. But even more unbelievable was the fact that nothing came up under any of those search terms except Cal's official website, pictures of him with a Close-Up Magician of the Year trophy, an interview in *Genii* magazine, and some paid-for clickbaits about his TV special.

She clicked frantically on the NEXT arrow at the bottom of the screen. Page 2, page 3…Here he was five years ago, entertaining celebrities at a fund-raiser. There he was a year before that, at a party held at the British consul's house in Hancock Park. Page 4, page 5…There was Cal's original headshot from the 1990s, with his then-crooked teeth. Another interview, this time for *Magic Magazine*. Page 6, page 7…At last, an obituary: "Brandy Clarke, née Sebastian, passed away late on Tuesday night. She is survived by her husband, Calum Clarke. In lieu of gifts, donations may be sent to Narcotics Anonymous."

Jessica began to relax. Everything was fine. Evelyn was just a confused old lady, and Cal's first wife had had a substance abuse problem. It was sad, but it wasn't nefarious. Except…on page 18, practically buried, was a link to an *LA Examiner* article from three years ago.

The headline read: "Local Magician Calum Clarke Questioned in the Death of His Wife."

Heart pounding, throat dry, Jessica clicked on the link.

It took her to a plain white page with black text: "This page no longer exists! Perhaps you've followed an out-of-date link, or perhaps it was never here to begin with."

She opened a new browser screen and typed in archive.org. The Wayback Machine maintained a database of every single publicly accessible page on the web. Surely a news source counted as such?

She copied and pasted the original link into its search box.

Another dead end: "Due to a direct request from the owner of the site, we no longer have a copy of this article. The Internet Archive strives to follow the Oakland Archive Policy for Managing Removal Requests and Preserving Archival Integrity."

Dammit.

Wait, why am I disappointed? This is a good thing. The Internet kept rumors, lies, hearsay, and misinformation alive forever—that was practically its purpose—so if there was nothing there, it meant nothing abnormal or alarming had surrounded Brandy's death.

Her heart rate slowly returned to normal.

She got up, poured herself a glass of water, and settled back into her desk chair. *Chill.* Crushing guilt set in. *How could you have entertained for even a second that he was a murderer? You should be helping your husband, supporting him, not imagining monstrous scenarios.* According to Claire, it was her job as a magician wife to be on the lookout for anything that could hurt Cal or hobble his career.

But where to start? She knew a little about other close-up magicians, and she'd sensed a rivalry between him and Jonathan Fredericksson, but those things seemed trivial with Cal skyrocketing to success because of the pilot. Then she remembered something else Claire had said at the WAGs brunch: The biggest threat facing their husbands was that YouTube guy. She decided to learn all she could about the so-called Hipster Magician and the damage he'd inflicted on the magic community. Cal certainly didn't have time to look into it right now, so she'd be his eyes and ears on the ground.

Most of the Hipster Magician segments on YouTube were three minutes long, and involved the little shit—wearing a Mardi Gras–style mask over his eyes, skinny black jeans, and vintage Pony shoes—dismantling the code of secrecy the majority of magicians honored. He'd uploaded thirty-seven videos so far, divided into categories like Coins, Cards, Levitation, Transpos, Mind Reading, Vanishing, and Reappearing.

At the beginning of each video, he delivered a nasal-toned manifesto.

"To the haters, know this: I'm helping the art. Only by burning down the forest can there be regrowth. Only by revealing the oldest, easiest, and, let's face it, *laziest* illusions of the past fifty years will modern-day mages be forced to go beyond their comfort zones. Magic isn't magic if it doesn't evolve, if it doesn't force its vessel to go beyond that which came before. This is my way of motivating magicians to be better, to provide a better experience for all who view their tricks. You'll thank me one day."

Jessica snorted. *Bullshit.* She subscribed to the channel's push alerts so she'd get a text anytime a new video went live.

She'd failed Cal today with her ugly distrust, but at least he and Claire would be proud of her for taking a step in the right direction.

Speaking of Claire…

She typed *Claire Frederickson* into the browser.

Did you mean Claire Fredericksson? asked Google.

At first glance, Claire seemed invisible online, subsumed by her semi-famous husband's presence. But on page 3, Jessica found an article in the *Modesto Bee* from 2005. It was a hometown-girl-hits-it-big puff piece that touted Claire's accomplishments since leaving the Central Valley. There was a picture of her graduating from Oxford, playing with her baby girl on the beach, and posing next to a publicity poster from Jonathan's national tour as the Monarch of Magic.

Jessica recognized the image—why was it familiar? Oh, right! She'd seen his show when she was thirteen, in Chicago. She probably had the original program tucked away somewhere. How funny!

Back when she was just an audience member, an outsider, life had been simpler. No magic tricks popping out at her from behind every cabinet or drawer. No strange women at mysterious, underground clubs talking intimately about her husband's bedroom habits.

"Someone's got a crush," came a low, singsong voice behind her.

Jessica screamed.

Cal chuckled. "Sorry, love. Didn't mean to make you jump."

"I didn't hear you come in," she whispered.

She must've have been so absorbed in her research that she didn't hear him jimmy the lock. Who knew what he'd even used? A pin? A credit card? He'd slipped in unnoticed because he was just that damn good. The realization hit her like a punch to the gut.

No locked door can keep him out.

"You're shaking." He rubbed her shoulders, and she tensed beneath his touch.

He gently turned her around to face him, and searched her eyes with his. "All right, Jessie?"

"Yeah, I'm fine, you just…startled me. Why didn't you ring the doorbell?"

"I assumed you were out since the door was locked. Why are you doing a search on Claire?"

Jessica took a few breaths, determined to keep things light. "Well, she *is* a stone-cold fox. Why didn't you tell me?"

"One does not typically refer to another woman as 'a stone-cold fox' to one's new wife." His accent sounded funny when he lobbed her phrases back at her. "Besides, I don't think of her that way. I've known her since Oxford."

"You, Brandy, and Claire went there together?"

"No, Claire was the only one enrolled. Brandy and I were wastrels. Townies, you'd call them. She's the one who introduced me to Brandy. They grew up together and convinced me to move back with them to the States."

"You married one of her friends, and she married one of yours?" Jessica asked.

"I wouldn't exactly call him a friend. Jonathan and Claire are the king and queen of the club. I am but a mere subject."

"Pssshh. You should be the king."

"Making you my queen?"

"Obvi. But Claire would have to teach me everything. She's like...*damn*. In control."

"Well, first impressions can be deceiving," he murmured. "Though I agree she's too clever by half."

"Are you staying for dinner?" Was it already six o'clock? The hours she'd spent online had flown by.

"Actually, I'm just grabbing a couple of things and then I'm back to the edit bay. Don't wait up, okay?"

"Oh. Sure."

He snapped his fingers, excited. "Before I go, I want to show you something I'm working on for Halloween. Come here."

She sat on the couch and he flipped open his wallet, pulling out seven small business cards.

"I don't want it to feel like a magic trick, though—I want it to feel like I'm reading your mind. Right, here we go."

He spread the cards out on the coffee table so she could see them. Each contained a gothic image, grotesque and detailed, drawn in thin black ink. A wasp. A child's old-fashioned doll. Two hissing black cats, one inside a 3-D square, the other outside it. A headless horseman. A jack-o'-lantern with a deranged grin. A bottle of poison with a skull-and-crossbones label. Two skeletons fucking.

"While my back is turned, choose one. Don't pick them up or move them in any way, just choose one in your mind."

After some hesitation, Jessica chose the doll. It was slightly less creepy than the others. But maybe that was the point—maybe he'd included it so she'd choose it. Or had he assumed she'd choose the amorous skeletons? The last thing she felt right now was turned on. She chose the cat. No, the grinning pumpkin.

She didn't want him to be right.

She didn't want him to know what she was thinking.

Pumpkin. He won't guess pumpkin.

"Got it? You're thinking of it?"

"Yeah," she murmured.

Cal faced her again. "Is there any way I could know which one you've picked?"

"No."

"You probably changed your mind a few times, too, didn't you."

She didn't respond. Why bother, if he already knew?

While he spoke, he gathered up the cards, flipped through them, selected one, and placed it into his shirt pocket, all while looking at Jessica's eyes rather than the deck. She couldn't see whether he'd chosen correctly.

"Is there any way I could've influenced you?" he asked.

"I...don't think so..."

"The hard part isn't getting people to do what you want, it's making sure they're unaware of it."

"Okay."

"What would you say if I told you I knew which picture you'd choose, before you even chose it?"

"I'd say that was pretty disturbing."

He grinned. "Excellent. I want it to feel as though I'm controlling you. Now. Moment of truth..." He placed the cards on the table again, facedown, and slowly turned each one faceup. Only the pumpkin was missing.

"Which one did you pick?" he prompted.

"The pumpkin," she said quietly.

He plucked it from his shirt pocket and turned it over. There it was, grinning madly.

She shivered. "Wow."

He can get into locked rooms. He knows what nasty drawing I'll pick. How do I go up against that? How am I supposed to fight that?

His eyes glinted. "Want to know how it's done?"

"No, that's—"

"It doesn't matter which one you pick—"

"Seriously, don't tell me—"

"—because it's not mind reading at all, it's—"

"Don't," she snapped. "I asked you not to."

He looked taken aback. "I thought you might enjoy—"

She stood up. "I don't want to know! Don't you get that? It's no fun for me anymore."

Tears spilled down her cheeks and she covered her face, ashamed, frustrated. Instead of coming home and steamrolling her with yet another of his new tricks, treating her like a feedback mechanism—she could've been anyone—she wished he'd come home to *be* with her, *talk* to her, have dinner as a couple and ask her how things had gone with her new client. *But then, what would I have told him? It was a nightmare, she accused of you killing Brandy? And if I'm totally honest with myself I don't know what to think of you?*

He pulled her into his arms. "Sweetheart, what's got you so edgy today? I won't tell you the secrets anymore, you're right, that was completely daft. What's going on?"

His phone rang.

She wiped her eyes. "Answer it," she said, miserable.

"No, I want to hear what you—"

"Just answer it," she demanded.

He sighed and picked up his phone. "…Yeah, I'll be there shortly. Right." He hung up. "They need me to approve the ad they're putting together."

"Sure." She sniffed. "It's fine."

He kissed her forehead and briefly stroked her cheek with his thumb, rubbing the last remnants of tears away. "I'm so close to being finished. I promise things will be different soon. We'll have loads of time together. I love you."

You hardly even know me.

"Talk tomorrow?" he said. "Jessie?"

She swallowed, nodded, and watched him walk out the door. Again.

With nothing else to do—she'd have killed for a drink, but there wasn't any booze in the house—she sorted through the mail, starting with the odd, lumpy box her mother had sent. A messily scrawled notecard inside read, "Your father sent this for you on your 18th birthday. I forgot. Mom."

No mention of Jessica's new life, her husband, or her move to LA. No acknowledgment that her eighteenth birthday was eight years ago. She would've been angry with the woman who'd birthed her, but she'd learned long ago that her parents lived in a world that scarcely included her. It didn't even include each other.

A fragile-looking music box sat within the duct-taped, folded cardboard. She lifted the music box's lid to reveal a bird automaton. It was pretty, she'd give him that. The crank to make it sing didn't work.

She wasn't surprised. It was as useless as her family tree. *Thanks for nothing, Pop. Awesome.*

Maybe she could fix it and sell it. Wait, wasn't that Kaimi's job? She snapped a picture of the music box and texted it to Kaimi with a question mark below it.

The rest of the mail (besides the horrible clown magazine) consisted of bills: phone, Internet, website hosting, and furniture. The last one was a bill from a website called Reputation Restorer, for a whopping fifteen grand. It was divided into payments, and Cal's first payment of twenty-five hundred dollars was due. *Whoa. Can he afford that, even with his TV money?*

She got back online and searched for Reputation Restorer. She knew what it was before she clicked on the link. She just didn't want to be right.

No wonder his online footprint was scrubbed clean. The company promised to remove or suppress any negative mentions on message boards, articles, websites, and search engines. If they couldn't be removed, they'd be pushed so far down in any search results that 99 percent of users would never come across them.

The service had been purchased August 3.

The day before she and Cal got married.

Kaimi

FINDING A BUYER for the Erdnase papers was easier said than done. Landon had been right about one thing: Everyone wanted them, but few could afford them. Half the magicians at Club Deception could barely rub two nickels together; just paying the annual membership dues was a hardship. The members who *did* earn high salaries didn't make them from magic; they were agents or doctors or lawyers who practiced the art as hobbyists, and couldn't justify spending six or seven figures on a half-torn set of papers. How would they explain it to their wives? And legitimate curators with public collections couldn't purchase stolen goods without fear of facing charges themselves.

The first three contenders, Calum, Jonathan, and Nigel Allen (who operated Magic Crossroads, the London equivalent of Club Deception), remained the only contenders in Kaimi's view, with Nigel as her number one prospect. Rich but unscrupulous, he was her ideal customer. However, Nigel was holding out until the second half of the instructions were added to the set, and according to Landon they didn't exist.

Nobody knew Kaimi didn't have the papers in hand yet. She was waiting for Landon to leave for New Mexico for a speaking engagement. Once they were in her possession, she'd off-load them as fast as possible and fly home to Hawaii before he even knew they were gone.

Landon texted her once a day in the evenings for progress reports. She'd ignored him for the past four days.

She told herself it wasn't shame that kept her silent, but indifference.

To keep her mind off waiting, she accepted Jessica Clarke's second lunch invitation.

Jessica had inherited an enamel music box and wanted Kaimi to assess its value. Kaimi had contacted a former professor whose specialty was authenticating watches and automatons from Paris. His initial theory was that it might have been manufactured by Pierre Jaquet-Droz over two hundred years ago, and based on Jessica's description, he was able to provide Kaimi with a checklist of attributes the music box ought to have. Looking at it in person would tell her whether it passed the test.

At noon, she arrived at the Clarkes', surprised to see Jessica wearing pajama shorts and a tank top, sans makeup. Her eyes were puffy, her smile seemed forced, and when Kaimi handed Jessica a housewarming gift (a personalized cutting board that read, THE CLARKES—MAKING MAGIC TOGETHER SINCE 2016), Jessica's eyes filled with tears.

Kaimi quickly shut the door behind her. "What's wrong? Are you okay?"

Jessica shook her head. "I don't know what I'm doing."

"What happened?" Kaimi's stomach was in knots. Her connection with Jessica was built on a lie, but that didn't mean she wasn't fond of her.

"Sorry. I'm a mess. Thanks for coming over on short notice. I made spinach-and-artichoke pasta if you're hungry," Jessica warbled.

"Sit down. Tell me what's wrong," Kaimi suggested. She

placed the offending cutting board out of the way, and she and
Jessica sat at the dining table.

"It's Cal. He's never home, and when he *is* home we barely
see each other. He never wants to meet up with people, or take
me to the club, and the other day I found this…" She showed
Kaimi the bill from Reputation Restorer. "I think he's hiding
something from me. Something big."

Kaimi studied the bill. "I've heard of them. They clean up
your online profile, right?"

"Yeah. But why did he get it done *now*? Look at the date—
just a few weeks after we met."

They met each other two months ago!? "Well…" She racked
her brain for an explanation. "His show's about to air. Maybe
it has something to do with that? All the attention he'll be
getting, he probably doesn't want anyone digging up embarrassing photos or an off-color remark from years ago. He
could be worried about bad publicity."

Jessica sniffled. "I guess, but…look how much it is. It's way
more than we can afford, or at least that I thought we could.
Why would he need to spend this much? What is he trying to
stop me from finding out?"

It might not be about you, Kaimi thought but didn't say. No
need to upset Jessica further.

She was disappointed about Cal and struck him off the list
of buyers. If he was spending that kind of cash before he'd
earned it, he was worthless to her. That left only two people,
hardly enough for a good bidding war. And time was running out.

"And what about the whole swinging thing with that group
of women at Table Six. What the *fuck*, you know?"

It took Kaimi a moment to figure out what Jessica was re-
ferring to. *Oh, right, we bonded over that, too—our mutual
sex-crazed magicians.*

"And then…" Jessica took a deep breath. "This is going to sound batshit, but I met up with Cynthia, one of the older WAGs, and her mom the other day to go through some old photos, and the mother told me…" Jessica dropped her voice to a whisper. "She told me something awful about Cal."

Kaimi frowned. "Does she even *know* Cal?"

"Probably not…and her daughter said she has dementia, but…"

"Well then, I think you can safely discount it," Kaimi said with a reassuring smile.

Jessica rubbed her forehead and got up to blow her nose. She washed her hands afterward and retrieved the casserole from the oven. "I don't know. But I can't sleep and I can't concentrate on anything." She dished out two servings and sat back down.

"That sounds rough. I'm sorry."

"What was your ex-boyfriend like?" Jessica asked. "The one from hell? You mentioned him at lunch?"

Kaimi froze. "Oh. You don't want to know."

"What did he do? I mean, if you don't feel comfortable talking about it, I understand."

"It's all right. He framed me for something, and got me kicked out of grad school."

"Holy shit."

"I know. But let me ask you something: How do *you* feel about Cal? Not *What do people at the club say?*, not *What did you find in his mail?*, not *What did a confused old lady tell you?*"

Jessica sniffled again, but when she spoke, her voice was clear. "I love him. That's what scares me the most."

"And how does he treat you?"

"When he's not working, he treats me like a goddess," she admitted.

"Okay. And when does the show wrap?"

"Next week. It airs two weeks after that."

"Here's my advice. Wait until he's done with the show, and see if things improve. In the meantime, do you still have your old ID?"

Jessica nodded.

"Set up a bank account in LA under your maiden name. Don't transfer your money into a joint one."

"What money?" Jessica mumbled.

"I'm serious."

Jessica nodded again. "You're right. Thanks. Who knows, maybe the music box is worth something and I can start with that?"

After they'd eaten, Jessica brought out the item in question.

"What's that stuck to the bottom of it?" Kaimi asked.

Jessica peeled it off and showed it to her. "It's just a photo of a clock tower. No message or anything."

In the background was the Bay Bridge, but the waterline beneath it was lopsided.

"It's not even a normal photo, it's all elongated and weird. I think it was cut out of a larger picture." She shrugged. "Whatever."

Kaimi turned the photo over. On the back, on the lower left corner, Jessica's dad—or someone—had written 126, 4B in pencil.

"Any idea what that means?"

"Nope," Jessica said. "An address, maybe, like Apartment Four-B? But One Twenty-Six where?"

Just in case it proved useful down the road, Kaimi snapped a few pics on her phone of the music box, the photo, and the numbers.

Then she put on gloves and picked up the music box. Best-case scenario, it was a rare enameled Griesbaum Automaton that would fetch five figures. For Jessica's sake she hoped it was.

She carefully wound a lever at the side of the box, which caused a clock-like reaction to occur. An oval lid on the top of the case opened, and a mechanical, feathered blue-and-gold bird rose up, singing, flapping its delicate wings, and turning from side to side.

She set the timer on her phone, and when the song ended her shoulders drooped.

"Sorry, Jess, but it's a replica." Kaimi set her magnifying loop down on the kitchen table.

"Are you sure?"

"It's sophisticated, but it's a replica all the same."

"I thought since I got the bird singing again, it might be worth something…"

"The bird's song is what tells me it's fake, actually. It lasts longer than it should. Also, the cam set—the part of the music box that makes the bird sing—isn't a perfect spiral. Lastly, it uses a going barrel instead of a fusee. You see the same issue with modern watches."

"Oh."

"It's meant to look like a Frisard, but it's not one. I'm so sorry."

"Thanks for the fucking knockoff, Dad," Jessica muttered. "Sorry for wasting your time, K."

"You didn't waste it," Kaimi said kindly. "It was worth looking into. I really wanted it to be authentic."

"I should've known anything that came from him would be garbage."

"I wouldn't go that far," Kaimi offered. "It's still a nice piece. The music is lovely. It's not a bad gift, it's just not real."

"It's the only thing I have of his," Jessica lamented with a bitter laugh. "It's shit, but it's mine."

They chatted blandly for another ten minutes, but Jessica's

gloom had sunk into the furniture and stuck to the walls like wet moss.

"I'm sorry I didn't have better news," Kaimi tried again, after a while. "I know it sucks."

"It's not your fault. Thanks for looking at it. What do I owe you?"

"Nothing. Happy to help."

"You're the best. And I'm sorry, I never said thanks for the cutting board."

Kaimi stood and wound her purse strap around her shoulder. "The pasta was great. Send me the recipe?"

"Sure, and here, take the leftovers." Jessica rose as well, and filled a Tupperware container with the remaining food.

She walked Kaimi to the door but stopped short before turning the knob. "God, I talked so much about myself today I never even asked how *you* are! I'm a jerk."

"Don't worry about it. Really."

"Things are good with Landon? He treats you well, too?"

"Yeah, he really does."

During the elevator ride down to the parking garage, Kaimi realized she hadn't lied.

Back at the Oakwood apartments, she pulled up Landon's website and subscribed to his newsletter. *Why not? Nothing better to do while I wait for him to skip town.*

Half a second later her inbox dinged with a new message.

Dear Friend,

If you're performing magic for any reason other than to give of yourself and your talent, screw you. No one

owes you jack. They don't owe you applause, let alone a date. Stop expecting the world and the women in it to bow down to you. The moment you use your gifts for any sort of gain, material or otherwise, you lose. Yes, some of you need to make a living. That's different. Honor your contracts and perform your best regardless of the price you're being paid or who's in your audience. But when you're not on the clock, using magic to make other people happy should be its own reward. When you truly embrace that aspect of your talent, and let go of any expectations or sense of entitlement, that's when love (and its corollary, sex) will come to you.

Dig deeper.

Stop picking only the supposedly pretty girls to come up onstage. If you took a look at the "second choice" you're using as a prop to make the pretty ones jealous, *really* looked at her, and saw how much fun she was having, how much she *enjoyed* your magic, maybe you would clue in that *she's* the one worth getting to know.

Dig deeper.

In my weekly newsletters, fresh to your inbox every Thursday, you'll learn about mindfulness, accomplishing your goals, and enriching your relationships, all through using your magic skills.

Kaimi laughed so hard her stomach ached. He was a con artist all right, just as he'd claimed. But he conned *men*, not women.

It was now clear Landon's racket consisted of three parts:

1. Marks paid to attend "sold-out" seminars on picking up women using magic. At the seminar, marks were advised

to select women they would normally ignore as their helpers, and then browbeaten into signing up for Landon's newsletter, where the "real" pickup information awaited them.

2. Marks paid to subscribe to the newsletter, which literally said "screw you" to them and steered them toward better behavior.

3. Marks were then bludgeoned by dozens of ads. In the margins of the newsletter was an ever-rotating series of links for magic products, DVDs, and downloads. Mentalism. Vanishes. FISM-award winning routines. Bar Magic. Gimmicks. Party tricks.

Each step presumably brought in respectable amounts of cash, but the ads were likely where Landon made most of his money. Purveyors of magic products and instructional videos, magic warehouses, and even mom-and-pop stores would pay a nice commission for such a precise target audience, hand-picked for their disposable income and interest in magic. The seminars drummed up initial interest but after that, the newsletter and ads were self-sustaining.

Bonus points for the word corollary, Kaimi typed into her phone. She was about to hit SEND on the text to Landon when she thought better of it. *Don't get attached. If you need a Landon fix, snoop his Facebook page.*

It had seemed peculiar at first, Landon's low number of FB friends, but that was only because he kept the group carefully curated—people he truly knew and liked. And they obviously cared a great deal for him, too.

Kaimi was his sixty-fourth friend.

She didn't fault herself for thinking he was full of crap when they'd first met. But she had to admit there were hidden depths to him that intrigued her. He'd been straight with her about one major thing from the beginning: Landon the Libertine and Landon the Actual Human Being were opposites.

His most recent update remained his new relationship status.

She clicked on the comments. (Her own FB status about Landon had received thirty-four "likes" but not a single comment.) In contrast, Landon's page overflowed with kind words from all over the city and country.

Good for you. I knew you'd get there. Love and hugs.

Hi, Kaimi! Good to "meet" you! Friend me?

Does this mean your mourning period is over? So proud of you.

Happy for you, bro. When are you two coming over for dinner, hahaha?

Congrats!! See you at Deception soon I hope. Charlie will want to meet her.

She's pretty. Must be smart, too, if you're with her. Let's double when I'm in town for Halloween!

Don't break his heart, Kaimi, we've got his back. But don't be afraid to call him on his sh*t, either ;)

It is so nice to see you looking happy. I've been thinking of you and that talk we had. I know it's been a long road for you. Don't ever think you

don't deserve this. What a beautiful piece of news
on my feed this morning.

On and on it went, each welcome warmer than the last. His announcement was as fake as Jessica's music box, but she felt special anyway. Like she'd joined a rarefied group of close-knit friends.

The thought of never seeing him again was oddly deflating. Surely they had more insults to fling at each other.

Suddenly a new status update appeared under Landon's name:

Just touched down in Albuquerque.

Landon lived in a quiet neighborhood on Pickford Way in Culver City, in a cozy, blue-and-white Colonial split-level house. *Not exactly the hit-'em-and-quit-'em vibe I was antici-pating*, Kaimi thought. She hadn't expected Ground Zero for Landon the Libertine's pickup operation to look like a single-family home waiting for its family to return.

She was surprised, but maybe she shouldn't have been. So far he had defied all her assumptions of him. *Don't think about that.*

Kaimi parked two blocks away and approached on foot, wearing a dark-gray hoodie and black leggings.

At dinner the week before, he'd asked her why she'd shoplifted as a kid. She hadn't known how to explain it, but as she walked toward his house, a familiar sensation overtook her.

Time was slowing down.

For this instant, she was innocent. She would remain innocent until the second she used her key to get inside his home without permission, at which point survival instinct would kick in, and all her problems, every single wayward thought, every frustration and rage from her past, would vanish. One objective would remain: Don't get caught. What a relief to feel only *one* thing, instead of many. What a relief to know the way forward, to see her world shrink down into a single directive, free from emotion, free from pain. That sort of relief demanded to be duplicated, and committing a crime was the only way she knew how.

She put her gloves on and got to work.

Her homemade key didn't glide in the lock as seamlessly as she'd hoped. While she jiggled it, she glanced from side to side, hoping nobody in the neighboring houses would head out for their nightly stroll.

The key didn't work.

Did you really think it was that easy? That you'd turn from a mall rat into Catwoman overnight? She took a few deep breaths and tried again, slowly, willing the grooves to catch. One more time, and…

Yes.

Hands shaking, she turned the knob and gingerly stepped inside the house. If she flicked a light switch, would that arouse suspicion outside? Hedging her bets, she moved to the living room and pulled the cord of a small desk lamp, which cast a thin triangular glow into a corner of the room.

A bay window overlooked a spacious backyard and BBQ pit. She imagined Landon in jeans and an apron, rotating skewers of grilled chicken and vegetables, the comfortable, easygoing host of a party.

His bookshelf took up an entire wall.

Let's see what he's got:

The Prophet by Kahlil Gibran. *The Expert at the Card Table* by S. W. Erdnase. (No surprise there.) *Bound to Please* by Simon Aronson. (That sounded a little kinky, but it wasn't S&M, it was a magic book.) *Zen Mind, Beginner's Mind.* (Whatever.) Kama Sutra. (That seemed more like him. Though the book looked new, pristine, uncracked.) An anthology of Mexican poetry, compiled by Octavio Paz, gave her pause.

Underneath it, on the bottom shelf, was a thick paperback turned spine-in. The pages were curled and yellowing. She removed it and flipped it over: *The Journey from Abandonment to Healing: Turn the End of a Relationship into the Beginning of a New Life.*

Inside the book, handwriting filled the margins, sometimes in pencil, sometimes in pen. Chapter headings were highlighted as well. Who had abandoned him? He'd mentioned a father, but no mother. Perhaps she'd split when he was young? Or did it refer to someone else?

She replaced the book the way she'd found it, title hidden.

A framed photo on the table next to the shelf caught her eye. Landon as a teenager, standing beside an older white guy—his dad, she presumed—in a panoramic view of a wide, low, grayish-blue building. Letters atop the building read PORT OF (big space) SAN FRANCISCO. Landon and his dad were the same height. They stood back-to-back with their arms folded, sunglasses on, posing like Will Smith and Tommy Lee Jones from *Men in Black*. It made her smile.

Focus, Kaimi. She moved to his office/guest room and silently opened the ironwork-and-glass French doors. Pulse racing, she searched his desk drawers, closet, and the boxes under the bed—nothing.

Because the manila envelope that housed the Erdnase papers sat on his desk, propped against his computer.

Oh, no. This is wrong. This is too easy. Why isn't it in a safe?

A locked cabinet? Landon wasn't careless, and he wasn't lazy. He meant for her to find it.

How did he know?

She undid the thin red cord, winding it tightly around her finger. It was a cumbersome task while wearing gloves.

She allowed herself to succumb to the fantasy of a six-figure payday.

She lifted the envelope flap and removed the papers.

They were blank.

A Post-it note attached to the top page read,

Nice try, Hustler. YOU'RE FIRED.

Felix

IN THE END, fear won.

To be more accurate, the *greater* fear won.

The fear of being ordinary.

So he bombed onstage—so what? What was the worst that could happen? He'd be a washed-up minor-league player? Guess what, he was already there.

But being ordinary…That was intolerable.

"I'm kind of searching, you know? This seems like a good way forward," he'd told his mother back in January, over flan and coffee the night before he accepted the job at Merlin's Wonderporium and moved into Paco's house. He'd read *What Color Is Your Parachute?* (well, most of it), his duffel bag was packed, and he'd made up his mind to pursue magic, but she'd tried to talk him out of it right up until the last minute.

"You're hopping from one thing to another like you have no choice. Baseball didn't work out so now it's magic all of a sudden?" she asked. "You haven't played with your magic kit since fifth grade."

"That's not true!" (It was true.) "And I loved it. Don't you remember how much I loved it?"

"*Sí*, okay, but making a living that way?"

"Not right away," Felix admitted. "But eventually, yeah. Why not?"

Dad walked in from the guesthouse where he ran his acupuncture business. He stole a sip from Mom's coffee and she swatted his backside.

It wasn't as though his parents were unhappy with their lives, but somehow that made it worse. They didn't *care* that they were ordinary. They didn't even *notice*.

Reinvigorated, he knocked on Claire's door, bagels and coffee in tow.

"Morning, sunshine," she said, and the relaxed lilt of her voice took him back to the filthy instructions she'd whispered to him on the phone.

She divested him of the carryout and placed it on the kitchen island.

She wore leggings and a mint-green T-shirt for some band called the La's. Her leggings begged to be peeled off her, and the T-shirt definitely had to go.

She snapped her fingers in his face. "Felix? Are you listening?"

His gaze was glued to her lips. "Hmm?"

"I asked if you were feeling better today."

He'd quit the magic shop via text, and gotten cursed out in a voicemail for not giving two weeks' notice or helping secure a replacement. A real man would've shown up in person and found someone to fill in. But she hadn't given him a choice.

Surely he deserved a little sugar for placing so much faith in her?

"Before we get started, wanna...?" He nodded toward the bedroom, gave her his best, sexiest smile.

"Absolutely not."

"Why?"

"*Why?* You haven't earned it."

He deflated. "How do I earn it?"

She handed him a deck of cards and proceeded to test him on his knowledge of card sleights. They went over Riffle Stacking, the Top Change, Palming, and various shuffles. She forced him to reveal his strengths and weaknesses while she jotted down notes in a pad.

Her favorite phrase seemed to be, "Did I say you could stop?"

When she brought over an egg timer to see how quickly he could perform eight Faros in a row (a type of shuffle in which the cards are interwoven perfectly, with eight being the number of shuffles required to return the deck to its original order), he felt like he was in basic training or something, trying to assemble a rifle in ten seconds flat.

Three hours later, his patience wore so thin it ripped apart. "Why are we doing all this? Can't we just get on with the routine?"

"There's a reception after the award ceremony. If anyone talks to you about sleights, you need to be able to speak knowledgably. Also, I need to know what you're capable of, and how fast you can learn. Because if we're going to do this, we need to *really* do this. Do you understand?"

He nodded.

"We only get one chance to fake it. So we better do it right."

He nodded again, but inside he bristled. By the time the contest rolled around, maybe he wouldn't be faking it. Maybe he'd just be good enough.

The rest of the day passed swiftly, with only water, snack, and bathroom breaks to look forward to.

She never softened, never let anything slide. *Did I say you could stop?*

If anything, she became more demanding after he demonstrated something correctly, because that proved he must have been slacking off in the other areas. No praise, of course, because that would waste time.

He would never have learned so much so fast without her drilling him, and in a weird way he liked having a personal trainer who showed no mercy. It reminded him of his 66ers coach.

What he didn't like was how sore his hands, wrists, and fingers felt on the drive home. A couple of tokes from one of Paco's joints wasn't going to come close to dulling the ache.

On Friday, Claire was even harsher, something he hadn't believed possible. He arrived at eight a.m. and they worked steadily until midnight. Instead of cards, they focused on coin manipulation, which he didn't have much experience with. She had him rolling coins up and down his knuckles and holding them in a variety of positions between his fingers to hide them. He also practiced Muscle Passes, the trickiest of all, in which he shot a coin upward with his left hand into his right, seemingly without moving them.

During the drive home, his fingers tingled as he gripped the steering wheel. Closing his fist was agony. He hadn't been in this much pain since his knees got jacked up.

Claire told him to do his hand exercises before bed, but he couldn't even hold a bottle of beer without his ligaments screaming in pain.

On Saturday, he nearly crashed his car due to exhaustion. He had no life outside his training, no life outside Claire.

On Sunday, his car broke down. He was downright ecstatic at the prospect of a day off, but Claire said she'd drive over and pick him up.

"Fucking great," he muttered before hanging up.

"Nice house. Who are all these people?" she asked upon arrival.

Partiers from the night before trickled out the door, squinting at the sunlight and looking for their cars.

Felix rubbed his eyes. "We had a little get-together last night."

Three more people exited.

"What's a *big* get-together?" she wondered.

He thought for a moment. "Usually involves a rented trampoline."

"When do you get any sleep?"

"I don't."

She pursed her lips, displeased.

"Come on in," he said.

He was relieved that the place was presentable. His housemates were either at work or, in Jamie's case, at an audition, and nearly all the visitors had left. However, he hadn't anticipated the return of Rocky.

Claire shrieked and leapt backward onto the porch when a brown-and-black-striped blur raced past and into the house. It was the girliest he'd ever seen her.

"What was that?" She practically hyperventilated.

"It's our raccoon."

If she hadn't been so freaked out, he might have enjoyed the visual of her breasts rising and falling as she sought to calm down.

"You have a pet raccoon?" she asked.

"Not really a pet. He comes and goes."

"So he's a feral raccoon."

Felix felt defensive. "Well, I mean, he's a city raccoon. He likes Marshmallow Fluff."

"He eats Marshmallow Fluff inside your house? He's probably diseased, Felix." She backed out farther, down the stone steps. "We need to leave. Right now."

"Agreed," said Felix, closing the door behind him.

Just then Jamie strode up the front walkway, carrying a grease-soaked bag of fast food. "Dude, Rocky's back!"

"*We know,*" Felix replied in a warning tone, which Jamie ignored.

"I brought him a burger, think he'll like it?"

Felix drew a line across his throat, and Jamie dropped the subject, only to change his focus, giving Claire a quick once-over. "Where you guys headed?"

"Far, far away from here," muttered Claire.

Behind Claire's back, Jamie made a thumbs-up sign at Felix and mouthed the word, *Nice.*

"When are you coming back?" he asked, in a louder voice.

"A few weeks," said Claire, dead serious.

At first he was excited to move in with her. It would be like dress rehearsal for when he ditched the Pussy Palace, give him a taste of independence and actual, honest-to-God rest. She set him up in the guest room and explained how the shower worked and where to find clean towels.

It was difficult to pay attention because Jamie kept texting him.

> *JAMIE:* what just happened!!!
> *JAMIE:* R U abducted
> *JAMIE:* i'd hit that

JAMIE: and then steal her social security checks
JAMIE: LOL
JAMIE: but seriously I'd hit that
JAMIE: unless she's all loosey goosey down there

Horrified, he dropped the phone and it clattered and bounced on the bathroom tile. Claire looked down at it and he scrambled to pick it up before she saw any of the messages. It vibrated again and Felix quickly shoved it in his pocket.

"Which reminds me," Claire droned on. "Under no circumstances are you to answer the phone. Also, since you don't have to drive here anymore, I want you ready to work at six tomorrow morning."

They returned to the living room and she opened a bottle of Pinot Grigio. Although she sat beside him on the couch, she didn't offer him any wine, and when he reached for the bottle she lightly slapped his hand.

"No alcohol until after the contest," she reminded him.

"But you're allowed to drink in front of me?"

"I can do whatever I want. And you're not much of a wine drinker, remember?"

"I could learn," he grumbled, eyeing the drops of wine clinging to the side of the glass. They beaded and slowly traveled down the curve to the stem. It reminded him of sweat gathering along a woman's arched back.

Claire patted him on the head. "You're blossoming. Like a little flower for Algernon."

He wasn't about to admit the reference went over his head, but it was obvious she was talking down to him. "If you're going to sit there and drink in front of me, could you at least do it in your gold nightie?" he said.

"What gold nightie?"

"You know, 'silk chemise…short skirt…'" he quoted from memory.

She took a sip from her glass and licked her lips. They were pink and shiny tonight. "Right. There is no gold nightie."

"What do you mean?"

"It's an illusion. Hate to break it to you, but that's the line of work we're in."

His shoulders slumped. "Aw, man. I was jacking off to a fantasy?"

"Masturbation is always a fantasy."

"But you were, too, right?"

"Maybe." She smiled. "Or maybe I was doing my tax returns."

He scooped up a throw pillow and tossed it at her. She held her wineglass out of harm's way and laughed.

He slid closer, so their thighs were touching. "I could *buy* you a gold nightie," he suggested.

"With what, my own money? No thanks."

"I feel like a prisoner," he groaned.

"In the lap of luxury."

"There's another lap I want more."

The stinging rebuttal: "Cute."

"Luxury." He rolled his eyes. "My place is bigger than yours. *And* it has a pool."

"Don't forget the relaxing atmosphere. No wonder you haven't been able to concentrate."

"I've been concentrating plenty!"

She recorked the bottle of wine, put it in the fridge, and went to bed, locking the bedroom door behind her.

Felix watched her go.

Eye on the prize, he told himself. This time next month he'd have thirty-five large in his bank account, concrete proof he *wasn't* like everyone else, he *didn't* have to fold and give in, settle for a life spent looking backward to his glory days instead of forward to the renewed fame that awaited him.

Not long now.

He took out his phone.

Jamie had text-screamed the same offensive question four times in a row.

> **JAMIE:** IS SHE ALL LOOSEY-GOOSEY DOWN THERE?
> **JAMIE:** IS SHE ALL LOOSEY-GOOSEY DOWN THERE?
> **JAMIE:** IS SHE ALL LOOSEY-GOOSEY DOWN THERE?
> **JAMIE:** IS SHE ALL LOOSEY-GOOSEY DOWN THERE?

His jaw clenched. It was bad enough Jonathan treated her like crap; he wasn't about to let his housemates sit around making fun of her. She was a kick-ass teacher, she was going to give him his rightful life back, and she deserved some g-d respect. At the very least she was his friend now and that meant he would protect her. He couldn't tell Jamie, Scooter, and Paco about the contest but he could defend her in a language they understood.

"Like a paper cut," he typed back, and powered down his phone.

Jessica

CAL WAS GONE, but his side of the bed was still warm. She never heard him leave. Jessica pulled his pillow close and wrapped her arms around it, inhaling the scent of cedar.

Another day, another MIA husband.

Kaimi's pep talk the day before had soothed some of her fears, but Jessica still felt a lingering sensation of wrongness in the air, and she found her anxiety increased the longer she went without seeing him. He'd sworn up and down he'd be home for dinner, so she had ten hours to find something before he returned. This time she'd search IRL.

She dragged one of the dining chairs into the bedroom and stood on her tiptoes to reach the top shelf of the closet. A binder labeled TAXES came back down with her. The tabs inside were separated into categories: WRITE-OFFS, TRAVEL, INSURANCE, MEDICAL, CAR PAYMENTS. *Go back, go back:* INSURANCE.

Neither Cal nor Brandy had a life insurance policy (or if they did, it wasn't contained in that particular binder), but they did have a list of personal assets. Well, Cal did. They included expensive magic equipment, a twenty-four-volume antique magic book set, and a deed to some land in Britain. Brandy's sole asset was a yacht insured for *two million*. A ripple of ice shot up Jessica's neck. Fifteen thousand dollars for

Reputation Restorer was a drop in the bucket compared with two million.

She slammed the binder shut. Stood on the chair again and felt along the top shelf with her hand. It returned lightly dusted. She tried again, reached farther, stretching her fingertips to the back of the shelf, and was rewarded with an unmarked VHS tape in a plain white box.

Twenty-five minutes later, she returned to the house with a rented VCR and remote from a vintage store called Hooray for Hollywood.

Ten minutes after that, she'd hooked the VCR up to his flatscreen and audio receiver.

If you're going to do this, you better do it now.

With no alcohol in the house, she couldn't fortify herself before inserting the tape in the player. She was forced to watch it sober, which made the Cal of 1995 seem even more like a stranger, since he was so often out of his gourd in the tape.

The handheld camera work was shaky, blurry, and occasionally out of focus. Sometimes the time stamps revealed a binge of narcissism—sixteen films in a week—other times, a month would pass between updates. "Life in the '90s on High Street in Kidlington" was the loose theme. Oasis and Blur CDs provided occasional background music. The one bedroom, ground-level flat where Brandy and Cal had apparently shacked up near Oxford contained a small, fenced-off garden out back. They didn't grow anything in the garden. The rusted, cracked flowerpots were used as ashtrays.

The focus was on documenting their drunken exploits, usually after the fact. Whoever was key to the story sat on a small black sofa inside, being "interviewed." Despite Brandy's insistence that Cal recount every detail of his recent adventures, she often grew bored with the retelling. ("Oh, my God, is there a gas station between now and the end of this story?")

Cal was pale, undernourished, and thin. His thick, dark hair stood on end, with sideburns that reminded Jessica of Rufus Wainwright. In the first scene he took alarmingly generous swigs of Gordon's gin straight from the bottle. Jessica could barely tell what he was saying; his accent was that thick.

When Brandy stepped out from behind the camera, Jessica leaned forward for a closer look. Definitely the same woman from the photo Cynthia had shown her. Cal's future wife was petite and gleefully evil, with a pixie haircut and sharp cheekbones. She was a cross between the dancing woman from the old Gap ads and the devil.

Her favorite pastime seemed to be saying something hurtful and filming her victim's reaction.

"There's a *gorgeous* new guy at the gym," Brandy told the camera.

"Oh, did you manage to go this year?" Cal teased.

She ignored his dig. "I might have to dump you for him. He's got an *ass* that won't *quit*."

"Oi," said Cal, "my arse quits halfway through. Halfway through what, I dunno, but it just up and quits, lazy fooker."

At that point, he pulled down his track pants and mooned the camera.

"It's blinding," cried Brandy. "It's a blinding white British ass!"

"It's luverly, it is," he said, giving his own cheek a smack.

He turned around and treated the camera to a full frontal view, swiveling his hips wildly and making his penis helicopter around in a circle. "Bet he can't do this, though."

Brandy cracked up. "You're gonna put someone's eye out."

He pulled up his pants and approached the camera. "You know who's got an arse that won't quit?"

"Who?"

He pointed to her and waggled his eyebrows.

"Gross," said Brandy.

In the next segment, Cal sat on the couch by himself, using a coffee table to fiddle with a deck of cards. He cut the deck one-handed, plucking a single card from the middle with his thumb and forefinger. It was the Queen of Hearts.

Jessica smiled. It felt like he was reaching out to her from the past. *I'm waiting for you on the other side,* she thought. *You just have to get past this phase in your life, and I'll be waiting here.*

He was sober, his accent less pronounced, and he sounded more like "her" Cal again. Maybe the lower-class inflection only came out when he drank.

He folded the card into a tent and set it on the table. Using an even fancier maneuver than last time, he retrieved two cards from opposite ends of the deck: the Three of Spades and the Three of Clubs. These were also folded and placed either side of the Queen. Then he tossed all three back and forth in rapid succession, over and under one another.

"Three Card Monte," he said to the camera. "Li'l bar trick to pay my tab. No one can resist."

It worked well as a segue; the next sequence took place in the outdoor eating area of a pub. Cal wore a formfitting suit with a classic-looking checked tie and hat from Burberry. He also had two black eyes.

"Look at him, he looks like a chav," Brandy cackled beside him. They sat at a wooden table, sipping from large glasses of lager. The sun hovered in the distance, going down. It was unclear at first who filmed them.

"We're hoping to induce heart attacks by the time we're twenty-five," Cal said cheerfully, tucking in to a platter of fish-and-chips.

"How'd you get the shiners?" asked a flat female voice. A *familiar*, flat female voice. Jessica sat up straighter, and her breath caught in her throat.

On-screen, Cal cocked his thumb at Brandy. "This one volunteered me for a fight."

"You gotta fight, for your right, to paaaaarty," Brandy sang.

"I leave you alone for two days and you wind up in the hospital?" the unseen female said.

"Who said anything about the hospital? I'll be your Nurse Nightingale, baby," Brandy cooed. She opened a bottle of prescription pills and shook them out onto the table.

"Where'd you get those?" the female voice asked.

"This chick I know reads to blind people at a nursing home. I tagged along and I was right: They have the best shit lying around."

"You stole from a nursing home?"

Brandy was giddy. "They don't even *try* to hide them."

"They don't *deserve* them," the female voice added sarcastically.

"They won't miss them. They won't even know they're gone."

"The strangest part of this story is that you know someone who reads to the blind," said the female voice.

"I know lots of good people," Brandy said.

"And they know one very bad one," Cal said. He picked up the bottle, marveled at it. "Can't believe you pilfered these from someone's dear sweet granny."

"You want some, or not?" Brandy retorted.

"'Course I do."

Brandy looked directly at the camera and rattled the bottle. "Clairey?"

Her suspicion confirmed—it *was* Claire—Jessica leaned in toward the TV.

"None for me," said Claire.

Brandy rolled her eyes. "Are you at least going to have a drink? Now that exaaahhhms are over?"

"No, not tonight."

Brandy was obviously annoyed by her friend's lack of in-toxication. "But we're at a *pub*." She tossed some pills down the hatch and swallowed them with a gulp of Black & Tan. "At least have one of your weak-shit shandies."

A nervous laugh from behind the camera. "God, how much have you had?"

"Not nearly enough to make you two interesting."

"I'm *so sorry* we bore you. Maybe you should get a hobby," Claire said.

"I'm taking over the show," Brandy announced. The camera turned sideways as it transferred hands.

Claire of 1995 entered the frame.

Jessica hit PAUSE. Watching Claire felt wrong. Forbidden. But there was no way she could stop now, and she was kidding herself if she thought otherwise. She felt a guilty thrill at the prospect of seeing Claire in her early twenties. *Almost my age. Would we have been friends? Real friends, not forced acquaintances?*

Claire of 1995 was bookish and awkward, a little tall for the room. She wore glasses that made her eyes look small, a SMITHS T-shirt, and cuffed, faded jeans over black ankle boots.

Her blond hair was long, thin, and straight, pulled back in a tight ponytail that trailed limply down her back, unlike the present day, where the thick tousle barely hit her shoulders. She'd learned to play to her strengths since her college days.

A rush of power flowed through Jessica and she laughed aloud. A little harmless revenge for the way Claire had treated her. *She wasn't always so put together, was she?*

Claire sat beside Cal, who wrapped his arms around her in a bear hug, pulling her closer to him on the bench. She almost squirmed with delight but edged away once it was over.

"Give him a kiss," said Brandy.

Claire laughed nervously again. "What? No."

"Why not? You've always wanted to. And he's so *debonair* with those black eyes."

"I am pretty adorable." Cal puckered his lips and made a smooching sound.

Claire leaned over to peck Cal on the cheek.

"No, no, no, a real kiss," said Brandy.

Claire blushed and looked at Cal. He smiled reassuringly.

She brought her face closer to his until their lips touched. He tangled a hand in her hair, removing the hair tie she'd used for the ponytail, and deepened the kiss, sliding his tongue inside her mouth.

Jessica goggled at the screen.

"Are you getting hard, Callie?" asked Brandy, zooming in. "I'm getting hard."

Claire wrenched her mouth free, breathing hard. She stroked her lips with her fingers, looking dazed.

Cal removed Claire's glasses and placed them on the table.

She looked painfully exposed without them, a snail without its shell. Her hair fell across her face and she tucked it reflexively behind her ears.

"Can you turn off the camera?" Claire asked.

The image cut out.

Jessica's stomach twisted in knots.

On-screen, some time had passed—a week? Cal's black eyes were mostly healed. He and Brandy, drunk and plotting something diabolical, sat together on the couch at their flat. The camerawork was *finally* smooth and stationary; they must've been using a tripod.

"We've decided that our dear friend Claire is too tense."

"Much too tense."

"We think Claire needs to get laid."

"Only problem is..." Brandy whispered, "she's a *virgin.*"

"Virgin. Virgin. Virgin," said Cal behind cupped hands, creating an echo.

"She's, how you say, skittish."

"But deep down she's gagging for it." Cal snickered.

"It's our duty, as her best friends, to make sure she doesn't stay that way."

"We'd never forgive ourselves."

"What's better than having sex with someone who loves you?" Brandy asked.

"Having sex with *two* people who love you," Cal shouted happily.

"We're going to teach her everything she needs to know about the *big, bad* world." Brandy swung both her arms in a wide arc, landing in a pointing position toward Cal's crotch, like a game-show hostess showing off the merchandise. "Wait'll she sees his uncut monster."

Cal grabbed at his junk. "It is a truth universally acknowledged that skinny blokes have the biggest cocks."

"Only because they look big in comparison to the rest of their bodies," Brandy said.

"We'll film it, naturally," Cal continued.

"It'll be a snuff film for her cherry," Brandy agreed.

"Rest in peace." Cal grinned and raised a glass.

Jessica cringed and hit PAUSE on the remote again.

She'd seen more than enough of her husband and his former wife to get a sense of their relationship. There was no reason to go looking for trouble by watching more.

But a sick, tenacious part of her needed to know whether they had succeeded in their plan.

She pressed PLAY.

Made a hundred vows to stop watching, and broke every single one.

Felix

ANOTHER WEEK WENT by at the House of Frederickson. Felix was pleased with his progress. Not only had he nailed three new sleights under Claire's tutelage, but he'd memorized the patter for the entire act; no small feat considering it was filled with jargon about quantum physics. Unfortunately, his pain was worsening; the tingling sensation had traveled up his fingers and hands to his wrists and inner elbow. On her advice he held his hands and wrists under hot water in the bath to soothe them, using the jets as a massage, but by morning they ached more than before.

Thursday night, he sneaked out of his room and stole a couple of swigs from Jonathan's stash of whiskey. *Enjoy the backwash, pendejo.* He'd hoped it would knock him out, but instead he lay in bed tossing and turning until he fell into an anxious dream. He was back on the baseball field during a play-off game, and he couldn't do one g-d thing right. He balked. He fumbled. He juggled. He couldn't keep a single ball in his mitt.

All he could do was sit there in chair position throwing dummy signals to Gutierrez, the pitcher. Only, they weren't supposed to be dummy signals. To Felix, they meant very specific things, things they'd practiced for weeks—cutters, splitters, four-seams, changeups—but to Gutierrez and everyone else they were meaningless. They lost run after run and hit after hit.

The smell of roasted sunflower seeds, freshly cut grass, dirt, chewing gum, and Jonathan's whiskey sank into his throat and nostrils, making him feel sick.

He woke up drenched in sweat, his fists clenched and throbbing.

Even his knees ached.

Friday morning, a different smell woke him up: sugar and bacon and buttery pancakes. Oddly, Claire wore a black pencil skirt and a sheer, see-through white blouse that showcased a black bra underneath, instead of her usual jeans and T-shirt. He mentally unbuttoned her blouse as she led him to the table and sat next to him. She'd already fixed him a plate and when he reached for his fork to dig in, she stopped him.

"Rest your hands."

He hadn't felt this demeaned since she'd made him fold her laundry. And yet he hadn't the strength to argue. Like a baby bird, he opened his mouth and she placed a forkful of food on his tongue.

How did this become my life?

He felt wrecked. He'd been battling a killer headache all night, he was scared what he now thought was tendinitis in his hands was permanent, he felt morally conflicted about the contest, he had no job, no income, no contact with the outside world, and no say in how he spent his time. *Jesus—I joined a one-woman cult. And now she's cutting up my pancakes and feeding me.*

When he polished off the plate, she brought him a thick

packet of papers and a fancy pen with the Club Deception logo on it.

"Here's your application to sign."

"What does it say?"

"It's boilerplate. Each act must be between six and ten minutes in length, blah blah. If you go over or under they can disqualify you, blah blah. A contestant's performance may be videotaped or recorded, blah blah."

He could feel impatience radiate off her; it gave her a sharp, fierce glow. He didn't want to invoke her anger, but he'd be pretty stupid not to read the contract before signing. When he got to the originality clause, he stopped. *The contestant asserts that he has the right to perform the act in question, and that it does not infringe on the rights of any third party.*

"But it's not my routine."

"Just a technicality," she said.

"It keeps saying here it has to be my own creation to be eligible."

"It is. You're the one who gives it life," she said. She placed a reassuring hand on his cheek. Looked him straight in the eyes.

Her palm was the softest thing he'd felt in weeks. Possibly ever. He almost wanted to cry with relief. To be touched again, when he couldn't touch himself anymore. To be touched again by the woman who'd been teasing and denying him all these days and nights—it was almost spiritual. He'd been fasting and now he could eat. He'd been dying of thirst and now he could drink. She'd taken all his senses away, and now she was giving them back to him, and he was so grateful he would've signed anything she asked him to. He would've signed his soul away to the devil. (Maybe he had. Maybe the devil looked like an angel.)

"You don't want these last few weeks to be for nothing, do you?" she asked. She smelled like raspberries and syrup.

He wrote his name on the line.

He didn't recognize his own signature.

She kissed him on the cheek. "Why don't you go back to bed?"

He nodded and stood on shaky legs to return to his quarters.

When he woke up, she was sitting on the chaise lounge in his room, reading a book. She set it aside and asked how his hands were faring.

"Honestly, they've never felt worse." He hated the sound of his voice, which was on the verge of cracking. But the emotional roller coaster of the past twelve hours, not to mention the physical pain, had made him sound like a teenager and turned his brain to mush.

Adding to his confusion was the fact that his bedroom was dark, the shades drawn, the sheets cool, and he had no idea if it was day or night.

"How long was I out?" he asked.

"Most of the day. It's okay, you needed the rest."

At least when his knees suffered in baseball he could wear a patellofemoral brace. That wasn't an option for his hands and arms. Neither were cortisone shots, which had ultimately cost him his career, anyway.

"I have something that will help," she said.

Dubious, he followed her out of his room and down the hall, to the master bedroom. To his disappointment they bypassed the bed and entered the bathroom. On the counter were all sorts of girlie products: tinted moisturizer, leave-in conditioner, sunscreen, lip gloss, perfume, a double-barreled curling iron. Now that Jonathan had moved out, she was taking advantage of the extra space.

Determined to regain a sense of equilibrium between them, even if it was false, Felix made a point of standing very close

and towering over her. "I know it was an insult," he said.
"When you called me 'Flowers for Algernon.'" (He'd checked
Wikipedia, which in turn prompted a vague memory of read-
ing the book in high school.)

"I was only teasing. What, I'm not allowed to tease you?"

"You can be a straight-up *perra* sometimes."

She looked amused. "Sometimes? Am I being that way
now?"

"No," he conceded.

"Sit," she said, pointing to the closed toilet.

He did so without a second thought, and then berated himself. *Good boy. Woof.*

"Paraffin wax," she said, and lifted the lid off a small plastic
tub that was plugged into the wall. Inside was clear, hot liquid.
She took his right hand in hers and dipped it repeatedly into
the tub until a white gel formed and solidified around his skin,
like a warm, thick, tailor-made glove. Then she did the same
for his left hand. Afterward, she wrapped both his hands in
plastic bags, and covered them with what looked like oven
mitts.

Felix sighed in pleasure and felt his tendons relax, soaking
in the heat.

"This," he said, gesturing to the wax with his elbow, "this is
how your skin is so soft."

"That's part of it," she said. "I also bathe in the blood of vir-
gins."

"You are so freakin' awesome."

"Not bitchy, then."

"Not bitchy."

"Keep your hands still for the next twenty minutes," she
said. "You want to go sit down somewhere more comfortable?"

"Okay."

Keeping his hands steady and level, careful not to whack them against the doorframe as he went past, he moved to the living room and sat on the couch. She propped two pillows on either side of his body so he had somewhere to rest his arms.

Claire retrieved a bottle of Cabernet and popped in a Blu-ray called *Galaxy Quest* that he'd never seen before. It was hilarious. She watched him watching it, and seemed pleased by his reactions. He liked seeing how entirely not-bitchy she could be. They spent the evening lazy and comfortable with each other, no talk of magic or preparations for the contest.

Halfway through the movie he peeled off the paraffin wax, and when the film ended, she told him about growing up in Modesto. It was neither Northern nor Southern California, just an endless urban sprawl in the Central Valley. According to Claire, only two kinds of things happened there: suburban horrors—satanic animal mutilation, underage prostitution, the Laci Peterson murder—or nothing at all. Their only *good* claim to fame was George Lucas. To escape, she moved to England after high school to study at Oxford. Her best friend, whose bank account was newly fattened by a deceased grandparent, came along for the adventure.

"You know what a pain it is to tell people you're from Modesto? I'd say California and they'd say, 'Los Angeles? No? San Francisco? No? San Diego? No? Are you at least by the beach? No?'

"It was incomprehensible to them. 'Why would anyone live in California but not be close to the beach?' And it's not like I blamed them. I started saying I was from Seattle."

He laughed. Even *Castaic* was cooler than Modesto.

He wondered if, once the competition was over, they might spend another evening that way. And another evening. And another.

He had a feeling it all depended on whether or not he won.

"When I came back to California," Claire finished, "I moved to Venice, a block from the water."

"With Mr. F?"

"Yes."

"Can I ask you something personal?"

"I don't know, can you?" She winked.

"*Dios mío*," he laughed. "You are *drunk*."

"What makes you say that?"

He mimicked her wink, doing an exaggeratedly slow version.

"Yeah, yeah," she muttered, a ghost of a smile playing at her lips.

It was true, though. Her wine bottle was empty. She'd opened it before the movie started, and per her rule, he hadn't touched it. Jesus, she really was the same as the guys at the club. She lived off cigarettes, alcohol, and cards.

"Go ahead," she said. "Ask me anything you want."

"Why did you put up with it? Him sleeping around on you? Didn't it make you angry?"

She sat quietly with the question, staring into space. He figured she wasn't going to answer and he thought about getting up and going to bed. But eventually she spoke.

"That part didn't really bother me. Not the way you think. But there was this one time…" Her voice caught. "It was when my daughter was about five. You already know I can't do magic myself. I mean, I can do it, just not…"

"With an audience."

"Right. Well, he'd left for his second tour. It was eight months long, all over the country, and I was stuck at home, hating myself for not going, hating him for leaving me behind. There was a woman in the Midwest. He hired her to be his assistant onstage for a two-week run at the Arie Crown Theater in Chicago. Essentially, he hired her to be me. They became…

involved, and she followed him to Indiana, which was his next tour stop. Jonny didn't like that. He didn't like her unpredictability. He'd broken things off but she wasn't listening, she was showing up at the stage door, showing up at his dressing room, wouldn't take the hint, kept chasing after him, even though she had her own family that she was neglecting. He gave me the woman's number and asked me to call her, make it clear that he was through with her, that he had a family, too, and that he'd go after her for damages if she didn't back off. He needed to feel relaxed and calm in order to have a successful show, and she was getting in the way of that." She looked at Felix then, as though he'd asked for a better explanation; as though she needed to defend herself.

"*We couldn't afford to fail.* We'd poured everything we had, financially, emotionally, into this tour, and when I couldn't be part of it, the pressure mounted even higher." Claire coughed, ran a tight hand through her hair. "So I did. Of course I did. I got her on the phone and let her have it. The worst, cruelest things I could think of, whatever I thought would be most likely to make her *stop*—and that night, she was upset, of course, she really thought he was going to be with her, I guess—she was driving erratically, swerving, and she crashed into another car. There was...a child in the other car, a little boy." She cleared her throat. "He didn't make it."

She picked up her glass of wine. There were only a few drops left. She lifted it to her mouth and tilted it, and her hand trembled when she set it back on the table.

"So no, the infidelity on its own didn't bother me. Our marriage was probably over when I froze up during our first show and had to be left behind. Things were never the same after that. I could survive it for my daughter's sake, and I did, but I will *never* forgive him for making me make that phone call."

Felix swallowed. She'd no doubt gone over the event a thousand times already, and he was positive no insight or opinion he offered would make a lick of difference to her.

"We didn't have any more children after that. I couldn't do it. I knew I didn't deserve them," she finished.

He reached over and laced his fingers through hers, gave her hand a squeeze.

"Jonathan's the one who doesn't deserve to live," he whispered fiercely.

She refused to look at him.

But a moment later, she squeezed back.

Jessica

WHEN CLAIRE CALLED that morning, Jessica let her cell phone ring five times before picking up. She wasn't trying to play hard to get; she needed a moment to compose herself.

She'd seen Claire doing exceptionally intimate things on videotape and couldn't figure out how it would be possible to conceal it.

Just seeing the caller ID put Jessica in such a heightened state of anxiety, guilt, and persistent, dragging lust that she could barely string a sentence together. She'd crawled into bed and feigned sleep when Cal got home at nine the night before. He'd pressed a kiss to her forehead and turned out the light as her heart thundered in her chest and her body thrummed and vibrated with unfulfilled desire.

"Hi-this-is-Jessica," she blurted in a torrent of words before the voicemail could kick in.

"Hi, Jessica, it's Claire. Is now a good time to talk, or are you busy?" Claire's low, flat tone managed to sound bored *and* alluring, as though she were issuing a challenge: *Bet you can't get me to change the inflection of my voice. Try, though!*

What *would* it take to make Claire's voice higher, expressive, full of passion? The way she sounded when she…?

Jessica bit her knuckles to suppress the hysteria that threat-

ened to burst forth. "Not busy. A time. Good. A good—time."
Get it together.

A pause. "Okay, good. I owe you an apology, and a second
apology for taking so long to do it. I'm sorry about the way I
treated you at brunch. It was atrocious, and—I'm sorry. I wish
I could do it over."

"That's okay," Jessica said quickly.

"It's not okay," Claire responded.

It's not? She'd never had someone try to talk her out of accepting an apology before, especially not the person who'd
apologized.

"As I'm sure you could tell, I'd had too much to drink. I
should probably take a page from Cal's book and abstain for a
while."

"Cal's not 'abstaining for a while,' he's three years sober." Jessica found that her voice came back fine when irritation took
over.

"Yes, of course, you're right. And while being drunk's certainly no excuse, it's part of the reason I overreacted," Claire
continued.

Jessica felt a familiar, bland acceptance make her features
go slack. How many times in her life had she endured this ex-
act conversation?

Her mother's version was less eloquent, but the message
was the same: "I'm sorry if I hurt your feelings, but it wasn't
me, it was the alcohol, so…" After which Jessica would reassure her: *Of course, I understand, you were drunk, it's not your
fault. (Let's just get this over with so we can go back to ignoring
each other.)*

But Claire surprised her again. "If you're willing, I'd like
to make it up to you. I thought we could get lunch and go
shopping today, and you could buy a new dress—my treat—
something to wear at the club."

Jessica's pulse raced. "When-like-right-now?"

"Sure, if that works for you."

"It works."

"Would you like to drive? It might be easier for you to learn the ins and outs of the city that way."

"Sure, good idea." Keeping her eyes on the road would prevent her from staring openly at Claire and seeing in her a past she shouldn't know about.

"I'll text you my address. And thanks for accepting my apology."

***

"I think it's good you're driving." Claire folded her long legs into the passenger seat of Cal's BMW and flipped down the sunshade.

The day was quintessentially Californian, in the low eighties, breezy, with a light hovering of smog in lieu of clouds. Claire wore Armani sunglasses, a black T-shirt that read I WANT TO BELIEVE, a pair of skinny jeans, and some strappy black heels. The T-shirt had been cut with scissors into a low V-neck. She filled it out in a way Jessica would never fill out anything, and Jessica couldn't prevent her eyes from flitting to the cleavage that was approaching her.

Claire kissed her on both cheeks—that weird Paris-by-way-of-LA thing people did on the West Coast. Jessica never knew whether to make a kiss sound next to the other person's ear, or to actually kiss their skin. Before she could decide, the moment was over. She fought the urge to reach up and touch the place where Claire's lips had brushed her skin.

She put the car in drive and glanced down at her cubic-zirconia-speckled flip-flops, picked because they'd be comfortable for walking around in, but now she wondered if that was the wrong choice. She admired Claire for the confidence to wear heels when she was already Amazonian size.

"I like your shoes," she said. "Is that what women go shopping in out here?"

"You know, I didn't even think about it. I'm so used to wearing them as an *eff you* to my husband. He hates it when I'm taller than him."

Does her husband know what's on that videotape?

Jessica pulled out of the driveway onto Edgecliffe Drive.

"Oh, my God, I meant to tell you, I saw your husband's show when I was a kid."

"I'm sorry."

"Why?"

"When was it?"

"I was thirteen, so, 2004? I really wanted to be called onstage but he'd already chosen his helper beforehand, I think."

Claire snorted derisively. "Sounds about right. He can't stand leaving any element to chance. If you're a good magician, it doesn't matter who you call up, it'll go off without a hitch. I mean, Cal never has any trouble choosing audience members. Case in point," she added under her breath.

Was that a dig? Jessica thought. Or a compliment?

"Let me guess, the woman you saw, she was tiny," Claire continued.

"I think so, yeah."

"Always are."

She flashed on an image of Claire and Cal and Brandy writhing together and blinked to cast it out.

How did the shy girl in those videos turn into you? Sexy and smart and everything I want to be?

Silence stretched on between them, and Jessica wondered if she should turn on the radio. But that might draw too much attention to the fact that she'd *noticed* the silence. Also, which station? Would Claire approve of the stations she'd preselected (KROQ; KIIS) or did they make Jessica seem young and unformed, her musical taste dictated by Top 40?

Did Claire like the temperature and fan level of air-conditioning Jessica had chosen, or was she an open-window kind of person?

She wanted the answers beamed directly into her cortex so she could do everything the way Claire preferred.

Claire flipped the shade down and examined her lips, using her middle finger to smooth out her lipstick. Jessica couldn't help staring at Claire's perfect mouth. A mouth that had thoroughly tasted her husband's. What would it feel like to kiss her? Would it bring her closer to Cal, provide a heightened connection, ease some of her loneliness?

She compiled a list of the times Claire had touched her. Outside the club, of course, when she'd rescued Jessica with the password; before brunch, when she'd leaned on her shoulder to put out her cigarette; in the hallway, encircling her wrist; and just now, with the cheek kisses. She was certain Claire didn't remember any of those moments, but for Jessica they were electric currents that tied her to Cal's past.

"Is your shirt from *The X-Files*?" Asking questions was always good. It put the focus on the other person and took the pressure off her.

"Yes. Did you watch it on DVD?"

"I've seen a few episodes. My mom watched it but I wasn't allowed. I remember going to bed on Friday nights when I was a kid and hearing the theme music."

Another silence filled the car and Jessica racked her brain for something else to say. When they reached the bottom of the canyon, the light at the intersection turned yellow. Jessica slowed down.

"You got it, you got it, run it, run it," Claire chanted.

Jessica gripped the steering wheel and moved into the center of the intersection, then yanked the wheel to the left. It was red by then.

Claire leaned over and honked at the person who had the right-of-way.

"Bravo," said Claire. "Well done."

Jessica blushed under Claire's praise, despite the fact that she was pretty sure she'd committed two moving violations in less than three minutes.

"Don't worry about the cameras, by the way," Claire said.

"Cameras!?"

"No one ever pays those tickets and they don't follow up on them."

Before Jessica could get more information about the cameras she hadn't even noticed, Claire pointed at the car ahead of them on the right. "Ugh, I can't stand it when people do that."

"Do what?"

"Dangle their arm all the way out the window like they don't have a care in the world. Like they're indestructible."

"The guy with the cigarette, you mean?"

"Yes."

"What's the alternative to his hand out the window, though?" Jessica asked. "Asphyxiating himself?"

"No, but he could be a normal, tense smoker, holding his cigarette close, not flapping his arm all the way down the side of the car like he doesn't even *want* to be smoking. I'd kill for a cigarette right now." Claire loosened her seat belt and rolled down her window. "Pull up alongside him."

"Um, why...would we do that?" She could accept the fact that the trip had turned into Mrs. Toad's Wild Ride, but she drew the line at deliberately sideswiping someone. However, she also had the distinct impression that it didn't matter who was behind the wheel; Claire was the one driving.

"Just pull up alongside him," Claire said. "Get close but not too close."

"Wait, what are you going to do?"

"Now's your chance, go."

Although she wanted to resist, Jessica did as told. When only a few feet separated their window from the other guy's, Claire reached out and plucked the cigarette from the guy's fingers.

"Go, go," Claire whispered urgently. She ducked below the view of the window, tucked the cigarette in her mouth, and took a deep, satisfying drag.

"Oh, my God." Jessica put the pedal to the metal, trying to make a clean getaway, but another car swerved in front, preventing her from zipping ahead.

She hooted with nervous laughter as traffic slowed to a halt at the light. They were stuck right beside their victim.

"Did you take my cigarette?" he yelled.

Using only her tongue, Claire flipped the lit end around and closed her mouth over it, then sat up in her seat as though nothing were amiss.

"No," Jessica called back. "You must have dropped it. Sorry!"

Claire leaned out the car window and gave a big, confused shrug. A tendril of smoke escaped from her nose and her eyes watered. He squinted at them a moment longer, but, having no proof, waved them away in irritation when the light changed.

Jessica hung back so he could pull ahead. Claire flipped the cigarette back around so it hung properly out of her mouth. The smoke she'd been holding in plumed out. She coughed and took another drag.

Jessica was incredulous. "How did you learn to do that?"

Claire tapped a caterpillar-size ash out the window.

"I learned it twenty years ago. It was going to be part of my act."

"I didn't know you had an act."

Claire tapped her forehead. "Only up here."

"But you wanted to be a magician?"

She continued looking out the window. "If you can't be one, marry one, huh?"

"I guess."

Claire turned to Jessica, a hint of a smile on her lips. "Never thought I'd have another reason to use it, though."

They both laughed and Jessica's heart soared.

The angular salesgirl at Maxine's boutique on Beverly Boulevard decided they were valid customers and doggedly pursued them around the store.

Armed with selections in black, midnight blue, lavender, and peach, Jessica drew the dressing room curtain closed. None of the dresses had price tags, which made her nervous. In high school she'd had to leave a consignment store when the prom dress she'd fallen in love with turned out to be more expensive than she realized. Halfway through being rung up, her mother threw a fit in front of the other customers.

"Um, Claire?" she whispered, ducking down toward the bottom of the curtain where she could see Claire's bare feet. "It doesn't say how much these cost."

The feet turned toward her. "That's okay."

"Maybe we should go someplace else. I just...don't want there to be any surprises."

"Do you like the dresses?"

She smiled. "Hell yeah."

"Good enough for me."

Jessica took a deep breath and zipped up the latest one: a Romona Keveza black dress with an asymmetrical neckline and thigh-high leg slit.

When the time came to pay, Claire kept a poker face at the register so she never did learn what it cost.

After shopping, they went to Murakami Sushi for lunch, and Jessica was proud of herself for trying eel and spicy tuna instead of her usual California roll.

Back at the car, Claire walked to the driver's side. "If you want, I can drive."

Jessica squinted into the sun. She'd left her sunglasses inside the car. "Was I going too slowly?"

"No, but you seemed a little stressed about it."

Only because you made me run a red light and commit Grand Theft Cigarette. "Oh, okay."

"So do you want me to take over?"

"Uh, whatever you want."

"Yes or no?"

"Yeah, that'd be great. Is that weird? Do you mind?"

"If I minded I wouldn't have asked."

Jessica tossed the car keys to Claire, who let them hit the garment bags and clatter to the ground.

"We're not the Dukes of Hazzard," she said.

Five minutes later they glided east on Sunset Boulevard. Jessica settled into her seat and tried to breathe normally. Their dresses hung by the windows in back, and it was nice not to be worrying about whether they would've impeded her sight line. It was also nice not to be worrying about her driving performance, battling traffic, getting pulled over for running reds, or generally keeping them both alive.

"What do you see yourself doing in ten years?" Claire asked.

"I know this isn't what I'm supposed to say, but I always just sort of wanted to be a mom."

"Nothing wrong with that."

It felt good to get the words out, to know she hadn't wasted a natural opportunity to say it. The honesty was liberating. "I want three kids, I think," she continued. "At least two. I was an only."

"Oh? Well, there are pros and cons to siblings."

Claire's phone lit up, buzzing. The screensaver was a picture of her teenage daughter. "Sorry, I have to take this." Claire didn't bother signaling, just pulled over to the side, parked, and answered the call in a low voice.

The image of Claire's teenage daughter was branded into Jessica's brain.

Oh, my God.

Oh my God, oh my God.

Claire and her husband were both blond.

Eden was a brunette.

Claire's disdain for Jonathan was palpable. But she always had a good word for Cal.

Claire continued her quiet conversation as Jessica's brain whirled.

"She's a Hitchcock blonde." "Too clever by half." He could deny it all he wanted, but their admiration was mutual.

Claire hung up and reached over to put the car into drive.

"Did you have your daughter before or after you met Jonathan?" Jessica asked.

Claire's hand froze on the gearshift. "That's an odd question."

"I didn't know if…I mean…forget it."

Claire sent her a look so icy Jessica nearly shivered.

"I just—the way you talk about Cal sometimes, I just—I wondered if, maybe…" She trailed off. Looked out the window and shrugged.

Claire grasped Jessica's chin in her hand and forced her to look at her. "Eden's dark hair comes from her grandmother. Cal was on another continent when she was conceived. Would you like the details of that night, or does that satisfy you?"

Jessica wrenched herself free. "Ow," she whispered.

Claire yanked the car into drive and peeled away from the curb. Jessica clutched the side of the door.

A tense, five-minute silence followed.

"Does Cal know you want kids?" Claire asked quietly.

"We haven't talked about it yet."

"Do you have *any* conversations?"

Something sharp and tough calcified in Jessica's throat. The only way to dissolve it was to lash out. "Yes. I know all about Brandy."

"I'm certain that's not true."

"I know she looked like the dancing woman from the Gap ads."

"What?"

"Brandy."

"Is it *possible*," Claire said, teeth clenched, "that you mean Audrey Hepburn?"

"Yes. Right."

"You think of her as 'the dancing woman from the Gap ads'?"

"Well, *obviously* she's from other things like movies, I know who she *is*, but that's what I first saw her in, okay? That's just how I think of her first or whatever. I don't have her IMDb page memorized, *sorry*."

"Unbelievable," Claire muttered. She slapped on her sunglasses even though the sun had retreated behind the mountains.

"I'm sorry," Jessica implored. "I just—I'm just trying to *know* him, and I'm in the house all day by myself, and I'm going stir-crazy. It was a fucked-up thing to say to you."

No response.

Claire's silence infuriated her. *Would you give me something?* "But, I mean, it's not *that* crazy to think. I saw the video, okay? So, I know you've been with him, and..."

Claire opened her mouth to speak, and then shut it again.

She didn't say another word until they reached her house forty-five minutes later. The drive back was endless. They hit every red light, found themselves in every slow lane. It seemed impossible that they had laughed with each other in the car earlier. They weren't just back to Square One, they were at negative numbers. And wasn't that the reason Claire had offered to take her shopping in the first place? As a do-over?

She shouldn't have watched the tape, and she *definitely* shouldn't have thrown it in Claire's face, especially not after Claire had spent a fortune on Jessica's dress and taken her out to nice places all day.

Sitting in Claire's driveway at long last, Jessica turned to Claire to apologize again. She was filled with shame, would've said whatever was necessary to make Claire understand. But Claire was faster. Her voice sounded different from before; it wavered erratically.

"I don't know what you saw—and I don't want to know—but there's more to Brandy than what's on those videotapes. And more to me."

"Of course," said Jessica. "That's true of anyone."

She'd succeeded in provoking Claire's high voice. It didn't feel like a victory.

"I suppose I'll see you next weekend," said Claire unhappily.

The Magician of the Year competition was on Saturday, with Cal's premiere party the following Monday.

"Okay," said Jessica tremulously.

"I'm sure you'll look stunning."

Tears gathered in Jessica's eyes. "You too."

Claire retrieved her garment bag and purse and shut the car door firmly behind her. When she passed by Jessica's open window on her way inside the house, Jessica blurted out, "Were you in love with Cal?"

Claire returned to the car. She looked furious. "I didn't love him. I didn't love her," she said quietly. "I loved *them*. I wanted to be a part of them, as a unit. The three of us. And that's more than you deserve on that subject."

Jessica's heart beat so rapidly in her chest she thought it might lift her off the ground. "Could you ever feel that way about me?" she faltered. "Me and Cal?"

Claire gave her a lengthy once-over, peeling away every protective layer Jessica had amassed in her life.

"No."

Kaimi

KAIMI KNOCKED BACK two shots of soju before making the call. Sweet and crisp, it was the first type of alcohol she'd tried as a kid; she was twelve, living in LA. One of her Korean friends (whose parents were first generation) kept boxes of it in the fridge. As in, itty-bitty, innocent-looking juice boxes that wouldn't be out of place in a Powerpuff Girls lunch box. The day before her family moved to Hawaii, she dared her friend to bring some to school, and they got smashed during lunchtime, which was pretty impressive since by then the juice boxes were room temperature and tasted like nail polish remover. Tonight she purchased her soju in bottle form, froze it for ten minutes, and shook it vigorously before pouring.

Ahh. Clean, smooth, cold, perfection.

Landon picked up on the fourth ring. "What do you want?" he demanded. "You're off the case."

She cleared her throat. "I have something important to tell you."

His voice was gruff, not his usual late-night-DJ purr. "What?"

"It's better if we meet in person."

"Why? So you can try to rip me off again? No thanks."

"It has nothing to do with the Erdnase papers."

Another long pause. "I'm waiting."

"Not on the phone. In person."

He laughed nastily. "Good luck with that."

"You're going to want to hear this."

"Well, I don't trust you," he hissed. It was the first time she'd ever heard him lose his composure, and her heart ached knowing she was the cause.

She bit her lip and released it, tasting blood. "Turns out, you're not an only child."

He hung up.

She poured another shot and waited for him to call back.

Fifteen minutes later, her phone lit up. Her heart leapt and she fumbled to answer.

"Hi."

"You know where I live," he said, and hung up again.

Too tipsy to drive, Kaimi hired an Uber, and on the way to Landon's she sent a text, trusting the recipient would read it right away and follow its instructions.

Landon waited for her on the porch swing. "Stay where you are. Talk."

"Okay," she said, standing awkwardly in front of him. "Where should I start?"

"Tell me why you needed the money so badly you were going to steal it from me. And then *maybe* I'll let you come in and tell me about this supposed sibling I have."

"And if I refuse?" Kaimi asked.

"Then go home. Wherever that is."

She sat on the porch step, feeling like an exposed wound and grateful for the soju-infused bandage around her heart. A deep breath and she was off and running with the CliffsNotes version of her downfall.

"I was working toward my master's in art history at the University of Hawaii, with a job lined up at a private auction house. My parents' intervention when I was a teenager worked; I hadn't stolen so much as a sticker from the Hello Kitty store in years. There was this guy—he sort of swept me off my feet. For, like, the dumbest reason. See, Benji and I—my little nephew—we were at Manoa Valley Park and he spilled the ice cream bowl I'd gotten him, and for I swear, a full five minutes, he was sobbing his eyes out. Nothing I did or said would calm him down. Here's a tip for your seminar. If you want a sure bet, go up to any chick with a kid, preferably not her own, and be super nice to the kid. She'll melt right into your arms. True story."

"Everyone's sweet to kids," Landon said. "Especially if they think it will earn them brownie points with moms."

"Or aunties. Trust me, I know that now. Anyway, he was sobbing, and Cole stopped the game he was in and came over from the baseball field, looking all toned and surfer-hot, and said, 'We've all spilled things. Don't worry about it. You know my friends and I are playing baseball over there. You want to be our rookie?' And the rest of the afternoon, he played catch with Benji and had him run around the bases, cheering for him and giving him high fives, all the kinds of stuff my brother-in-law didn't have much time for. He was so patient and so kind, and I fell for him within, like, five minutes. I was such an idiot."

Landon's expression remained passive, giving nothing away, but his eyes crinkled in sympathy. "What happened?"

"We had a good couple of months. At least, I assume we did; he might have been cheating for all I know. He was definitely dealing coke. Grace, my sister, she figured him out right away and told me to ditch him. But I was completely blind." She shook her head, wishing she had something else to drink. Sobriety crept up on her from all sides. "That's not true, though. Part of me knew he was up to something, and

I *liked* that about him. As long as I didn't know the details, I could pretend it was okay. But one day when I was in class, he a hid a bunch of cocaine in my apartment, and when he got busted, to save himself he told them where it was and let me take the fall. I was lucky, in a lot of ways. The judge went easy on me because it was my first offense and I was in grad school and everything, but I had to go to rehab, and my parents had to pay for it out of their retirement fund. All the money they'd saved for so many years and earmarked for an active seniors' place went toward this long, expensive treatment I didn't even need. And now they have to live with Grace and my brother-in-law and Benji, in this tiny one-bedroom place, and Grace is pregnant with another kid, and there's no *room* for everyone.

"The auction house job I mentioned, the one I had lined up for after graduation, cut me dead, which was of course the least of my worries. With a criminal record, an incomplete transcript, and no thesis, I'm basically unemployable. No gallery, museum, or brokerage firm will go near me. Even the antiques store I cashiered for one summer won't return my calls. But the worst part, the *worst*, is my sister. She forebade me from seeing Benji anymore, because of my 'drug habit.'"

Landon was stunned. "Even though it wasn't true?"

She nodded. "I used to pick him up from kindergarten once a week, take him to the park." She felt her eyes mist up at the memory of the day she had to tell Benji she wouldn't be seeing him for a while. "I know that's not really the reason; she *knows* I never sold drugs. She's punishing me for hurting our parents. She thinks they've rescued me enough times. She and her husband and Benji all share the master bed, and my parents sleep on the foldout. It's not good for them. It's not good for anyone, and I need to make things right."

Landon made room on the swing and patted the spot beside him. Kaimi stood from the steps, her legs sore, and sat by him.

"I got greedy," she conceded. "I thought, if I can sell the Erdnase papers for the whole amount instead of a commission, I can fix everything right now, and go home a hero. I should've worked harder, faster, and smarter, instead of expecting one big score. And I shouldn't have tried to steal them from you. I hated you when we met, but then I got to know you, and…If it helps, I was having second thoughts the whole time I was in your house."

They sat next to each other in strangely companionable silence.

"You hated me?" he asked after a while, in mock surprise.

She pinched her forefinger and thumb together. "Just a little bit."

He stood. "Here's the thing. Your arrest was in the public records, but I didn't know the details. I needed someone willing to work outside the law. I can't exactly be mad you tried to hustle me, considering that's why I hired you.

"Come on," he said, and held the door open for her.

"How'd you know I'd break in when I did, though?"

"I didn't. But I followed you to the valet. *That* was bizarre, you taking a photo of my keys. So I had my friend Patrick keep his eyes open, watch for you outside my place."

She was shocked. "He knows about the papers?"

"No, no, I just told him you were crazy."

"Oh, thank you so much!"

"Yep, crazy jealous Kaimi, my new girlfriend, looking for evidence I was cheating."

"Wonderful," she muttered, stifling a laugh.

"He says you marched right in like you lived there and then looked at my bookshelf for damn near an hour." A booming laugh filled the air. "What kind of person breaks into a house and looks at the books?"

"The kind of person you hired, I guess."

"Drink?"

She followed him into the kitchen. "Please."

Beers in hand, they sat in the living room. Landon's leg bounced up and down. "Now what's this about me having a brother or sister? Did you say that just to get my attention?"

"It's a theory I'm working on. I'm ninety-five percent there, I just need a little more info. Tell me about your dad and we'll see if the pieces fit."

He exhaled. "Let's see. Single dad, raised me alone. Worked as a chauffeur, which got him into contact with all sorts of people, you know, flying into and out of LAX. He also worked a lot of high-end parties."

"How'd he come across the Erdnase papers?"

"No idea. Maybe he overheard something or saw an opportunity at one of the houses and took it."

"And he knew enough to know they were worth something, so he had a passing interest in magic."

"Right. Yeah, he did tricks here and there, mostly for poker games. And he taught me a few moves. He's the one who told me to use it as an icebreaker whenever I felt threatened by kids at school or whatever. He also ran scams. Mostly when we lived in San Francisco."

Kaimi set her beer down. "What kind of scams?"

"Returning merchandise to Best Buy. Like, we'd pick up some big-box purchase, a flatscreen TV, speakers, microwave, and always pay cash, and then the next day we'd bring the receipt back in—and ask to return it for some reason. But we wouldn't be returning the one we bought. You feel me? I sometimes helped with that one. We furnished a whole apartment that way."

"Did he leave behind anything besides the papers for you, when he passed?"

"Uh, yeah. It's all in that cigar box on the table behind you."

She opened it and she and Landon went through it together. The first thing Kaimi retrieved was a book called *Art Forger's Handbook*.

"Ha. We read this in one of my restoration classes. Was your dad into art fraud?"

"I think he dipped his foot in—but not with paintings. Just decorative objects, small items."

"Such as…?"

"Just like, tchotchkes," he told her. "No Fabergé eggs or anything."

"Jewelry boxes, maybe? What about music boxes?"

Landon's eyes lit up. "Yeah, the birds! Those singing birds. Claimed they were Frisser somebody."

"Frisard," Kaimi corrected him.

"Sold 'em for ten times what they were worth. What's this got to do with—"

"I'll get to that. What's this?" She handed Landon an envelope.

He lifted the flap and poured the contents into his hand: a card and a small key.

"What do you think it opens?" Kaimi asked.

"Something small."

"That's your contribution? The small key opens something small?" she asked drily.

"Well, give me a second. I haven't thought about it in a while."

She grinned. They were back to their old sniping, and it felt good. Comfortable.

"Safe-deposit box?" she suggested.

"No, I already took it to the bank and there were no matches."

The doorbell rang, and Landon stood.

"Wait," Kaimi said. "Don't answer it yet. My next question is sort of…delicate."

He moved to answer the door. "I can handle it."

"Wait!" She grabbed his arm. "Do you know if your dad had any other families? Not in California, necessarily?"

"No."

"Does the name Deverell ring a bell?"

In shock, Landon dropped his beer. It spilled out onto the wood floor. "That was an alias he used with marks."

"I'll mop up the beer, you get the door," Kaimi said.

In an apparent daze, Landon did as told.

"Hiya. I brought pizza," said Jessica. "But why am I here?"

"Who are you?" Landon asked in response.

Kaimi entered from the kitchen, paper towels in hand. "Jessica Clarke. Formerly Deverell," she explained. "A while back, her dad, whom she's never met, sent her a music box. I think your key opens it. And I think the other half of the Erdnase papers are inside."

Jessica was silent for a long time, mulling things over. Kaimi didn't think Jessica had a mean bone in her body, but she worried that the shock and stress might manifest in an ugly way. A surprise family member of a different race who had apparently been raised by the man who'd stepped out on her, and…

"Are you sure?" she asked finally.

"We'll do a DNA test, too, but I think the easiest thing to do now is see if the key fits."

"How much are they worth?" she wondered. "Those papers you have?"

"The buyers we're talking to, one here and one in Britain,

said they're willing to pay half a million for the full set," Landon said.

"Shut the fuck up," Jessica said genially. She turned to Kaimi in awe. "How did you figure all this out?"

"Did you bring the items I asked for?" Kaimi replied.

"Uh-huh."

"Photo?"

She handed the long photo to Kaimi, who walked over to Landon's bookshelf and picked up the framed panoramic image of Landon and his dad. She held the two pieces together to form a complete image of the San Francisco Port.

The feeling Landon's picture meant something had nagged at her for days, so she did a Google image search of the location, and realized she'd seen the other half of the photo at Jessica's. "I think he wanted to tell you about Landon but he chickened out. He cut this picture in half the same way he cut the Erdnase papers in half. It was a clue. You said he met your mom in San Francisco, and…"

"But that's such a huge coincidence—"

"Then there were the numbers and letters he wrote on the back. It's from the Thomas Guide."

Kaimi turned Jessica's photo over and showed Landon the bottom corner. 126, 4B.

"I remember those," Landon said. To Jessica, he added, "They were these big-ass maps, spiral-bound paperbacks, that everyone had in their cars. To find an address, you looked up the coordinates. The first part is the page number, the second part is the grid."

"Your dad was telling you where he lived," Kaimi told Jessica. "I looked it up in an old guide and it led me right here to Landon's house."

"He lived here till the day he died," Landon confirmed.

"If he wanted me to find him, why didn't he just call me?

Give me his address?" Jessica asked. "He wasted so much time. Why the fucking treasure map?"

"He always did stuff like that," Landon said. "Never straightforward, never easy."

Jessica took a deep breath and let it out.

"So where's the music box?" Landon asked.

Jessica retrieved it from her bag. "Here you go."

Landon handed Jessica the key. She turned the music box over in her hands and slid the key into the slot.

It slipped right in and turned effortlessly.

Jessica's face lit up.

Without opening it, she handed the box to Kaimi, turned to Landon, and threw her arms around his neck. "I always wanted a sibling!"

"Me too," said Landon, squeezing Jessica tightly back. "I was just saying that to Kaimi, what, a few weeks ago? How I always wanted a sibling. Tell her, Kai."

"He was. It's true."

"We have to talk," Jessica said. "About everything. So, he raised you? With your mom?"

"Just him."

"So I had a single mom and you had a single dad. Why didn't they bring us up *Brady Brunch*-style? What's wrong with them?"

"I don't know. Maybe he figured we each got one parent and that was for the best? Or one of them didn't want to move?"

"Do you think he looked like me at all? And look at *you*— you're so handsome. I was telling that to Kaimi, wasn't I, Kaimi? I mean, I don't think it's weird to say. My handsome brother. Big brother, right? When were you born? And you're dating one of my friends. How cool is that?" She barreled ahead before he could answer any of her questions.

Kaimi walked backward toward the door.

"I'm going to let you guys get acquainted. I'm glad something good could come of this, even if I'm not on the job anymore."

"What do you mean, not on the job?" asked Jessica. "You're getting a commission for sure. Don't even think of arguing. Twenty percent, right, bro?"

Landon and Kaimi looked at each other for a charged beat.

"Right," said Landon. "Thanks for everything, Kaimi. See you around."

Kaimi sat at her desk that night, composing a letter on the most expensive stationery she could find. She took her time, printing neatly and pausing every few words to make sure it came out the way she intended. She'd begun with the only two Korean words she knew.

Dear *eomma* and *appa*,

I have good news...

Jessica

JESSICA WOKE THE next day feeling lighter than air.

A brother!

She had a kind, handsome brother!

Not to mention…a friggin' fortune. Well, once Kaimi and Landon sold the papers, and who knew how long that would take. But it was on its way.

If, God forbid, she ever needed to bail on Cal, she had someplace to go now, a family member who would take her in, and money to protect her.

She and Landon had stayed up until three talking and eating cold pizza. They both liked pepperoni and mushrooms, which Jessica chalked up to a "sibling thing." She had sibling things now!

When she got home, Cal was asleep. The role reversal was extremely satisfying. Best of all, she had a secret from *him*, now. A fucking whopper.

Her euphoria was heightened when Cal treated her to a memorable wake-up call. From his position between her thighs, he gazed at her adoringly, his brown eyes dark and tender. His tongue swirled against her, setting off a chain reaction, as though little lightbulbs were popping on along her spine.

As she climaxed, an image slipped into her mind. Claire's

face at age twenty, unguarded, smooth, and free of tension, her mouth forming a perfect, soft O.

Gasping, she clutched Cal's hair in her fingers. She assumed he would crawl up her body and finish himself off, but after seeing to Jessica's bliss, he left the bedroom and returned with a breakfast tray: turkey bacon and avocado omelets, toast, OJ, and coffee. She stretched languorously.

"This is nice," she purred. "What's the occasion?"

"The show's done, so I planned a day for us, and tonight's the Magician of the Year contest if you're up for it."

"Definitely."

"Until then, today is all about you. I'm ashamed to say it's long overdue. I should've done this when we first arrived."

She didn't disagree. "You were working," she reminded him. "It's okay."

"In that case, Jessica's day begins..." He glanced at his watch. "Now. When you've finished breakfast, pack a swimsuit and come with me."

They arrived at their destination two hours later.

Her first guess was Santa Barbara. They'd headed north on the 101. Realizing that didn't exactly present the best views California had to offer, Cal had swept up the 405 to the 5 and then the 126—a dizzying array of freeways that eventually broke into a two-lane road surrounded by dry, sleepy farm towns that in anticipation of Halloween boasted haunted train rides for kids and murder mystery rides for grown-ups. They passed tree orchards, wineries, orange groves, and roadside stands selling strawberries, honeycomb, and pumpkins.

Five minutes shy of their destination, he pulled over to the side of the road and blindfolded her for the big reveal. She remained sightless when his BMW pulled into a parking space. He turned off the engine, opened the passenger-side door, and led her carefully out of the car, up the road, and onto an elevated platform. Warm breezes threw her hair into turmoil. The steady crash and fall of waves in the distance, the smell of salt water and muggy sand told her they were at the beach. He guided her by the elbow over some uneven ground, and she held on tightly to him so she wouldn't trip. Seagulls squawked, kids yelled, dogs barked, and music poured from radios nearby. Yet they weren't walking on sand. The ground beneath her feet was firm yet seemed susceptible to weight; it swayed with their steps.

A pier.

Twenty more paces and Cal stopped.

He tucked her hair into the back of her shirt and removed the blindfold.

She squinted as sunlight burst across her vision. When she could see clearly again, she discovered her guess was correct: the beach, on a warm, cloudless day.

"Welcome to Ventura Harbor," said Cal.

It was almost October but summer lasted as late as November out here, she'd been told. She occasionally missed the foliage from the Midwest, but right now it was impossible to yearn for Chicago weather.

"I've a confession to make," Cal continued.

Her stomach flip-flopped.

"I wasn't always in the edit room. Sometimes I came here to fix up a surprise for you, and now it's ready."

Cal pointed to a sleek, fifty-foot-long boat docked several yards away. "This is her."

Made of wood and fiberglass, spacious but uncluttered, it seemed like a natural extension of the loft. Compared with some of the boats farther along the coastline, which were dou-

6 Sarah Skilton

ble its size and had complicated-looking rigs and multiple masts, Cal's boat was clean and simple, with one mast and two sails.

Jessica stared at it. It was the yacht. The one he'd inherited after Brandy's death.

She looked to the right, where a statue of a mermaid playing a flute leaned elegantly above the rocky coastline. "How far outside the city are we?"

"Quite a way north." He followed her gaze to the statue. "That's Soter's Point, and up the coast is Marina Park, and then a private beach. I thought about docking her south, in Marina del Rey, but when I go sailing I want to get away from it all, not just head to a different kind of noise and crowd."

She nodded, unable to speak.

"Did you see the name?" he asked.

Painted in dark yellow cursive on the side of the boat were the words, GOD BEHOLDS.

She occasionally looked up the meanings of baby names online, including her own. The name Jessica meant, alternatively, "Rich" and "God Beholds," which had stuck with her because they were both so painfully untrue.

"What do you think?" he said. "Do you like it? I thought about putting 'rich' but that seemed to be asking for trouble." He chuckled. "'SOS. This is the USS *Rich* calling with an emergency! SOS! Harbor Patrol, do you copy?' 'Well, why don't you just throw some money at the problem, you rich prick?'"

She forced a laugh. "What did the boat used to be called?" she asked.

"It didn't have a name," he said. "Until you."

"But—wasn't it Brandy's?" she exclaimed.

He tilted his head. "What?"

"The boat—it belonged to Brandy. I was, uh, cleaning, and I saw the policy."

He gave her a long look, his face blank. "Did you? Dusting off my personal files, were you? How thoughtful. When was this?" He'd never spoken so acidly to her before, yet it wasn't completely unfamiliar. It was the way he sounded on the videotape. *That damn videotape.*

"Just—when you were out."

His cheek twitched. "As a matter of fact, Jessica, the boat was always mine. She hated the water, never went sailing with me. I put it in her name when we were dating, to keep her solvent in case I kicked off first. Of course, that's not what happened, but I suppose you know all about that, too, don't you?"

She swallowed tightly.

"Tell me, Jessica. Any other concerns you have about the state of my finances?"

She trembled even in the warmth of the sea air. Twice now he'd called her Jessica instead of Jessie. Such a minor thing, but it set off alarm bells. He hadn't called her that since they'd first met.

Again, she couldn't form words.

"Do you even want to see it, or should we forget it and go home?" he said darkly.

She felt self-conscious in her bikini. The midafternoon sun seemed to highlight her scars, and tiny as they were, they stood out because of the sheer number of them. A few wouldn't have been noticeable, but at that moment she felt lit up like a constellation chart.

Watching Cal, shirtless, check the lines and hoist the sails should have made her happy. His strong, lean body, sinewy arms coated in sweat, worked the boat like a pro. Which, she reminded herself, he had been. He'd spent ages sixteen to

twenty as a crewmember, "one step above a scullery maid," as
he put it. Somehow, this made her feel uneasy rather than secure. In a few minutes she'd be helpless, completely alone with
him in the ocean, far from shore.

The boat began to move. Cal strolled the deck and made a
few adjustments. "We want the wind at our backs, but also our
sides," he explained, and came over to sit next to her.

The waves were light but still dizzying, and reminded her of
their honeymoon, a twelve-day cruise from Bali to Singapore.

Technically, she and Cal hadn't been guests on the cruise;
his after-dinner magic shows paid for room and board on
an otherwise unaffordable trip. Their cabin was half the size
but twice as fun as those of the paying guests. Okay, it was
cramped beyond measure, with nowhere to stand, but that
just meant they had to be creative. And they'd been *very* creative.

After some complaints from the other passengers about the
sounds emanating from their room at two a.m., the cruise
manager threatened to leave them at the next port. For the re-
mainder of the trip, Jessica bit down on a deck of cards at her
most climactic moments, which solved that problem. She'd left
the indented pack behind in the bedside drawer like a Gideon
Bible.

Those carefree days were only six weeks ago, but it felt like
years.

"You've been unhappy." He touched her knee. "Tell me
what's wrong."

"I don't like being left alone all day. I don't like being in a
new city without you," she admitted. "So yeah, I let my fears
and worries get the better of me. And what I've realized is
there are so many things I don't know about you."

"We'll get to all that in time. It'll happen naturally, we don't
need to force it," he said gently.

"It just feels like you've got so many secrets," she added.

"You've got quite a few secrets of your own, you know," he said.

Oh, God. Does he know about Landon somehow? The Erdnase papers? She swallowed and put on her best "confused" face. "What do you mean?"

Cal stretched out next to her and pointed to the scars dotting her skin. "What's all this, then?" he asked in a kind voice.

"How come you've never asked before?"

"I didn't want you to think it mattered. And you don't have to tell me if you don't want to."

She nodded, not trusting herself to speak. They sailed another half hour in silence, watching the horizon, until Cal checked his watch and stood up to reverse their course. He released the sheet from the winch on the windward side and pulled it to leeward to get them back on their way to shore.

Sailing together reminded her of their first real conversation, when they'd walked along Lake Michigan, looking out at the endless water.

"I can tell you. I want to." She took a deep breath. "I used to go outside in the summer without insect repellent on and I'd let the mosquitoes eat me alive."

"Why?"

"Because then my mom would use cotton balls and calamine on them. It was the only time she acted like a real mom. She'd go slow, make sure she got every spot, every bump. Have you ever used it? It's cold, and pink, and it smells sweet, almost like putting ice cream on my skin. Even so, I'd scratch and scratch in my sleep, they itched like a mother, I couldn't help it. And the next morning and the next night she'd go over them again, so I kept doing it, every summer until high school."

"I hate that you had to hurt yourself to get her attention," he said softly. "But I'm glad you told me. Thank you."

He kissed each scar, mark, or slight discoloration along her arms. Kisses that weren't designed to lead anywhere and expected nothing of her in return.

"When it's just you and me," he murmured, "it's perfect. It's when other people jump in, that's when it gets tricky."

"But I want there to be other people. I want to have dinner parties and go out and meet up with friends. How come you haven't taken me to the club?"

"We're going tonight," he pointed out. "And on Monday."

"You know what I mean."

"Why haven't I taken you to the club?" he repeated. "Staggering cowardice, mainly. I didn't want to be grist for the gossip mill. I knew they'd fall in love with you, and that would reflect well on me, make it easier for me to return. But they frightened you, instead. Even though I asked Claire to look out for you, they got to you."

Jessica nodded.

"They told you I killed her, didn't they? What's the latest story, strangulation? Push her out a window?"

"Nobody told me specifics, there was just this weird vibe everywhere, you know? Whenever I introduced myself."

"There were whispers when I left town, too, and I'm sure they grew louder while I was away. The truth is, we hated each other at the end, but I never would have hurt her. Not physically. We hurt each other in other ways. If Brandy and I could snort it, smoke it, inhale it, or fuck it, we would, and anytime she had second thoughts, or I had second thoughts, we'd pull each other back in.

"We lived together a long time, but we were only married a year, all of which I spent blitzed because I was miserable. And so was she."

"Why were you miserable?"

"Well." He looked at the sky, avoiding Jessica's gaze. "Loads of reasons."

"Pick one."

"She fed the worst parts of me," he said finally. "And when someone does that, you'll do anything to keep them around because otherwise you might have to change. I fed the worst parts of her, too." He closed his eyes. "God, it's a wonder Claire even speaks to me."

"Claire?" Her heart rate sped up, the way it always did when Claire was mentioned. She considered telling him that she'd watched the tape, but she couldn't bear for him to stop talking, or become more disappointed in her than he already was.

"We tried to drag her under, too. But when she married Jonathan, everything changed. He took her from us," he added bitterly.

"How did Brandy die?"

"Overdose. It didn't occur to me to be scared. In my wonderfully considerate state, I figured 'the dumb bitch' didn't measure right. So I took everything that was left and spent the week after her funeral loaded to the gills, falling into bed with anyone who'd have me."

Ah. *"You stole their favorite toy."*

"I don't know if I thought that was the fastest way to join her in the ground or what. When my supplies ran out, and I had to take a look at myself, I hated what I'd become. What I'd been becoming my whole life. The only way to fix it was to be someone better. And the only way to do *that* was to stay alive."

"That was three years ago?"

"Almost to the day. And I didn't just give up drug and alcohol. I gave up all forms of hedonism. Sex included."

Something occurred to her and she covered her mouth.

"What?" he said.

"I ruined you."

"No, not at all! It wasn't permanent. I mean, no drinking is permanent. But the sex thing, that was always temporary." He swallowed. "I was waiting for the right girl," he said. "And here you are."

She felt guilty, and strangely proud. "I've never ruined someone before."

"Well, you *are* extremely naughty. But never have I been so thrilled to be ruined." He wrapped his arm around her and she rested her head against his warm, strong shoulder. "I've been an arse since we got to Los Angeles. Can you forgive me?"

She nodded and snuggled closer.

She closed her eyes and drifted off as the waves carried them back to shore.

Claire

THE NIGHT BEFORE the competition, Claire sat on the porch, smoking, a bundle of nerves and nausea. Felix was well prepared, unquestionably, but was that enough?

What if he flat-out choked the way Claire had so many years ago on the eve of *her* debut?

She'd sent him to spend the night at the Chateau Marmont so he'd get plenty of rest and pampering. To her surprise, she missed his company. He'd moved in almost immediately following Jonathan's exit, and their constant work together had eased her through the transition from married to not.

I've grown accustomed to his face.

It amused her to think he was sleeping down the hall from Jonathan, who'd been sure to tell her his exorbitant new address. He'd also hinted she would need to find new quarters once Eden came home for Thanksgiving and they told her about their split.

Best-case scenario was sixty-five thousand dollars of prize money. It was good but it wasn't great. In Los Angeles, 65K wouldn't last long. And if Felix didn't win, she'd need a new plan, fast. Perhaps something in consultancy? Her magician Rolodex stretched for miles—surely someone at the club could use an extra set of eyes, fresh patter, or a booking agent.

But who would vouch for her? And how could she possibly

prove she'd been invaluable to Jonathan, when they'd both kept it a secret for so long? Anyone who tried to corroborate her claims with her soon-to-be-ex-husband would hear a very different story from him. She *knew* he'd go scorched earth on her.

Her cell phone buzzed and she smiled at the caller ID. "Hi, Felix. How's the Marmont?"

"It's dope. You should come see for yourself, help me test out the bed…"

She laughed. He never gave up. "Thanks, but I wouldn't want to tire you out before the big day."

"Oh, man, you're killing me."

"How are you doing? Nervous?"

"Not really," he said. She could hear a baseball game on TV in the background. "The last rehearsal was perfect, I thought."

"I did, too."

"Are *you* nervous?" he asked.

"Extremely." She took a deep breath. "Not because of you," she added quickly, which was a half-truth. "You're going to be great. I just…get nervous."

"Don't be. You want to know why?"

"Why?" she asked.

"Because no matter what happens, we're in this together."

"We're in this together," she repeated numbly.

"I'll take care of you. I promise."

But she didn't need someone to take care of her. She needed a partner, and Felix wasn't up to the task. He was a strapping windup toy, preset to perform a series of actions in a certain order and in a certain way. He wasn't capable of deviating from them, and if he did, he'd be doomed.

Baseball had come easily to him, she could tell; he'd probably assumed this would, too. But magic wasn't a job or a calling, it was an art. Despite their marathon practice sessions, he simply hadn't had enough time to grow, organically, as a performer. There were no guarantees he wouldn't crash and burn tomorrow.

Unlike his previous career, where a bad game could be swept aside and relegated to the stats book to make room for twenty new games, this was his sole chance to perfectly perform Schrödinger's Cat. He'd essentially gone from batboy to starting lineup at the World Series, and everything hinged on a single inning.

After she hung up the phone, her head swam, her guts roiled, and she raced to the bathroom to be sick.

The next afternoon, having ingested nothing but saltines and Vitaminwater, Claire struggled to maintain focus during her drive to Club Deception. She hovered in the board members' back room as the sun went down, emerging right before the show began. She sat in the last row of the theater and managed to stay upright in her seat even though every instinct she possessed told her to curl into a ball on the floor and close her eyes until the show was over.

It was common courtesy at the club for seasoned professionals to sit in the back row, so the bug-eyed newcomers and their even more bug-eyed guests had the chance to sit closer and experience magic the way it was intended, for laypeople.

When Jonathan first started out as a magician, Claire could scarcely bear to watch him. She knew his punch lines and applause cues by heart, knew the reactions his routine ought to elicit, and at which points he'd be rewarded by gasps, catcalls, or even stunned silence (the best sound in the world).

But that didn't mean the audience always cooperated. She'd considered them the enemy for a long time, unworthy and unpredictable.

What if someone noticed he'd transferred a card from his pocket, swapped it for a lemon behind his briefcase, or distracted an audience member into closing his or her hand around a coin that was in fact already gone? What if he *dropped* something? Since the manipulation and misdirection were obvious to her, she always feared they might be obvious to others.

Worse, if someone *did* notice, would they snicker, point it out to a seatmate, or, God forbid, yell about it? *I saw you. I saw that.* What if there was a drunken grabber in the audience who destroyed a delicate prop? A disobedient volunteer, a spoiler?

How could Jonny stand to go up there, night after night, and open himself to abuse or ridicule? How could any of them?

As the years passed, she stopped watching Jonathan altogether. Instead, she watched the people in the seats. How they squinted, leaned forward, covered their mouths in shock, or turned to one another in delight.

Unlike Claire, they weren't privy to the secrets. They probably hadn't been to a magic show in years, didn't realize magicians had grown up just as they had, that magic could be sophisticated entertainment, not just kid stuff.

They didn't know that the card-to-lemon trick was fairly standard; to them, it was baffling. Unique. Creative. *Magical.* Watching the audience became her entertainment, her own private show.

Tonight, however, she kept her eyes glued to her estranged husband.

For the first time in twenty years, she had no idea what he was going to do.

At intermission, Claire ordered a Perrier and brought it up-stairs with her to the balcony. The Classics were done; Orig-inal acts were up next. Most of the audience mingled down below and it felt nice to retreat from the chaos.

Jonathan waited for her in the shadows.

"What did you think?" he asked.

When he'd appeared onstage in an authentic 1920s suit, pale makeup, and a slicked-down, retro hairstyle, with his light-blond hair dyed dark brown, she almost hadn't recog-nized him. He'd been transformed into P. T. Selbit (real name Tibbles, spelled backward, minus a *b*), whose 1921 act he du-plicated word for word.

She'd suggested, as an insult during their last argument about Schrödinger's Cat, that he perform in the Classics com-petition. He'd done a fine job emulating the other man, but it was a step down for him. Reproduced Classics were consid-ered the appetizer for the main course of Original work.

Apparently, though, he hadn't had time to come up with a fresh act without Claire. It was flattering in a way. Less flat-tering was the fact that Becca, the bimbo he'd slept with in Claire's bed, was his assistant. Her role was large. P. T. Sel-bit's biggest contribution to magic was the concept of sawing a woman in half.

Originally, magicians cut a boy in half. But in January 1921, on the London stage in Finsbury Park, P. T. Selbit shocked and titillated his audience by using a gasping, gimlet-eyed ingénue instead, and suddenly there was an outlet for all the rage men were feeling over women's suffrage.

The infuriating result of which was the century-long stan-dard of all-powerful male magicians dominating over glam-orous, nonspeaking, disposable females. Nonspeaking unless you counted screams, of course.

Jonathan's act included a custom-made wooden box, similar to a coffin, and a large handsaw, both of which would have been used at the time. Later versions introduced buzz saws.

Even in 2016, the symbolism hit close to home.

"I'm surprised you didn't make her pretend her name was Claire," she remarked.

"I was going to, but Becca does her best work when she's not unduly taxed with words."

"I thought I recognized her. It was hard to tell since she was wearing clothes."

"But what did you think?" he repeated.

She shrugged. "It seemed accurate. Your accent could've been better."

"But what did you *think* of it?" He was almost pleading. "Claire."

"It was good."

The way his shoulders fell told her he read her loud and clear. "But not Stage Magician of the Year good."

"What do you want me to say? Besides, it doesn't matter what I think. Not anymore."

"You know what's funny? After all these years, I don't even know if you *like* my magic. If you ever did."

"If all you wanted was to be adored, you have your groupies for that."

"I wanted to be adored by *you*." He rubbed his eyes.

"When do I get to see Doctor Faustus?" she asked.

"He's living with my nephew in Manhattan Beach. Is that all you have to say to me?" Jonathan asked.

"You took him just so I couldn't have him. That's...wow."

They stood on the balcony, overlooking the crowds and the stage. Unbeknownst to anyone below, it was their last appearance together as king and queen of the club, surveying their subjects.

"Did you ever love me?" he asked.

"Of course I did."

"But there's no chance of reconciliation."

She swallowed. "Do you really want there to be?"

He shook his head.

"Do you remember the Easter egg hunt at Candyland, when Eden was six?" she asked.

He seemed thrown by the question. "I'm not sure."

"She corralled a group of preschoolers into doing all the work for her. She knew from experience they'd been learning the Clean Up song in class—'Clean up, clean up, everybody everywhere; Clean up, clean up, everybody does their share'— so she sang it to them while holding out her Easter basket. They didn't understand the concept of an Easter egg hunt. They thought they were cleaning up the park. They scurried around gathering the eggs, bringing them to Eden, and putting them in her basket."

A smile graced Jonathan's lips. "Diabolical."

"She won first prize by a landslide. I'd never been more proud. Or more appalled. I kept thinking, *She's ours. We made her, this extraordinary creature. We made her. She's ours.* And no one can take that from us."

"I was faithful for a long time after Indiana," he said. "Years. But it was never enough for you. It was never enough."

"It didn't make us any happier," she offered. "It didn't fix what we'd done."

With five minutes left of intermission before the second wave of shows, Claire went back downstairs to ditch her drink.

Felix would be up next.

Her near-empty stomach clenched. How to distract herself?

Ahh.

There was Jessica, dripping off Cal's arm in her new dress, which perfectly underscored her slim, lithe body. Her caramel-colored hair was pulled into a loose, wrap-around French braid that ended in a ponytail. Cal drank her in with his eyes as though she contained all the alcohol he could ever need.

In short, the Clarkes looked stupidly happy, which set Claire's teeth on edge. Why had Cal been allowed to move on without a scratch from Brandy, while Claire's personal life lay in ruins?

Neither of the lovebirds had seen her yet, so she waited until Cal was pulled into a conversation with one of the judges before winding her way through the crowd toward Jessica.

"I can see why he's so enamored with you," Claire remarked. It wasn't a lie. Jessica was as wholesome-trashy-mischievous-sweet as ever. It was incredibly appealing, and incredibly unfair.

Jessica blushed. "You're the one who bought me the dress."

"You look beautiful. Truly."

"So do you," Jessica said quickly. Her lips were wobbly-shiny with gloss.

"I'm sorry for how we left things—"

"I never should have—"

They smiled shyly at each other.

"Do you think I could get a third chance?" Claire asked. "Last time, cross my heart."

Jessica beamed. "Yeah, okay."

"Thank you. I won't squander it."

Claire tucked a loose strand of Jessica's hair behind her ear and let her fingers fall down the side of Jessica's neck. Jessica swallowed, and her pupils widened.

"You have a little…" Claire motioned to her mouth.

"What?" said Jessica, sounding alarmed.

"Oh, it's nothing, just a little too much, you know—" She touched a finger to her own lip to indicate there was extra gloss there.

"Shit." Jessica looked around. "I don't have a napkin or anything to dab it." She raised the back of her hand to smear it off but Claire stopped her.

"Here."

She leaned down and kissed Jessica on the mouth. It was a soft, swift kiss, could barely be categorized as a peck, but Jessica closed her eyes to receive it and she seemed on the verge of going in for more when Claire pulled away. She stared at Claire, breathing hard.

Claire used her middle finger to spread the transferred lip gloss across her own bottom lip. "Better. Though I might have to start calling you Peaches."

"It's my favorite…"

"I remember."

"I'm just going to…I think I better…" Jessica motioned to the bathroom. She blushed furiously. It was fetching, and painfully indicative of her state of mind. Claire could practically feel the heat pouring off her.

Claire watched her go and pressed her lips together to even out the color.

A low, accusatory voice rumbled in her ear. "What. The hell. Was that?"

She turned, amused. "What, with me and Peaches?"

Cal walked around the table so they were facing each other. "Buying her that dress, kissing her just now? *I saw you.*"

"It was a peck."

"She has a crush on you," he divulged, running a tense hand through his hair. "I'm trying to discourage it."

"Why? Could be fun."

"No, Claire."

Her eyes sparkled. "Why not? Jonathan and I are separated."

"I'm sorry to hear that."

"No you're not."

"But Jessica and I are monogamous."

Claire ignored him. "She's a real pleaser, your wife. She practically quivered with the need for my approval when we went shopping. And at lunch she opened right up. Mama was a drinker, Papa was a rollin' stone…"

"She admires you. Don't take advantage of her. I mean it."

"I bet she's a crier, too. Does she cry when you make love to her, Callie?"

"You know who you sound like, and it's not a compliment," he said darkly.

"Maybe she could act out all her mommy and daddy fantasies with us. It'd be good for her, like therapy." She made her eyes go wide, like something had just occurred to her. "I know, we could *videotape it.*"

He tensed.

"How could you let her watch it? How could you?" she hissed.

"I didn't! I—I didn't even know—I didn't—I wasn't—" He shut his eyes, pained.

"You're stuttering," she deadpanned.

His brown eyes searched hers desperately. "I'll talk to her. She shouldn't have done that. I had no idea. But, please, don't mess with her head."

"The way you and Brandy messed with mine?"

His hand clenched around his bottle of club soda. "I know I have no right to ask, but I'm asking anyway."

Claire rounded the table and stepped close to him. "That's true. You have no right to ask."

"How can I turn this around, make things right?"

"You can't," she whispered. "Because you know what I think? I think, if you crawled over to her right now and pulled her thong off with your teeth, it would practically smell like me. Enjoy the rest of the show."

Felix

THE WELL-DRESSED, sixty-something master of cere-
monies took to the stage and read from a notecard. "Welcome
to part two of tonight's competition for Stage Magician of
the Year. Our next category is, of course, Original Magic Act.
Our first performer promises to astonish you with his feats
of…" He squinted at the notecard and broke out into a smile.
"…alchemy and time travel. How about *that*? Please welcome
newcomer Felix 'El Gato' Vicario."

Behind the velvet curtain, Felix held his breath during the
polite applause that followed. Anything more enthusiastic
than golf claps had to be worked for. He couldn't imagine a
tougher room.

They'd opted to keep his real name (plus *El Gato* tied in to
the use of a cat in the show), which he now suddenly regretted. A stage name to hide behind would be a relief.

There would be no friendly or familiar faces to focus on in
the audience. He wasn't even a *member* of the club, yet here he
was, attempting to bypass the natural order of things and collect its highest honor.

This is insane.

What made us think we could get away with this?

One of Claire's books said there were no such things as magicians, only actors playing the role of Magician. Jamie, his

actor roommate, could probably do just as well or better right now if Claire had coached him, he realized glumly. *Okay, so maybe that's true—but Jamie's not up here, I am.*

Why squander a great opportunity just because it arrived early in the game? He would earn his bona fides later. See, everybody wins. Well, maybe not *everybody*. Not the magicians he would displace in the contest, the ones who had come up with their own routines and spent years—*stop. You can't think that way. You worked your ass off, too, no one can deny that.*

Tonight was the beginning, a necessary launching pad, just so he could score the cash he needed to get his own place and honor his potential. Yes, honor his potential. That was the right attitude. *I'll make good on this,* he vowed. *I'll be my own man after this. Forge my own path.*

But first he had to win.

The judges would be using a scoring system for each aspect of the show:

Originality and skill
Level of difficulty
Stage presence
Audience reaction

If you displayed talent but no charisma, you were out of luck. If the audience adored you but your routine was derivative or simplistic, no dice. Claire believed her routine was foolproof but it was still up to Felix to be that fool.

He took a deep breath and walked onstage. *You can do this. You're El Gato. You always land on your feet.*

The timer started.

Per Claire's instructions, he plunged right in. No wasting precious seconds with "Good evening, ladies and gents" or "thank you for being here."

"I have three curiosities for you tonight. They are not tricks. They are not illusions. They are real. And because you cannot accept the fact that they are real, you will try to pass them off as sleight of hand, or a trick of the light."

The lights went out.

Someone shrieked in surprise, and then giggled. A tiny moment, yet vital to establishing a connection. A small hook to hang his hopes on: At least one person was on his side.

A moment later Felix was visible again, but only by the light of a flashlight, which he held under his chin. It was meant to give his face an eerie, fragmented glow, like a kid playing around a campfire.

Felix lifted a cardboard box and directed the flashlight beam through a small slit. The light went through it and emerged in two separate, distinct locations, visible on the wall stage right.

"Same source, different outcome. Electrons and photons. Some pass through, and others are reflected. One light, two images."

Felix clicked off the flashlight, enshrouding the entire room in darkness once more.

Sound of a finger snapping.

Full house lights came back on and the curtain opened, revealing Felix's stage: a small lab and chemistry classroom set, complete with smoking beakers, a chalkboard, a desk and a chair.

"Three curiosities. Why three? Three is a magic number. Three acts tell the perfect story. Beginning, middle, and end. The first act is transmutation."

He fanned out a deck of blank cards, all of them bright white, front and back.

He took out a knife and cut his arm. The blood pack hidden in his sleeve punctured instantly.

The audience gasped and squealed in distress.

He squeezed a large drop of "blood" onto the blank deck of cards and fanned the deck, to show that the red suits—Hearts and Diamonds—had formed on half the cards in a dripping-wet red smear. All the symbols and faces seemed to vibrate, alive.

He wrapped his bleeding arm in a handkerchief, walked to the beakers, and lifted one out. "Blood to blood, dust to dust. Behold, the dust of my bones."

He poured the dust on the deck of cards, closed them, and opened them to reveal that the black suits—Spades and Clubs—had now formed, spreading like the ink of a Rorschach test, changing from gray dust to black imagery, darker and darker.

Applause. He didn't realize—or maybe he'd forgotten—how intoxicating applause could be.

"These are my cards, the devil's picture book. Or, if you prefer, 'Now I'm playing with a full deck.'"

Chuckles followed, half a beat behind. Felix moved so quickly the audience had trouble keeping up.

But it was really Claire moving quickly.

The fact that few people could keep up was one of the reasons he'd been so drawn to her. That and her loneliness. Maybe each ensured the existence of the other. He was glad he couldn't see her out there, golden-haired and terrified, mouthing along with the routine.

"How do I know these are my cards? They came from my blood and from my bones. Alchemy died out two centuries ago, but we still look to it for our magic. Rabbits into mice, charcoal into gold. Blood and bones into cards. Breath into fire."

He took a quick swig of a beaker labeled MAGIC SPIRITS, tossed a flash paper in the air, and blew. It ignited in a burst of light and flame.

Careful applause. They needed more. Flash paper wasn't rare enough.

"If a magician came up to you and granted you one wish, what would you wish for? Most people say money, wealth, fame, power, invisibility...I'd want time travel. Think about it. With time travel, there is no path not taken; there is no unexamined life. What people don't understand is that time travel doesn't go forward or backward. It goes sideways. You don't move up and down along a continuum, because that would create a vacuum. No, you must move between worlds.

"Remember the flashlight?" He performed the light through cardboard again. "One light, two outcomes. One life, two paths. One person, two worlds."

Lights out.

Flashlight on.

Lights on.

Felix suddenly appeared at the chalkboard.

He drew a line on the chalkboard, and then a second line branching out from the first and curving around so it eventually became parallel. "Look, it's like a map of Los Angeles. San Vicente, I think."

Laughter.

He labeled one line "You—A" and the second line "You—B" and drew circles to signify two people.

"With time travel, you wouldn't move earlier in your own life, you'd swap places with a different version of yourself: the you that's in a different world. The difference between the worlds isn't huge. It's not as though suddenly we all have lizard faces or have evolved into different species because some asshole stepped on a butterfly, apologies to Ray Bradbury."

I was supposed to cut that line, Felix berated himself. *Is my timing off now? Will I go past the ten-minute mark and be automatically disqualified? How much time did it add? And how much time am I adding by thinking about this? Oh, God. What's the next line? Difference between worlds...right.*

"No, the difference between our world and another, parallel world is as small as the difference between picking the Two of Hearts and picking the Two of Spades. You are still you. You've just made different choices, and different choices have different consequences."

He moved to the front row with his deck of "bloody" cards in hand. The people there collectively recoiled and he smiled. "I won't hurt you."

No one budged.

"Here, take the deck."

A woman shook her head, vehement.

"It's okay, the blood has almost dried."

"Disgusting," she said, to nervous titters all around.

"I don't blame you for being uneasy. But if you please, pick a card."

She gave in.

"This is not sleight of hand," said Felix. "This is not misdirection. This is not an illusion. You have picked the card of your own free will. Think of this deck as a living thing—it came from me, after all—I breathed life into it. Each card has a role to play, and they are all entangled with one another. The deck is a closed, coherent system."

He gave the woman the rest of the deck. "Hold out the deck to your neighbor and ask him to pick a card, then pass the deck along. Neighbor, once you've selected yours, do the same: Turn to the next person and ask him to pick a card.

"As it travels row by row, there will be fewer choices. If I pick the Two, you can't pick the Two; I've affected your options. My picking the card precludes you picking the card. The more picked, the fewer possibilities remain."

He returned to the chalkboard for some quick scratches:

```
52 CARDS = 52 WORLDS
51
50
49
48
```

Some audience members shifted impatiently in their seats.

"The first four rows hold fifty-two audience members, which is of course the number of cards in a deck. I'm going to predict with one hundred percent accuracy which card all fifty-two of you will choose.

"How am I able to do this? Because these are the only cards you could pick and still be in this world. If you were to pick differently, you would no longer be here; you would be part of a different world, in which you picked a different card, in that world's version of this trick.

"Before you sat down tonight, I prepared my predictions. Each card has a perfect twin; each card in this deck is entangled with another card; they each do what the other does. Einstein hated entanglement. 'Spooky action at a distance,' he called it. Well, of course it's spooky action at a distance," Felix roared. "*I'm a magician!*"

And at the moment, he believed it, with his whole heart, which thundered in his chest as beads of sweat gathered on his forehead. More than that, he believed it would be true always, from that point on.

He wiped at his brow, suddenly out of breath. Took a moment to compose himself and clear his throat. "Under each chair I've taped a sealed envelope."

"Oh, my God," someone said.

"Yes, underneath each chair, taped to the bottom—don't

touch them yet—are envelopes. Inside each envelope is a card. A prediction of your choice.

"Don't avert your eyes; that won't stop me from making you participate. Pick a card and pass it on. Don't think too hard.

"While you're all passing the deck along, I'd like to prepare my finale, the third act, for which I'll need the help of my feline assistant. He is going to time-travel."

Felix disappeared behind the curtain and returned carrying a black cat with a white splotch on his forehead. The cat's left paw was also white.

"Aww," went the audience.

"This is my cat, Schrödinger."

Felix kissed Schrödinger's forehead, and set Schrödinger on the floor. Next he retrieved a large, white, velvet-lined box and held it aloft.

"This box represents Hilbert space. All the possibilities of the universe are inside it. Has everyone finished selecting their card?"

Felix removed a small manila envelope from his pocket.

"Schrödinger has a very important role. Inside this envelope is a prediction card, just like the ones under your chairs. He's going to hold on to it for me."

He placed the envelope in the cat's mouth, set Schrödinger inside the box, and closed the lid.

"We'll return to him in a moment. Remember what I said in the beginning? That I would predict precisely, with one hundred percent accuracy, which card each of you picked? Well, the cards you pick determine whether he lives or dies."

Chaos from the audience. Shouts, some angry *Shh*s, then silence.

"Yes, you heard me. A quantum system is nothing until it's measured. It doesn't exist. Looking at it and making an observation about its qualities brings those qualities into being and destroys the system. When multiple possibilities are brought to a single outcome, we experience quantum collapse. Everyone done? Everyone have a card? Let's all reach under our chairs and remove our envelopes. Don't be shy."

"Holy shit, he got mine right," someone yelled. Arm movements, cacophony, as more and more people reached under their chairs, held up their cards, and ripped open their envelopes. Shrieks and laughter overlapped, along with more announcements of successful predictions.

Felix was pleased. "Yes, I know it's surprising…Especially because half the cards were dipped in poison."

Sounds of people screaming and throwing their cards made Felix want to grin maniacally, but he held back.

"And half of them were not. Because the cards are entangled, we can predict with certainty that if the card you chose has poison on it, so does its twin, in the envelope. Only trace amounts, not nearly enough to hurt you."

Someone in the second-to-last row stood up. He was the final person to participate in the trick.

"I've got the Ace of Spades," he called. "But there's no envelope under my chair."

"That's true. I'm glad you pointed that out. You're absolutely correct. Schrödinger has your card."

"No way!"

"But was it a poisoned card, or no?" Felix asked.

"*No! No!*" shouted the audience in a desperate chant.

"Are you sure?"

"No!" they yelled again.

"A poisoned card can't hurt *you*, but for a cat…well, it could be deadly."

"*Yes!*" / "*No!*"

"Shall we see?"

Felix lifted the box.

The cat was dead. The envelope remained in his mouth. Poison from the card had seeped through the thin paper and killed him.

Nobody made a sound for a long, long time.

Then a woman cried, "Bring him back. Make him come back."

"Impossible. But it's okay. Don't you see? In the other worlds, Schrödinger's alive. In the other worlds, the poisoned card was not chosen. Think how happy your other self is. She's clapping. Can't you hear her clapping?"

"Make him come back."

"Bring the cat back to life!"

"Very well. Perhaps Schrödinger can time-travel back to us by switching with another world's version of himself."

The clock was running out. The warning light in the overhead booth flashed, signaling the nine-minute, thirty-second mark. If he went beyond ten minutes, everything would be for naught. He'd be disqualified even if the judges liked him the best.

If.

Lights out.

Lights on.

The switch had occurred. The "dead" cat (a taxidermy of Schrödinger's late sibling) was gone. He and the live Schrödinger had swapped places.

Schrödinger got up, stretched, hopped out of his box, and walked to the front of the stage near the lights, where he proceeded to *bow three times.*

A cat, the most notoriously difficult animal to train or manage, had been killed and brought back to life. And then the cat had *bowed*.

Unbeknownst to the audience or the judges, one of the footlights on the floor of the stage had an extra element inside, next to the bulb: Schrödinger's favorite toy. He wasn't bowing;

he was leaning over to try to grab the treat with his mouth through the glass.

The room exploded with cheers.

It didn't matter that the next competitor swallowed fire, or that the one after that balanced five plates above his head. The contest was over, and everyone inside the theater knew it.

The Mexican Inquisition, as he came to think of it, turned out to be easier than Felix expected. He'd overprepared. The judges certainly wanted to chat with him at the post-ceremony cocktail party, but their questions were rooted in awe rather than distrust.

Watching him onstage, they'd reverted to wide-eyed little boys just as Claire predicted they would, and the young man several decades their junior with the shaved head and smooth brown skin was their strange new god. After all, Magician of the Year Felix Vicario was the total package: a jock magician with a science habit and a sense of humor. It gave the art a much-needed update. They'd known for years that magic was no longer the purview of old men, and here was the proof! Now they could compete with those arrogant cardists in the court of public opinion. Just like Penn & Teller, Derren Brown, and Michael Carbonaro before him, he was changing the face of magic.

While Felix had rehearsed the act that won them over, he'd also rehearsed having the kind of personality that would've created the Schrödinger's Cat routine in the first place. Felix the science jock had supposedly audited physics classes whenever possible, none of which he received grades or credits for (and thus wouldn't appear on his transcripts if anyone looked into it), but such was his love for the topic. This was in actuality the type of thing twenty-something Claire would've done, though he wasn't sure if she had. Despite all the time they'd spent together, and how much she'd infiltrated his psyche, he still knew very little about her. The thought was surprisingly depressing. All of the free drinks and congratulations paled in comparison with what he wanted to do with Claire, whom he now associated with the greatest night of his life. She'd warned him beforehand she couldn't stay and celebrate or indicate in any way that the victory was shared.

If he could have, Felix would have bent her backward in a full-body dip and delivered a showstopping kiss for all to see. He pushed that image aside and focused on entertaining the judges with his made-up personal history.

Helpfully, visitors to the club who wanted photos with Felix interrupted the conversation every few minutes. Their chatter allowed him to duck any questions he didn't like, or take his time forming answers. Reporters from *Magic* and *Genii* magazines asked to set up profile interviews. The second- and third-place winners came over to congratulate Felix and slap him (a little harder than necessary) on the back.

Mr. Fredericksson, who'd come in second place for his category, had stormed out following the announcement of the winner. He certainly wasn't joining the afterparty, even at his own club.

At two thirty in the morning, Felix called it a night as well. Besides the nice fat check, winning the contest meant a life-long membership to the club. He could come back every night of the week if he wanted. He was still pumped up with adrenaline, so he headed west to Sunset Boulevard and the Chateau Marmont, where he'd spent the previous night in obscene luxury. His old room had been taken, but he could upgrade to an eight-hundred-dollar suite. Why not? He had the money. He deserved it.

He also deserved a new car. Some tailored suits, custom shoes. After all, if tonight had taught him anything, it was that all he needed to do was *look* the part to *become* the part.

While the concierge set up his new digs, Felix turned on his cell for the first time all night.

Twenty voicemails!

Four were from Claire, time-stamped throughout the evening, starting from five minutes after he won the grand prize.

10:47 p.m.: [incoherent scream of joy, followed by laughing sobs] "Felix. I am so proud of you. You were brilliant. You were…you were…pure magic. [pause] There *was* that time when you could've—no, no, I'm not going to critique anything. You were brilliant."

11:23 p.m.: [car door slams] "Felix. Me again. I'm at home. You could call me at the house, but I don't expect you to, we can catch up later. Have fun at the party. You deserve it. Jesus, the place erupted at the end. They loved you. *Loved you.* [pause] I wonder if there was a point where we should've added a mention of quantum superpositions, or whether we should've been more explicit about how the poison was standing in for radioactive atoms…but maybe that's too pedantic…it was great. I mean it really couldn't have gone better. The old farts were speechless. *Well done.*"

Midnight: "Hi, hi, hi, I'm opening a bottle of champagne. Just wanted to say again what a success it was, hope you're being feted appropriately. Can't wait to hear every detail. Take notes. Ha-ha but really, I would like to know what people are saying. What did they like best, et cetera? What surprised them the most? Does anyone know how the multiple card selection was achieved? Let me know. [kiss sound] Mwaaah."

In the last one, recorded at half past one in the morning, slightly tipsy from champagne, her voice rumbled in his ear, low and sultry. "I think you can afford that gold nightie now."

His pulse raced, and he almost ran outside to collect his car and speed over to her house. But she'd left the message two hours ago, and was probably asleep, so their reunion would have to wait. Imagining it would be fun enough for now.

When his head hit the pillow, though, he fell instantly asleep. He didn't dream. There was no need to. Everything he'd hoped for had come true.

Kaimi

IN HAWAII NO one she knew had car insurance because it was too expensive, but at least there were cops everywhere to direct traffic around even the smallest potholes, so drivers tended to be careful under so many watchful eyes. In comparison, LA was a free-for-all on crack. *I don't want to die in Burbank*, Kaimi thought for what felt like the millionth time, having been cut off three times while attempting to merge onto the 101 South.

Ten a.m. on Monday, she and Landon met at Club Deception to sell the papers to Jonathan Fredericksson. The buyer from England hadn't returned Kaimi's latest messages, and even if Cal had the money—which Kaimi doubted—they couldn't stop his wife from providing him a copy of the papers for free. The sooner they off-loaded the goods, the sooner Kaimi could get back to her family and set everything right.

"Don't mention Saturday's contest," Landon advised Kaimi as they rode the elevator down to the depths of the club. "He came in second and it's a sore spot."

"Got it."

"Once it's handled, want to meet up tonight for Cal's premiere party? I told Jess I'd be there."

She grinned. "Sounds good."

Landon held the elevator doors open so she could exit first.

Jonathan waited for them in the Silver Room, at the head of a long table.

"This is where the board meets," Landon told Kaimi as they walked in.

"Leave the gun, take the cannoli," she quipped. The room was dark, lit by a silver chandelier. A silver carafe, surrounded by goblets filled with ice water, sat in the middle of the table. A silvery blue, abstract sculpture of a naked woman's torso was attached to the wall. Her breasts shone as though someone had spent considerable time polishing them. Kaimi rolled her eyes at it.

Jonathan glanced up when they sat across from him.

Kaimi set the Erdnase papers, encased in plastic protective covering, down so Jonathan could see them.

He barely acknowledged them. Wrote a check with a silver pen, tore it from the ledger, and slipped it across the table to Landon.

Kaimi squinted at it. Five thousand dollars. *What the—!*

"You're missing a few zeros there, pal," said Landon, sending the check back to Jonathan.

"Where'd you *get* these, 'pal'?" Jonathan retorted with a smirk, stabbing his finger on the table next to the Erdnase papers.

"I inherited them."

"We agreed to five hundred for the full set," Kaimi snapped. "Well, guess what, here's the full set."

"Becca agreed. I did no such thing."

"She was speaking on your behalf—"

"You'll sell them to me for five, or you won't sell them at all." Jonathan capped his pen, set it down, and folded his hands.

"What!" Kaimi exploded.

"I'll spread the word they're fabricated. I'm very well connected. I'll hold a meeting of the board, right here in this room, send out a special-edition newsletter to all our members, get the interns to post about it on every magic-related message board. I have an expert in magical artifacts who'll verify what I say, warn every magician from here to China not to touch them because they're worthless."

Landon jumped to his feet. "They're not worthless!"

"They're only worth what someone is willing to pay for them."

"You can't do that," Landon warned him.

"Keep your pit bull on a tighter leash, Kaimi," Jonathan said.

"What did you just call me?" Landon asked, dangerously quiet. "I am a *member of this club*."

"You're a snake oil salesman. Your little self-help scam has made you some enemies, you know. Nobody will be surprised to learn you're peddling Erdnase imitation goods."

Kaimi stood next to Landon, forcing herself to sound calm. "You don't want them? We'll sell them to Cal. Good-bye, Mr. Fredericksson."

Jonathan called her bluff, though not for the right reason. "If you think Calum Clarke can afford them, you're delusional."

"He's not the only interested party," Kaimi retorted, and packed up the papers.

Jonathan remained seated, a permanent smirk on his face. "Nigel Allen at Magic Crossroads? Who do you think my expert is?"

Kaimi stared at Jonathan. Her limbs felt weak. "You planned this with him?"

"Face it, kids, we're the only game in town. What'll it be? Five? Or should I make it two, at this point?"

Outside the club, Kaimi let out a muffled screech into the sleeve of her cardigan. Tears of rage filled her eyes.

"I already wrote my parents. I told them I was going to take care of them, that help was coming. I sent the letter yesterday."

"We just have to think," said Landon, punching his fist into his hand. "We just have to think…"

"He's not getting away with this."

"No, he's not. We're not going to let him."

Felix

THAT SAME DAY, Felix woke in his room at the Chateau Marmont feeling confident. It had been two days since his triumph at Magician of the Year, and the online chatter about it was increasing hourly. He'd spent half the night poring over the message board threads devoted to his astonishing, "rags-to-riches" victory, copying and pasting the best ones to email to Claire. Then he drove to Merlin's Wonderporium for a good old-fashioned Fuck You Very Much with his ex-co-workers.

"Whoop-whoop," he said, arms in the air, fists pumping. "How's it going, dickheads? You miss me?"

"All hail the conquering hero," Roy deadpanned.

Spencer crouched on the floor and used a Swiss Army Knife to open some boxes. Didn't even look up.

"Want me to sign anything while I'm here? Programs from last night's show are fifty bucks on eBay and climbing," he said.

Spencer finally deigned to acknowledge Felix. "Sure. We'll add it to the Hyuks items."

Out of habit, Felix squatted down to grab some books and help Spencer shelve them. "What do you mean?"

Spencer yanked the books out of Felix's hands. "We know you didn't turn into some kind of savant overnight."

"It wasn't overnight," Felix huffed. "I worked my ass off."

Roy and Spencer looked at each other and smiled. Some kind of unspoken agreement seemed to pass between them.

"I have two words for you," said Spencer, crossing his arms. "Jonathan Fredericksson."

Felix's heart blasted in his chest like shotgun reverb. "What about him?"

"He was here five minutes ago looking for you," said Roy happily. "He's out for blood, says you stole his act. Which is the only way this makes sense."

"What? No. He's out of his mind, man. Anyway, I have to go."

Felix's thoughts raced as he bolted from the store.

"Yeah, that's what I thought," Spencer yelled after him.

On the sidewalk, moving briskly to his car, he punched Claire's number into his phone, but she didn't pick up. He didn't want to say anything incriminating on her voicemail, and he couldn't show up at her house—what if Jonathan had gone there next?

Where on earth would it be possible for him to run into her?

The answer was so obvious he almost didn't think of it.

You're a lifetime member now. You can hang out at Club Deception anytime you want.

Jessica

ON THE WAY out the door to Cal's premiere party, Jessica just barely remembered the cupcakes she'd baked that afternoon, running back inside to grab them from the fridge. She still felt bad about the way things had gone down with the club receptionist, not to mention the weird skinny guy Claire had insulted. She wouldn't feel right showing up with bad karma following her around. Being Cal's wife meant she should be *extra* nice to people there, not act like a diva. She wanted them to treat her nicely because she deserved it, not because they wanted to kiss Cal's ass.

Cal was quiet on the ride over. Jessica chalked it up to nerves. This was the first time his peers would see the result of nearly three years' worth of work. Naturally he'd want to impress them.

They stopped at a red light. "When this is done, we should talk about some things," he said.

"You sound like me," she pointed out.

"I'm serious. About boundaries, and privacy, and what we expect from each other."

She didn't like being scolded.

Not that she blamed him.

She quickly changed the subject to one she knew he would get lost in.

"When I was watching Jonathan's show last night, I had the weirdest sense of déjà vu," she said. "Did I tell you I saw him when I was a kid?"

His eyes gleamed. "Ha. It was probably the same act. He never was one for switching things up."

"The assistant looked so familiar."

"Most assistants do; they have to be a precise size and shape to fit inside the props," he said.

Traffic stalled them further, and by the time they arrived they were forty-five minutes late.

"Cal! Great to see you. Congrats on the show, the big night, everything!" said the sour-faced receptionist, predictably, when they walked in. She avoided Jessica's gaze, but Jessica strode toward her with a big smile.

"These are for you," she said. She peeled back a corner of the Tupperware lid.

"What? Why?"

"We sort of got off on the wrong foot last time and I just wanted to let you know I appreciate how hard your job is and I didn't take it personally. I hope you like raspberry buttercream frosting."

"You're not from around here, are you?" she asked, peeking inside the bin.

"No, she's not, she lives on a planet of sweetness and goo," said Cal, smiling at Jessica.

The receptionist struggled to understand. "Wait, so, all of these? Are for me?"

"Yeah! You can share them with whoever, or take them home."

"Um, thanks. Wow. Thanks."

"So bygones to all that? We're bygonesies?" Jessica asked.

"Yes."

"Oh, wait, sorry, I need to take one back," said Jessica.

She lifted the lid off the cupcakes and scrutinized her options.

Once downstairs at the bar, she scanned the room for the Ichabod Crane–looking guy Claire had humiliated. He stood in the corner where she'd first met him, as though he'd been backed into it, eyes watchful and guarded. There seemed to be a force field around him.

"What are you doing?" Cal murmured in her ear as she moved toward him. "He's a hanger-on."

"It won't take long." She approached, cupcake hand outstretched. "Hi. This is for you. I never meant for you to feel bad. I don't know if you remember, but you showed me a trick when I first arrived and you did it really well. You didn't flash."

Ichabod regarded her with suspicion. Didn't even look at Cal. "Claire's the one who should apologize," he said sullenly.

"I wouldn't hold my breath," Cal joked.

Ichabod's eyes swiveled up to land on Cal. He mumbled something and made a hasty retreat, which ended up being a sort of sideways maneuver since his back was to a wall.

Cal took Jessica's hand in his. "Now that you've spread a little sunshine, we have a clip show to introduce."

The screening room sat fifty people in plush armchairs. Each chair had its own small, circular table, upon which sat a tiny lamp (with room for a cocktail beside it). Typically, the room was used to broadcast old TV magic shows from the '70s and '80s, or current magic specials airing only in London and Tokyo, with panel discussions afterward.

When Cal and Jessica stood at the podium to make a few remarks, a waitress approached with a tray of champagne flutes, shimmering like gold. Cal stared at them and Jessica could feel his body tighten, like a coiled spring waiting to leap.

"None for us, thanks," Jessica said quietly.

"What's that?" the waitress asked.

"None for us," she repeated. "Thank you." She pushed lightly at the tray in an effort to send the waitress on her way.

Cal watched her go, his eyes fixed on the glasses, and then on the recipients of the champagne. He fiddled with his necktie and cleared his throat.

"Hello everyone, and thank you, really, for taking the time to come out tonight. Please tune in tomorrow at eight, and then I swear I'll shut up forever about the damn thing. However, if you *don't* tune in, I have ways of finding out, and in that case I'll keep talking about it. So those are your choices. You've been warned."

Light laughter and applause followed.

The lights dimmed, the screen unrolled from the ceiling, and the clip show began. On-screen, Cal performed his impeccable Bottle Cap trick at the Gold Coast Hotel. Jessica watched proudly, and then her jaw dropped. There she was, on-screen next to him.

Cal paused the projection and turned to Jessica, whose smile grew even wider.

"I performed a version of this trick nationwide, almost all fifty states, and on two separate continents," Cal told his friends in the room. "We filmed every single version. But this one is special, because it takes place the night I met Jessie." He cleared his throat again, looking emotional. "To my wife, Jessica."

"To Jessica," the crowd repeated, lifting their glasses. Jessica blushed and gave a little wave, reminding herself to stand up tall.

On-screen, the paused image lived forever. In a moment, he'd tap the bottle cap against the bottom of the bottle, and it would magically appear inside, trapped. But until then, it was just Cal and Jessica, falling in love.

He unpaused the video and whispered in Jessica's ear, "A little souvenir."

"Thank you," she whispered back.

Next came a montage of Cal performing close-up magic around the world, on the street, in restaurants and bars, ski slopes, and even inside a hot-air balloon. The scenes were intercut with a brief documentary-style getting-to-know-you interview in which he revealed the reason he'd gone into magic.

"Anyone growing up in Britain in the mid-eighties will remember the Paul Daniels show on BBC. When I was ten, he had a special that blew my mind right open. He was placed in a wooden box on a racetrack, while a car sped toward him. We all thought he was going to escape, but he didn't! He wasn't fast enough, and the car smashed straight into him, crash, boom—we thought he was dead. Then the box opens up, revealing that Daniels is gone. And *then* the car that ran him over came to a stop—and who exits the car but *Daniels*. Absolutely classic. Never forgot it. But it was his smaller, more intimate work that really got me going. Aces in a wineglass, cups and balls, I wanted to do it all. I moved on to studying Cardini after that. Basically, I had no life. I was a real hit with the ladies, as you can imagine," he said self-deprecatingly, which of course served to charm the pants off anyone watching. He was so damn cute, so damn unpretentious, so damn fuckable.

When the show airs, women all over the country, maybe even the world, will see him and want him for themselves, but they can't have him, Jessica thought. It was a massive turn-on and she intended to collect on it later tonight, maybe even on the car ride home.

As the teaser clips played on, she and Cal moved to the back of the room.

"It's hard to come here and not drink," he confided. "It's such a part of the ambience. That's another reason I haven't escorted you here as much as I should have. Ordering juice, or water, or club soda depresses me more than it should. And I look around at everyone here, who can stop at one or two or three drinks, who can just decide to *stop*, and I envy them. I can't even have a sip of champagne at my own party. It's pathetic."

"I understand," she told him. "We don't have to stay."

"Good, because I don't think I can." He tugged anxiously at his necktie.

"After this, we'll take off."

But the guests had other plans for Cal, and they couldn't escape as easily as they'd hoped. His friends and admirers wanted to chat, and he was engulfed by well-wishers immediately following the show. He shot Jessica a hangdog look before turning to them with a practiced smile.

Claire emerged from the crowd, wearing a floor-length gown. She held two flutes of champagne. "He might not be able to, but you still can," she told Jessica, discreetly pressing one of the glasses into her hand.

Jessica felt guilty because she *did* want one. What was a celebration without bubbly? But she couldn't very well stand there drinking when Cal couldn't. Of course, if he didn't *see* her, maybe it didn't count…

"Thanks," she said, and took a large sip. *Get it down quick…*

"I'll block you," Claire offered. She slipped the fingers of her free hand through Jessica's and led her toward the screening room's exit. Claire's thumb caressed the side of her hand, just once, but the swipe gave Jessica a little electric jolt. It turned into the happy flicker she got whenever someone took care of her.

She mentally added it to her list of times Claire had touched her.

Once they were safely ensconced in a corner, Claire let go. Claire's makeup was subtle, her dress modest and almost conservative; it didn't show an inch of her legs. Jessica chose to believe it was a considerate choice; she hadn't wanted to draw attention away from the Clarkes on their big night. Because who could ignore those legs?

"There's a lot of overlap in the crowd from Saturday," Claire said quietly. It took Jessica a moment to interpret what Claire was saying. "You don't want people to think you only have one going-out dress," she added.

"But it's kind of true," Jessica said. "And I love this dress."

"It was true for me, too, not that long ago. So space it out more, add some different accessories. I know, that's what we'll focus on during our next shopping trip."

She hadn't dared hope for a repeat shopping trip. Insides warm from champagne and the idea of more excursions, she smiled at Claire and wondered idly if she'd worn too much lip gloss again. Maybe she should have done it on purpose, to keep their little game—whatever it was—going that much longer.

Jessica downed the last drops of her champagne and looked around for the waitress. She was either going to give her back the empty and leave it at that, or sneak another glass while Cal was otherwise engaged. But the decision became moot when Jonathan Fredericksson showed up and all hell broke loose.

Felix

OUTSIDE CLUB DECEPTION, there was a line to get in. Which wasn't the image the club wanted for itself. First, it alerted people to the club's existence. Second, it implied there was a way to get inside if one waited there long enough, which simply wasn't true. Some celebrity must have tweeted about it and now random jerks were hoping to catch a glimpse of the place.

Felix was ushered inside ahead of everyone in line.

Downstairs was packed for Calum Clarke's TV premiere party. Felix had first read about the show last year, when he was barely making a living hawking gimmicks at Merlin's Wonderporium. Since then, he'd become involved with the wife of the club president, wiped the floor with his former idols at a major competition, and become a coveted member of an underground club he hadn't thought he'd ever see the inside of, let alone join.

This can't be my real life.

But it is. Act like you own it.

He nearly jumped out of his skin when he saw Jonathan in the corner, speaking to the *flaco* creeper who'd eyeballed Claire the first time he'd come. Jonathan and the pale, skinny guy (who was inexplicably eating a pink-frosted cupcake) laughed together like they were old buddies.

"I'm not disagreeing with you," he heard Jonathan say. "She's an ice queen."

They're ragging on Claire, he thought angrily. Fighting his urge to confront Jonathan, he ducked into the screening room to find her.

He scanned the room and saw her hand Cal's wife a glass of champagne. Was Claire chaperoning her? Or trying to get her into trouble?

He tried to be casual as he sidled up to Claire.

"Jessica, Felix. Felix, Jessica." She didn't look at him. "Keep walking."

Taking her cue and looking anywhere but at her, as though they were in a spy movie, he whispered, "I need to talk to you."

"What's wrong?" she whispered back.

"Your husband is stalking me—"

"He's not my husband anymore—"

"He showed up at the shop, I just saw him here now, and—oh, God, incoming—"

As though summoned from hell, Jonathan materialized at the entrance of the screening room.

He was more than a little drunk.

Felix braced himself for Round Two of *The Frederickssons Go Batshit.*

"There's the rat-faced thief," he roared, pointing at Felix, who instinctually stepped away from Claire. "This guy stole my routine. He's been screwing my wife, and she gave it to him." Jonathan wheeled around theatrically to include anyone in the vicinity. "Did you all know that?"

"I'm surprised to see you here," Claire countered loudly. "Considering you told me about a dozen times you wouldn't be ca-caught dead at Cal's premiere."

Jonathan seemed pleased by her loss of finesse.

Felix's fist clenched.

"Schrödinger's Cat is mine," Jonathan asserted. "And I can prove it." From his suit pocket he fumbled to retrieve a piece of paper. "I patented the trick. Look! See that?"

Claire's eyes widened, and she reached for the paper. "Give me that—"

He yanked it tauntingly out of reach. "Filed it months ago."

"What? Why would—why on earth would you have scrapped it, then?" Claire asked. "If the trick was yours, why wouldn't you have gone through with it? The award-winning trick—*Felix's* trick—if it was yours, why wouldn't you have…this makes no sense, you haven't got a leg to stand on," she sputtered.

"You gave him my trick and you thought I wouldn't notice?"

Her voice lowered abruptly to such a degree Felix almost couldn't hear her. "*It's not your trick, Jonathan*," she hissed.

"I've already launched an official inquiry with the board." He regarded Felix coldly. "You're *done*. I am going to *ruin* you."

"Everyone who saw me last night knows I'm the real thing," Felix replied, oozing ice back. "What are you good for, besides stepping out on Claire and coming in second every year?" He shoved Jonathan roughly back.

He wanted to do a lot more than that but he doubted Claire would approve.

Jonathan straightened his lapels and swiveled to face Claire again. "And *you*—as of next week, the house is up for sale. You have until the weekend to vacate the premises."

The people around them had either crept out of the room in horror or inched closer to find out what was happening.

Claire seemed to be reeling from the unexpected threat of homelessness, and Felix felt his stomach lurch on her behalf as well as his. The evening was spiraling out of control.

Jonathan suddenly noticed Calum Clarke's wife. "Hello. You look fun. Freshen your Jell-O shot?" he quipped.

"Leave her alone," Cal said. He stepped between Jonathan and Jessica and took off his suit jacket, tossing it onto one of the chairs.

Jonathan grinned like a shark. "Interesting. Who is she?"

The young woman struck a defiant pose. "I'm Jessica Clarke. Which you should know considering he introduced me up there."

"Sorry, just arrived," he demurred. "This is *killing* you, isn't it?" he asked Claire. "She's hardly older than Eden."

"I have no opinion about it," she replied.

Jonathan sidestepped Cal and leaned in close to Jessica. "You know, you have to watch out for your husband and Claire."

"That's enough," Cal warned.

Jonathan was slurring his words now. "Let me explain something to you." He cocked a thumb in Claire's direction. "*This one* doesn't know how to love anybody. That's why she's always a third wheel."

"The term you're looking for is *fifth wheel*. A third wheel serves a function, of balance," Claire said.

"Oh, *shut up*, Claire. You don't speak for me anymore."

"A fifth wheel is unnecessary. Isn't that what you're trying to say? That I'm not anything on my own?"

"She latches on to other people's lives and leeches off them, and she thinks because she's smart, she's immune to any fallout. And Cal's just as bad," Jonathan boomed, "never letting her move on." He wobbled even closer to Cal's wife, as close as he could get. "Although maybe I should be thanking him. He broke her in for me. Sexually. Like a horse." He poked Cal on the shoulder. "Want me to return the favor?"

Bam.

Cal felled Jonathan with a single, lightning-fast punch, right in the face, and Jonathan tumbled backward. Jessica screamed.

Felix wished he'd been the one to do it.

Jessica worriedly examined Cal's hand. "You shouldn't have done that," she said. "Are you okay?"

"She's right," said Jonathan from the floor. Everyone stared down at him, surprised. The blow had been strong enough to knock him unconscious. His mouth was bloody and he looked slightly deranged. "You shouldn't have done that. I'm suing you for assault. I'll alert the press about it tomorrow before your show airs."

Cal looked like he wanted to kick Jonathan over and over until he turned to mush. "You mardy tosser…" he seethed.

Felix had no idea what that meant but agreed with the sentiment behind it.

"You can't sue your way out of everything," Claire added.

A few older men—board members, Felix assumed— finally intervened, flanking Jonathan and helping him to his feet. "Let's get you washed up and get you home," one of them said.

Half an hour later, standing outside the valet line waiting for their cars to arrive, Felix and Claire spoke in low tones. She looked shaken.

"What are we going to do?" he asked.

"I'll take care of it," she snapped. Seeing his startled expression, she lowered her eyes. "I'm sorry. This isn't your fault."

He'd envisioned their first post-show meet-up many times since Saturday. It usually involved carnal acrobatics. Right now that seemed about as likely as snow falling on their heads at this very moment.

"How?" he asked. "How will you take care of it?"

"I'll speak to him tomorrow when he's calmer, explain to him why forcing an inquiry with the board will backfire. Because it *will*. Because it's *not his trick*."

It's not mine, either, he thought.

Her plan was too vague. It couldn't possibly work. *Talking things out? Really?* "What if they take the money back? What if he *does* ruin me?"

Her eyes flashed. "I'll see him dead before that happens."

"What was he talking about back there, anyway?" Felix asked.

She sighed. "Which part?"

"The part about how you, like, 'latch on' to other people?"

"Oh, in his version of our narrative, he rescued me from Cal. Gave me back my self-respect. And I bought into it for a long time, but the truth is, Felix, I never *lost* my self-respect. Anyway." She paused. "Give me twenty-four hours. Don't try to get in touch, don't text or call, don't do anything. Just let me handle this."

She was using her best class-is-in-session voice and it would be such a relief to follow her lead and let her make the decisions, the way he usually did. "I don't know. I don't like this."

She touched his arm, gave him a beseeching look. It took all his willpower not to pull her into his arms, keep her from going off tomorrow to deal with Jonathan on her own. What if she made him even angrier? What if she put herself in harm's way? What if she cost Felix everything?

"Come over tomorrow night after Cal's show," she said. "We still have some celebrating to do." She looked suddenly shy. "I mean, if you want to."

He *did* want to—but anxiety and adrenaline had overtaken him the moment she'd uttered the words, *"I'll see him dead before that happens."*

What if, for once, he took care of something for *her*? After all, he and Jonathan were staying at the same hotel tonight. He'd see Jonathan before Claire would. He kept this thought to himself and bid her good night.

Claire

ALONE ON THE couch twenty-four hours later, Claire watched TV as though from a distance, or under water. Her mind lay elsewhere, trapped.

When she'd seen Jonathan that afternoon at Ca'Del Sole, he'd agreed to lay off Cal, whom he'd admitted to provoking. (Although Claire believed his real reason for backing away from alerting the press about their fight had more to do with the fact that he'd lost the scuffle.) But in regard to everything else, he'd doubled down on his threats: She'd be homeless by the weekend, and Felix's burgeoning career would be destroyed. Claire's lawyer assured her it wasn't possible for him to kick her out of the house that easily; in a no-fault state like California, it would take six months for the divorce to be finalized, and even if infidelity on both sides could be proven, it was irrelevant. Still, he was the one who'd paid the mortgage; her name wasn't anywhere on it, and she worried all the same.

Where Felix and the prize money were concerned, she felt a white-hot rage that smoldered in her veins. The money was hers. The award was hers. He would *not* take it from her.

She'd noticed something gross and exaggerated about his behavior; it marred the surface of him, like a used Band-Aid or a sticky ice cream wrapper in the sand of an otherwise clean beach. Why was he being so petty?

She'd reminded him he hadn't *wanted* to do the trick, that *he'd* been the one to end their marriage; if he'd toughed it out a few more weeks, he'd have been crowned Magician of the Year, not Felix, and they could've gone their separate ways afterward, as was her original intention.

Then she told him she'd scheduled her own meeting with the board, in which she intended to reveal that he'd been embezzling from the club ever since being elected president three years ago. It wasn't true—probably—but it *could* have been, and it would at least buy her some time and call Jonathan's character into question, which in turn might derail his claims that Felix had stolen from him. She'd also be sure to mention how he'd been exploiting the interns for years now, using the club's reputation to secure them.

And if none of that worked, she told him, she'd use the nuclear option, full exposure—tell the board that all of Jonathan's prior placements in the competition were due to Claire, and that when she'd offered her expertise to someone else, he couldn't handle it. He had no more right to sue Felix for copyright infringement than Claire had to sue Jonathan for using her work in the past. Lawsuits among magicians were messy and made everyone look bad. They would want it covered up as much as Claire did. Jonathan might even be stripped of his presidency for such a hypocritical abuse of power, and his standing in the magic community would plummet.

Jonathan didn't believe her. He said the board wouldn't, either. He practically guffawed in her face.

"You'll choke up just speaking to them around that long table. And you expect them to believe you came up with all my routines? When you can barely spit out a sentence if people are—" Here he gave a sarcastic gasp. "—*staring* at you?"

She'd wanted to slap the triumphant look off his face. Forever. But she couldn't draw attention to their argument at a public restaurant. The only way to shut him down permanently would be—

The sound of the doorbell interrupted her train of thought. The credits on Cal's show were already rolling, and even though she'd watched the entire, hour-long special as it aired, she couldn't recall a single minute of it.

The doorbell rang again.

Oh.

Right.

I invited him.

When she opened the door, Felix stood on the porch in jeans, a T-shirt, and a baseball cap. He looked as yummy and boyish as he had the first time he came over for a lesson. The difference was, this time he seemed one hundred percent sure of himself.

In his left hand, he held the trophy for Magician of the Year. It hadn't yet been engraved with his name.

Dangling off his forefinger was a fiendishly small gold nightie.

"I'm not sure that'll fit," she said.

"You won't be wearing it for long," he replied.

"Tell me I was good, that I did everything the way you wanted," he demanded softly once they were in her bedroom. "Tell me I did everything right."

"You were good," she assured him. "You did everything right." For some reason she felt tears gathering at the edges of her eyes.

The superfluous lingerie slipped teasingly against her skin and she had to admit it felt nice; she hadn't worn anything like it in ages.

They kissed slowly, experimentally, getting reacquainted with each other. In some ways he was already familiar, though. Not because they'd kissed before, but because he was a magician. It was all so shamefully predictable of her. *Of course he'd be a magician.* For some women there was no escape. Some women were sawed into thirds, divided, and given away, never to be reunited with their former selves. Claire was no different.

The top of her body, which housed her brain, her logic, her reason, her pragmatism, and her survival instinct, had gone to Jonathan. Her midsection, where her heart lived, along with all her passionate, emotional, foolish impulses, had gone to Cal (and Brandy). At this moment, everything below the waist belonged to Felix and though he was making it worth her while, it preoccupied her that he was another magician.

But he wasn't *really* a magician. He was a baseball player.

Yes. That worked…

The fantasy created itself. She wore a thin sundress that clung to her skin and he wore his dirt-flecked uniform and he took her right there on the baseball field, which smelled of grass and sweat and testosterone. No, he took her from behind, standing up, slamming her against the chain-link fence. It shook and rattled from his thrusts, and she had to turn her face to the side and grip the unforgiving metal wires tight with her fingers so she wouldn't fall.

"What are you thinking about?" Felix asked. "Where'd you go?"

"Hmm?"

"You told me you always think about other people when you…you know…screw Jonathan…?"

"Oh, don't worry, I'm thinking about you—just…as a baseball player." She smiled sheepishly.

He frowned. "Why not think about me like I was onstage? The crowd? The rush? Isn't that a good fantasy, too?"

She tapped his lip with her fingertip. "No, that'd be like making love to myself."

"Cute," he said, in a moderately successful imitation of Claire. (Okay, an entirely successful imitation.)

She chuckled. "Brat."

"That's the worst you can come up with?" he chided her. "'Brat'?"

She grabbed two fistfuls of his T-shirt, helped him pull it off, and coasted her hands across his chiseled abs and chest. There wasn't an ounce of fat on him. Just tight skin stretched over muscles.

"Oh," she breathed appreciatively.

At his insistence, she lay back on the bed and held her arms above her head, gripping a pillow, while he paid particular attention to parts of her body she'd forgotten could be erogenous: the backs of her knees, her belly, the smattering of freckles on her shoulders, which he made a point of kissing individually. He peppered the inner part of her elbow with love bites, nibbled her earlobes, and touched every centimeter of her face—her lips, her eyelashes, chin, jaw, neckline, temple— with reverence and awe.

It didn't occur to her until then that she'd been resigned to never being touched that way again. Brandy was dead; Cal had remarried. She figured there were parts of her, figuratively and literally, that would never be revived. What a blessing to be wrong.

They made love in earnest and she felt light-headed and pleasantly dream-like. He built up his pace, clutching the sheets on either side of her, his muscles rippling, his hips and back rising and falling.

She entered a state of delirium as they surged against each other.

"Hey," he whispered. "Look at me."

She kept her eyes closed. "I can't…"

If she looked at him, she'd have to acknowledge everything that had led to this point. The dissolution of her marriage, winning the award that proved she was the best, and then having to watch while Jonathan tried to take it from her.

"Please. Open your eyes," he said.

She shook her head.

"We're in this together," he said. "Look at me. *We're in this together.*"

Slowly her dark lashes lifted and they locked eyes, green to brown.

She climaxed in a wave that flooded down her legs and straight to her toes, numbing them in ecstasy.

Despite the sweat coating both their bodies, she felt cleaner now than she had in years. Cleansed—of the past, of settling for anything less than what she'd just received.

Reborn.

Jessica

TUESDAY NIGHT AT T minus five minutes to show-
time, Jessica made microwave popcorn and opened a bottle of
sparkling grape juice. She hadn't watched live TV since junior
high, but this was a special occasion. Cal had a bag of frozen
peas pressed against the hand he'd used to punch Jonathan
Fredericksson the night before, but his free hand gripped Jessica's as they sat on the couch together, waiting for their lives
to change in real time.

Her phone lit up twelve times during the show with what
she assumed were texts from well-wishers and friends back
in Chicago, so she ignored them. During the last ad break,
she sneaked a peek, and her heart leapt into her throat. They
weren't texts after all; they were push alerts from the Hipster
Magician's YouTube channel, linking her to his latest videos.
Twelve new videos in the last forty-five minutes? What the—?

The time stamps varied. Each one had been released to correspond with the West Coast feed of the show. The instant
one of Cal's tricks aired on TV, the Hipster Magician had responded with a ready-to-go explanation.

"Oh, shit." Jessica scrolled frantically through the videos.

"What? What's wrong?" Cal leaned over to look.

Hands trembling, in a state of slow-motion futility, she
showed Cal her phone.

On TV, Cal finished up his signature illusion.

Ding, went her phone, and a new message overtook the screen. Alert! A new video is available from the Hipster Magician! The link led straight back to YouTube, where the Hipster Magician had uploaded the secrets behind the Bottle Cap trick.

"First off," he intoned in his nasal twang, "the cap is never *not* in the bottle. Which should tell you all you need to know." Of course, he then proceeded to explain the illusion in detail.

"Jesus fuck," roared Cal, eyes wild. "How many people have seen this?"

"It's okay, it'll be okay—" Jessica stammered.

"How many people?

"I—I don't know yet."

He snatched the phone out of her hand. "It says three hundred and one plus. That's not too bad."

"Uh…well…that means they've frozen the count to check for bots."

"Why would they need to check for bots?" he demanded.

"Because it's…a lot of activity."

"It's getting so many hits so inhumanly fast they think it's *robots*, is what you're telling me."

"Couple hundred thousand, maybe? It's okay—"

"How is it okay? How is it bloody okay, Jessica? It's the worst possible thing that could've happened. Do you understand that?" His accent was growing more pronounced the angrier he became.

In his haste to move away from the couch, he dropped the bag of peas and spilled the sparkling grape juice bottle onto the area rug. "Oh, that's just great."

"I'll clean it up."

He shook his hands out, flinging more sticky droplets everywhere. "You know, I'm not a child, I don't need to drink *grape juice* and pretend it's champagne."

Her eyes welled up. "I'm sorry."

He headed for the door.

She followed him. "Where are you going?"

"Out. I don't know."

She grabbed the car keys. "I want to come with you."

"Well, *I* want to be alone," he snapped.

"When will you be back?"

"I don't know, Jessica," he said with exasperation. "I have to get out of here."

"You're scaring me," she said quietly.

He stood still. "I'm sorry. I don't mean to take it out on you. I just need to be alone for a while, someplace where I don't have to keep saying I'm sorry. I'm rotten company right now and it's nothing to do with you." He grasped her face with both hands, gave her a swift kiss, and headed out into the night.

Her mind raced.

She didn't know the city well enough—she didn't know *him* well enough—to hazard a guess as to where he'd go.

She had an overwhelming urge to call Claire and ask for advice, where she thought Cal might be headed. But before she finished dialing, a second thought hit her like a slap to the face.

The only way the Hipster Magician could have uploaded his pre-recorded rebuttals so perfectly in time with the live airing of Cal's show was if he'd known beforehand which tricks Cal would be doing. He hadn't revealed every single one—only the ones from the teaser montage they'd shown the night before at the club. Which meant the Hipster Magician had been a guest at the party.

He was someone they knew. Someone they trusted.

Her eyes filled with tears and she sank to the floor.

Claire

LESS THAN AN hour post-lovemaking, the past came knocking at Claire's door.

Banging, really.

Pounding.

"Are you kidding me?" she muttered.

"Want me to see who it is?" Felix asked.

"No, I'll be right back."

Slick and raw from their coupling, she stood on wobbly legs and pulled on a bra, her Liz Phair EXILE IN GUYVILLE shirt, and her frayed jean shorts from the closet, the ones with the British flag on the back pockets.

From the corner of her eye, she saw Felix pluck the gold nightie off the floor and place it over his face like a washcloth.

"No having fun with that until I get back," she said.

He gave her a thumbs-up from under the silky tent, and she walked down the hall to the foyer.

She turned on the porch lights, but that hardly helped; one of them was broken. Maybe Felix could fix it for her tomorrow.

She opened the door. In the dim light, Cal was disoriented and disheveled. It was a sight she knew well, and it filled her with a combination of dread, excitement, and anger. (Of course, unlike in the old days, he didn't wear track pants and a ratty T-shirt when he fell off the wagon. Present-day Cal wore a tailored button-down and Helmut Lang trousers to do it in.)

"Do you know how late it is? Why are you here?" she asked.

"I did something terrible." He reeked of gin. "You have to help me."

"Get in here." She looked behind him into the darkness and opened the door wider.

He plunged inside the house, arms flailing. "I'm going to lose her. I'm going to lose everything. Please, Claire, you have to help me."

She regarded him calmly. "Why should I?"

He seemed gobsmacked by her denial of him. Of course he did; it was a first. He grabbed her wrist. "Are you still mad about the video? That wasn't my fault."

She yanked her wrist free and he stumbled backward from the unexpected force of her action.

"No, you prick, it's not about the video." It was the first time they'd been alone together in three years. She followed him to the kitchen, backed him up against the island, shoving him, pushing him, unleashing the tumult of emotions she hadn't realized she'd been suppressing. "You were supposed to come back for me. Three years ago you left me. You *left* me. When she died, I was alone. And I'm still alone. You prick."

He stood there, arms limp at his sides, and took it. He was contrite, baleful, wet-nosed. He knew he'd been bad. He was a puppy returning to its master. Only Claire had never been his master. Their master was gone. Maybe that's why it had taken him so long to come home to LA, come home to her, and why he'd needed a new wife to do it. They didn't know who they were to each other without Brandy. They were scared to find out.

When she'd exhausted herself berating him, he clasped his hands together prayerfully. "I'm sorry. I'm sorry. Please,

Claire, I'll do anything. But you have to help me. I can't go home like this. I can't let her see me this way."

"Okay," she relented, mostly to keep him quiet. "You can stay in the guest room. I'll call Jessica, make something up, tell her you're tired and you'll see her first thing in the morning. We'll get everything sorted then."

This sent Cal into a fresh torrent of tears and hair rending. "She can't know I've been drinking. Her mother is a drunk. And I love her. I want to be with her forever. I want to be like that skeleton couple they found who were holding hands for fifteen hundred years while they decayed. The Romanian couple."

"Where have I heard that before?" she muttered.

"This time I mean it."

"You always do."

He looked desperate and sweaty. "Claire, I'm sorry. Forgive me? Forgive me."

"Stop, okay? Stop."

He was on his knees now, hugging her tightly around the waist, pressing his face into her groin, her hips. "Claire. Claire. My Claire."

It was at once nostalgic and infuriating, and sent her into a tailspin of sense memories and misplaced arousal—she could still feel Felix inside her, hard as an iron bar dipped in velvet. She shifted her legs and tugged at Cal's hair, trying to extricate him. "Get ahold of yourself. I said I'll help you. But I want you to know I'm doing this for Jessica, not you. I like her more than you right now. She deserves better than this."

"I know she does."

Of all people, it was Jonathan's words that came to her then; how Jessica was barely older than Eden. She felt an overwhelming urge to protect Jessica, to cover up whatever might need covering up until Cal got his act together again. Everyone in AA backslid at some point; now it was Cal's turn. She had no idea why he'd chosen tonight of all nights to go on a bender—shouldn't he have been enjoying the show? Living it up in fame and glory? But she didn't have the energy or inclination to get into it. He was incoherent now anyway.

As if to emphasize her low opinion of him right then, he actually *grabbed her leg* and looked up at her, accusatory. "You have someone over. There's a car outside. Who is he?"

"None of your business," she snapped.

After she forced him to drink some water, ushered him to the guest room, and called Jessica, she returned to Felix in the master, who asked her the same thing.

"Who were you talking to? Who's out there?"

"No one," she said warily. "No one at all."

Felix

THE SECOND TIME they had sex there was no gazing into each other's eyes, no mutual effort to ride the crest together. Claire was aggressive, almost frustrated, as though she were trying to pull a response from him that he couldn't give her, because he didn't know what it was.

Not that it stopped him from attempting a third round before breakfast, which he hoped would be the same pancakes she'd made him the morning he signed the application for Magician of the Year.

Claire was cuddled up under his arm, half asleep. He pointed to the tented sheet over his junk and said, "Hey look, instant reset." (An instant reset was any trick in magic that could be performed again right away. He thought it was pretty clever.)

She had just enough time to indulge him with a smile when a distant voice sounded outside the front door, accompanied by a series of knocks.

"Police. Answer the door, please."

They both jumped.

"Claire, you might want to get out here," urged a tense, British-accented voice.

"Is that Cal?" Felix said. He was up off the bed in half a second, frantically searching for his clothes.

Claire was slower to rise. "Yes, he crashed here last night. Let me see what's going on. Stay here."

He didn't need to be told twice. He was already choosing which window would work best as an escape. She pulled on the same clothes she'd worn to answer the door a few hours prior. Felix swiftly stuffed himself inside his boxers and jeans and stood on the other side of the door, hidden from view, as she opened it, stepped out, and closed it behind her.

Low, muffled voices, both male, filled the air. The calm, regimented sounds were indecipherable for a long stretch, stacked on top of one another, and then wrenched apart by a high-pitched wail.

"No, no, no, no..."

It was Claire, stuck on a loop of repetition. Felix's throat swelled and before he could think better of it, he opened the bedroom door, just a crack, using Claire's hysteria as cover for the sound of the knob.

She was on the ground, boneless.

One of the police officers crouched beside her. "We're going to need you to come down to the station to identify the body and answer a few questions. Do you have someone you want to call?"

"No," she said again, this time almost a whisper.

Horrified, Felix backed away from the door and nearly stumbled over his shoes.

While he laced them up, Calum Clarke was Mirandized and arrested for the murder of Jonathan Fredericksson.

As he ran along the reservoir, feet kicking up dirt from the pedestrian path, concealed by the other, normal, good people who were out for their morning jogs, Felix had one thought: *They weren't supposed to hurt him.*

Jessica

THE FIRST PHONE call was bad enough.

According to Claire, Cal was spending the night in her guest room. She was vague about the details, just said there was nothing to worry about, Cal was safe, he loved Jessica very much, and he would explain everything to her in the morning.

Jessica felt like she'd been socked in the stomach. Either he'd gone to Claire's straightaway, looking for solace after his show was exposed, or he'd ended *up* there after some kind of binge. Had he gotten drunk? Tried to buy drugs? Hooked up with someone?

And why couldn't he find solace in me?

The second phone call, eight sleepless hours later, was worse.

This time it was Cal, calling from the police station.

Jonathan's body had been found in a hotel room at the Chateau Marmont. He'd apparently been living there the past six weeks, separated from Claire. He wore a mask over his eyes and skinny jeans that didn't really fit, just like the ones worn by the Hipster Magician. On the table in front of him was an empty bottle of beer.

He'd been poisoned.

The police's theory was that Cal must have figured out

Jonathan was the Hipster Magician and gone after him for exposing his show the night it aired. The guest log in the hotel's lobby held Cal's signature, and the empty bottle of beer in Jonathan's room had Cal's fingerprints on it.

The part that baffled investigators: The glass beer bottle contained its own bottle cap inside, and no one could figure out how to extract it. This was of course Cal's signature trick, which the Hipster Magician had taken such delight in ruining.

The final kicker was that an entire roomful of people had witnessed Cal attack Jonathan the night before.

Motive, method, means.

He had no alibi during the hour of death. He told the police over and over that he hadn't gone near Jonathan, didn't know he was living at that hotel, and had no idea he was the online prankster who'd tanked his show. He explained that he'd walked to the Liquor Cabinet on Sunset, where he paid in cash, no receipt. He'd wandered aimlessly, drinking gin out of a paper bag until he rode the bus to Silver Lake.

The Cabinet's security camera was strictly for show, so there was no video confirmation to back up Cal's story. He'd already hired counsel, and Jessica should expect a visit from the police sometime that morning.

"What should I tell them? Should I say you were with me all night? That you didn't leave once, not even for a second? I'll say anything you tell me to say—" She gripped the phone so tightly her entire arm shook.

"No, tell the truth—they already know I went to Claire's, that's where they picked me up this morning."

"I love you. We'll get through this," she said, though she had no clue how.

His arraignment was set for Friday, two days away.

News outlets tried to outdo one another's headlines.

Variety: "Cursed Conjurer Accused of Calamitous Crime"

LA Times: "Magic, Mayhem, and Murder at the Marmont"

LA Weekly: "TV Wizard Calum Clarke Can't Make These Murder Charges Disappear"

Facedown on the floor of the living room, crying into her arms, Jessica heard her phone chime. She crawled slowly toward it, sore-muscled and dizzy. The alert said a new video from the Hipster Magician was up.

But how could that be, if Jonathan was supposed to be him?

She rubbed her damp face, took a deep breath, and tapped the link.

A young man wearing an eye mask, T-shirt, skinny jeans, and bright kicks stood alone in a stark white room. "Rumors of our demise have been greatly exaggerated," he said. "For we are legion."

In a blink, the original guy was surrounded by twenty other Hipster Magicians, all male, of differing ages, shapes, and sizes, in the white room. All wore the same outfit. The camera swooped and swirled around them before rising above them and shooting straight down.

"However," said one, looking up at the camera,

"Jonathan," said another,

"Fredericksson," said another,

"Is not," said another,

"And was not," said another,

"One of us."

The effect was eerie, like they were part of a hive.

Reset camera, back to the main guy, solo again: "Our sincere condolences to Mrs. Fredericksson and the members of Club Deception. We regret your loss. Out of respect we will be taking a month off from posting new videos. Be good to each other."

Blackout.

Jessica's pulse raced. This would change everything for Cal's case, wouldn't it? It had to! She emailed the video to Cal's lawyer.

The lawyer responded within five minutes. Thanks for the tip but unfortunately it doesn't matter whether or not the victim was the Hipster Magician. It only matters if prosecution can prove Cal **believed** he was, and that he acted on that belief. Why else would Jonathan Fredericksson be dressed in that outfit?

TO FRAME HIM, Jessica wrote back in all caps before she threw her phone against the wall, cracking the screen straight down the middle.

Claire

"MRS. FREDERICKSSON, I THINK you're in shock," Lieutenant Douglas said. He was tall, with thick, slightly graying hair, and a wide nose and wide stance. "It's understandable. Can I get you anything? Coffee, water, cigarette? Of course, we'd have to go outside for that."

She desperately wanted a cigarette but she'd promised Eden (again) that she would quit. It was the least she could do for her now. The very, absolute least.

She shook her head. "No, better not."

"You sure?"

She ran a tired hand through her messy blond hair. "Let's just get this over with."

They went back and forth for a little while until she told him to find the other magician, the one who hated Jonathan. Find that man, and in that way he would find the killer.

Killer.

But that wasn't the right word, it couldn't be.

Wasn't it only yesterday she'd seen him? Nothing could change that fast since *yesterday*.

But now he was...

Her brain shut down that line of thought. Everything was fine. None of this was real, none of this was happening. Everything was fine. Everything was okay.

"A lot of magicians—the good ones, anyway—lead a double life," she told the lieutenant. "On the other hand…he might make us float. He might make us fly."

"Is that why you married Jonathan?" he asked.

"No. I wanted to disappear. And that was the only way I knew how."

During the ride to Robbery/Homicide (as though the two were comparable; as though the two could be slashed in half as equals) she'd sat next to Cal, who was handcuffed. Not for long, of course. She'd prepared for that. When she entered the opposite side of the sedan, she leaned her head down toward him and he pulled a bobby pin from her hair. Immediately the arresting officer barked at her to sit up properly and put on her seat belt. Cal used the bobby pin to undo his handcuffs.

It wasn't a dramatic prelude to a daring escape and life on the run. He just wanted to hold hands with Claire. They reached for each other in unison. When he gripped her hand with his, it was as if a crank turned, cords pulled tight throughout her body and locked into place, tethering her to the world.

She remembered the first words he'd ever spoken to her, twenty years ago, at the library in Cambridge: "Would you like to see a magic trick?"

She'd fallen in love with magic that day, and with him, too, though not in a conventional sense…Perhaps she should have kept his existence to herself, but she'd told Brandy about him, and Brandy had demanded an introduction. Suddenly all Claire could do was watch from the sidelines as they intertwined into a co-dependent mess.

If she'd never met Cal, or if she'd somehow met Jonathan first, would magic have captured her attention in the same way? Was the message more important than the messenger?

"I swear I didn't do this," he murmured out of the corner of his mouth.

"I know you didn't."

She thought now of the night she'd met Jessica. How she'd told her that *WAGs* stood for "widows and girlfriends." She'd meant it as a joke, but what if the act of saying it out loud had worked as an incantation, a spell? After all, a woman with a deck of cards was essentially a witch. A tarot reader.

Was she a witch? A danger to the townsfolk, cackling into her cauldron, something to be burned alive or drowned?

Was that the real reason so few women pursued or felt any interest in magic? Men performing magic were untrustworthy, but women doubly so, simply because they were women.

Making potions.

Making poisons.

"Tell me about Felix Vicario," said the lieutenant.

"Hmm?"

"The car parked outside your house is registered to one Felix Vicario. Seems you had quite a few male callers last night."

"Two hardly constitutes 'quite a few.' Cal's a friend, and Felix is…also a friend."

He gave her bed-head hair a once-over that suggested he didn't believe her. "Where is he?"

"I don't know."

"But you admit he…spent the night? Were you lovers?"

"Sure." *Barely one night, but sure.*

"Some of the guys are working on an alternative theory. Me, I don't buy it, I think Cal's the one, through and through, but…some of the other guys have a theory and it goes like this: You got your lover boy to do the dirty work for you. Or maybe you didn't know about it, but he did it for you, thinking now you can be together, the lawsuit goes away, you keep the money from the stolen magic show."

"It wasn't stolen," she gritted out.

"What was that?"

"Nothing."

"So tell me. Did Felix have something to do with this?"

"He's not smart enough."

Lieutenant Douglas raised his eyebrows.

"Felix is pulchritudinous and sweet but not much else," she said.

Pulchritudinous was one of her favorite words with which to test people. Did the lieutenant think it was an insult or a compliment? It *sounded* like an insult, but of course it meant physically attractive.

She didn't actually know if Felix was sweet in general, but he was sweet to *her*. She craved his sweetness like a cloak she could wrap around herself. He would save her, protect her from whatever was going on right now. She wanted to return to last night, bury her face in his hard, warm belly. He wasn't *El Gato*, a cute tabby—he was a jungle cat, and she *liked* his simpleness, his *suppleness*. His lack of ulterior motives.

"Could Felix have tipped Cal off, had a hand in it, or conspired to do something on your behalf?"

She snapped out of her daydream. "I really don't think so. You know, I like the other definition of *smart* better. 'To be painful.' I think to be smart sometimes is to be painful," she said.

He shot her a confused look. "Well, speaking of painful, can I ask...why are you wearing these shoes? Why not sneakers? Flip-flops? Officer Cleary told me you insisted. Those must have taken five minutes apiece to lace up, and they look uncomfortable."

"Jonathan hates it when I wear shoes that make me taller than him," she said.

And if I do something he hates, that means he's still around to hate it, otherwise I wouldn't be doing it. It made perfect sense. She would wear the shoes every day from now on if she had to. "He wishes I weren't so tall," she added.

The lieutenant's voice was soft but emphatic. "I think we're done for today, Mrs. Fredericksson. Stay close to your phone. Are you planning on doing any traveling? Because if so, you'll need to cancel those plans."

Outside the station—it was already afternoon; how long had she been in there?—she pulled out her phone and dialed Felix.

"Are you okay? It's me. Where are you? Why'd you run out?"

He acted like she was nuts. "*Everyone* knows you gotta book ass when the cops show up."

"Well, now they think you had something to do with this."

"Shit, shit, shit."

"What's wrong? They're not right, are they?"

"Uh..."

Her eyes widened. "Felix?"

"So I kind of...asked my roommates to do something for me. As a precaution."

"What did you ask them?"

"I told them where he's been staying, what room number at

the Marmont—I knew I'd be with you last night, see, like an alibi, and—"

"How'd you know his room number?"

"I told the concierge we were supposed to session and I'd forgotten the number. I figured that's probably been happening a lot the last month, magicians going to hang out in his room and work on stuff, and that she'd be used to it."

Claire was weirdly impressed.

"So then I asked them—my roommates—to put on masks, grab a baseball bat, whatever, and go over there and screw with his head a little. Tell him to back off from us."

"You *what*?"

"They weren't going to jack him up, just scare him. And anyway they didn't do it. Look, I'm home right now and they just told me they didn't do any of it. They got stoned and watched *Stranger Things*. Unreliable motherfu—"

"This is good. You're in the clear. But you have to come in, right now, and tell them all this."

"If I come in, I might never come out! You don't get it, you're rich, you're white…"

"Please, offer yourself up for questioning. Make it easier on everyone. You have to help yourself here, Felix, I'm begging you."

"Okay, I'll do it," he said quietly, reluctantly.

She walked back inside the police building and looked around for Lieutenant Douglas. She felt like she was hovering outside her body, watching herself go through the motions. It was not unlike stage fright.

When she found him at the coffee machine, she told him she was picking up Eden at LAX that evening and that someone could accompany her if they wanted; if they were worried she was a flight risk. In fact, she'd *like* someone to accompany her. She wasn't sure she could drive. Would that be possible? A police escort? She could even pay them...

The truth was, she was terrified of being alone with Eden.

Jessica

AT HOME AFTER THE bail hearing, Jessica succumbed to another bout of stomach-heaving sobs. She'd kept it together at the courthouse because she wanted Cal to see her being strong for him, but when she emerged alone from the building, TV news reporters and their camera crews chased her to her car.

TMZ was the first to post: "Poof Goes the Bail! Killer Magician Denied Bond."

Standard bail in murder cases was one million dollars. She'd hoped to put the boat and loft up as collateral, or use her share of the Erdnase money to bring him home before the trial, but the judge believed the evidence against Cal was too strong. On the drive back she'd had to pull over twice in case she was sick. What if Cal *never* came home? What if the night his show aired was the last night they ever spent together? *Our last moments as a couple, and we argued.*

She scrubbed lightly at her face and took a long drink of water. Then she called Kaimi and Landon. Both of their cell phones went immediately to voicemail.

She called Cal's producer and asked him to email her the raw footage of Cal's show. She regretted invading his privacy by viewing the videotape of Cal and Brandy, but this was different. This was life and death.

The man was reluctant to send them over. "What do you need them for?"

"He performed the Bottle Cap routine all over the country, and I was thinking, *That's how someone could get their hands on a bottle with his fingerprints*, because he lets the volunteers keep the bottle as a souvenir. Right? If I watch them all maybe I'll recognize someone, or the police will."

It was the eighteenth version of the trick that did it.

Claire

THE SECOND TIME Lieutenant Douglas brought Claire in for questioning, she glimpsed Landon the Libertine and his girlfriend being escorted into a separate room. What did *they* have to do with anything?

This time, Douglas was less prone to tangents. Less curious about Claire's life with Jonathan and whether she was privy to his magic secrets. He had a partner with him, a younger man with a smattering of acne on his cheeks and neck. Had he been brought in to provide a counterpoint to Douglas's questioning? She couldn't imagine the younger cop intimidating anyone.

The room, though: *That* was intimidating. Sparse, uncomfortably small, and blindingly white, with a single fluorescent rectangle on the ceiling and a black camera mounted in the upper right corner, Claire felt herself shrinking down into nothing. She had nowhere to hide, nowhere to look, nothing else to focus on. She'd read somewhere that LAPD interrogation rooms employed the same proportions as the confessional at the Santa Barbara Mission. Both projected the same effect:

Confess.

Confess.

"You've been holding out on us," Douglas said. "Turns out you were the last person to see him alive."

"We spoke that day," she conceded. "At Ca'Del Sole, I'm sure they have a record of it…"

Her mind wandered. She didn't even hear the words she was saying. They were drowned out by another voice.

I don't understand, Mom. Why was he at a hotel? Why wasn't he at home?

Because… well, because he…

Why was he at a hotel? They said he was there for weeks, Mom. Why was he at a hotel?

Well… It's just that… there are things that…

Mom. Mom! Why wasn't he at home? Why wasn't he at home, safe, with you?

The baby-faced cop chimed in, startling Claire out of her painful recollection. "Your boy Felix had a lot to say. How it wasn't fair that Jonathan was going after you, because you were the one who came up with Jonathan's act. That you've come up with a lot of his material over the years."

She sat ramrod-straight in her chair. Didn't blink. Didn't move.

The original lieutenant, Douglas, took over. "Do you know what I think?" He inched closer to her. "I think *you're* the magician. The one who hates him. Isn't that what you told me? That if we found that person, we'd find our killer."

Before she realized they were forming, tears dripped down her cheeks, and she took several rapid, gulping breaths.

The younger cop seemed alarmed. He looked to Douglas for his cue on how to react.

Douglas placed a light hand on her shoulder. "Is there something you want to tell me, Claire? Mrs. Fredericksson. Do you have something to say?"

No matter how fast she wiped at her face, the tears replenished. She cried, hard, for a straight minute, until she felt emptied out. Until she felt certain she couldn't produce a single tear more.

"No one's eh-ever…called me a magician before," she said, and it turned out more tears weren't just possible, they were necessary.

She leaned over onto the table and buried her face in her arms.

No one moved for a while. Eventually the door opened. Still facedown, she heard a third person enter the room, followed by hushed voices—"Are you sure?" / "Yeah, it's over. Let this poor woman go home."

Then a voice close to her and more distinct: "Mrs. Fredericksson, you're free to go. And please accept our sincere condolences on your loss."

Claire straightened up from the table. Her sleeves were damp, sticky, wrinkled. Her face ached.

"Why?" she asked softly. "What's happened? What's going on?"

"Captain's holding a press conference in an hour," said Lieutenant Douglas. He held his hand out for her to grasp. "I'll walk you out."

Dazed, sleep-deprived, and battling a headache, Claire swayed on her feet as Douglas guided her down the hallway. They didn't make it around the corner before a bloodcurdling scream erupted in Claire's ear.

"You! You *witch*!"

Confused and discombobulated, Claire watched in slow motion as her husband's mistress struggled against her captors, thrashing wildly toward Claire, reaching out with blood-red nails as through trying to slash the air between them and propel herself closer.

Douglas thrust Claire behind him and his younger partner covered her from the side until Becca was subdued.

"You don't know who I am, do you?" Becca cried out, slower, sounding sad instead of angry now. "You don't even know who I am."

Jessica

THAT EVENING, JESSICA watched the press release live on the local news and read the report online six or seven times because she couldn't quite believe her nightmare was over.

Having recognized a man from Cal's footage, Jessica had picked up her cracked cell phone and frantically called Club Deception.

"Veronique speaking. Password, please."

"Veronique, it's Jessica Clarke, listen, I need—"

"Oh damn, Jessica. How are you holding up?"

"I need the name of a member, he's a…" *What had Claire called him? An amateur? A probationary something?* "He's not a full member, I think he still needs to pass the test, but he's older, real skinny, and he, like, skulks around, does card tricks…"

"That describes a *lot* of—Oh wait, you said he's not a member yet? There are only three provisional members right now."

Jessica closed her eyes and bit her cheek. "Provisional, right. Who are they? *Please*, I need their names."

"Normally I wouldn't do this—but since it's you, Cupcake Girl…let me see…Richard Moore, Toby Joyce, and Leon Krause. With a K."

"Thanks, you're a lifesaver."

Fingers tripping over one another at her keyboard, Jessica opened three browser screens for three separate image searches and typed in the names.

"Leon," she whispered.

It was the skinny, grudge-holding man she'd dubbed Ichabod.

In the unused footage from Cal's show, Ichabod had sat next to Cal while Cal performed his Bottle Cap trick for seven or eight audience members. He'd held out a napkin and asked for Cal's autograph, which explained how he'd perfectly forged it at the Marmont's guest log. Although he wasn't the one who'd helped with the trick, he managed to walk offscreen with the bottle—holding it at an odd angle with the signed napkin so as not to muddy Cal's fingerprints.

She called it in to the station and prayed for the first time in years. *Let it be enough. Please let it be enough.*

In the news clip, Leon was seen from behind, wearing handcuffs and keeping his head down as he passed through a barricade of reporters and camera crews.

The anchor intoned: "His motive is currently unknown but police have in custody a second, unnamed suspect, whom they will also be questioning at length."

Jessica puffed up with pride at the next voice-over: "A tip from original suspect Calum Clarke's wife—we're told they're newlyweds—led to the warrant necessary to search Mr. Krause's apartment, where police discovered the original clothing worn by the murder victim."

Cut to a slick-looking reporter outside the police station, struggling to be heard above the din of competing TV news crews. "According to his website, Leon Krause was a talent manager whose lead client, Rebecca Winstrom, recently performed in murder victim Jonathan Fredericksson's magic show as a woman who gets cut in half. Becca, as she's known to family and friends, was apparently following in the family footsteps. As Channel Four has exclusively learned, Becca's mother was *also* a magician's assistant, way back in the summer of 2004, when Becca was nine."

An old photo of Becca's mother filled the TV screen, then shrank to half size to make room for Becca's professional headshot. Seen side by side like that, they almost looked like twins. Jessica's feeling of déjà vu at the Magician of the Year contest made sense now. She had seen both of them onstage doing a similar illusion, albeit many years apart—she'd seen the mother in Jonathan's show in Chicago as a girl.

The first few days after Cal's return, Jessica worried incessantly. Part of it was leftover anxiety from his time in lockup, and part of it was a delayed response to his actions on the night of the murder. He'd fallen off the wagon, hard, which was of course the only way *to* fall. To her relief, Cal started going to AA meetings every day—sometimes twice a day—which was something Jessica's mother had never even attempted.

The night he came home, they kissed in a mutual tempest of emotion.

"You saved my life," he murmured. "You beautiful, brilliant woman."

He lifted her and she wrapped her legs around his waist so he could carry her to the bedroom. He set her down on the silk sheets and reached over her to open the bedside drawer.

She didn't have to look to know what was inside.

Her pulse quickened deliciously but she pushed him away. "My turn," she said.

"Oh?"

She took the rope from him. "Wrists above your head."

He looked surprised, but game. "Okay."

The rope was soft but thick. She was afraid of hurting him, so he walked her through the knot-tying process. When she was finished, Cal remained fully clothed in his dress shirt and slacks, his wrists tied to the bedposts above his head, with his legs spread open across the mattress, ankles secured at either end.

She hovered over him, and he strained upward so that he could brush his lips against hers. But at the last second, she moved away, and he let out a noise of frustration. The ropes held tight, preventing him from pursuing.

"This, right here, how you can't touch me, is how I felt around you for a long time," she said quietly. "Like you were just out of reach, like I was only getting *some* of you instead of everything. I had to learn about you from other people. I wanted to be close to you so badly, but you wouldn't let me."

To further make her point, she sat down in a chair across the room.

He looked straight at her, eyes full of guilt. "I didn't mean for you to feel that way."

"I know you didn't. That's why I'm telling you. That's why I want it to stop."

"Can you come back, please? Just be close to me."

She hesitated and he gave her a sad smile.

"I won't distract you," he promised. "I can't touch you at all, remember? You're in complete control."

She strode back to the bed and turned off the bedside lamp so they were shielded, at least, by darkness. The conversation wasn't going to be easy, but it was necessary. She laid her head on his chest and he sighed with contentment.

"Why did you marry me so fast?" she asked.

"You first."

"Because you were my dream guy. And I knew if I didn't lock you down, it would never come around for me again. Plus, have you *seen* you? And that accent—come on. You've got to know how sexy it is."

"Oh, this? I keep it around strictly for seduction purposes. 'Howdy, Pard-ner,'" he drawled. "That's my real voice. I'm a red-blooded American."

"Shut up, we're not all from Texas."

"It'd be fun if you were, though. All that big hair."

"I'm trying to be serious."

"Okay. Here's the truth. The day I met you, I couldn't take my eyes off you, because even though you got the biggest tips, you didn't keep them. You organized a pool."

She shrugged off his awe. "We all work harder when everyone's paid equally."

"If *I and everyone I know* had gotten the biggest tips, we'd have kept them for ourselves," he remarked. "You took the blame for a broken glass so the new hire wouldn't get sacked. You were the reason people loved coming back to the bar; you chatted and laughed with every customer, made them feel welcome. You were everything I wish my friends and I were like. Everything I hoped for in another person. And I knew if I left town and went on with my tour as though I hadn't met you, if I left without at least *trying* to be with you, I'd regret it forever."

She wrapped her arms around him and rested her face on his chest, feeling bashful. "Okay."

"I like myself, now. With you. I didn't before."

"I like you, too."

"Mmm, I had noticed that." He nuzzled the back of her neck and gave her a tender kiss, all of it misdirection for the sneak-attack tickle against her ribs.

Her eyes widened. "You jerk."

"What? Oh. Right."

"Your hands have been free this whole time?"

"Well, yes, what kind of magician would I be if I couldn't get out of a simple sailor knot? What kind of sailor, for that matter?"

"But the whole point was that you couldn't touch me," she cried.

"And I *couldn't*. Because you didn't want me to."

"But you could've stopped me at any time. You could've grabbed me and held me down."

"I would *never* grab you and hold you down. I love you."

She licked her lips, tasting the slight saltiness of her tears. His gaze was steady and she held it for a charged beat. "What if I *want* you to hold me down?"

"Then all you have to do is ask."

"Cal," she said, twining her fingers roughly through his thick, dark hair, "hold me down."

He gripped her wrists in his strong hands and flipped her over so she was flat on her stomach, facedown, divesting her of her clothes at the same time. She wiggled her butt at him and he pounced, gripping her hips firmly so he could slide home.

She gasped and he kissed her neck at the spot where it met her shoulder, right where she most loved it, and whispered in her ear.

"The French call orgasms *le petit mort*," he murmured. "It means 'little death.'"

"I'm dying," she wailed, a minute later, breathing frantic lungfuls of air, "I'm dying…"

"You're living," he corrected forcefully, slamming so hard that her body slid forward and her face dangled over the foot of the bed. Still he didn't stop.

Two weeks after his release, Jessica threw a dinner party. She'd been eager to introduce Cal to Landon, and to spend more time with Kaimi, whom she'd come to consider one of her closest friends. She invited Claire and Felix over as well, though Claire had been noncommittal about their presence. Jessica didn't even know if they were still seeing each other.

Landon was the first to arrive. "Heyyyy, sis," he said. "I love saying that."

"Me too," she squealed. "Cal, look who's here."

Cal and Landon shook hands. "Thanks for coming tonight, it means a lot to us." Cal clapped him on the back for good measure.

"Hey," Jessica added, "when I talk about you, can I call you my—"

"Nope," Landon interrupted.

"My brother from—"

"Nope."

"Come on. 'My brother from another mother'?"

"No," Landon said sternly. Then he grinned. "Okay, fine."

She clapped her hands and did a little dance.

Let the party begin.

Felix

THE NIGHT OF Jessica's party, Felix pulled up to Claire's house on Edgecliffe, his future still hanging in the balance.

In deference to her tragedy, the board members of Club Deception had put off voting on Jonathan's accusation that Felix had stolen his act, with Claire facilitating the theft. But now they'd set a meeting for Tuesday. His entire future was at stake, and he had no idea what Claire thought about it. They didn't talk much anymore, didn't go out.

When they first met, he'd wanted to fuck the sadness out of her. But now that they were actually fucking, she seemed sadder than ever.

A few days ago she'd insisted they do it at his house in Glendale, surrounded by junk food and dirty dishes and laundry. She wanted to rub her own nose in the mess she'd made. They'd been having sex when Jonathan was killed, so her punishment to herself was to keep having sex with him. That's how it felt, anyway.

Cut her some slack. Her husband was murdered, her daughter's pissed at her, she might not have a place to live soon...Of course she's sad.

Standing on her empty porch now, he remembered their first conversation. How she'd leaned against the doorway, cool as hell, drinking wine and pointing out his mistakes. Within an hour of talking to her and seeing what a genius she was at magic, he'd become infatuated.

Today she looked run-down and threadbare in a loose, knitted shift dress, wet, tangled hair pulled into a ponytail, eyeliner thick and wobbly. She was no longer precise.

He knew the rift with her daughter was flaying her alive. Eden blamed Claire for Jonathan's death. She had it in her head that Claire had kicked him out, and that if he'd been happily living at home rather than banished to a hotel he'd still be alive. She'd hightailed it back to Rice University and wouldn't be returning until her dad's memorial next month, where she planned to perform the ceremonial breaking of Jonathan's magic wand, because "Claire couldn't very well do it in good conscience, could she?" (Eden's words.)

So when she invited him to dinner at the Clarkes' it was a pleasant surprise. Even though she asked him to bring her a joint for the drive. Claire smoked two-thirds of it on the way over.

"This is a lot stronger than I remember it being fifteen years ago," she said. "Wooooo."

"Maybe you should take it easy," he replied.

She coughed and motioned for him to turn left, and to park in the underground lot, so they pulled up behind Cal's BMW in the tandem spot. When Felix pointed out that she'd hogged all the weed, she inverted the joint so the lit end sat inside her mouth. He rolled up the car windows and she shotgunned the rest of the smoke toward his mouth. After that they were still early for the party, so they did it in the front seat. She straddled him in the driver's seat and it happened so fast—jeans unzipped, dress hiked, angle adjusted, bounce-bounce-bounce—his head spun and "God!" He slumped against her. "Why are you even doing this?"

She flexed and rotated her neck. "I need to eat, and I assume you need to eat..."

"Not the dinner party. *This.*"

"Because…" She extracted herself from his lap and sat on her side again and wiped herself clean with a Carl's Jr. napkin, which seemed the most wrong of the things they'd just done. "I feel something with you and I want to keep feeling it," she said at last.

A seed of hope grew and flourished in his chest. "What's that?"

"As though I might actually be here. And that someday, I may even want to be."

It was a start at least, and she kissed him and brought his hand to the right spot to finish her off, and then they got out of the car, looking sloppy and half stoned, which was what they both were.

"Do my eyes look red?" she wondered.

"Yeah, sort of."

"Oh well, they'll just think I've been crying."

He was a little taken aback. "Haven't you been?"

She shrugged and that probably upset him the most. He had never known Claire to be anything less than certain about, well, everything.

***

While the other guests mingled, Felix took his time looking at the magic posters on the wall and admiring the view from the windows. He'd love to live in a place like this, right on Sunset Boulevard. It all depended on the damn board review.

Across the room, Calum wrapped an arm around Claire and she sagged against him, letting him comfort her. They melded together, a merging of dark and light.

Felix pushed down a spark of jealousy. He'd been inside her not ten minutes ago, but you'd never know it by looking at her.

She remained unknowable, fathomless as the ocean. It seemed fitting that he still couldn't say if her eyes were blue or green. Either way they signified a storm coming.

Jessica wore some kind of cute tweed dress that swished when she walked toward Claire.

"I never really told you how sorry I was," she offered. "How sorry I *am*. I only met him the one time…"

"How lucky for you, then."

Cal looked enchanted by every word his wife uttered. They seemed so happy and so in love that Felix felt weird watching them kiss, so he looked away. Claire didn't suffer from the same problem; she watched them like a hawk.

Once everyone sat down and began eating, Kaimi's phone buzzed repeatedly.

"Sorry, everyone, it's this guy Nigel from Magic Crossroads. He wants the Erdnase papers, but he's trying to screw me on the price."

"What's Magic Crossroads?" Jessica asked.

"The Blighty version of Club Deception," Cal explained. "They think we're a bunch of wankers, and we think the same of them."

"They're both right," Claire chirped, high as a kite.

"I'm a proud member of both," Cal added with a grin.

Claire clapped her hands together and everyone looked over. "Kaimi, tell Nigel that Cal is making his copy of the Erdnase papers available to every member of our club for a fee. His own members will be furious when they find out he had the chance to buy them as well but opted not to. Tell him to charge a thousand dollars each and he'll make back his investment in a month."

Kaimi beamed at Claire. "Perfect." She tapped away at her phone and grinned at the response she got. "We're in business."

After their excitement died down, Landon turned to Felix. "So, you ever go to the brunches?"

Felix felt on guard. "What brunches?"

"For the wives and girlfriends? 'Cause you're sort of like Claire's wife, right?"

Felix set his fork down. "The hell?"

"I'm just joshing you, man. Congratulations on Magician of the Year."

The way Landon said it told Felix he suspected the truth. He wasn't alone. After the original avalanche of online worship had subsided, critics began to chime in.

"Where did Felix come from?" they demanded. "How come no one's heard of him before this?"

"You know what, no," Landon said a moment later. "I can't keep pretending I don't know. This came in an hour ago."

He tapped his phone on and pulled up a website.

"Is it the Hipster Magician again?" Claire asked between bites. In thrall to the munchies, she'd gobbled up two helpings of chicken and half the table salad. "He, or they, swore they were taking a break."

"They didn't post a video, but they linked to something about Felix," Landon said.

Felix shot up from his chair and everyone gathered around Jessica's desktop computer, since Landon's phone was too small to view.

The link sent them to Tragic Magic. Spencer and Roy at Merlin's Wonderporium had apparently digitized the security cam footage of Felix stumbling around with the Foiled mask on.

The title of the post read: "Club Deception thinks THIS GUY is the best the magic world has to offer."

The video was grainy, but that just added to its authenticity. There was Felix, silently flirting with the coed, then attempting to impress her by demonstrating Foiled. There was Felix, lurching forward, accidentally groping the girl's dad, spinning, falling, destroying the Hyuks display, and knocking himself out cold on the floor.

For three long seconds, the Clarkes' loft contained nothing but stunned, mortified silence, until, "Ha-haaaaa!" Claire's uncontrollable laughter burst forth like a geyser. Fat tears of mirth rolled down her cheeks. She couldn't breathe, and then when she could gulp in air again, it was to double over in a fresh keening sound that swirled around the room.

Twenty separate GIFs had already been generated in the comments section. They ran on repeat, inescapable.

"I gotta ask…" said Cal, running a stiff hand through his hair, and trying not to smile. "How *exactly* did you become Magician of the Year, and does it by any chance have anything to do with Claire?"

To his own frustration, Felix looked to Claire for assistance, which didn't do much to support his cause.

"We may as well tell them." She wiped her eyes. "It's going to come out now anyway."

"What you need to do," Jessica said, "is use this to your advantage."

"What do you mean?" said Felix. "How?"

Having heard the story of Felix's transformation, everyone gathered in the living room to discuss damage control. Kaimi and Landon perched on extra folding chairs from the kitchen, while Cal, Jessica, and Claire sat together on the couch. Felix stood, alone in the middle of the carpet, feeling acutely out of place.

"First, you have to own it. It's like a sex tape," Jessica explained. "Sure, it's embarrassing, but there's no better way to get clicks." She pointed to Claire. "And here's *your* angle..."

"What? No. I don't have an angle," Claire said firmly.

Jessica barreled ahead. "Co-opt the image of Felix crashing into something, that's your intro, and then, 'If I could turn *him* into Magician of the Year, imagine what I could do for *you*.' Right? And then you upload weekly tutorials behind a pay wall."

"Tutorial...? Like instructional videos?"

"Yeah, why not. Start with a low price point, or give the first one free, or whatever, get people hooked—"

"People could subscribe to your channel," Kaimi chimed in. "And eventually order compilation DVDs, bonus material, *products*..."

"And I'll advertise it on my newsletter," said Landon. "I think it's a great idea."

Jessica beamed at him.

"No—no, I don't...I don't perform," Claire said faintly. "I mean, thank you, but..."

"You won't be performing, you'll be teaching, and you're a freaking rock star at that," Felix told her, getting into it. It wasn't the way he'd envisioned the next step of his magic career, but it was better than nothing. *Own it. Co-opt it. Use it.* He walked over to the couch and squatted in front of Claire as though he were proposing. In a way, he was. *Let's keep the partnership going.* "It would just be you and me on video, no audience or anything, just us and a camera." He looked at Jessica for confirmation. "Right?"

She nodded eagerly.

"And then one thousand nasty user comments about vagicians, or how I *sound*, or how I *look*, or how my hands can't palm things the way men's do..." Claire said.

"We'll disable comments," said Jessica. "Or no, we'll vet them first. And fuck that other noise."

"We'd need a studio—good lighting, good sound, it can't look cheap," Claire said.

"There's a nice spot on Pico that rents by the hour," Cal said. "You should really think about it, Claire."

She gave him a cautious glance. "You think so?"

"Yes, I do." He gave her shoulder a squeeze. "You'd be brilliant."

She seemed to consider the possibility but then shook her head. "I don't know how I would fund it."

"I'll invest," Jessica said. "I want to invest."

Claire's expression changed from hesitant to excited. Felix could practically see a lightbulb go off above her head. "It should be you," she said.

"What do you mean?" asked Jessica.

"It should be *you* in the videos with me. I can teach *you*. We need more women in magic."

"Men might not pay for it if it's a woman teaching a woman," Landon remarked. "It's lame, I know, but…just being devil's advocate."

"They will if the woman looks like Jessica," Claire retorted. "And if the instructions are clear and useful, which they will be."

Jessica ducked her head and blushed. "Okay. Okay! I'm in!"

Cal looked alarmed. "Don't underestimate your own appeal, Claire, you don't need Jessica to…"

"I'm so in," Jessica repeated.

"And who cares if some men are put off by it?" said Kaimi. "They're not the only audience. Go after female viewers. Maybe if women see other women doing magic, in a way that's accessible, it won't seem so foreign. There might even be a big market for it, *Landon*."

Landon laughed good-naturedly. "There might! I'm on your side. You need a catchy name, though."

And just like that, everyone started talking at once, coming up with concepts, titles, lesson plans, graphics...

Felix felt ill.

He grabbed his car keys and walked out the door.

Claire didn't need him. She never had. She needed a project, and now she had a new one.

Claire

ON A CLOUDY, late-October day, Claire pulled into Jonathan's reserved parking spot at Club Deception.

She remembered the day they'd first become members, how excited they were. He'd passed the skills test handily, and in typical Jonathan fashion decided to run for a board position right away. It never occurred to him to wait. He'd always been so self-assured, so confident. Always walked the line between confidence and arrogance.

Blind, willful arrogance.

How could you not recognize her, Jonny? How could you sleep with both of them and not realize it?

At Lieutenant Douglas's request, Claire had gone back to the station to corroborate Leon Krause's claims during his confession. What she learned was upsetting but not exactly shocking; hadn't she been waiting for years, in some hidden corner of her mind, for the other shoe to drop?

Becca's mother was the woman whom Jonathan had had an affair with thirteen years earlier. Jonathan hadn't made the connection, as he tended to view his assistants as interchangeable amalgams of dark hair and petite frames, opposites of Claire.

Leon Krause was Becca's maternal uncle. He hated Jonathan for sleeping with his married sister, couldn't forgive the way it ended. Their breakup—the one Jonathan had forced Claire to instigate over the phone—had resulted in that fatal car crash. Though Becca's mother survived, she suffered partial paralysis and jail time for vehicular manslaughter, not to mention the lifelong pain of causing the death of a child. Ichabod watched her transform from a vibrant wife and mother to a disabled, divorced single mother in one fell swoop. After helping to raise Becca, he followed his niece to Los Angeles to manage her show-business aspirations. In his free time he studied magic and joined Club Deception so he could track down the man responsible for ruining his sister's life. Against Leon's wishes, Becca had accompanied him to a party where Jonathan was performing, and fell under his spell just as her mother had. (Yes, Claire told Lieutenant Douglas, that was true; she'd witnessed the aftermath firsthand.) When Leon discovered the bastard repeating his predatory ways with Becca, he stepped up his plans for revenge.

Once he told Becca the truth about her new boyfriend, the girl was horrified and enraged. The original plan was for Becca to poison Jonathan herself. She'd wait to strike until after the contest, in the hope of receiving a portion of the prize money if he came in first. But when he lost, he angrily fired her, and she no longer had the necessary access to commit the crime.

Becca and Leon's lawyer claimed that Becca had a change of heart after the contest and "withdrew from the conspiracy." Acting alone, Leon showed up at the Chateau Marmont after approaching Jonathan at the club in the guise of becoming his new manager and helping him launch a TV career.

Having secured a bottle with Cal's fingerprints at a show six months before, and knowing (as most local magicians did) of Cal's and Jonathan's hatred for each other, Leon had planned all along to frame Cal. After his TV special was ruined by the

Hipster Magician, Leon used that to his advantage, particularly since a crowd of people had witnessed Cal and Jonathan fighting the night before.

Leon and Jonathan chatted cards and had a drink together in Jonathan's room. When the poison took hold, Leon dressed him in the easily purchased Hipster Magician costume to complete the frame job.

Claire had asked Lieutenant Douglas about Kaimi and Landon's connection to the crime. Apparently they'd been questioned for sending Jonathan threatening texts the day of the murder, regarding a payment they felt was their due. Kaimi had told the police about Becca's relationship with Jonathan around the same time Jessica had called in the information about Leon. Douglas's team was able to establish their connection shortly after.

At this point, Leon's only priority was protecting Becca. He provided a full confession in exchange for the conspiracy charges against his niece being dropped.

Claire didn't blame him. She would have done the same for her daughter. Her daughter, who still wasn't returning her calls but who'd sent a terse text last night: I love you, Mom. I just need time to process things on my own.

She'd read the text every hour since it arrived.

Sitting in the Club Deception parking lot and remembering those early, happy years, she mourned the version of Jonathan she'd first married. The man who worked himself to the bone, seven days a week, fourteen hours a day to support his pregnant wife. The man who, when he planned his first tour, wanted his family with him so badly that he wrote them into the act. She mourned the life they were supposed to have lived.

Now she braced herself for a tongue lashing of extraordinary degradation. Everyone, it seemed, knew about her troubled marriage and the part Felix had played in ending it. The all-male board of directors would no doubt side with Jonathan when it came to Schrödinger's Cat.

In her more frustrated moments over the past few years, she'd referred to the board members as "misapplied phlebotinum" because they used their limitless powers for the most mundane and trivial of tasks. ("Should the club logo be two millimeters taller on the letterhead?" "Is it time to retire Eskargot font?" "Do we want to be known as a place that serves Absolut vodka, or Grey Goose?")

But today she would learn the old goats were shrewder than she'd ever given them credit for.

For one thing, the three men who'd shown up in the Silver Room—Secretary Williams, Treasurer Pelletier, and Trustee Grossman—stood when she entered the room, and offered her a bottled water and a fruit plate. They'd also covered the sculpture of the naked woman's torso with a black silk. Perhaps it had finally occurred to them Claire might not enjoy having to look at it for hours on end during meetings. Whenever she'd sat in for Jonathan and taken notes on his behalf, she'd been all but ignored. The Invisible Woman.

"Thank you for coming in, Claire," Treasurer Pelletier said once she was seated. A copy of Jonathan's ridiculous patent sat on the table in front of him.

"Of course," she said quietly, hands folded in her lap. "I think I know where this is going, but…"

"You seem to have a pathological aversion to taking credit for your work," said Secretary Williams. He peered at her over his small spectacles.

She looked up, startled. "How do you mean?"

"It's time we call a spade a spade, don't you think? Jonathan's always been quick to blame others, quick to hire lawyers. For that reason alone we were skeptical of his claim that his show was stolen. As you pointed out when he confronted you"—she cringed remembering the brawl at Cal's premiere party—"if the show were his, he would have performed it. Also, his patent is half gibberish; he didn't include some of the best portions of the trick, almost none of the patter, and…we believe it was your routine all along."

She held her breath. "You do?"

"We do. Just like we know who's kept this place running during Jonathan's tenure as president. The newsletters, the password system, the swap meets, the trick of the week on the menu cards. We know it's you. You're the beating heart of Club Deception."

They all nodded.

"Without you, it would fall apart in a week," said Williams.

"A day," corrected Trustee Grossman, and shot her a warm smile. "Less than a day. And since Jonathan is no longer with us…we want you to take his place. At least until the formal election in January, though longer, of course, if you like. Will you be our interim president? We value you. We need you."

Stunned, she didn't reply right away. They must have interpreted her silence as dissatisfaction, because Treasurer Pelletier hastily added, "We're willing to give you a generous stipend, if that will help in any way."

"Yes," she said, standing, preparing to shake hands and leave as quickly as possible, before anything could alter the precious alchemy of the moment, before they could change their minds, shift the terms, take it all back.

"However…" Secretary Williams began.

Here it comes.

"In light of the video posted at Tragic Magic…I trust you've seen it?"

She nodded.

"We can't allow Felix Vicario to retain his prize, or his

standing. We want this to go away. He's no longer a lifetime member, or any other sort of member. He is no longer Magician of the Year. It'll be a blank spot in the record books. The prize money will be funneled back into the club."

She closed her eyes for a second. She didn't like hanging Felix out to dry, but she didn't want to push her luck or appear ungrateful, either.

"Could he…work his way back in?" she asked.

"How?" Trustee Grossman looked skeptical.

"Take the skills test, like anyone else? When he's ready, I mean." *If he's ever ready.*

Felix had never been lazy—he'd been impatient. When she gave him specific tasks, he worked valiantly and diligently until he completed them. But he wasn't good at managing his time; he wanted everything to happen quickly.

"I don't know that we want someone like him to be a member. Someone willing to pass off another person's"—he motioned to Claire—"routine as his own."

"I pressured him, though. It's not his fault. If I could've done it myself, I would have. And he really does love magic. I think, given a year or two, he could surprise you."

"Well, we'll think about it."

It wasn't ideal, but it was better than an outright ban. Still, breaking the news to him wouldn't be easy.

She opened the heavy club doors and stepped out into the smoggy autumn air.

Cal stood outside, leaning against his BMW, which was parked beside hers. He wore sunglasses (despite the clouds), khakis, a white T-shirt, and a Harrington jacket. In short, he looked like a *GQ* pinup.

"Hello, Claire."

"Where's your peachier half?" she said.

"Where's your nubile boyfriend?"

"Jealous?"

"Always have been, always will be."

She stood next to him, against his car, and folded her arms. They silently regarded the brick wall of the club's entrance.

He took off his sunglasses and cleaned them with the hem of his T-shirt.

"We never had a moment to be us, did we?" Claire asked.

"No, we didn't," he agreed. Placed the sunglasses in his pocket.

"If you really thought I was going to be divorced by the time you came back, why didn't you wait for me?"

"I thought about it, I did—but then I met Jessie, and…she seemed like a fresh start."

"But you thought about it," she pressed.

"Why do you suppose that out of the hundreds of hours of footage Brandy and I shot over the years, the only tape I kept was the one with you in it?"

"Yeah, thanks for reminding me of that," she said, but there was no bite to her tone.

He turned swiftly and cupped her face in his hands. Surprised, she met his gaze, drawn in by the same ineffable magnetism that had first attracted her.

"Hey," he said, thumb stroking her cheek. "You know you're amazing, right? The cat—the whole show—it was tremendous."

She tilted her head and gave his palm a warm, lingering kiss. "Thanks."

"We would've made a great team," he said wistfully.

"I thought so, too. Once."

"But not anymore."

"Not anymore," she agreed.

He let his hands drop from her face. Cleared his throat.

"Why are you here?" Claire said.

"Did they choose an interim president yet?"

She smiled. "You're looking at her."

"Oh. Oh! *Really?*"

"Yes," she retorted.

"Sorry, no. That makes sense. Congratulations. That's sort of why I'm here, actually. Without the show, I've lost a lot of my day-to-day focus. I need something to keep me out of trouble. You know how it is. I'm dropping off the paperwork so I can run in January."

She cocked her head. "For a trustee position?"

"No, for president. But this is great, you can give me insider tips and all that."

"I don't plan to step down in January," she said slowly.

"Quite right. Hold down the fort until after the holidays, ensure a smooth transition. When does the election take place? The last week?"

"I don't plan to step down at *all*," she reiterated.

"But . . . you're not even . . . I need this, Claire."

His frustration triggered her own.

"I need it, too," she said. "You expect me to step aside and prop you up like I did for Jonathan?"

"He never appreciated you the way he should have."

"Neither did you," she spat out. "And I'm certainly not giving up the post because you're feeling bored, or unfulfilled, or, or . . . *weak*."

"Well, that makes this a little easier, then."

"Makes what easier?"

He walked toward the entrance. "I'm running for club president, and I'm going to win."

His conceit might have mystified her, had she not been so

accustomed to it in just about every man she knew. (Which really meant, every magician she knew.) Even Felix hadn't been prepared to work as hard as he needed to, at first; he'd just assumed things would fall into place for him.

Now Cal was convinced he'd make a better president than her, despite the fact that he'd been out of town for three years and had no clue how to run the club or optimize the experience for its members, all of which she'd been perfecting behind the scenes.

Behind the scenes, behind the scenes. Her natural habitat.

Well, not anymore.

She'd told herself countless times that real magicians didn't take credit for their work. If they did, there'd be no magic at all. You couldn't go around crowing about your achievements. *Guess what, it was magnets. Double-sided tape! I memorized the deck!*

Jonathan had fed into this belief, of course.

"No one walks onstage and says, 'This joke is from so-and-so, this illusion is a variation of Triumph, my wife came up with the first and third punch lines.' That would ruin it. You get to be part of the magic, Claire. The hidden component. That should be enough for you."

Claire didn't deserve credit for his shows because she wasn't taking on any of the risk, she wasn't onstage. He'd drilled this into her head so relentlessly she'd internalized it. Just like she'd internalized his excuses for cheating on her. How she didn't "deserve" a faithful husband because it was her own failures that prevented them from having the life they wanted. She didn't deserve *this*, she didn't deserve *that*, and later: There *was* no this, there *was* no that. Later still: *There was no she.*

She had disappeared from her own life.

Well, she wasn't going to settle anymore, step aside, or shy away from claiming her due. If Cal thought she wouldn't fight him for the club presidency, he was in for a shock.

She stood up straight, tall as she could be.

She would take up as much space as she damn well pleased.

"May the best magician win," she said.

Acknowledgments

Thank you to the wonderful Victoria Marini of Irene Goodman agency for finding this book the perfect home. Thank you to my editor extraordinaire, Maddie Caldwell, who saw its potential, knew how to unleash it, and made the story infinitely better. I am exceedingly grateful to you both!

Big thanks to publicists Daniella deSantos and Tiffany Sanchez, cover designer Elizabeth Turner, production editor Yasmin Mathew, copy editor Laura Jorstad, and Marie Mundaca at Grand Central, illustrator Sylvan Steenbrink, and Penelope Burns at Gelfman Schneider/ICM Partners.

Love to the fearless few who read the NSFW, down 'n' dirty original version: Sarvenaz Tash, Amy Spalding, Lisa Green, Hope Larson; and the equally helpful readers of later drafts: Dana Davis, Lynne Kadish, Kathy Foley, Mark Herder, Rachel Murphy, Maggie Lehrman, Leslie Rose, Julie Musil. Thanks to Kristen Kittscher and Katharyn Sinelli for writerly support. Thanks to RWA, Sisters in Crime, and Mystery Writers of America for the terrific meet-ups and events.

Lovelovelove to Joe Skilton for supporting me in every possible way while I wrote this, answering my questions about magic, and fixing my various blunders. ("This doesn't mean what you think it means…") Any mistakes are my own.

Some of the books I read for research and pleasure while writing (by no means a full list): *Art & Artifice*; and *The Last*

Greatest Magician in the World, by Jim Steinmeyer; *The Magician and the Cardsharp*, by Karl Johnson; and *The Magician's Lie*, by Greer McCallister.

Thanks to Zach Waldman for use of the "card shaved into chest hair" trick. And to the Academy of Magical Arts, the Magic Castle, and the Magic Circle...thank you for existing!

Thanks to my family, near and far, the Hoovers, Skiltons, Jays, and Murphys for your endless encouragement.